# HIS OWN MAN

# His Own Man

## EDGARD TELLES RIBEIRO

TRANSLATED FROM THE PORTUGUESE
BY KIM M. HASTINGS

OTHER PRESS   NEW YORK

Production Editor: Yvonne E. Cárdenas
Text Designer: Julie Fry
This book was set in Bauhaus and Bembo.

10 9 8 7 6 5 4 3 2 1

*Library of Congress Cataloging-in-Publication Data*
Ribeiro, Edgard Telles.
  [Punho e a renda. English]
  His own man / by Edgard Telles Ribeiro ; translated from the Portuguese by Kim M. Hastings.
      pages   cm
  ISBN 978-1-59051-698-0 — ISBN 978-1-59051-699-7 (e-book)
  1. Brazil—Politics and government—20th century—Fiction.
2. Dictatorship—Brazil—History—20th century—Fiction.
I. Hastings, Kim M., translator. II. Title.
  PQ9698.28.I1547P8613 2014
  869.3'42z—dc23

                                                      2013047561

*Publisher's Note*

*For Angelica*

*For Ivan Junqueira and Luiz Augusto de Araujo Castro*

*I don't claim to paint things in themselves,*
*but only their effect on me.*
—Stendhal

*In the presence of certain realities,*
*art is trivial or impertinent.*
—George Steiner

# PART ONE

# 1

Writing a country's history may be difficult, but tracing a man's story presents its own challenges. For a country, there is a vast array of information in the form of books and treaties, maps and images, leaders, legends, and archives. But a man? What kind of history does he have? Where would his secret maps be found? Or his boundaries? What might be hidden beneath his façade or detected in his gaze should he give in to temptation and study himself in the mirror one night?

My first memory of Max dates back to 1968 in Rio de Janeiro and was to some extent foreboding: his shadow cast over my desk at the ministry. Without my hearing his footsteps or picking up on his presence in some way, he had appeared behind my high-backed wooden chair and casually leaned over the document I was working on. I was writing by hand, as was customary at the time, on loose sheets of paper that would later be typed up by my secretary. At the Ministry of Foreign Affairs (which I had joined slightly less than a year earlier), such familiarity — appearing out of nowhere and peering at what a colleague was drafting — was a privilege reserved for senior personnel.

The shadow hadn't set off any alarms for one prosaic reason: right then, my eyes were staring off into the distance, searching for the word that would best complete the sentence I was struggling with. Although the text, on the whole, was decidedly bland, that particular line wasn't. Given how dear symmetry is to the young, the irrelevance of the whole demanded a term that would glint like a blade in the sun. *"Fortuitous,"* the shadow murmured.

As I turned toward the voice, the stranger cocked his head and smiled, repeating as if in encouragement: *"Fortuitous.* That's the word you need there. From the Latin."

By then I was standing. I knew him only by sight; he worked at the secretary-general's office. Extending a hand, he introduced himself. "Marcílio Andrade Xavier. You can call me Max."

"Max?"

"My initials. My ex-wife came up with it." Leaning against the desk, he crossed his arms, giving the conversation just the right touch of informality. "She couldn't pronounce my full name. She was American." He corrected himself: "She *is* American. She's alive. Very much so, in fact." He laughed somewhat bitterly, then added, "The name caught on here at Itamaraty because of the initials we use on our memos. So I became Max for good. With any luck, for posterity."

I smiled at the joke but still wondered what he was doing in my office.

"I came to invite you to lunch," my visitor explained. "At the suggestion of a mutual friend, whose name I won't reveal just yet. He asked that we join him in his office and wait while he finishes up a report. He assured me that your dynamic personality puts you high on the list of lunchable colleagues."

"Lunchable colleagues?"

"According to him, you're among the few people one can share a meal with and not suffer the after effects of *indigestione acuta* brought on by the rampant tedium of our environment."

*"Taediu,"* I ventured.

And so, laughing and exchanging half a dozen phrases in Latin, we went out in search of our mutual friend. I remember feeling quite pleased with this new colleague, and more than a little gratified to be receiving the attention of someone higher up—adviser to the second-in-command at the ministry, no less.

The conversation flowed easily. When we're young, with our whole life ahead of us and a vague sense of immortality hanging over our heads, we crave virtuosity of every kind. Shining the spotlight on ourselves, we make outrageous statements and conjure affinities that will root us in familiar ground.

Max and I shared at least one affinity. A meaningful one, we would soon find out as we strolled between stairways and corridors: a passion for reading. We had devoured the same authors: Joyce, Proust, Flaubert, Chekhov, Fitzgerald, Machado, Borges, but also (and with equal appetite) Debray, Gramsci, Chomsky, Lukács.... As such, we spoke by way of metaphors. We could, whenever necessary, place unbridgeable barriers between us and our colleagues. This was largely because many of them seemed incapable of voicing a single thought unless it was first strained through the filter of reason and simmered over a low flame. But not so between the two of us—as became clear in fifteen minutes of conversation. In an environment where discretion prevailed, our behavior bordered on the irreverent. Without taking chances, of course—we avoided criticizing our leaders too pointedly, or exposing those in power to their own vulnerabilities.

Affinities of this nature pave the way for greater expectations—and for probing questions. Max showed curiosity regarding my background. He knew I was the son of a diplomat, but this alone wasn't enough for him. He was interested in verifying the legends that circulated about my father at the ministry. Had he really come from such humble beginnings? Gone through the public school system? Toiled as a geography teacher at suburban schools? How had he managed to work his way into Itamaraty?

"He studied theology as a young man," I explained. "He read a lot...."

"Even so," Max persisted. "Quite an accomplishment."

And it was. My father's obituary the previous year had made a point of saying so. The paper had emphasized his origins. Only a rare few of his social class spoke other languages or had the wherewithal to devote themselves to studies that would grant them access to the Ministry of Foreign Affairs. Max's persistence made me realize that the subject was of great importance to him. As for myself, I don't recall being curious about his family roots just then. The urge to dig deeper would come as the years went by, spurred by a succession of events that gradually provoked the need for some explanation.

Deciphering Max's inner workings thus evolved from initial feelings of affection to an atmosphere verging on unease and, later, duress. During this slow process, I would find out that Max descended from the more modest branch of the Andrade Xavier family, who hailed from the interior of Minas Gerais (and not Rio de Janeiro). This made him "doubly unlucky," as he put it—given how near and yet removed he was from the wealthier, more aristocratic branch of the family. Max had lost his father while still a young boy. Following that loss, his mother had seen all the doors of her husband's family close for reasons never explained. At the ministry, where Max felt he rightfully belonged, he had found the opportunity to reclaim the social status of his childhood.

This made me understand why the subject of ancestry, which didn't matter much to me, was a concern for him, tied up as it was to his distant past. Why else would he have dedicated himself to painstakingly tracing the genealogies of his colleagues and superiors? And why would he feel compelled to refer to the good marriages some had made as being merely alliances that would advance their careers? I surmised that his marriage to the American, which had lasted just two years ("a youthful mishap," he liked to call it), must have failed since it didn't serve this purpose.

Be that as it may, and concerning this social topic, I came away from our lunch with the clear impression that in my new friend's mind, the simple fact of my father's acceptance into

Itamaraty had made him an aristocrat and, by extension, made me a second-generation member of a stately family. Those were probably the real roots of my "lunchable" status.

I remember trying my best that day to live up to expectations created about me. I spoke of films and literature. I praised *Eros and Civilization*. Having read Marcuse earned me points. I cited verses by Pound. I talked about politics, sports, and samba. Lowering our voices, we criticized the military and the coup of 1964 with a frankness unusual even among the younger set. I also knew to laugh at Max's stories (which were quite good) and those of our mutual friend (which weren't bad). We swapped secrets about women over dessert.

At twenty-eight, Max was older and more experienced than us—not to mention divorced. He dazzled us as the man of the world we took him to be, full of wisdom that he seemed ready to impart in the form of advice or suggestions. He spoke of the birth control pill as the only significant invention of the twentieth century. And he considered the budding feminist movement the greatest opportunity ever offered to *men*, whose appetites would now be sated as never before. Over coffee, Max flattered me with an invitation to join him and a few friends getting together to listen to some new Art Blakey and Thelonious Monk albums he had received from New York. He gave me the address of his small waterfront apartment in Urca and revealed that he hosted a weekly jazz show on Radio MEC. He alluded to his gifts as an announcer and the stories he would make up to fill airtime when, out of laziness, he neglected to prepare material.

As though struck by sudden inspiration, I asked if he could recommend a tailor. He then made me the beneficiary of advice received from a veteran ambassador: "Make *few* suits." Long pause. "In *London*."

As I listened to Max, I realized how refined our ministry was in terms of language and hidden codes. Words, rhythms, and implied italics could imbue sentences with an entirely distinctive

Proustian flair. Such minor details, I believe, were what made me like Max right away: his ability to play with the mind and to conjure ideas, sometimes important, sometimes childish, with the lightness of a bird. Nothing, in my opinion, better exemplified Itamaraty and the diplomat's role back then better than my companion's levity, which the imprudent called savoir-faire. They couldn't imagine what strain lay behind my new friend's personal efforts.

On our cab ride back to the ministry after lunch, we heard on the radio that the Military Security Council was meeting with the President of the Republic at Laranjeiras Palace. That night we all saw in the shaky black-and-white images on our TV sets—and heard through our open windows, in successive layers of sounds that arose from streets, neighborhoods, towns, and cities across the country—that the generals had imposed Institutional Act Number 5 (AI-5), which severely curtailed civil liberties. It was December 1968 and there was clearly nothing fortuitous about the blades glinting in the sun around us. The nation was preparing to plunge into a period far darker than what had already come to pass—and far more suffocating.

Years would elapse before I recognized the deeper significance of Max and my having met that day, a Friday the thirteenth, no less. Only then was I able to associate the shadow he cast over my desk with that which would gradually take over the country.

# 2

Those who admired Max would say he was a pro; to others, he was simply an opportunist. And, inevitably, there were some who saw him as a scoundrel. I personally think Max, like many before and after him, might simply have been a victim of his own inherent contradictions—and not just a gentleman with a sword for hire. A gentleman, it's worth recalling, whose path would end up being defined by a singular set of accomplishments. There were few among us like him, so readily adapting to the ever-changing conditions of that time with such charm and competence, swiftly scaling the ranks of our hierarchy over the twenty years of military rule, and then going on to achieve further triumphs after the return to political normalcy—when everything indicated he should have been exiled or, with any luck, retired.

I imagine there must have been cases similar to his in the countless hidden corners of our federal administration. But no other setting lent itself to the particular sleights of hand that Itamaraty afforded its actors. This fact might be attributed to the subtlety with which those transactions were negotiated, since the foreign offices are known for their discretion. On the other hand, the presidential palaces in Rio de Janeiro and, later, Brasilia, as well as the embassies abroad, served admirably for the elaborate charades staged by bureaucrats eager to ingratiate themselves with those in power. For while the horrors took place in the military barracks and prisons, at formal state dinners the regime showed its finer skills, seating torturers and gentlemen side by side.

As for Max, he always seemed to be involved in bigger projects and causes, which far surpassed the routine tasks entrusted to us. That these might shift imperceptibly over time in focus (or *axis*, as he liked to say) never seemed to disturb him. At most, they would prompt him to make a comment or two about the transitory nature of ideologies—comments that enabled him to drop moral considerations from his personal equation. Once, when I criticized an individual who had adapted with remarkable speed to the political realities of the new times, Max simply smiled, as though listening to the ranting of a child, as he spun a crystal paperweight on his desk. *Changes*, his gesture seemed to imply, *are a part of life.* And the corollary, also unspoken, was as vivid as the crystal spinning before my eyes: *You had better learn how to deal with them accordingly.*

Anyone who sees Max today in official photos, decked out in his uniform, with white gloves, sword, and plumed hat, presenting his credentials in some foreign court, can't help but be impressed by his majestic appearance. The self-confidence, dignity, and poise that emerge from these images convey a supreme composure—albeit born of illusion. Not that Max deceived everyone—that was never the case. But for someone like me, who met him when he was young and thrilled to have recouped his family's former splendor, one fact stands out: he deceived himself above all. So how not to feel a special tenderness, even now, on receiving the photos he periodically sends us in the diplomatic pouch with a friendly postcard from some far-off land, images of himself in full dress, adorned with feathers, silk, and lace? How not to appreciate the idyllic scenes of Itamaraty banquets recorded with just as much enjoyment in Brasilia?

Oh, the Itamaraty banquets... How many were there then, paying tribute to kings and queens, among other foreign dignitaries who honored our generals with their presence? Partygoing people, who indulged in everything—except suspicions?

"How could they be willing to play along?" I would grumble to myself, wrestling with irritation that would turn to indignation as my friend lingered over the men's dress coats and uniforms, as well as their numerous decorations, or let himself become entranced by the women's gowns—and the jewelry they wore with calculated nonchalance.

My friend... That's still how I picture him on that late morning, when he whispered "fortuitous" in my ear and invited me to lunch. From the very start, he fascinated me. For his congeniality and intellectual brilliance at first. And, as the years went by, for something I always had trouble pinpointing but would today define as a kind of wistfulness, which would lead him to try to recover his lost childhood—knowing only too well that, of all his dreams, this would be the only unattainable one.

To make his social ascent feasible, and for added emotional support, Max surrounded himself with a diverse group of friends. The circle included young people of assorted leanings ranging from idealism to full-blown alienation. The fact that he was accepted and courted by his peers gave him added confidence in carrying out his projects. The group—whom I met when I accepted my new companion's invitation to listen to jazz in his apartment and into which I was quickly integrated—essentially consisted of Max's girlfriend, Ana, a young actress I had already seen onstage in Rio de Janeiro more than once; Moira, an artist who lived in Santa Teresa (inundated with debt and cats, according to Max); Olavo, a millionaire who owned a silver-gray Lancia in which he would cruise around Rio late at night, and whose appeal owed a lot to the jazz albums he would bring back from his trips to New York; Efraim, a poet whose genius was celebrated by Max alone, since no one else had access to his verses; and, finally, Flávio Eduardo, a film critic who would later get caught up in political militancy, go underground, and die a few months later in a bank robbery.

Each of us unwittingly played a role in Max's master plan. Mine was having lived in countries he knew only through literature and speaking (without an accent) two or three languages Max had taken great pains to learn at his boarding school. Ana's consisted of shining onstage and being courted by theater and film bigwigs, who envied our friend because once the night came to a close, it was his bed the beauty would seek. Olavo's could be summed up as flying his fiery meteor along the city's deserted streets, awaiting the tree that would eventually kill him. The young poet Efraim's was pondering verses with the implicit condition that he would remain unknown. I never understood what Moira was doing in our midst, which in a way also confirmed the group's unorthodox profile. Flávio's role would be unveiled only after his disappearance: dying for a lost cause. And even this extreme case would leave the impression of having to do with some whim of our friend and host.

But all of these hidden clues would become clear to me only as time went by. The afternoon of my initiation, finding the street-level door open, I'd gone up to the building's third and top floor, from which voices and music were drifting down. Max seemed to have forgotten that he'd invited me. He looked surprised at first but quickly recovered: placing a hand on my shoulder, he asked everyone to quiet down and lowered the stereo, relegating John Coltrane to the background — utter sacrilege. He then formally announced, "This guy has read everything. Even more than I have." He made the statement as though bestowing a title of honor on me — yet the brilliance was all owed to him. Ana, to whom I hadn't yet been introduced, confirmed my perception with an amused wink, which I caught by mere chance: *Max* was the benchmark to which the achievements of others were compared.

Without further ado, Max turned the stereo up, bringing John Coltrane back to the scene, and I was thrown into a rarefied atmosphere, as if I'd suddenly been given access to a greenhouse filled with exotic plant species.

We were young, we drank a lot, and the country was imploding at our feet—without our realizing what exactly was taking place. What was censored was more telling than what was revealed in the media, giving rise to a host of rumors. And these only grew. *Dead, missing, tortured*...The imagined horror magnified the actual, since it had no defined shape or limits. What could we do? Take up arms? Jazz symbolized freedom. The louder and more abstract, the better. Drinking, fueled by anxiety and chaos, took care of the rest. The word of Flávio's death, however, eventually brought a particular depth to our silence, which went far beyond pain and confusion: our safe haven had been violated.

In spite of it all, during those early days, I never stopped seeing Max through admiring eyes. He in turn gradually adopted me as a younger brother: an honor, true, but one that reflected a distinct hierarchy—assigning the role of mentor to himself. After my having built Max's pedestal with such enthusiasm, it took me years to dismantle it, in a tormenting, drawn-out process.

Looking back now, and considering everything that transpired in Brazil after the military coup—particularly following the AI-5 decree—I see Max as one of the most pitiful symbols of our country at that time. All the same, the decision to tell his story was difficult, requiring four decades. The urge to do so, initially daunting, ended up becoming inescapable. Not so much in order to reveal what we always knew within our group: namely, that the devil was in our midst. Not even because of the alternately perverse and tragic circumstances of the players involved and the sad situations they lived through. But out of my own need, as a witness to the adverse effects the period had on people I cared for.

The statements bordering on confessions that Max made to me over the years, often thanks to too much whiskey, or in response to remarks of mine—which weren't always kind or conciliatory—I have included here in order to give a fuller sense of other complex aspects of his character. The rest—no small amount, as will become evident—I gathered, often unexpectedly, from reliable sources close to Max (his ex-wife, former superiors, subordinates, acquaintances, friends, enemies), people who admired or abhorred him, as well as those whose careers may well have been jeopardized by his actions—but who nonetheless fell under his spell.

# 3

Max had been appointed to the first position of his diplomatic career more than five years earlier, in August 1963, after finishing his studies at the Rio Branco Institute.

The military coup of April 1964 was only months away and the country was seething with prerevolutionary Marxist ardor. The leftists, to use the language of the old-timers, were rolling up their sleeves, while the right held back and got organized. There were so many leftist groups that one had the impression the right didn't even exist. Or if it did, it lacked teeth. At the universities, Socialists and Communists voiced greater misgivings about the right-wing students than about the military, for those stocky young men were going around armed and preying on intellectuals—who were almost always frail by comparison. They wore their repression with pride—outwardly and aggressively, in contrast with the more conservative Tradition, Family, and Property movement.

Besides Brecht, Mayakovsky, and Sartre, Max read selected works by Mao and Che Guevara—among others attuned to the moment. Thanks to his journalist friends, he enjoyed direct access to Rio's intelligentsia. He would go to hear jazz musicians at the Beco das Garrafas and circulate among the boxes at the Municipal Theater. In bohemian circles, he expounded on Godard's films, which he said he preferred to those of Resnais. And he regarded those of Truffaut with a condescending smile.

Max had originally been assigned by the ministry to serve in the Middle East division. However, before he assumed his duties there, he received another offer. Through the intervention of a senator—for whom Max, as an intern in the ministry's consular sector, had secured a diplomatic passport in less than an hour—he was invited to switch divisions and serve in the minister's office.

Despite the good news, Max was worried about the repercussions of this unexpected distinction. What luck that the senator happened to be a friend of the minister. But what would his colleagues say? Wouldn't his move run the risk of being misinterpreted? And how would he concoct an apology to the head of the Middle East division, who was awaiting him with open arms and to whom he'd made a commitment just two weeks earlier?

On Max's first day at the ministry, he had all the forced seriousness of a young man who wished desperately to appear older than he was. The effort wasn't entirely successful, however, for it was contradicted by his natural exuberance. In his right hand, he carried a briefcase of worn but fine leather, which for the moment held only the day's newspaper. To offset the sobriety of his dark suit, he allowed himself two concessions: his hair, without being long, extended beyond his jacket collar, and his shirt was of a relatively striking color. Max sailed past the reception area staff, who regarded him in silence. Ignoring the swans in the pond, he made a right upon reaching the stately row of palm trees on the Itamaraty Palace grounds and headed toward the Personnel Department.

The head of Personnel, informed of the transfer by a phone call from the minister's office, was waiting for him. An unhurried older fellow, short and stout, with a thin mustache, he had witnessed similar—and even swifter—maneuvers in his time, but rarely involving someone so young, who hadn't yet officially joined the ministry. This point, in particular, intrigued him: that the first act of a play could occur before the curtain went up, in a kind of secret prologue to which the public hadn't had access.

Max hesitated in front of the man. Should he settle into one of the two armchairs? His superior, who was seated, had asked for the official transfer papers, which he was rereading now in silence, as though looking for some error or inaccuracy. Like a new recruit, Max waited, standing between two empty seats. He had put his briefcase down but was unsure what to do with his arms; not wanting to cross them, he simply let them hang at his sides. He wanted to smoke but didn't dare, despite noticing the used ashtray on the desk.

In less than an hour he would be ensconced at the minister's office, but right now he found himself paralyzed before this simple public servant. Three whole minutes had already elapsed, an inordinate amount of time for Max on that chilly winter morning. The hand on the wall clock kept marching forward. Max was undergoing the defining moment of his career. Like many a colleague before him, however, he was unaware of the fact. In that modest setting, a far cry from the more sumptuous ones that awaited him, he was relinquishing a substantive job that could have brought him great professional satisfaction in favor of the choreographed roles he'd surely be offered in the minister's office, where he'd probably do nothing but open doors and receive files destined for more capable hands.

The head of Personnel, who kept Max waiting, was well aware of this. His experience told him just what kind of path Max would follow from then on, and where it generally ended up.

"Good luck," he mumbled as they parted ways. But his farewell went unheard, since Max was already disappearing down the hall, his heels echoing on the marble floor.

The career Max had just embarked on was extremely competitive, with strict criteria for advancement, contingent on a sequence of promotions. It took thirty years, on average, to move from bottom to top. The faster the ascent, however, the brighter the panoramic view from above, not to mention the associated perks, among which was the most coveted one of all: the exercise of power. Very few ever made it to the highest offices, let alone gained access to the major posts abroad. Thus the frantic competition. For contacts, invitations, and prestigious positions, as well as for smiles and pats on the back from those in power.

This was the environment in which Max was to navigate. Difficult under normal circumstances and unpredictable in a context of randomness and ambiguity, as would become clear over the subsequent twenty years. But it was still a few months before this more disturbing scenario began to take hold. For the moment, the military was still champing at the bit in their barracks, while Max did the same in the solitude of his room in Humaitá, the neighborhood where he lived with his mother. It would be two years before he relocated to the more upscale Urca. In the meantime, he earned his place in the minister's office—but not in the man's heart.

The minister hardly knew him, given the complex internal system that, like everything around them, followed protocol. Even when Max first shook the minister's hand, the conversation he'd been rehearsing all week was cut off by a phone call from the president's office. Max created a mental montage based on that first meeting, splicing together a half-truth and a half-lie. He would tell his colleagues that his meeting with the minister "was interrupted by a call from the President of the Republic"— which had the benefit of being true. From there, however, he would go on to fabricate an imaginary conversation with his superior, embellishing it with a wealth of details that would vary depending on his audience but that always revolved around the minister's interest in what *he* had to say.

His colleagues would listen in silence, without betraying their feelings, hiding as best they could the envy eating away at them. And Max in his somber suit would remain undaunted, as he continued to spin his tale, attempting to disguise the bulk of his impudence. If he handled the challenge gallantly, it was because he sensed that the burden would be only temporary. To his dismay, however, he didn't feel welcome in the minister's office. His name had been suggested to the minister by an outside source, meaning the idea hadn't come from within the institution itself. Max reasoned that someone else must have been under consideration for the position, which increased his insecurity: he didn't know whom he might have been competing against.

He wasn't treated poorly. Far from it. But he was assigned menial tasks that he considered beneath him, such as reading the newspapers each day and cutting out anything that might warrant his superiors' attention during their morning coffee. This obliged him to arrive before eight o'clock. And since no one left work before eight in the evening, his daily routine ended up being exhausting. Most of the time he was dying of boredom, but he made it a point to appear busy whenever coworkers or visitors stopped by, constantly opening drawers in search of some nonexistent document, or making an unnecessary request of someone nearby, in a voice that often sounded too loud even to his own ears.

The furniture, rugs, paintings, and decorative objects were all museum-worthy. His first day on the job, he discovered there was a Corot painting on the wall behind his desk. Astonished, he mentioned the fact to a colleague, who not only deemed this completely normal but added in a blasé tone, "That's nothing compared to what's in the minister's office." The remark stung, not only for belittling his discovery but also for making his lack of access to the big boss all too obvious.

The small painting depicted a pastoral landscape in grayish tones, with a few cypresses swaying in the wind. In the foreground, two stooped peasants were carrying hoes as they made their way toward a shack. Although the work measured only sixty by eighty centimeters, excluding the ornate, almost baroque frame, the artist's signature was quite visible in the bottom right corner. Max realized that the painting was worth a fortune. Still, its presence soothed him. It enabled him to go home again—to the idealized family home he'd dreamt about throughout his childhood.

Max's desk was imposing and well proportioned. Seated, he could barely stretch out his hands to the far corners, and it took some effort just to reach his pens and ink. On the far right corner of the glass top protecting the varnished surface, Max set out a portrait of his mother. It remained there less than an hour—just long enough for him to realize that his coworkers' desks held nothing but file folders and papers. Lacking the courage to take the picture back home, fearing that his mother would notice, he ended up hiding it in the back of a drawer.

To his pleasant surprise, however, he soon found out that simply by occupying a seat in that particular area, he had become a key player in the eyes of those who came to meet with the minister or his chief of staff. It was an illusion—of which he himself was the first victim.

It didn't matter. Max was delighted by his position's inherent magic. Gradually, like a plant warming to the sunlight, he garnered strength by nourishing himself on the respect of others, proudly noting how the secretaries and typists, all young women from good families, appreciated his suits and ties. It was the first of many mirrors he'd face throughout his career— that of vanity. Mirrors that would lead him farther and farther from himself.

After his first two weeks, once the weight of his shamelessness had lessened and his somber suits felt lighter, he was able to have a few relatively spontaneous exchanges with his coworkers. For the first time, he discovered that he was being listened to and, before long, that he was being seen. Whereupon he realized that he had finally *arrived* at the minister's office. That same night, he paid for dinner among a circle of friends. The novelty didn't go unnoticed. His peers were as fascinated as they were flushed—the latter for having drunk three bottles of Château Duvalier, the label of which hardly hid the wine's true provenance.

He reported directly to the chief of staff, who over time began to exchange a few words with him. Nevertheless, Max would still be interrupted by other diplomats just as he was about to wrap up something he was saying. He would keep his composure despite feeling indignant, and even managed to smile at his colleagues—as they completed, in a rather mundane way, a thought that had been his own. Thus he learned, at great personal cost, to control himself, thereby initiating a circuitous process that would lead him to laugh at bad jokes at the right time, rounding them out, whenever possible, with a phrase that made them more amusing.

All in all, he remained unhappy. Matters always went sweeping past him without his being able to examine and elucidate them so as to produce a trace of a more substantive idea that would call attention to him in that environment, where each and every toehold was ferociously fought over. After a few weeks, despite all the business cards he collected while zealously distributing his own (with the title "Assistant to the Minister"), he began to grow impatient. He didn't allow himself to become completely discouraged, however, convinced that he simply needed to stand his ground and persist. And so he contemplated his Corot—and daydreamed.

Where he felt most at ease was with his inner circle of colleagues, who continued to be impressed by his appointment. When they got together for lunch or went out at night, his friends couldn't resist the temptation to ask questions about what went on in that august sphere. Max would give terse replies or pretend not to know. Which only increased his standing within the group, causing them to conclude that he was the keeper of state secrets. His silences were given more weight than his answers.

Max gradually absorbed into his personality the illusion he projected, creating a formidable image based in part on a priestly model suitable to the grandeur of his office. Moreover, he availed himself of penetrating looks when reading memos and telegrams, letting half words slip out here and there, fragments that would reflect the secrets he was believed to keep.

During this stage, Max lacked only substance. That would soon come, thanks to divine intervention. For, oddly enough, the gods are as attentive to dishonorable men as to the rest.

# 4

The months leading up to the military coup of 1964 spawned all kinds of naïve and contradictory rumors. Despite the intellectual climate of the time, with its myriad speeches, articles, conjectures, provocations, and challenges, an almost childlike innocence prevailed. Everything was taken into account except the obvious: that the military, convinced that values were disintegrating around them, were going to move their old tanks into the streets and intervene in the political arena.

No one, aside from the small circle of conspirators, was seriously considering this possibility—even though many in the middle class expressed fear regarding the populist direction the government was headed in, and participated in large demonstrations, organized by the most traditional sectors of society, with the open support of members of the clergy. Reflecting rifts occurring all over the country, the clergy too had splintered, into both a progressive wing, sympathetic to the peasants, students, and union leaders, and a conservative wing, whose most outspoken leader was the solemn Cardinal Archbishop of Rio de Janeiro.

It was in this capacity that the cardinal had asked to meet with the minister. Max had been enlisted as note taker for the session, the first time he'd been entrusted with such an important task. He didn't know to what he owed the honor—and would have been surprised to learn that the assignment had first been offered to his other colleagues, all of whom had declined, on one pretext or another, under the assumption that the cardinal was merely paying a courtesy visit, possibly seeking support for some charity event.

This was not the case, as Max would realize on transcribing his notes. Only as he reread them—he'd been quite nervous throughout the session—did he uncover the real reason for the flowery conversation he'd witnessed: the cardinal's deep concern regarding changes in foreign policy, which seemed to reflect an incomprehensible desire to move the country away from its traditional Christian-based mission and place it dangerously close to certain atheist regimes, with their appalling executions by firing squads—from which not even priests had been spared.

The foreign minister, a career ambassador professionally respected within the ministry for his intellectual strengths and personal integrity, was an affable man. The Brazilian left, lost in its own aspirations—and contradictions—couldn't have found a better face to present to the world. The right, pressed between the greedy elite, which considered nothing but its own interests, and a military machine seduced by the large-scale potential for power, had their own legitimate representative in the cardinal—for one simple reason: his hierarchical superior lived in Rome and counted on direct access to heaven.

The two men's backgrounds thus ended up lending a certain charm to their conversation. Glued to his seat and silenced by the seriousness of the occasion, our note taker had focused on his task. Only his hands moved, the left securing the writing pad, the right flying across the sheets of paper. In this latest encounter between old rivals, the two speakers, both worthy heirs of venerable traditions, replaced with metaphors and pleasantries the cauldrons of scalding oil that their predecessors had poured down on one another from their castle walls.

The minister had removed from his bookshelf the silver-framed photo in which he and his wife appeared in the company of the Pope and placed it prominently on the small central coffee table. The cardinal brought the minister a box of sweets, recalling that his host had revealed on a previous social occasion that he had a weakness for them. And no one made them quite like the nuns of his archdiocese. The two men regarded each other with a certain curiosity. They would have been better friends were it not for their distinct missions: in the minister's case, giving shape and continuity to an independent foreign policy; in the cardinal's, ensuring the greatest possible distance between Brazil and hell.

The minister, given his extensive background, sensed the simple truth that their disparate points of view, which at the moment seemed irreconcilable, were so only in appearance—just as yesterday's troubles cause us to smile today and lose their meaning by tomorrow. Without referring specifically to Evil, he did his best to suggest that, like anything in life, it shouldn't be seen as unchanging. Especially since it could, potentially at least, one day come close to Good. And he illustrated his point with remarks about the foreign policy of other eras, the aims of which, put in perspective, seemed far less compelling or important on that spring morning.

They spoke for an hour. The fact that they were sitting in what had been the Baron of Rio Branco's office during his lifetime—the room where the great wise man had worked like few others on behalf of our country, and in which he had eventually died, surrounded by maps, books, papers, and tremendous admiration—didn't escape either of them. At no point did they become contentious. Anyone who overheard their conversation might even have imagined they were taking part in an academic seminar on topics of no great relevance to the real world.

Max had remained attuned to the rhythm of their words. Lulled by them, he had sensed that his fate would need to follow the narrow path he glimpsed between the two men. There, among their mellifluous tones that harmonized with the breeze rustling the palace's imperial palms, he would see to it that his career came to flourish.

The young man who had entered the minister's office that morning in a smart suit and tie, pen and paper in hand, emerged from those chambers in a monk's habit and Franciscan sandals. He accompanied the cardinal to his car and kissed his ring with fervor and humility. The gesture had deeply moved His Eminence, who would not forget it that night in his prayers. The cardinal's secretary, who had not taken part in the meeting with the minister but remained in the waiting area, reciting the rosary, had gone one step farther: he had made a point of writing down the kind diplomat's name and home phone number. Divine intervention takes many forms. Sometimes as insignificant as a few lines hastily scrawled in a random notebook and tucked away in the pocket of a worn cassock.

# 5

Months later, as the military coup unfolded, the now former minister naturally assumed he might be imprisoned at any moment. Hours after his dismissal, he packed a black leather suitcase with pajamas, a change of clothing, and a collection of Machado de Assis short stories, along with a few toiletries and a pair of slippers. Then, sitting in the living room with his wife, he awaited the car that, by his calculations, would be coming to get him.

While exchanging a few words with his wife, he noticed their photo with the Pope, which he'd retrieved from his office that same afternoon along with a few books and personal papers. He then recalled the cardinal's visit. If he were imprisoned, would he receive sweets from the prelate? Deep down, he knew he probably wouldn't be arrested or experience further disgrace. These seemed reserved for the workers, students, and intellectuals who would inevitably fall into the hands of the repression. But he did feel certain that his career would end here. He consoled himself with the prospect of finally beginning the first volume of his memoirs. Three weeks earlier, which now seemed so distant, one of his staff members, whom he'd gotten used to calling by his nickname, had offered to help with this undertaking.

*Max*... To keep from dwelling on unpleasant subjects, the ex-minister focused briefly on the curious personality of this recent graduate of the Rio Branco Institute. In their few months working together, the efficient assistant had never ceased to amaze him. It all had started on the day of the cardinal's visit. That morning, the young man had gone completely unnoticed, as though he were part of the furniture. But the quality of his notes had left an excellent impression, capturing with absolute faithfulness what the two men had said. There was more, though, something only a discerning reader would have picked up between the lines: the two men's *thoughts*. To convey these, the young man had used parentheses, interspersed throughout the text like random brushstrokes, and inserted within them were his own brief comments.

At first the minister had been annoyed. But on examining the text more closely, he'd given in to the charm (and effectiveness) of the novelty. He had then told the chief of staff, "Keep an eye on this guy, he's a mind reader." And, without batting an eye, he had added, "I want him at all future meetings." For if Max could read his thoughts—and decipher those of the cardinal with equal skill—he surely had other talents.

Word had soon spread around the minister's office. From then on, everyone listened to Max without interruption, except to praise or reinforce what he was saying. The minister submitted documents for Max to edit and offer suggestions. It was up to him to decide on the number and frequency of quotes, as well as to balance these with objective data that would accurately reflect the reality of Brazilian society.

The young assistant had been part of the select group of diplomats accompanying the minister to the United Nations. All versions of the celebrated speech given by Brazil at the opening of the UN's General Assembly had been run past him, without, truth be told, his contributing a single word to the original. But the fact that the drafts had been sent to him for review at the minister's orders spoke volumes.

So thought the former minister, from the depth of his sofa, his eyes on the Pope—and on the suitcase by the door. So thought the veteran diplomat, as he considered the abyss into which the country would now sink. Oh, well, one or two generations would be sacrificed; clouds of intolerance and arrogance would hang over the country, possibly over the entire region. But one day, the truth would reign once more—it was simply a matter of time.

At that very hour, in his room in Humaitá, Max was busy exploring different worlds. His fantasies were soaring in sync with the Bach prelude he was listening to. The room was dark, except for the reddish tints from the blinking Coca-Cola sign at the corner bakery not far from his window. Max smiled, his face alternately shadowy and red. He had just received a reassuring phone call regarding his fate from the Cardinal Archbishop's secretary, with whom he'd discreetly kept in touch since the meeting between His Eminence and the ex-minister. True patriots would not be hounded or harassed by the military, he had been told. And there was more: a place had been reserved for him at the celebratory mass at Candelária Church. In the eighth pew, where the colonels would be seated—and, with any luck, if they arrived from Rio Grande do Sul in time, two generals.

Over the weeks that followed, Max's colleagues, who were just embarking on their careers, felt lost, like actors stepping onto a set without knowing their lines. Being very young, they were disoriented. Their studies had prepared them to enter an institution whose scenarios and realities were now suddenly gone. Ideas, commitments, and loyalties had been swept away. Like the baby swans precariously balancing on their feet on the palace lawns, they sought signs on their superiors' faces indicating which direction to take.

Seen collectively, the seasoned diplomats could be considered "right-minded liberals," in other words, moderates, who could readily serve the left, as they'd done in recent years, or the right, as they were preparing to do—provided the latter presented itself in a palatable form. These moderates set aside the past and confronted the future with a clinical eye, claiming to serve the State, not the Government—given that any administration was temporary by definition. As such, they wove a large, accommodating veil under which they would soon seek shelter.

For Max's group, who received third- or fourthhand the scraps of rumors circulating along the corridors of the recently established power, the biggest surprise turned out to be the smooth landing of their most distinguished colleague. Max, as might be expected, left the demoted minister's office. But, contrary to what had happened to his former colleagues—who were relegated to obscure, menial, or insignificant jobs—he wound up in another prestigious office, that of the ministry's new secretary-general.

To those who were astonished by his effortless transfer, given that it had occurred against a jarring backdrop of dislocations and revenge, Max explained that the *Revolution* (he pronounced the word with a hint of irony) needed to find men, within the ministry, who would "help ensure a smooth transition to the new era." He jokingly added, as if he'd really had no other choice, "men who can not only think but *write*."

*So it was a kind of personal sacrifice* was what the more naïve came to believe. A sacrifice that would enable him to assist in the effort to preserve the institution to which they all belonged. Even if to do so (and here our hero, with a show of modesty, had lowered his eyes) he had to surrender his personal convictions—which, incidentally, as he also hastened to make clear, "had never been thoroughly aligned with the previous populist regime." Thus, poised at the crossroads, Max once again felt the unique burden of his position.

Being the disciplined man that he was, however, he learned how to use his next years at the secretary-general's office to deepen his contacts and solidify alliances, within and outside the ministry. He handled South American issues, prepared the documentation for meetings, reviewed the speeches that would be given at regional events, and took part in high-level conferences. He didn't exactly formulate policy but helped implement it. Day by day on the job, he gained experience in treating matters objectively—along with something else that he himself would have had trouble defining but that his colleagues had no problem identifying: Max was discreetly, but systematically, consolidating his own authority.

"It was something," a diplomat who dealt with him often at that time confided to me, "that came through primarily in the *tone* of his voice." Far from the feigned humility that had characterized his speech during his first few weeks at the ministry, his tone had become steely. "There was a hint of impatience to it, even in mundane situations." This colleague also detected what I would later confirm: the almost imperceptible conceit with which Max addressed superiors he didn't particularly respect, as though he were sharpening his claws and suggesting the obvious: that the years separating them denoted age, not experience.

At my first lunch with Max in 1968, I was intrigued by the fact that he was still in Brazil after five years of service. I remember mentioning this over coffee, though only in passing, since we were not yet close friends. Instead of staying in Rio de Janeiro, he might have opted for a post in Europe, as was customary after a long stint at headquarters. Had he left, his path might have gone the way of so many others who paid lip service to the current regime and retreated into the landscape without further damage to their personal image.

It just so happened, however, that Max had gotten used to living in the precincts of power. The chemistry that bound him to its scenarios and players was so intense and intoxicating that he could no longer do without it. "In Paris, I would have the Seine, the Louvre, the Champs-Elysées," he once told me, lighting one of the Cuban cigars he used to smoke back then.

"Here," he added between puffs, "I have the ear of those calling the shots."

*The ear of those calling the shots.* What could be more exhilarating? No one who has worked in government would fail to appreciate such an enticing treasure, albeit hard to put into words. Being one of the anointed, having it reinforced daily over a shared cup of coffee—such intimacy undoubtedly conferred an exquisite sense of fulfillment. "The minister's office kindly requests that..." The velvety opening phrases perfectly conveyed the tone imposed by the higher-ups: they demanded, to be sure, but they did so with the utmost courtesy. The order was thus delivered with a soft touch, almost a caress. That the request couldn't be refused was a fact that went unnoticed. As unnoticed as the servers who circulated among them in silence with their trays of water or coffee.

6

Although no one suspected at the time, it would surface later that from the very onset of the military regime Max had helped build a bridge between the ministry and the *security community*, the seed of what would become the National Intelligence Service—the much-feared SNI.

It all began at the casual, seemingly offhand suggestion of the cardinal's secretary, a man with good military contacts whose name would eventually appear on the list of the privileged few who received a daily phone call from SNI headquarters. "I think I have just the man for you," the priest had said at the time.

Although Max's special connections weren't common knowledge at the secretary-general's office, where he performed the same kinds of tasks as his colleagues, no one could overlook one particular anomaly in that environment: his desk wasn't in one of the main rooms, where staff sat clustered in groups of three or four, but in a separate area, the entrance to which remained shielded by a partition diplomats rarely passed through.

Not that their entry was prohibited. Far from it. But since it wasn't a high-traffic area, leading from one room to another, or to someone else's office, no one came by there—unless summoned. And these individuals slipped in discreetly.

A friend who served at the secretary-general's office at the time remarked that the little room was not so much seen as imagined. Perhaps that was why, in order to demystify the secrecy associated with his secluded corner, Max often visited his colleagues' work areas, under various pretexts, which then allowed for informal conversations about what he liked to call "assorted agenda items." He would make these rounds without his jacket, which remained hanging on the back of his chair. He wasn't the only one to go around in shirtsleeves, but he was among the few to do so around the younger staff, which, in everyone's view, contributed to his elevated status on the hierarchical scale governing our lives.

In those early days, the SNI, or its first incarnation, was located in downtown Rio, on the thirteenth floor of the Treasury Department. One of the building's main entrances faced Avenida Antônio Carlos, not far from the Maison de France, one of the hubs of Rio's intellectual life due to the new wave films first shown there and the plays (Brecht and Ionesco, interspersed with Feydeau or Dürrenmatt) that brought together well-known casts and select audiences.

Max went regularly to the Maison de France and could often be seen at the restaurant next door indulging in a sandwich before some show. On at least one occasion, however, he was also spotted on the notorious thirteenth floor of the treasury building. But twenty years would elapse before a connection could be made between his presence there and his secret activities. The person who saw him in the waiting room at that fateful address late one afternoon, and greeted him with relief, had come seeking information on the whereabouts of a relative who had disappeared—and couldn't imagine that Max was there for a different reason. After embracing our friend, with an intensity that presumably reflected shared fears and concerns, this person had discreetly whispered an affectionate "good luck" on seeing Max give a wave and slip through a door.

To some extent, and like many of our generation, I too let myself be fooled by the nature of Max's activities. Since he took part in our group's most conspicuous tasks, I considered him a member of our team, one whose duties might occasionally have been confidential but entirely owing to the sensitive nature of the matters he dealt with.

In retrospect, we all seemed to be part of a large-scale puzzle, of which numerous pieces were missing. Today it would be easy to put together this long, sprawling mosaic and deduce the reasons that led some of our colleagues, passed over for promotion, to choose the stairs when they saw Max approaching the elevator. But how could we have known then? And how could we have found out what led Ana, the talented actress our hero seemed to get along with so well, to slowly pull away—to the point of not even greeting him in public?

Anyone who knew the couple simply thought that Max had swapped the young woman for the daughter of a well-known banker. Along with his circle of five or six friends, they could be seen at the Jockey Club or in the pergola at the Copacabana Palace, where they were photographed for the social columns. By then, the old group from Urca had already split up.

At this stage, Max incorporated Pascal and Saint-Simon into his extensive readings, perhaps out of a need to go back in time and brace himself for the transitions still to come. He was also careful enough to relegate the works he had devoured in his youth to the top shelves of his bookcases and obscure them with photos and knickknacks. Beyond that, he immersed himself in jazz with feverish intensity, as if he'd found an outlet that would help him deal with the contradictory world he currently moved in. Except that now I was the only one who joined him on these lonely voyages—which became increasingly rare.

Many years later, after democracy had been restored, a diplomat of his generation gained access to documents that confirmed Max's ties with the intelligence community. Finger raised, he confronted him with the proof. Max did not back down. He simply said, "But what did you expect, my good man? *Someone* had to play that role." His smile suggested, *You all were lucky it was me.* Besides, he soon added, his participation had *merely been sporadic.* Attributable to the geopolitical options of the government at the time. He claimed he hadn't been at all involved with the persecution of diplomats. Especially since, according to him, those accusations had resulted from special political inquiries, which he would never have taken part in.

It's possible. Just as it's possible that, at that stage, he had indeed been acting solely on the level of ideas. Particularly because the generals, fascinated by a power to which they'd never had such unrestricted and complete access, discovered they were statesmen. Therefore, they needed theories that would legitimize their goals and priorities, not just anticommunist propaganda. Even if this had been adequate to put them in power, slogans alone would never keep them there.

Max had read everything, from Confucius to Walter Benjamin, from Machiavelli to Hans Morgenthau, from Proudhon to Arnold Toynbee, not to mention Gramsci, Adorno, Max Weber, and Hannah Arendt. He knew how to adapt, simplify, and, above all, manipulate the information he would occasionally take from each of these sources. Furthermore, he was truly knowledgeable about South America. He embraced Marshall McLuhan's ideas with such enthusiasm that all were convinced of the need to censor the media at once. He had had access to a copy of *Strategic Intelligence Production*, the work of a US general, which he had absorbed like few others—and would use as part of his personal rhetoric, alternating quotes from it with lines by Sun Tzu ("As is written in *The Art of War*," he would declare, narrowing his eyes and giving his version of a Chinese accent, "every battle is won... before it is ever fought").

His sense of humor was much appreciated for allowing everyone to demonstrate their wit and intellectual nimbleness by laughing at his jokes. But his strength derived from the theoretical information needed by the lower military echelons on whom the new leaders depended. The War College officers would regularly call him for informal conversations, which would last all night and include, as a final touch, a stroll along a nearby beach to watch the sun rise and a new Brazil emerge.

# 7

Max met Marina, the banker's daughter he would eventually marry, on the train from Rio to São Paulo. She was, he would tell me months later, "a shy but tenacious girl." Marina, who was in her early twenties and had not yet experienced true love, had been charmed by a man whose calm demeanor reminded her of a younger version of her father. The same deliberate gestures, the same clearly enunciated speech, as though he were reciting lines of poetry.

Marina was nearsighted and wore glasses. Max had dismissed her beauty at first, picking up on it little by little, as if the figure in front of him needed time to emerge from the shadows in order to come into focus.

She was tall and dressed with a casual elegance that bordered on reserved. The women in our group would never fail to notice the quality of her clothing, usually by some renowned designer. At least initially, they treated Marina with hostility. And even though she pretended not to notice, it stung nonetheless.

With his discerning eye, Max had immediately noted her composure when she came into his compartment. The young woman's poise had led him to lower his newspaper.

"Pardon me," she had said softly, "but I think this compartment was reserved for me." Only then had she looked straight at him.

*She must be right*, he had thought, both surprised and disconcerted. Sharing a cabin with a young woman on a night train didn't actually make much sense to him. *Had there been some mistake?*

He searched his jacket pocket for his ticket.

"Could be," he started to say as he stood. "But I'm afraid...I think I'm in the right compart—"

"No," she interrupted politely, after leaning over his ticket and pointing to the number on the door.

Max had, in fact, been mistaken. Not only was he in the wrong compartment, he was in the wrong car! Embarrassed, he apologized and folded his newspaper. The woman watched with amusement as he hastily gathered his belongings.

Later, when they came across each other again in the restaurant car, she smiled and invited him to join her, extending her hand warmly, "Marina Magalhães de Castro."

"Marcílio Andrade Xavier."

"*Andrade Xavier?*"

"Yes...*and no*," he was quick to reply. "It's a long story."

"It's a long trip," she offered.

And the train continued along its tracks, only now at a livelier pace. A bottle of red wine appeared as if by magic. The two glasses the young woman drank took a greater toll on her than his six. Then came the name game. They had mutual friends, both in and outside Itamaraty. And although they didn't travel in the same social circles, they frequented the fringe world of artists and intellectuals. With the thrill of those on the brink of larger discoveries, they confirmed that they had other favorite haunts in common: from seaside restaurants to the Da Vinci bookstore, from the movie sessions at Paissandu to the nighttime races at the Jockey Club. Marina's father's bank had financed several Cinema Novo films. They had attended the same previews without knowing it. And this now tickled them, as if the news might foreshadow other exciting moments.

Max had had no trouble pinpointing his companion's social status. Her roots could be traced back to an old agrarian aristocracy on her mother's side, and a fortune built and consolidated in the financial market on her father's. She, in turn, had noticed that her fellow traveler didn't fit the usual diplomat stereotype. Although well mannered, he didn't have the pretentious airs or affected behavior of his colleagues. He showed genuine interest in what she said, without seeming to think his own words carried any special weight. Everything about his appearance suggested seriousness—yet he acted as if the last thing he expected was to be taken seriously.

Perhaps because of that, or the slight hope that takes hold of someone shy confronted by the unexpected on a night train, Marina ended up being the one to utter the decisive line of the evening. After talking at length about their respective journeys in the somewhat nonchalant tone of people who didn't harbor unrealistic expectations, Max pointed out that, with the train's arrival at the station, their paths would part once more. She swallowed one last gulp of wine and took a deep breath before throwing down the gauntlet: "Unless fate works its wonders and brings us together again."

Not even the jesting tone in which the line was delivered had stripped the words of their subtext as Max heard it: fate...wonders...and fortune, he had mused to himself.

The next day, Marina confessed to a friend over the phone, "I don't know where I got the courage to say something so ridiculous." Before adding, not very convincingly, "It must have been the wine." (*If you say so*, her friend was probably thinking on the other end of the line.)

Marina knew perfectly well that her boldness was born of old longings. But she was unaware of the underlying cause: the flames of the small hearth fire built for two on that night train had been carefully kindled by Max.

After dinner, the two had stayed in the dining car for more than an hour, peppering their conversation with longer and longer pauses. Marina gazed out at the small towns and villages they were passing through in the middle of the night, which seemed like apparitions, but in a shared dream. Every so often the train would go through a tunnel, and the two travelers' profiles suddenly became visible in the fogged-up window, only to disappear again into the landscape. This left her feeling as if they'd gone off together toward glorious destinations, whereas the man seated across from her, contemplating the same scenery, saw things more pragmatically.

Suddenly, as if overcome by a profound weariness, they retired to the cocoons of their respective sleeping compartments. They wanted to replay their conversations in the dark, to the rocking of the train, with no witnesses other than their own hopes and desires.

Marina had admired the straightforward candor with which Max had spoken of his separation, even though the subject tugged at her heartstrings. Listening to details about the breakup of his relationship with his ex-wife, she discovered how alone she too had felt throughout her adolescence and early adult life. Without realizing it, she had wandered into unfamiliar territory, the sort of place where soul mates sometimes meet.

Max didn't sleep at all that night. Watching the succession of shadows that flickered on the ceiling of his cabin, he weighed the implications of this chance encounter. It seemed that suddenly, due to a whim of the gods, he would be able to take a decisive step toward reacquiring what he had always seen as his, thereby sealing the promise of a stellar future that had begun with his entrance into Itamaraty.

He would say little about this encounter to his colleagues. For months, Marina remained shrouded in an aura of mystery, from which she rarely emerged, save in a photo published in some paper or the hushed sound of her voice on a whisper-filled phone call.

I owe the detailed description of the train scene to her. We became friends over time, sounding each other out as we conducted separate investigations into the enigma that was Max. Whereas I sought more objective truths bearing on the realities of my career, Marina's search would probe deeper, taking the form of an obsession in years to come.

Why, Marina would ask herself, had Max stopped loving her as intensely as she did him? Why, after the wedding, had he begun to withdraw—compelling her to entangle herself even farther in their desperate relationship? What could possibly have gone wrong?

The more she anxiously turned to her husband, childishly exposing herself by calling him persistently and giving him gifts of records he hardly listened to or books he barely read, the more Max seemed to retreat. The game had intrigued her at first but soon became frustrating, leading her to have recurring nightmares of quicksand and free falls in space.

Life hadn't prepared her for major challenges, and surely hadn't endowed her with defenses against situations of this kind. She couldn't identify its origins or the reasons for her malaise. She had even fought with her older sister, who had simply tried to put the problem in perspective by saying, "Maybe he just doesn't like women... these things happen all the time among diplomats."

Marina didn't know how to deal with a man who, after showing initial interest—and desire—in a thousand ways, gradually distanced himself from her, albeit almost imperceptibly. She didn't know what to make of a husband who had shown so little passion on their wedding night, before falling immediately into a heavy sleep beside her, leaving her alone as if suspended in the dark.

That night, while the wedding guests slept peacefully, dreaming of overflowing seafood platters, a troubling seed had embedded itself in a forgotten corner of her being—the same one that, years later, would lead her to seek comfort in the arms of other men out of loneliness and spite.

Max, for his part, was deluded into believing that being with Marina made him immune to all types of threats and dangers. He thought that, with her at his side, no one would be able to touch him. In one respect, he was right, as she would remain his companion on a socially irreproachable path that enhanced his career during the twelve years they lived together. But if Max led a double life at work, in the private realm of his relationship with Marina he ended up committing far more painful kinds of duplicity, leaving in their wake countless wounds and scars.

He would be surprised, even angry, should someone reveal that, in spite of his formidable defense mechanisms, he loved his wife. To preclude the anxiety and fear of such a discovery, he had chosen to keep his feelings in check. Thus his tendency to respond almost indifferently to the affection directed at him. And to position himself as his wife's tutor rather than her partner. After all, he thought, she was young and had much to learn. Such prosaic truths give rise to misunderstandings. And disappointments.

Of the saga I've taken up, I know only what was told to me piecemeal and diluted over time. But my impression of the couple's failed relationship is clear: unlike his secret world, which he managed for better or worse, Max would pay a much higher price with the failure of his marriage.

Far beyond remaining the rich wife who brought him the social and financial support he deemed necessary, Marina ultimately became a painful counterpoint to his life—deep-rooted in abandonment. Would he ever have suspected that he used his wife like a mirror, to hide evils of another nature?

One thing is apparent, however: this state of affairs might have contributed to his withdrawal from himself—and from all of us. Socially adrift since childhood, simultaneously dazzled and intimidated at work by circles beyond his reach, Max would respond poorly when confronted with his wife's increasing vulnerability. He had to believe that Marina was strong: he needed her. The way a warrior needs his shield.

Less than a year had gone by between the Rio–São Paulo train ride and the wedding reception at the Santa Teresa mansion where the Magalhães de Castros lived—a party I attended along with a significant portion of carioca society and most of Itamaraty.

Dressed in an understated silk gown and adorned with flowers, Marina had come down somewhat belatedly to the mansion's ground floor. In the garden, where she was met with cheers from the guests as a flight of white doves was released, Max greeted her reverently with a chaste kiss on the forehead. A first sign of what would lie ahead.

# 8

The twelve years of Max and Marina's marriage would largely coincide with the worst phase of the dictatorship in our country. And during the tense political situation that marked the end of this period ("slow and gradual easing up," as the authorities liked to remind everyone), their personal ties would finally unravel.

It is hard to fathom how Max's two worlds—his professional and private lives—coexisted. I don't think they ever really came into contact. But Max had to remain constantly on the alert.

Although his in-laws' clan was traditionally conservative, they never backed the military, from whom they distanced themselves to the greatest extent possible. And if their social class had benefited from the repression imposed on the country, particularly in regard to control of unions and the undermining of workers' expectations, it's also true that not all who belonged to this segment of our society stood by, or cooperated with, the regime. There were those who sought to remain discreetly neutral. A dignified stance, compared to the position of those who openly approved of the dictatorship—or financed it.

The Magalhães de Castros' fortune, moreover, was solid enough that family members weren't afraid of retaliations and could therefore act independently. For a few years, Marina's father continued to fund plays and films produced by progressive intellectuals and refused to stop advertising in leftist newspapers that had initially managed to survive thanks to attitudes like his.

The *Correio da Manhã*, to cite just one example (and there were many political and literary magazines among them), wouldn't have lasted as long as it did were it not for the clan's support.

Their Santa Teresa mansion served as an oasis in Rio de Janeiro for many years. Despite the atmosphere in the city and the country, people could speak their minds freely within its walls. Every time we entered the gateway to the property's sprawling grounds and drove past the pool from which friends and acquaintances would wave, drinks in hand, we felt we were entering paradise.

It was in this same privileged environment, at one of the Sunday luncheons Marina's parents would periodically organize in order to see their now-married daughter, that I met a colonel friend of Max's from the Brazilian Coffee Institute.

I was somewhat taken aback by the way he greeted me. He clicked his heels and bowed his head rather formally. Then he shook my hand firmly and whispered, "Colonel Cordeiro," in a low voice as if "Colonel" were his first name, the equivalent of João, Marcelo, or Pedro. This was of course customary among the armed forces, giving rank and surname in a single breath. But the fact that I heard it in such a protected space, and that it sounded so irritatingly natural besides, made me feel the stench of oppression right under my nose.

Of average height and muscular build, the colonel was about fifty years old. He smiled a lot, but somewhat gratuitously, a trait that gave him an air of perpetual politeness, vague and undefined, which did little to ingratiate him with those present. Ironically, his surname, Cordeiro, the Portuguese word for *lamb*, also called to mind the fables of Aesop and La Fontaine, suggesting there was a wolf in sheep's clothing in our midst—and not even the banality of the cliché comforted me. The colonel's pointy white teeth contrasted sharply with his friendly appearance, as if at any sign of discord something unexpected might happen. Aside from his teeth, however, I didn't detect more overt suggestions of contained violence. On the contrary, his body language remained relaxed. Yet in five minutes of conversation with me, discussing various topics, he twice declared, "But this, you have to admit, is a matter of principle." And with that, one of his many masks came off.

I don't recall exactly what we were talking about, but hearing "you have to admit" followed by "a matter of principle" conjured for me a sinister world of innuendos in which compromise would prove impossible should differences of opinion arise.

If linguists one day undertake a more refined study of speech from this authoritarian period, they'll find that numerous phrases during those dark times went from being innocuous to intimidating. We were to hear "But this, you have to admit, is a matter of principle" at Itamaraty countless times over the next few years. The interjection "my good man" would often be thrown in for emphasis, as if the term of endearment held an additional veiled threat.

But to return to Max's friend, at one point, as we were speaking of the Coffee Institute, the colonel raised his eyes skyward and sighed. "The revolution hasn't gotten there yet." Right after that, in a theatrical gesture, he lowered his head and devoted himself to a moment of almost melancholic reflection. As if, in his view, the "revolution" hadn't reached a number of places. Which would thus explain the corruption prevalent in them.

The idea of a Greater Brazil wasn't yet being broached. It would take a few years before that entity bared its fangs in the economic and commercial sectors. And we hadn't yet won the 1970 World Cup, which would boost our national pride considerably. Even so, the colonel turned out to be a harbinger of those times.

What intrigued me most that day, further illustrating my naïveté with respect to Max and his labyrinths, was the fascination this character held for my friend. Evidently Max hadn't reached this stage through an admiration based on moral or intellectual values. Or through more trivial motives, which sometimes lead a man to value in others talents he himself lacks. No. To my surprise, his fascination had darker origins, as he himself would hint to me one day, in a conversation about the colonel.

"It's that he's different from us," he explained at the time, averting his eyes.

"Different how?" I asked innocently.

And Max murmured, "He's killed a man."

Certain revelations leave an indelible impression on those who hear them. Clearly that anonymous death had deeply affected Max. It was as if by taking a life, the colonel had made his own less insipid.

# 9

The armed forces never really worried about Itamaraty as a focal point of subversive activities. The ministry was held to be an elite group, given the rigorous admission process that had been in place for generations. The generals tended to regard leftist leanings that might exist within it as more intellectual than radical in nature. Besides, they were dealing with far more serious challenges on other fronts.

The military commanders nonetheless needed to find people to monitor us, people who would blend in, since the idea of having SNI agents infiltrate our environment was unthinkable. At first, as had been done in other government offices, a Division of Security and Information (DSI) was created at Itamaraty. This proved to be merely a smokescreen, a seemingly innocuous oversight agency. Behind it, however, lay the real agents, selected from among our own diplomats. Thanks to them, the regime had access to everything we wrote. Though few in number, these intermediaries wove an invisible, intimidating web around the rest of us. Their names would remain largely unknown, even after the regime was over.

Since none of this was common knowledge, we lived in a nebulous world, dealing with international issues that seemed strangely removed from our government's stance. This often led to some bizarre situations: in a right-wing country, we were increasingly allowed to formulate a left-leaning foreign policy. As a result, we would be the first government to recognize the independence of Socialist Angola and, to the astonishment of our own military, one of the first to reestablish diplomatic ties with Communist China.

It was a way for us to retaliate, thought the more naïve among us. Or to delude ourselves, concluded the more realistic. Because even if we could achieve an independent foreign policy, we would be dismissed and jailed, just as one of our colleagues had been, were we to go public regarding the torture and missing persons on the rise in Brazil.

Amid these contradictions, as young apprentices, we also kept a close watch on one another, not knowing if we were sharing an office with some enemy or were "lunchable" for dubious reasons.

Since Max was my friend and, at the time, I knew nothing of his covert dealings, I felt comfortable opening up to him about the widespread mediocrity overtaking the government, particularly in our more restricted environment. He would laugh heartily, agreeing with some of my venting but never failing to tactfully add a few favorable words about the military. Nothing that made me suspect he had an incestuous relationship with them, but his comments always seemed somehow to endorse the regime.

Although I continued to find conversation with him amusing, it pained me, as the intellectual I took myself to be, to imagine that a person I trusted and admired could have become so closely identified with such a system. When I called him to account, he claimed to have reached the conclusion that the populist republic needed to be dismantled so that other realities might now be examined. When I pressed further, condemning the increasing intensity of the military repression, he reminded me of the alternatives proposed by our small, now disbanded group from Urca: take up arms—or work within the system.

"*Within* the system?" I asked. "But *for* or *against?*"

"As if there were a difference..." He laughed in response.

One day, concerned about the activities of a colleague who was deeply entrenched with the right, I asked Max if he thought that *lives* might be at stake as a consequence of the man's actions. He launched into one of his tirades: "But, my friend, if it were only lives we were dealing with..."

From then on, I felt Max's integrity was being corrupted by indifference or cynicism. Paradoxically, these attitudes didn't seem to prevent him from showing a certain aptitude for criticizing the regime. His detractors would later say that he was serving, in this capacity, as an agent provocateur, ferreting out colleagues he could inform on.

Today, I prefer to think that such displays were simply escape valves in which he indulged, so as to keep face among us. These forays in the Legions of Good, as Max called them, allowed him to revisit ideals that had been part of his upbringing, and in which, I want to believe, he still had faith. I've come to think that at some level he never stopped seeing himself as a Socialist at heart, although he had given in to the right (as he used to joke) *while it needed him.* This hidden conviction may even have been what enabled him to move toward the left when such shifts became expedient. Undoubtedly, others in our midst had behaved the same way.

What bothered me most about Max at that stage wasn't so much his defense of the right, no matter how cynical it sounded to me at times. Nor was it his tendency to downplay the abuses committed by the military. (Despite the censorship, we received word of these regularly.) After all, we had met when he was at the secretary-general's office, working quite closely with those in power. No, what bothered me then, perhaps from what little I knew of him in other contexts, was a more troubling flaw, because it was rooted in one of the most vulnerable aspects of human frailty—flattery. He was a master in the refined art of pleasing those in power by appealing to intellectual qualities they rarely possessed.

Influenced by his readings, he upheld a theory of vanity that he continued to perfect throughout his career. For him, the only true antidote to vanity was pride. When someone was said to be "a man without vanity," he was most likely an individual with a strong sense of pride. According to Max, because the proud were so confident, they "didn't need others' stamp of approval." It was as if they were immune to some lesser evil.

Despite the unsavoriness associated with the sin of pride, for Max it implied greatness. And since this trait was becoming scarce at the ministry, he was left with the more prosaic alternative of dealing with the vain.

He moved well on this fertile ground, however, whatever shape it took—and there were many, which in turn required good judgment and a certain selectivity. In order to set himself apart from other colleagues also competing for favors, Max had chosen a single course: literature.

In this particular field he had no rivals. He worked with the precision of a surgeon, able to wend his way with a scalpel through the most twisted and delicate passages. "One doesn't praise a poem the way one does a necktie," he would declare.

He earned the trust of his superiors, who submitted their manuscripts to him. He would eloquently extol the virtues of texts that deserved eternal damnation. Or he would comment on poems with tears welling in his eyes—and then later reread these to me while howling with laughter. As such, he encouraged mediocre authors, within and outside Itamaraty, to publish their works in books or offprints, assuring them that they didn't deserve the obscurity to which they'd been relegated.

Even though his victims didn't rank among people I particularly respected, I felt sorry for them without exception. In the more modest pantheon of lesser evils, it seems to me, there is no greater sin than taking advantage of others' weaknesses to further one's own cause. And Max proved to be a pro at this, great pretender that he was. When the targets of these maneuvers happened to be the bosses' wives, when the poems (or canvases, or embroidery, or pottery, or whatever else they may have created in a moment of inspiration) were theirs, the cruelty was even worse—for it often affected the innocent and the naïve. "Secretary Xavier said that my poems are *intriguing*," a major's wife once shared with me, twisting the white scarf she held in her hands.

"*Who?*" I asked in surprise.

"Your colleague. The secretary..."

"Oh, *Max*. And what was it he said?"

"He said"—and here she lowered her voice, sensing that certain things aren't to be repeated with impunity—"that my poems are intriguing."

The major was traveling on business to Montevideo, accompanied by his wife. Max and I were also a part of the mission. The proximity of our airplane seats had provided for a certain intimacy among our foursome during the flight. We had chatted about beaches, barbecues, sports, and TV shows. After lunch, the major and Max had fallen asleep, each in his aisle seat, leaving us trapped in the middle of the row.

"You don't say," I replied cautiously. "*Intriguing...*"

She took a deep breath and, slightly embarrassed, glanced at her husband as if making sure he was still asleep. Quietly, she recited the poem for me. It was long and mostly unintelligible, as it competed with the noise of the engines and her companion's snoring. But the last stanza was perfectly audible. In it the hero returns home at dawn, his olive green uniform stained with blood: "*From where would he be coming, my holy warrior, at the break of dawn?*"

Her reverent tone made me realize she was totally unaware of her husband's activities, and yet it seemed eerily prescient. Where indeed were they coming from, these holy warriors? Where were they headed? And what deeds were they performing on their nightly raids that might give rise to a romantic poem in one home—and such grief in others?

# 10

That trip to Uruguay, although only three days long, ended up having an important impact on Max's career, since it was there that he met one of the most sinister Brazilian career diplomats of the time: the head of our embassy in Montevideo. The man displayed a singular efficiency in that universe laced with secrets and conspiracies. A dramatic starkness was evidenced in his speech and gestures—even in his attire. On formal occasions, he had a habit of donning a black waist-length cape over his dark suit, a throwback to another century. He was, in this sense, a courtly figure, but of frosty demeanor. For many at Itamaraty, who spoke of him only in hushed voices yet didn't think twice about embellishing the myth, he was the kind of man who would carry a dagger at his waist. *With a diamond-encrusted handle*, the more inspired would add.

Arriving at a reception—with no shortage of witnesses on hand—the ambassador would casually loosen his black cape and allow it to drop, following his grand entrance, certain that the servants or, in their absence, some younger diplomat in charge of protocol, would rush to retrieve the illustrious cloth before it touched the ground.

Positioned to the right of the right ever since his youth, this high official focused his energies on the all-out battle against communism, in whatever form it might take throughout the international political scene. He admired Karl Marx's work, but only on the conceptual level—since the spirit of those theories tended to confirm the inherent danger of dreams and utopias. But what really riled him was Marxism's growing appeal in Brazil, especially following the Cuban revolution. He considered it a curse that this admiration had created roots (which he judged to be romantic and, therefore, dangerous) among the formulators of Brazilian foreign policy prior to his esteemed "Revolution." To his way of thinking, the association between Marxism-Leninism and the populist traditions of Latin American politicians (*politicians* with the smallest *p* available in good Western typefaces, he liked to emphasize) would destabilize the region. Being an intelligent man, he knew that social changes were necessary, and that delaying them for another hundred years might prove unwise. But like many of his generation, he thought it would be better to let them evolve through predictable patterns and processes, whose repercussions would be under constant scrutiny, than to import foreign ideas formulated for other cultures.

On the night of March 31, 1964—as he would later disclose to Max—the ambassador opened the small refrigerator in his lodgings, where he had kept a half bottle of the finest French champagne stored for months. Wrapped in a silk scarf and dressing gown, he toasted the new times from the balcony of his residence. In contrast to several of his colleagues, who had quickly aligned themselves with the military, he had opted to remain behind the scenes—recognizing that his ideas were too well known.

What he sought and, as was discovered later, had already accomplished at the time I refer to was to form an elite network, within and outside the ministry, which would help the military consolidate its power until it became inviolable. (In less formal circles, or when he had a second drink, he used to introduce a more conciliatory variant into this equation of his: "Or until the people learn to vote.") Should there prove to be interest, we would not shy away from sharing experiences with other countries. As a simple exchange of ideas, naturally. And there was no lack of interest around us, as History would soon reveal.

By one of those coincidences that well-organized social events sometimes afford, Max happened to have a private conversation with the ambassador during a reception the embassy held for the Brazilian delegation visiting Uruguay. This occurred with utmost discretion, as did almost everything else taking place at the residence that night — the guests tiptoeing, doing their best to occupy the least amount of space possible, and soundlessly taking care of their personal agendas.

While I concentrated my best efforts on subtly serving myself a second helping of the excellent lobster salad from the lavish buffet, Max wandered, whiskey in hand, through rooms and hallways, studying paintings, etchings, and Persian rugs, quietly taking note of the mysterious and seductive objects in that collection of antiques set against walls covered with brocades and textiles from other eras. Until he came across the library — and our host on the phone. He quickly retreated, but not soon enough. The ambassador, who was just hanging up, invited him, with a friendly gesture, to peruse the shelves of leather-bound books in his company.

The conversation that followed drew them closer together, although the actual bridge that would ultimately connect them remained hidden for the time being. Well before falling into the orbit of the ambassador's political influence, Max allowed himself to be seduced by his literary prowess, evidenced in the library's collection, as the two discussed books and authors in an exchange of ideas that had gradually mapped out their personal preferences.

Several guests, myself among them, saw Max return to the living room with the ambassador's hand resting on his shoulder in a familiar manner, as if the two, at the end of that conversation, had shared an intimate moment. Both then made a concerted effort to rejoin the reception and casually insert themselves into different groups.

Later that night, once the foreign guests had left and only the Brazilians remained ("the inner circle," in the tired expression someone always used on such occasions), the ambassador probed Max on his personal plans for transfer abroad. During their talk, our host acknowledged that his young colleague must have had a specific foreign post in mind, access to which would be facilitated by his having worked at the secretary-general's office for years. He added, however, that Max shouldn't rule out Montevideo as an option — given his experience with South American issues. According to him, the fragile state of the local democratic regime, combined with the concentration of exiled Brazilians of all social levels and classes, "beginning with our ex-president and his deranged brother-in-law," made work in Uruguay highly stimulating.

"A broad leftist coalition has formed here too," he said at one point, hands crossed over his chest, eyes fixed on the ceiling. "And if they win the next election, there's going to be trouble. A *great deal* of trouble..."

After a sober pause, during which no one said a word, the ambassador continued, "And that's not all."

He went on to sketch the geopolitical picture in neighboring countries, doing so with cool detachment. To my ears his conclusions seemed to point to an imminent series of Greek tragedies. In fact, as he predicted, without lowering his eyes — as if the script of the calamities to come were etched on the ceiling — Uruguay did become the domino piece that, after Brazil and Argentina, would complete the shadow the military cast over the region. The one that would herald the next coup, this time in Chile.

"I'm leaving for the Kingdom of the Tupamaros!" Max would announce to me days later when we had returned to Rio de Janeiro, in a euphoric tone that made me think of a Crusader on the way to the Holy Land.

I wouldn't have been any more surprised had he unsheathed

a sword. But it was his next line that really struck me: "In exchange, I even got a promotion. I'll be going as first secretary."

And in a lower voice, which enhanced rather than contained his joy, he added, "Leapfrogging forty-seven colleagues, to boot."

His fate was sealed. Because if up until then he had acted like an amateur whose information the military appreciated, in Montevideo, under the ambassador's tutelage, his opinions would soon earn accolades as doctrine.

# 11

Max's transfer abroad coincided with the beginning of Itamaraty's move from Rio de Janeiro to Brasilia, which in a way reinforced my feeling that we had both gone into exile. In fact, the new Brazilian capital in early 1970 looked more foreign to my colleagues and me than anyplace beyond our borders. Max, in Montevideo, quite likely felt closer to Rio than did those of us who imagined we were on Mars.

We began to exchange letters regularly through the diplomatic pouch. Mine were long and typically reported on the deteriorating political climate we were living in. Max never commented on my criticisms. On the contrary, he tended to share details of social life on weekends in Punta del Este or trips to the countryside. Marina had friends in Uruguay, the children of bankers her parents knew, who had opened their stately homes to the new arrivals.

Whenever the couple came to Brazil on vacation, or took advantage of some long holiday to leave the post, I almost always found a way to travel to Rio de Janeiro to be with them, which also enabled me to see my family. We would have dinner together in small groups at the Casa da Suíça in Lapa, or at the Château, a lovely restaurant on Anita Garibaldi in Copacabana, which, to our dismay, disappeared a few years later. In these two settings, which rarely varied, we would swap stories about our experiences, bad-mouth our bosses and their wives, and philosophize about the future. Max hardly ever referred to his job other than in very general terms. From what he led us to believe, he was primarily involved in technical cooperation. And he belonged to a poker group, to Marina's displeasure, since she was home alone two nights a week.

During these trips to Rio, the visitors would usually hold a big luncheon for friends and acquaintances at Marina's parents' place. Colonel Cordeiro never failed to show up. Often, when coffee and liqueurs were being served, he would retreat with Max to some remote room for a private talk, the content of which, despite my many attempts, I never managed to learn.

At these gatherings, I slowly began to realize that I no longer saw Max as a mentor of sorts but simply as an older colleague with whom I shared a broad range of interests regardless of our ideological differences. At the same time, and on another level, I sensed Marina was gradually withdrawing. Once full of joie de vivre, she now seemed downcast, which, in my view, didn't correspond to her condition—since, at that stage, she was pregnant with their first child.

It's at large parties that we sometimes share truly private moments, as Fitzgerald memorably remarked, and this is precisely what happened to Max and me at one of these lunches, in 1970, when something he said shot through me like a warning.

We'd had plenty to drink and he allowed himself to get caught up in an unexpected reverie, centered on his boss, whose personality and political opinion were known to all. At some point I asked, half joking, how far to the right Max found himself now. Would he continue to be buoyed by the respectability of the conservative wing, or had he given in to more radical schemes, the secret nature of which I kindly declined to mention?

Max laughed a little at my nerve, but his expression soon grew serious, as if he'd distanced himself from me for a few seconds—and even from the little room to which we'd retreated. I didn't push it. In fact, I began to think I'd gone too far, particularly because I'd never, not even in jest, engaged in conversation with him on such a sensitive subject. But he took one of his Cuban cigars out of his breast pocket and was preparing to light it, which, in the past, typically meant that he wished to think aloud with me, in the unmistakable tone of a man talking to himself. I settled at the opposite end of the sofa where he was seated. It was a long piece of furniture, Italian leather, which would fit four people comfortably. We each kept an arm draped over the back, his left hand holding the lit cigar.

Max began to speak somewhat evasively, as if preparing to launch into a series of reminiscences. Except that his voice, which was usually upbeat and energetic, sounded like that of an old man at the end of his career, concerned with recalling scenes from a distant past. I understood that the withdrawal in some sense protected him, as though sparing my friend from threatening memories. Unsure where Max was headed, and imagining that he too was unclear as to what he really meant, I listened closely, aware of a wistfulness behind his words. Thus my surprise when, at a certain point, and completely off topic, he turned to me and asked, "Have you ever asked yourself why some people collaborate with the military?"

He went on, without awaiting my response: "Out of fear, in some instances . . . or for money, in the case of minor players."

Here he settled back into his seat, further distancing himself from me, and continued. "In our line of work, it's never for money. At most, it's out of fear. Or, more often, for access to power. The *expectation* of access to power."

As luck would have it, I had taken up smoking again that week. A politically incorrect admission today but one that bought me time right then. I pulled out a cigarette and searched my jacket unsuccessfully for a lighter.

Max raised his, flicking it at my eye level.

"How about you?" he asked. "Are you afraid?"

"All the time," I confessed, unblinking, as I lowered his arm and lit my cigarette.

I wasn't lying. But I surprised myself. I wasn't sure where that unexpected revelation had come from. After a long first drag, I added, "Every time I land in Geneva for work, I feel I'm entering another world. Not another country, but another *world*."

# 12

"Such an intriguing notion, fear..." He seemed to be warming to his topic.

*Intriguing?* I remember thinking. Fear could be everything, from chronic to unbearable, from dreadful to dark. But *intriguing?*

Max continued: "Take the guerrilla's fear, for instance"—and here he looked at me, seeking a tacit sign of approval, it would seem, for not having used the then-common term *subversive*—"the guerrilla's fear as he weighs the odds of being caught. Which, depending on the case, might mean *being tortured and killed.* It's a concrete, objective, almost tangible fear, which runs as deep as his beliefs."

He winked at me, as if making an amusing side comment. "As the ambassador has a habit of saying, from the depths of his favorite armchair in his Montevideo office, 'It's fear shrouded in bravado.' A fine phrase, isn't it?"

I no longer knew if he was kidding or serious. I remembered a colleague who loathed him and was always professing, "Max's problem is that he lies all the time." Was he lying? Or simply having fun with me, creating a character inspired by his sinister boss?

He repeated the line, so that I could savor what was to come. "'Fear shrouded in bravado...that only comes to a head when skilled hands—*pop!*—burst the bravado like a bubble.'"

Unable to contain himself, he proceeded, "You can't imagine how happy he is when he goes *pop!* He's like a kid."

He exhaled deeply, long enough for the ambassador to take shape between us, eyes flashing maliciously, the poor blood-covered victim hanging in chains, his bravado undone.

Max calmly went on. "Now, what you were referring to earlier—the fear of someone unaware of why he feels afraid—*that's* something else entirely."

He turned to face me. "Like you, for example. You don't know why you feel afraid. You just know that's how you feel. It's what you tend to think about before you go to sleep. And almost always what you think about when you wake up. Without your having a single thing to feel guilty about. Extraordinary, isn't it?"

I remained silent.

"More than dread or fright, it's an insidious sensation, the strength and *utility* of which come from its constancy." His voice had taken on a professorial tone. It was his boss talking through him.

"And that constancy, do you know what it feeds off? Hundreds of sources at once, from censorship of the press to rumors that someone's disappeared, from doubts about a neighbor's real identity to the possibility of tapped phone lines, from statements by certain colonels who threaten to tighten the screws even further to the decision that political crimes will now be judged by military courts. Year in, year out, nothing changes. And nothing will change. Except for minor details. Because what we're dealing with here, my friend, is a huge and mysterious *oyster*, a self-contained bureaucratic corporation, which depends on absolute cohesion to survive. Its members will fight among themselves and no one will know a thing out here. The head honchos will indeed change. But not their profiles, or their uniforms. Even if these are replaced by suits, there will always be uniforms. The generals will always prevail. And everything will remain that way beyond our generation. Even the fear. *The fear, above all.*"

He briefly smiled at me and concluded in a soft, almost gentle voice, "Because it spreads by contamination."

"Like Camus's plague," I added.

"Exactly."

He got up and found an ashtray, which he set between us on the coffee table. It was high time, since our ashes, which had remained precariously perched, now threatened to fall onto the rug.

Marina came in just then. The carpeted hallway had prevented us from hearing her footsteps. I was taken aback when I saw her, as if I had come face-to-face with a ghost, welcome though the encounter may have been. Only then did I become aware of the angst that had taken hold of me.

Marina seemed overwhelmed. Despite her lovely pregnant form, it was her weary expression that struck me. And the sadness I detected in her eyes.

"Marcílio," she protested, "our guests are looking lost without you."

# PART TWO

# 13

It would be thirteen years before I saw Marina again. After the birth of their son, the couple rarely came to Rio. My trips to Geneva, on the other hand, became more frequent. This wasn't altogether a bad thing, since I'd been shaken by my last conversation with Max in Santa Teresa. I would cross paths with him only in Brasilia, when he periodically returned to Brazil for work. Always alone, never with his wife. So we ended up growing apart, Marina and I. Later, when I was transferred to Los Angeles, our contacts became fewer and farther between. Max, I still saw occasionally. But not her.

As the years went by, there came more news, some good, some less so. Marina had another child with Max, a daughter born in Chile. Four years later, when the couple was living in Washington, she left him. In 1983, however, while on vacation in Rio, I heard of her father's death and went to the wake. I imagined I'd find Marina there with her children. To my surprise, however, the person who kept an arm protectively around her, and remained at her side the entire afternoon—as if a spouse or partner—was Nilo Montenegro, an actor I quickly recognized, who had performed in several Teatro de Arena plays and Joaquim Pedro de Andrade films, and helped produce the first *Opinião* shows. Marina's father's bank had financed several of his plays in the 1960s, when the openings would invariably be celebrated at the house in Santa Teresa, with parties that would go on all night—and be faithfully reported in the next day's papers.

Smiling tearfully, Marina hugged me and said affectionately, "You two know each other, don't you?" Before we could
answer, she added in a tender voice, "Nilo Montenegro..."

From down on his small satin pillow, surrounded by flowers, Marina's father seemed to be smiling at us. I stood beside his
coffin for a few minutes. The longer I looked at him, the more
he seemed to smile. He must have somehow sensed the growing line of artists and intellectuals in the small São João Batista
chapel, made up largely of men and women whose works owed
much to his altruism and whose attendance also represented the
dead and the disappeared.

Marina and I made plans to get together and ended up seeing
each other the following week, on a night Nilo had traveled to
São Paulo. When I arrived at the small apartment the two shared
in Jardim Botânico, she greeted me with a photo album in hand.
Leafing through it while Marina fixed me a drink, I could see
nearly fifteen years of her life unfold before me, in Uruguay as
well as in the cities that had come after Montevideo. I saw that
Max had put on weight with the arrival of their first child, and
had grown a beard after the birth of their second. All the while
collecting medals and decorations, visible on his jacket lapels
in some photos, pinned in rows to his gala uniforms in others.
Even so, as often happens in such cases, he started to appear less
and less on each page, until he didn't show up at all. Nothing
like a family album to let us see, far beyond the ravages of time,
the personal and emotional hardships that shape our lives.

As I expected, Marina got to talking about her ex-husband.
That was when she told me the train story in full detail, while
I continued to flip through the album, now from back to front.
She described the encounter with Max in the wrong cabin
and spoke of the long dinner that would change her life. "It's
strange," she added after a pause. "When I met Marcílio and we
spent a good part of the night talking in that deserted car, I
was positive that endless possibilities would open before me. And

all for one ridiculous reason: simply because he was listening to me. No one had ever listened to me that way before, with an intensity that shut out the rest of the world.... It was just an illusion, of course."

She looked at me with some small hope that I would be able to grasp what she was trying to say. And she continued, "I was barely twenty years old, a victim of one of those classic adolescent infatuations. With someone I mistook for a father figure. Someone who knew how to play his part adeptly, giving me the attention I desperately craved—and hadn't received in my childhood."

She took the album from my lap and chose a photo at random. "Santiago," she said. "The worst time of my life. And the country's." She then told me about a lover of hers back then, an Italian photographer named Paolo. I had the impression she was talking to herself as her tone remained impassive.

Since I said nothing, she fell silent. And began to turn the album's pages without lingering, until she pointed to an image of utter desolation: a snowman lost in the middle of a completely white yard, with two bare, black trees in the background. She sighed. "Washington. "The kids built the snowman but disappeared at picture time. They went to get a carrot for the nose, tomatoes for the eyes, string beans for the mouth. I don't think they could get the vegetable drawer in the fridge open. And they forgot about me. They went to watch TV, leaving me standing out in the yard. Kids...So I took the snowman's picture."

I set the album aside. Her sadness had only increased with each photo.

"I felt completely alone," she continued. "The house was far from the city. My marriage, already a sinking ship, ended up going under for good. One day I packed up the kids and left."

We talked about other things, but in circles, without getting anywhere. One painful impression gradually came over me: the hour spent together had produced incomplete fragments rather than the tapestry I had hoped the two of us would weave. The remarks about Max, which had reflected a whole series of truncated perceptions, the revelation about her Italian lover, the abandoned snowman in the yard, the questions I didn't dare to ask—and the photo album itself, incomplete as they always are—all made us feel farther apart.

When I showed signs that I wished to leave, our gazes converged on the empty whiskey bottle. We realized we'd drunk too much—and yet remained sober.

Marina closed her eyes, as if lost in thought. She seemed to be mustering the courage to face a test beyond her strength. "One cold winter afternoon, walking around Montevideo, I bumped into Nilo. We hadn't seen each other in years, since I was a kid, back when he used to spend a lot of time at our place. What a happy coincidence. It was as if a whole past full of joy, hope, and creativity had suddenly sprung up at my feet. We weren't just two Brazilians lost on a corner of some distant city. We didn't even feel the cold! For a few brief moments, we rekindled memories of Dad's parties for his artist and intellectual friends. We were surrounded by Cinema Novo and the theater, swept up by pop music..."

The jitteriness with which she lit a cigarette belied her subject. "We were both elated," she went on. "I still remember the corner we met on: Sarandi and Ituzaingó...*Elated*," she repeated.

Something in her demeanor had changed. She stopped short for a second, like a horse that balks before an obstacle. "Nilo was living in exile in Uruguay." She seemed ready to move ahead now. There was no turning back. "He wanted to know what I was doing in Montevideo," she continued in a controlled voice. "He asked casually, as though still caught up in the thrill of our meeting. And with the same ease, I answered that I was married, that my husband was a diplomat and worked at the embassy. I added that I'd just found out I was pregnant."

A new pause, this time to settle against the sofa cushions. She'd hurdled her obstacle, but landed on the other side depleted. "A shadow flickered across his eyes. Just for a second. He must have made a heroic effort to control himself. *Only it didn't work.*"

I removed my arm from the back of the sofa.

"He pulled away from me. As if I suddenly no longer belonged to his world."

I turned toward her. Her eyes were dry. Her story had already taken its toll of tears from her.

"Even worse: as if I no longer belonged to *my world*, as if all the memories that had enveloped us moments earlier had vanished."

She lowered her voice. "At first I didn't understand a thing. I stood completely bewildered on the sidewalk."

Her hand moved slowly toward the ashtray to snuff out her cigarette. An almost languid gesture, which seemed to emerge from that gray afternoon in Montevideo. A farewell gesture.

"He turned and slowly walked away, without a word, hands in his pockets, shoulders hunched over. I started to understand then. Each step he took, I understood a bit more. By the time he rounded the corner and disappeared, I had realized everything. *Everything.* One block was all it took. A single block."

She turned toward me. "Then I began to comprehend the reticence of our colleagues' wives, the young ones, especially. They treated me quite formally, in contrast with the courtesy the ambassador's wife showed me. She and the military attaché's spouse would always invite me to lunch or suggest going to a movie whenever Marcílio was traveling for work. The attaché's wife was actually even kind. But her husband..."

She was offering up a new character, as if wanting to leave that corner of her past for good. "He was a terrible man. Once, at a dinner at our place, I heard one of Marcílio's colleagues telling a new appointee that the attaché had formerly served on the police force, where he'd killed people. He said the man was a known torturer."

She closed her eyes again. "The young man who was listening had his back to me, but the one speaking was facing me. When he saw me standing there, with my tray full of desserts, he grew pale. It was the first time in my life that someone"—I had to lean in to hear what she was saying—"*looked at me with fear.*"

We hugged again, as we'd done on my arrival. What mattered most were those two embraces, two parentheses around a conversation so intense that it had withstood all the alcohol we had consumed.

As she walked me to the door, Marina spoke up again. "Many years went by until, desperate, I got up the courage to seek out my father. By then, my suspicions were driving me crazy. I was afraid of confronting so many doubts. My father listened to me in silence. When I was done, he drew me close to him. And, to my surprise, since we were alone in his living room, he whispered very softly in my ear, 'Sweetheart, anything is possible in Brazil these days. But listen to your father: *focus on your children.* And leave the rest for later.' Only then did I realize the reason for his caution: *he too was afraid...* afraid that someone might be listening."

Here, she paused briefly and finished with a wistful goodbye smile. "Fear had even wormed its way into our old house in Santa Teresa. My last stronghold had fallen."

# 14

By the early 1980s, Brazil's military regime was in its death throes. The most recent general who had been appointed president went around sullen and scowling, hidden behind dark glasses, distant from the country and its people. He paid more attention to his horses and barbecues than to the government, giving everyone who watched him closely—his uniformed cohorts included—the impression that he no longer felt comfortable in his skin. There was speculation that his discomfort had something to do with the very institution he had helped devise at the initial stage of the coup: for this man had been second-in-command of the National Intelligence Service in 1964. The monster had turned against yet another of its creators.

This sad figure was the fifth and last of the parade of military presidents who had emerged two decades earlier. The country around him had altered dramatically, and the national security system, overloaded by a perverse combination of incompetence, dishonesty, and arbitrariness of every kind, had succumbed to its own contradictions. The population, driven by the ghosts of their dead and encouraged by the press, which grew bolder each year, returned to the streets in growing numbers demanding justice and, above all, changes. These would come—in a form that couldn't be ignored. Throughout South America, the domino effect would again come into play, this time in reverse, toppling dictatorships.

This was the backdrop when, less than four months after my reencounter with Marina, I returned to Brazil from Quito to spend Christmas with my family. One evening, entirely by chance, I came across Max at the wedding reception of the son of a mutual friend at an old colonial home in Alto da Boa Vista.

As sometimes happens in situations brought on by fate, we ended up seated at the same round table in the garden of our hosts' residence. I had greeted him from a distance. Not out of callousness or unease but because right then the newlyweds had flown by us like two birds at the beginning of a journey, doling out hugs and kisses. By the time the young couple moved on to neighboring tables, we were already seated, busying ourselves with unfolding our napkins and watching, with warm smiles, as the bride gathered the train of her white gown and the groom proudly and confidently greeted friends. As far as I recall, this bridal party fly-by—marked by bursts of laughter, hearty congratulations, and brief waves—provided me with the only light moment of the evening.

There were eight of us around the table, which was decorated with white linen and a floral centerpiece bearing a corresponding number of candles. Of the group randomly brought together, only the two of us were from Itamaraty. The others were lawyer friends of the bride's father or architects and journalists associated with the groom's family. The only woman present, wed to one of the lawyers, was seated to my right.

During the hour we spent together amid this group of strangers, we didn't exchange two words. Max talked plenty, but to the others. And I had followed his example, which ended up being easy as we were opposite one another at the round table. Waiters circulated serving food, wine, bread, and occasionally relighting the candles that would go out every so often with the soft breeze. At one point, I had helped the woman next to me redrape a shawl over her shoulders. The property was near the woods, and a chorus of cicadas had welcomed us moments earlier—only to fall silent, like a theater audience when the lights go down and the curtain rises.

Max had come with a young woman he would marry a few months later, who was seated some distance from us. He remained inflexible where protocol was concerned, never sharing the same table with a wife or girlfriend on such occasions, just as he never sat beside them at restaurants or group gatherings. At his home, before leading us into the dining room, even when we were among close friends and there weren't more than eight or ten of us, he would always insist, "No lovebirds together." And he'd add, "Preferably at opposite ends of the table." For Max, only a provincial couple, intimidated by someone else's radiance—whether real or imagined—would choose two seats together, a nearness he considered "socially incestuous."

Two or three times that evening, perhaps putting those strict rules to the test, his companion had risen from her table and walked across the lawn to him. She had whispered a few words in his ear before pulling a cigarette or a lighter out of his jacket pocket. Watching her stroll back between the tables, I couldn't help but agree with the message her body was sending: her curves were indeed lovely. Good thing, for the journey she was preparing to embark on with Max would hardly be straightforward.

Max, on the other hand, had put on weight. And he seemed tense, if not nervous. This tension, which first manifested itself as an occasional drumming of his fingers on the tablecloth and then evolved into the two cigarettes smoked between the main course and dessert, ended up being detected by the others for a more apparent reason: the way he imposed or defended his arguments, no matter what the topic of discussion happened to be.

From the very start of the meal, as was his habit, he had dominated the conversation on his side of the table. And, given the increasing silence around him, he had extended this domination over the entire small group. He had invited me more than once with his eyes to join the discussion, even if it were to disagree with him, as long as he wasn't left alone speaking in the arena. It wasn't a call for help, brought on by the eventual awkwardness, which he was either unaware of or pointedly ignored. Rather, it was a sign of distinction: in that social context, he considered me his equal. I pretended not to notice his appeals and revisited a topic already covered with the woman to my right, or raised my eyes skyward in search of some constellation of stars to console me as sadness set in.

I wondered how the man seated across from me—whose erudition had given way to an intellectual frostiness that barely hid his personal disenchantment (with life, the country, the economy, technology, and even soccer) and whose speech, once so forceful, amusing, unpredictable, and full of life, had become cynical, if not bitter—could possibly be the same individual who had won me over in the early days of our career, sending a mysterious and unexpected *fortuitous* my way.

When I first met him in 1968, I had the feeling that our paths had crossed socially as well as intellectually, which I took to be the basis for a solid friendship. But now, the scenario around us held little of that past. Something seemed to have cracked behind the façade of my old mentor, as if the suit he was wearing once again weighed heavily and his body could no longer support the burden. This detail, imperceptible to the others, seemed to have embittered him—and explained the silence that had come over our group, in an awkward contrast with the peals of laughter that arose from the surrounding tables.

This charged scene only grew bleaker, especially once the waiters stopped relighting our candles, convinced there must be some reason for the evening breeze to concentrate its energy on us, leaving all the other tables peacefully aglow. Consequently, as soon as dessert was over (and some were left untouched), the six guests seated around us had taken off in various directions, one of them tipping over his chair in the process.

The eager stampede made us laugh and the unexpected opening instantly transported us back to our youth. "I think I scared off your friends," said Max, standing to replace the toppled chair.

"As usual," I bantered back, preparing to leave the table.

In the meantime, however, he had sat back down, and one of the waiters came by with coffee. I could no longer walk away without being impolite.

"You've been following a rather obscure career path, haven't you?" he asked with a dose of sarcasm after serving himself, as if he didn't know what posts I'd worked in. "Los Angeles, Guatemala? Where else?"

"And you, after South America and Washington, you're roughing it in Paris?" I inquired in the same tone. "UNESCO, right?"

He laughed again, only this time shaking his head. *Still the same old guy*, he seemed to be thinking. Had the time come to call him to account?

"The system is imploding, Max," I said then, in a cordial tone, accepting the cup of coffee being offered to me. He continued to shake his head while stirring his coffee. "Haven't you noticed?" I persisted. "It's falling apart."

The constant movement of the spoon in his cup seemed to suggest conceptual consistency: the country, like me, would never change. "You must have taken part in all the protest marches," he finally remarked, between sips.

"No, I was out of the country. But I followed everything closely. The youth movement in particular. It's interesting that this generation projects such genuine indignation. Despite not having lived through what we did. The slogans, the raised fists, the enthusiasm in their eyes — "

"*Elections now! Out with the military!*" he exclaimed, echoing the cries that could be heard all over the country. He held up his empty cup as if proposing a toast. How many times had he raised crystal goblets in honor of various foreign dictators, not to mention our own?

"That's right, Max," I went on, giving in once more to the irresistible temptation to provoke him. "And how are you going to get along in this new Brazil that's emerging?"

"Better than you," he teased, offering me a cigar, which I accepted.

"I don't doubt that," I answered coolly. "But what I wanted to know is... *with yourself.* How are you going to get along with yourself?"

"Games? Must we, my friend?" He sighed with an ironic smile. "Have you already forgotten our crystal paperweight?"

No, I hadn't forgotten the crystal sphere that, years earlier, he had spun before my eyes, trusting in the variety of its facets to deal with my doubts and hesitations. But the fact that *he* recalled the episode surprised me. I would have thought he'd forgotten the moment long ago. But Max never forgot anything.

# 15

That crystal sphere and the accompanying fear I had felt at the time were hardly subjects I wanted to talk about during a reception. But it was inevitable that they would come up in a conversation that, sooner or later, we had to have. So let it be now, I thought.

I remained quiet at first. Max's utter stillness intrigued me. Unlike mine, his was the silence of *one who waits*. It reminded me of an animal between the attack and the retreat. What he was waiting for, neither he nor I knew exactly. Our conversation evoked a similar one that had taken place twelve or thirteen years earlier in Santa Teresa, when I had said little—and he had done more probing than talking. Only now the roles were reversed. Except that probing wasn't part of my plans.

"You had a theory about fear, remember?" I asked when he finally lit his cigar. "You spoke of constancy, of instruments of a system that would last beyond our generation. You spoke of intimidation as though reciting a recipe or the steps of a weight-loss program. But for me..." I paused. I knew that he was eyeing me from his corner, yet the feeling was far from unsettling, as I found myself retrieving something that I hadn't been able to articulate during that long-ago discussion.

"But for me," I repeated, "*fear had a shape*, which at times seemed so dense as to be almost tangible. Like a thick fog, the kind that leaves us feeling clammy and makes our clothes cling to our bodies."

A waiter approached with a tray of liqueurs. We both chose cognac.

I continued. "It wasn't a fear that we in Brasilia could associate with violence, insubordination, or arbitrariness, because none of us had ever seen anyone jailed or tortured. Horror lived next door."

"That's a good line, excellent," he cut in with a laugh. "It'd make a great movie title."

After a puff of his cigar and a brief moment of reflection, he added, "It's better in the present, though. *Horror lives next door.* Don't you agree? It has more of an edge to it. *Horror lives next door.* The story is still to come...."

"Lived next door," I repeated deafly, as if his comments were mere background noise. "It lived in the police stations in Rio, in the cellars of military barracks in São Paulo and the rest of the country. Just as, years later, it would live in the lost villages of the interior, the backlands of Bahia, and dozens of places we'd never heard of, which were always far removed from Brasilia."

Max kept smoking, but his eyes avoided mine. It didn't matter much to me, that starry night, what direction his thoughts might have taken. Today I could speculate about a few likely possibilities. A stop at the Sorocabana Café in Montevideo, to make initial contact with a British agent named Raymond Thurston? Or a round of poker with the military attachés, from whom he extracted information for his own use (and at times neglected to pass on to his superiors)? An additional visit to the feared National Stadium of Santiago, where he had witnessed scenes that still haunted him? Or could he be thinking about the informers he had planted at the request of the SNI among the community of Brazilian exiles in Uruguay?

"That's what gave Brasilia its surreal quality," I went on in the same tone. "The fact that decisions were handed down from the silence of the highlands. And that their outcomes, in the form of rumors, whispered hearsay, or guarded conversations, got back there, giving rise to further, identical operations. But the screams, the despair, and the horror *never reached us*, the first wave of young diplomats transferred to Brasilia. We had been living cloistered in one of the nation's architectural masterpieces, amid reflecting pools and baroque Brazilian artwork, and felt utterly lost in a city that looked more like a stage set for a play featuring cold and sterile beauty along with tension, silence, and—"

Fortunately, Max interrupted my rambling monologue. But in a casual tone, not at all unpleasant or aggressive. "You know I missed that first phase of the move to Brasilia. I was transferred to Montevideo months earlier. I didn't live in Brasilia until 1981. They say the city had improved a lot compared to the initial period you're referring to."

With that, he had concentrated on the objective part of what I'd said and remained on the outskirts of the real conversation. So what would be the point of pressing? I asked myself. Deep down, maybe he was even right. What were my motives in bringing up the twelve- and thirteen-year-old shadows of Brasilia on a peaceful Rio night in 1983? Me of all people, a bureaucrat who, as Max was aware, had never experienced real danger—nor taken a stance that would warrant retaliation by those in power?

I knew full well that I'd been no hero. I hadn't criticized my superiors out loud, I hadn't resigned, following the example of two colleagues who quit as discreetly and anonymously as possible, I hadn't taken up arms. On the contrary, I'd become part of an orchestra—in which Max was the soloist. But he would hardly have stood out if all of us weren't, to some measure, playing around him. And if I had pounded a few bar tables in the way of protest, I'd done so in the company of friends whose indignation matched mine, in keeping with the number of beers consumed. Heroism had thus eluded me by a long shot. I just wasn't convinced that I hadn't cowered in certain circumstances. Not that this represented a serious character flaw. It was, rather, something bordering on unease, a kind of incorrectness. I could, for instance, have ceased to shake hands with people I knew to be involved in criminal activity. During my year and a half in Central America, I hadn't hesitated to dutifully socialize with known tyrants of the region, to whom I was introduced at dinners and receptions. I had even played Ping-Pong with one of them at the dismal end of a party. ("If you beat me, I'll kill you," he had joked, revealing the gun tucked into his waistband while gnashing his teeth.) More than once—and this sometimes kept me awake at night—I could have disagreed with a superior on a matter of principle instead of keeping my mouth shut. Or even worse, agreeing—with a smile that would have me brushing my teeth back at home until my gums bled. But my irritation with myself was limited to the bloody stream of spittle, which quickly went down the drain.

Since I said nothing just then, facing the unequal struggle I'd had for years with my own ghosts, Max correctly inferred that he could go in for the kill. He propped an elbow on the table and rested his cheek against his palm, shrinking the distance between us. Moving aside the centerpiece while holding my gaze, he prepared his attack.

"Enough of this dull chitchat about Brasilia in the early days. It's tiresome. Let's talk about something more interesting—about this new Brazil that's being heralded, willing to reexamine the injustices of the past. Take Itamaraty, for instance: what specific cases do you know of injustice committed in our realm? Aside from the people expelled from public service by the commission convened by the military?"

"Of whom there were many," I interjected. "Forty-four civil servants."

His voice, amiable until now, hardened. "Of whom *only thirteen were diplomats*. And I'll tell you more: compared to the other public sectors, that wasn't many. In most cases, the oustings and forced retirements were more than deserved."

"How can we know that? If the accused didn't even have the right to defend themselves?"

He relit his cigar, then tried to pursue the tenuous thread he thought he'd picked up on in our conversation. "Maybe so. But one thing is certain: for better or worse, we implemented a foreign policy that sparked general interest—and has inspired respect for its independence."

"A foreign policy that presented an interesting paradox," I remarked in the same steady tone. "Considering the regime it came from." I hesitated a moment, annoyed with myself more than with Max. I didn't want him to be the one to praise the small group of visionaries who, at considerable personal risk, had safeguarded the ministry's ideals and upheld our dignity abroad. But this remained a moot point because Max took it upon himself to redirect the conversation.

"Countries thrive on such paradoxes. Mutatis mutandis, the same thing happens in the United States. Consider recent examples: Nixon, a Republican, established relations with China, the same way Reagan is the one who negotiates best with the Soviets today. The Democratic Party, with whom we share affinities of another sort, only holds us back. They're essentially protectionists."

"Besides their inconvenient obsession with the issue of human rights—so aggravating!"

"You can kid all you want." He laughed. "Anyway, that's not what I wanted to talk about. I wanted to talk about your more personal grievances. From that difficult time. At the ministry."

"My *grievances*, Max?"

"The ones you didn't share with me. All you did was grumble. At most. I always asked myself why. Considering our long-standing friendship..."

The sweet-sounding cicadas that had greeted us earlier were in for a treat.

# 16

"What did you feel was unfair? Or absurd?"

"*Everything* was absurd, Max. Starting with the stifling conditions we were living under. And still are."

"Okay. Tell me about the dictatorship, then."

"Max, what interests me, what ought to interest you, is something else altogether. It includes the ministry but goes beyond. *Well* beyond..."

"I'm all ears."

"Okay. Compared to the acts of violence that took place throughout the country, the cases that occurred among us obviously don't seem so grave. There was no physical aggression, no bloodshed, torture, or rape to speak of, no cases of young children seeing their parents in chains, or *parents watching their children being tortured*. There was nothing comparable to the electric shocks applied to nuns' vaginas or adolescents' rectums."

"Exactly."

"*Exactly?!*"

"I'm reacting to *your* words, my friend. I'm trying to figure out what *you're* getting at, not evaluating the intensity of a shock to someone's anus. I'm the first to regret that things like that happened. *If* they happened."

"What I'm getting at is this: the bloodshed and violence aren't enough to evaluate what happened in our midst. At the ministry, to begin with, there were individuals who remained indifferent or cynical. Some threw their career out the window, reducing a worthy profession to a mere job. That kind of atmosphere, transposed to poorer or more radical social contexts, could have led hundreds of people all over the country to despair, possibly even to suicide."

"Or worse, to armed conflict."

"How is that *worse?*"

"From the point of view of the military, of course."

"Of course."

"*And...?*"

"Max, how many people were baited, pressured, corrupted by the regime? People who under normal circumstances would never have gone off track, abandoned their values, whether ethical, moral, or religious? And who, later on, when confronted by relatives and friends regarding the consequences of their actions, were driven to depression or despair, if not more extreme measures, without ever being tallied among the horrors? Without even becoming so much as a footnote in the annals of the dictatorship?"

"You know what I think about all this?" he asked wearily.

"No, Max. What do you think about this? I'd love to know."

He took a deep breath and said, "When the history of this period is written, impartially, without being manipulated by one side or the other, it will become clear that these weren't acts planned by the military or political leaders, much less by bankers or businessmen, as rumor would have it. *They were works orchestrated in absolute secrecy.* As if the CIA had commissioned Merce Cunningham, who was at the peak of his career in the sixties and seventies, to choreograph the series of coups to happen in rapid succession, so that the entire region would fall like a house of cards."

I couldn't resist the temptation to add my two cents, albeit with a heavy heart: "In unison with the ballet dancers who collapsed onstage as soon as the lights faded, the curtains closed, and the middle class applauded."

Without acknowledging the irony, Max digested my remark and went on. "Maybe so," he said. "The difference is that there was no audience. Because the theater remained empty. Outside, the people were being roughed up as usual. Until, twenty years later, long after the spells cast by the Cuban threat and Allende's rise to power, the theater would gradually fill up again. In a matter of months, the curtains would open to full halls. And the house of cards would go up again before everyone's eyes, to the applause that would then celebrate the restoration of democracy."

The student had clearly surpassed his master, as the ambassador in Montevideo faded into the shadows of the past. I listened in silence to Max's conclusion: "Except that the people would remain abandoned in the streets. They were no longer beaten or tortured. But their conquests would amount to little more than that. Should you ever quote me on this, however, I'll not only deny everything but say that I always sensed there was something off-kilter about you."

I clapped my hands together six or seven times, in the slow, cadenced kind of applause that produces silences as expressive as the sounds. Applause that echoed mournfully in the middle of the night. It was moments like this that enabled me to see just how well Max understood his own tragedy—and the hell he had gotten himself into. Or so I thought.

"You know what's even worse?" he asked, aware that he'd caught my attention. "That in twenty or thirty years, no one in Brazil will talk about this anymore. By the early twenty-first century, not even historians will be interested. *No one will broach the issue except in passing.* Bookstores will shelve works on the subject in the history section. *In alphabetical order.* Depending on the author's name, an account of torture in Brazil in the 1970s might be located between a volume about gold mining in the colonial period and one on African influences in Brazilian folklore. If it's there at all."

"Could be," I conceded. "*Because we'll be busy paying the price of impunity.* Which will always be a part of the country's realities from here on."

Besides feeling powerless and indignant, I was furious with myself. And with fate, for having directed me to sit at Max's table. I stood up. "Anything else? Or am I free to go, wishing you luck on the banks of the Seine?"

"There is indeed something else. Sit down, my friend. And see if you can handle it. Because it's not very pleasant."

He seemed intent on taking our conversation to its conclusion. "If some of the dead and the disappeared you and the press are always referring to," he said after I sat back down, "not *all*, but *some*, could one day return from heaven or hell, or wherever they are, they would kneel before their friends and relatives, *they would kneel at their feet*, and beg forgiveness for the grief they caused. That *they* caused."

"Max..."

"For the childishness of their actions," he continued deafly, "for the stupidity of their decisions, for their immaturity in embracing lost causes. And for the way they let themselves be manipulated by the cunning old foxes of the left. They would be on their knees, begging forgiveness for the suffering they caused. Not of their victims, generally young soldiers (because these were the poor souls who died, not their superiors) or simple bystanders, like the unlucky managers of banks that were held up, or foreigners that the amateur guerrillas mistook for CIA agents. No. They wouldn't have to ask forgiveness of these individuals, because they were just accidental victims, as we love to say in our line of work. But they would beg forgiveness of the friends and relatives they had loved. And left devastated—if not wounded or mutilated. Because many were imprisoned and tortured *simply for the sad privilege of knowing them.*"

"Max," I tried to interject, "what about the military, responsible for everything that happened beforehand? Beginning with the coup? And their accomplices and business backers, the team that covered for the torturers? And trained them? Or provided financial support?"

"They're better off, relatively speaking."

"How can that be?"

"Because they would only have to ask forgiveness of their victims. 'Forgive me, my dear man, but we were at war, you were on one side, I was on the other. And I killed you. Because it was you or me . . .' Much easier than asking their loved ones, right?"

Given my silence, he proceeded. "Think about facing your sister, who was raped and tortured for days *just because she happened to be your sister*, with absolutely no connection to the insurgents. And try to open your mouth. Let's say you're able to do so. Open your mouth. What words would come out? 'Lenin and Guevara were right, the party was wrong'? It's tricky, don't you think?"

"Max!" I exclaimed, both awed and astonished. "*A world without victims or culprits . . .* What about Nuremberg? How would that fit?"

"No, my friend. It's just the opposite: a cruel world in which all are to blame. By action or default. A world in which the borders between good and evil aren't vague or inexact; they simply don't exist. Or when they do exist, they shift easily, depending on what part of the globe you're in."

"*History as written by the victors* and so forth?"

"A lesser vision, that saying. Superficial, like everything that deals with subjects of this magnitude. But if you want to put it in those reductive terms, yes."

"And where do notions of aggressor and defender, of victim and perpetrator, fit into these scenarios of yours, devoid of values?"

"Where they always were: in the minds of men."

He looked straight at me for the first time. "Upon arriving in Paris and assuming my duties, I decided to reread the preamble of UNESCO's charter. Do you remember the wording? Did you ever read it?"

"I must have. I don't remember."

"No, my friend. You *didn't* read it. *Because if you had, you wouldn't have forgotten.* It alone accounts for the existence of the United Nations. Poetically, I should add. And its simplicity is stirring, more so than the reams of reports that the UN has been churning out over the course of nearly four decades."

True to form, he would keep me in suspense. Then, eyes on the stars, he quoted: " 'Since wars begin in the minds of men, it is in the minds of men that the defences of peace must be constructed.' " He took another puff of his cigar. " 'In the minds of men,' " he repeated. "According to which side they're on, of course. What happened in Brazil and continues to happen in South America is a microcosm of what occurs in the world at large. Wherever there are conflicts. And, from the look of it, the universal trend will only get worse. Particularly because we're talking about a cultural melting pot that thickens with hunger, poverty, and ignorance. And these three ingredients, as we know, are only going to increase."

I decided to cut to the chase. "If that's the case, why did you feel compelled to take a stand in 1964? To switch sides without even batting an eye? What happened in the mind of Marcílio Andrade Xavier?"

Unflappable as always, Max looked me head-on and asked, "Who told you I switched sides?"

# 17

I glanced around. Apart from a waiter, we were the only ones left in the garden. The other guests had disappeared into the house, from which muted voices, interspersed with laughter and the strains of a piano, drifted. Then I heard Max saying, "Convictions are a luxury, my friend. Reserved for those who don't play the game. *I played the game.*"

Still silent, I slid over the clean ashtray the waiter had just set on the table and snuffed out my cigar. I took my time with this activity, as though pondering some final plan that would lead me to victory in a battle whose hidden meaning almost eluded me.

Max slowly stood and crossed his arms, as he bestowed his professorial treatment on me. "The truth," he declared, "is that we'll never know what would have happened to the country if the military *hadn't* staged the coup. Quite likely we would have done the same had we been in their shoes."

Voices and laughter continued to drift from the house. The piano chords, however, had given way to a Chopin étude, which seemed to be missing several crucial notes. I was beginning to feel somewhat helpless.

Calmer, almost relieved, Max concluded in a casual tone, as though now dealing with secondary details, "As for the rest of the population, other than the group who took up arms (and then regretted it, as they themselves will admit someday), or those who chose exile, everyone adapted to the new realities. And tried to get on with their lives as best they could."

It was my turn to stand. I felt more nauseated than tired. I hadn't had that much to drink. Or so I thought. I took a few steps across the lawn, breathing deeply, while Max, who remained where he was, appeared to be looking for the other guests. He hadn't noticed that we were alone in the garden, lost like two ghosts in a landscape overtaken by darkness. He made his way over unsteadily and placed his right hand on my shoulder, probably hoping we might still salvage some vestige of friendship between us.

Unable to move, I decided to react. "Not everyone, Max," I managed to say. "Not everyone, to use your words, *tried to get on with their lives as best they could.* More than six thousand people were thrown in jail in the two weeks following the coup. Those who remained incarcerated, for months or years, or who eventually died from mistreatment or starvation, left behind families who couldn't rebuild their lives."

To my relief, since I no longer had the energy to duel with him, Max nodded. Whether it was in agreement or from drink, I couldn't guess.

"The others resisted in their own way," I went on, more forcefully, gradually regaining my strength and, with it, a certain degree of lucidness. "Without taking up arms but defending their principles. They too would pay a high price. University professors were fired. They survived by giving private classes. I studied with several. Hundreds of members of parliament were ousted and had their political rights suspended. For ten years—an eternity, considering they were in the prime of their lives. *Ten years...* Union leaders were tortured. The ones who survived quickly learned to keep their mouths shut."

Max kept nodding, as if he could read my mind and was already waiting for me at the finish line. I forged ahead nonetheless. "Liberal professionals lost their contracts and saw former associates crossing the street to avoid them. I knew of dozens of such cases. Shameful, humiliating cases, because the damage affecting us seldom had anything to do with blatant violence. It happened in out-of-the-way places, sometimes in modest home settings frequented only by the victims and their closest kin. In alleyways, rather than in the town streets or squares. Beneath torches, so to speak, not searchlights or high beams."

I was inspired. If Max was awaiting me somewhere, he'd best set up camp. "Others had their loan applications denied. Your ex-father-in-law's bank was one of the few that continued to help those it shouldn't have, according to the regime. This led to bankruptcy. Many of my friends had to pull their children out of school. Others had to move to a different neighborhood or city. Marriages fell apart, from pure tension or fear, leaving behind a legacy of lost, insecure children. A considerable number of these people went into exile, uprooting entire families. We're talking about thousands and thousands of human beings, Max."

Here he held up his free hand, in a clear sign of assent, implicitly recognizing the validity of the points raised—as well as of others I might yet wish to bring up. "*Almost everyone*, if you prefer," he amended. "Almost everyone tried to get on with their lives as best they could."

We took a few steps toward the house, his hand still resting on my shoulder. He seemed pleased with the fact that some scrap of conversation could still take place between us. And when he began to speak again, his voice sounded untroubled for the first time. Not aggressive or annoyed, nor impatient or ironic—but tranquil and thoughtful.

"In general, engineers and architects constructed buildings that were praised and inhabited by numerous families, doctors and dentists treated their patients, teachers gave their classes, farmers and workers planted soy and coffee, lawyers practiced law, judges judged, bureaucrats clocked in, without ever failing to take their vacations and sabbaticals. And virtually all received their salaries at the end of the month, including you and me.

*Almost all*, for twenty years. *Almost all stood by.* Some out of conviction. Others, I recognize, because they had no other option.
Or because they imagined that things would change over time.
Just as we at Itamaraty did, living isolated from the real world,
moreover. Here and abroad."

Under the pretext of drawing a cigarette from my jacket
pocket, I managed to free my shoulder from his hand. *Isolated
from the real world*...Might as well give up, I decided, flicking
my lighter. And, for the last time that night, I contemplated
the stars. As if, from the universe beyond, they could deal with
the frustration I felt. Meanwhile, Max allowed himself to slump
into a chair. He appeared to be on the verge of surrendering. To
fatigue, however, never to me. Only it was a fatigue far greater
than I could ever have imagined, *nearly two decades old.*

"We're going to have to wait and see," he said quietly. "It
will take the Argentineans a long time to overcome the nightmares they were victims of. What happened among them was
beyond terrible. The scars remain deep and won't heal quickly.
Two long and brutal periods of dictatorship, separated by a short
neo-Peronist interval and capped by a ridiculous war. *Thirty
thousand dead in seventeen years*...No election can fix that. President Alfonsín will take over chained to cadavers; he'll govern
amid ghosts. The smell of death hangs over the country."

He might as well have been talking about something that
had happened on Mars, the mere fault of inattentive gods.

He continued in the same tone. "The Chileans will live
through their hell for years to come. There, they talk of five
or six thousand dead—*for now.* Because, unlike Brazil"—he
allowed himself a glance in my direction, to verify that I was
following closely—"in Chile there's no solution in sight. From
what I could understand of the country during the time I lived
in Santiago, the right is entrenched. It will hold firm for a long
while. When inspired, my ex-boss in Montevideo used to assert,
'If there are worthy disciples of the old Prussian military school

remaining anywhere in the world, it's in Chile.' He would say this with pride, as if he himself were Chilean."

With tenderness, he went on to touch upon the least dramatic of the tragedies—in his view, at least. "The Uruguayans suffered even greater human losses, proportionally speaking. But the chaos took a different toll there. For a nation that proudly flaunted the most democratic traditions on the continent, those were *eleven long years*. Enough time to affect the population's most precious resource: its pride, its dignity. We, on the other hand..." He'd come full circle and was now reaching what he took to be the crown jewel. His tone was no longer distant. As if the entire region he had referred to—its dead and its disappeared included—had become part of the same mural, set on a curved wall in a museum. "We will solve our problems easily... despite these never-ending twenty years."

He grew quiet, then straightened up in his chair and gave a forced yawn to downplay his remarks. The performance didn't hide the essential: Max was moving on, taking his first steps toward the future. Just as he'd done years before in a moment of inspiration, kissing the ring of the Cardinal Archbishop of Rio de Janeiro. It was a fascinating and pathetic moment to witness. A moment that, in the case of some animals, involves shedding fur or a skin, but for humans occurs on a subtler level—when some sense of the self survives personal devastation.

Max's revelation seemed to represent a tribute to me, a proof of trust. It was, at heart, a final demonstration of friendship. In a matter of minutes, we were going to go our separate ways. And many years might pass before we spoke again. Whenever it was we next met up, he would be *another person*. A brand-new Max, brilliant and shining. *The Max of my younger days*, I thought, overcome by sadness. The Socialist Max who had joined the office of the country's last progressive foreign minister. If I met him again at this new stage, and closed my eyes, who knows? Maybe I would see him as he had once been.

I felt a little dizzy from the liquor and from certain verses running through my head that we used to recite at Itamaraty, while strolling in the shade beneath the imperial palms of the old palace, circling the reflecting pool where swans glided:

*Time present and time past*
*Are both perhaps present in time future*
*And time future contained in time past.*

Perhaps Eliot would open the way for our reconciliation? All I had to do was forget the current Max and concentrate on the former one, who had just been reborn in front of me. Just as the country was preparing to do: to rescue the future from the past. I noticed that one of the porch doors at the house had opened, casting an intense yellow beam across the lawn. This was soon filled by a shadow, which, after a brief pause, had taken on contours and become a silhouette. The shape began to move toward us, with such languidness that identifying its sex was unnecessary. Max slowly rose from his chair.

"Goodbye," I whispered.

"Goodbye," he replied.

# 18

My conversations with Marina and Max, just months apart, led me to address at last my misgivings concerning my old companion's contradictions. Since no one holds on to a friendship poisoned by doubt, I decided to shake off my lethargy—which, at this stage, was bordering on complicity. I began to give greater credence to the rumors circulating about Max and recalled some of the ambiguous comments he had made during our past discussions.

Over the years, I investigated various sources in piecing together the puzzle that was Max. And in 1993, I came across what I later realized was the most damning one, an article in *Foreign Diplomatic Review* titled "Operation Condor." The report had been written based on the dreaded secret organization's archives unearthed in Paraguay by one of the operation's victims. "*Prisoners thrown from airplanes into the sea,*" blared the headlines. "*Thrown alive...Bound or stuffed into burlap sacks. Still conscious, hurled from five to eight thousand meters up...*" And this was merely *one* aspect of the famed operation, whose name derived from a bird that fed off dead flesh. It was all there: the monthly frequency of the missions, the number of prisoners loaded onto each flight, the drugs administered to the victims before departure "*to sedate them without their losing awareness of what was happening.*"

But the report didn't end there. On a list topped by Argentina's notorious Angel of Death, and followed by references to the infamous DINA gang—the Chilean National Intelligence Directorate, with its chief, Contreras, up front—the names of Brazilian torturers and agents figured prominently. Among them was Colonel Cordeiro, in thirty-seventh place, just below his near namesake, the Uruguayan Manuel Cordero.

Although shaken by the piece, I didn't associate it with my friend—despite his connection with the man from the Coffee Institute. For me, the article merely represented an extreme example of the macabre shroud that had been lowered over the region for thirty years. I filed it away, but it stayed in the back of my mind.

Two years later, though, whatever had seemed vague or incoherent acquired an unexpected shape and gained a sense of urgency. It all happened thanks to a colonel from Rio I met in Vienna—a man with whom I forged a strange and short-lived friendship. His name was João Vaz.

It was 1995, and more than a decade had elapsed since the end of the dictatorship. The colonel and I were part of a delegation in charge of drafting a convention on international crime at a dull UN meeting. Already retired by then, he had been included in the group as an adviser. One night, we wound up having dinner together. The colonel was much older than I, and in his burliness and gait reminded me of an old circus bear, the kind that develops a gentle temperament with age. One of the most disturbing novelties of those years of political transition was, for me, at any rate, the sudden humbleness and congeniality that military personnel of nearly all ranks now tried to project when in contact with civilians, as if their constant smiling indicated that none of them had been at all involved with the terror the country had gone through.

That night, however, this thought didn't even cross my mind. I was simply happy not to be dining alone yet again. As is fitting in Viennese restaurants in the wintertime, my companion and I exchanged pleasantries in front of the fireplace.

We spoke of family first. And soon afterward, of our travels, of the countries in which we'd lived. Remembering the years he had worked at our embassy in Uruguay, the colonel casually brought up Max's name. He asked if I knew him. I said yes but without going into detail.

"What a character," murmured the colonel, without shifting his gaze from the flames in the fireplace.

I instinctively straightened up in my chair and, for the first time, faced the colonel with my full attention. I awaited some other sign from him, slight as it may have been, something that would better explain the strange look in his eyes.

"He worked for the British," remarked the colonel, as though addressing the fireplace.

"For the *British*?" I couldn't help but exclaim, letting out a surprised laugh.

"*That's right*, MI6," continued the colonel. "*He was working for the British secret service. Working* may be an overstatement. Let's say he was *cooperating* with them. The ones who alerted us were our friends in"—he tapped my arm with a familiarity that boded well—"Washington! We at the SNI *were informed by the CIA!* Isn't that something?"

"Unbelievable!" I cried out.

"You knew, at the ministry, that he was part of the *system*, didn't you?"

"Of course," I answered without hesitation, adding in the same tone, "But this story about MI6...To my knowledge, no one at the ministry ever knew *that*."

"It took us two years to find out. And when I think that we even played poker twice a week at my house..."

"*Poker!?*" My attempt at nonchalance barely hid my surprise. It was a miracle I hadn't choked on my wine.

"Max was the only diplomat at our table. He almost always lost, but he was a good loser. At any rate, we didn't play high stakes. A hundred dollars or so was the most he'd wager per night.

At the time, that was still real money, considering that we played twice a week." He frowned. "Sometimes he did win." Then an almost heartfelt admission: "But I never caught him bluffing!"

Fortunately, the UN conference would go on for eight more days. During that time, to the growing satisfaction of the colonel, who had found in me a friend always willing to listen to the recounting of his adventures, we dined together on three other occasions. The Max I discovered thanks to my dinner companion turned out to be a far more complex figure than the one with whom I had developed a fine friendship early in my career. He had split his personality in 1964 and, apparently unsatisfied with that particular accomplishment, had subdivided it further in Montevideo, as though trying to progressively reduce his individuality into less and less visible niches.

But when I raised this theory with the colonel on our last night—when we'd drunk champagne as well and our tongues were wagging loosely—my companion managed to briefly set aside the effects of the alcohol he'd consumed and threw me a bitter look. "Could be," the colonel admitted, "but, from what I knew, he never lost sight of his own objectives. He never played fair with his bosses; his peers; us; the Brazilians, exiled or not; the Uruguayans; or even the Brits. And he didn't toy with the Americans, because he sensed that's where he would get burned. That bunch was too powerful to mess with. His actions were..." He paused, in search of the expression that would best convey his thought. "His actions were those of a strategist *with a personal agenda*. Max's team had only one player: himself. Our friend realized very early on that his superiors, within and outside the ministry, would come and go and lose power and prestige, gradually disappearing, whether from age or ill-formed alliances, while he advanced in his career. So he used them strictly for his own needs. No more, no less. He gave each an amount of attention proportional to his potential usefulness. And he knew better than anyone how to buy low and sell high."

After signaling to the waiter for some water, he asked, "Did you know him well?"

"Yes...and no..."

"Funny, you sounded just like him then. Depending on the subject of discussion, that's how Max would often reply. In that regard, he reminded me of an American I got to know pretty well in Montevideo. A true friend I still keep in touch with these days. Whenever I asked him about certain topics, he would almost always respond, '*Yes...*,' then pause and add with a sly grin, '*and no...*'"

The colonel hesitated, staring at me somberly through the haze of whiskey, wine, and now champagne, as if weighing the pros and cons of continuing. Then he shrugged. All things considered, he was much closer to the end of his life than to its beginning and no longer feared anyone.

He leaned forward. "Eric Friedkin, that was my friend's name. We remained in touch, even after we were retired. Our girls attended the same school. A very expensive American school, I might add."

He lifted the champagne bottle from the bucket and, after glancing over at my glass, which was still full, topped off his own.

"He was the agricultural attaché at the American embassy. Actually, as I quickly surmised and eventually confirmed as we became better friends, he worked for the CIA."

I greeted the new topic of conversation with a generous gulp of champagne.

"Eric headed the CIA office for all of South America. In other words, the supposed agricultural attaché at the US embassy reported directly to *James Pyne* in Washington, the same guy who had alerted Kennedy about the existence of Soviet warheads in Cuba during the missile crisis. And just as I'm doing with you now, here in Vienna, although without this beautiful fireplace—"

"And without the champagne..."

"Without the champagne," he echoed, before taking another brief pause. "I remember we were in a bar when Eric spoke to me for the first time about Max. Among other things, he told me that he spent countless hours discussing with his colleague from MI6 which of the two secret services should approach Max, the Americans or the British. That's how highly Max ranked in everyone's eyes."

"Approach Max?" I asked, unable to contain my disbelief. "But for *what*?"

# 19

"Easy, my friend," laughed the colonel. "Take it easy. It's a funny story. And a good one at that."

He was right: now that we'd plunged into the past, I needed to let him speak freely, without voicing my own concerns.

"Despite Max's understated position in the embassy's hierarchy, he was soon noticed by the secret services of both countries, the US *and* Britain, which had bugged several foreign missions, ours among them—'a regional power to be reckoned with,' in Eric's words. Max's intellectual brilliance stood out in the recordings."

The colonel again turned to the bucket, retrieved the bottle, and this time stopped at my glass before pouring into his. "I don't know how well you knew Max. As I learned from Eric, he was cold and calculating above all, traits that are greatly appreciated in this field. He also had a rare quality valued by the foreigners who were watching his moves closely: he was *extremely adaptable*. Depending on who he was talking to, he could just as handily swing to the left as embrace the right. The guy was an artist!"

I kept my mouth shut, other than to take another sip of champagne.

"Max's words had *intellectual clout*. That was how Eric put it. He could hold his own in serious conversation with professors, journalists, politicians, and supporters of the most diverse causes. Even with militants connected to the Tupamaros, during the lead-up to the military coup in Uruguay..."

As the colonel spoke, I noted how naturally he had resorted to the term *coup*. In which he had been involved up to his eyeballs, albeit in a secondary role.

"Max was worth his weight in gold," my dinner companion went on. "He was brilliant, subtle, discreet. A natural. No one compared to him, and everyone coveted him."

Just then a curious notion took hold of me. That the former head of the CIA in South America was now a peaceful retired man, probably on a bowling team and helping to raise his grandchildren. But he had once been a protagonist in events that had affected the fate of several countries in our region—not to mention the unhappy destiny of some of their inhabitants. I wondered if Eric Friedkin and Max had ever met.

It didn't occur to me to ask—nor did it seem important to know. But that same night I learned other things. Among them, that the CIA had come to the conclusion that its police and military training center wasn't achieving optimal results with the Uruguayans and Chileans. Due to "cultural differences," Friedkin had told the colonel. The CIA had then decided to ask Brazil for help, suggesting that former Brazilian trainees who had completed the program go on to lend "technical assistance" to the Uruguayan and Chilean police forces. "But not to the Argentineans," he had emphasized, "because they had learned everything they knew from the French mercenaries, people who trained during the fall of Indochina and honed their skills during the Algerian War."

I took advantage of the colonel's excellent performance to interrupt. "But *where does Max fit in*? How did he get himself into all of these . . ."

The colonel smiled, evidently pleased by my amazement. "They ended up splitting Max. Don't you get it? The two secret services made use of Max by shared agreement." The colonel reached for the bucket.

"What was Max in charge of at the embassy?" he inquired.

"Technical cooperation...as far as I recall," I replied hesitantly.

"Exactly. *Technical cooperation*... That, let's say, was the CIA's domain, the confidential part. Max's task was to make sure the Brazilian police officers and their Uruguayan counterparts understood one another, so they could carry out their efforts with maximum efficiency. That was the CIA half."

"And the other?"

"The British. And it wasn't just confidential, it was top secret. For more than two years, no one knew what it involved. That's why the CIA, concerned about a lack of transparency on the part of the Brits, began to keep tabs on MI6! According to Eric, it wasn't the first time, and he suspected that the British secret service occasionally returned the favor. So it's possible—as my ex-boss, our attaché in Montevideo, reasoned—that on receiving the first signs that something serious might be going down, the CIA burned Max along with the SNI. Particularly because, at that point, our hero was about to be transferred to Santiago. And, as far as he knew, in Chile, the CIA... Well, the CIA wanted Max for themselves...."

"But what were the signs? *Of something serious?*" I persisted, casually pouring myself another half glass of champagne. "What did they have to do with?"

"That, Eric only told me about superficially. *He mentioned uranium smuggling, nuclear energy, and Germany.* From a few other garbled remarks, I assumed that the British must have smelled a business opportunity in the nuclear market with Brazil. And they might have tried to cut Germany out of the deal, *but without letting the Americans know.* So they wouldn't enter the field, of course."

"Which they couldn't prevent," I said. "Westinghouse ended up selling us the Angra 1 nuclear plant. But that's as far as it got. Because in 1975, the Americans became outraged when Brazil signed a nuclear agreement with Germany."

"Exactly." The colonel sighed, as if he were the one who had lost a billion-dollar deal. "And KVD, a subsidiary of Borgward-Stitz, was the one that made a fortune in this transaction." He consoled himself by digging into his sizable dessert.

"Anyway," he remarked after two forkfuls, "heaps of money were at stake. The matter is of course clearer seen today. But back then, it was all guesswork. Before serving in Montevideo, our ambassador had headed the Brazilian mission in Germany. And from then on, he'd spend his vacations in Bonn, all of them. *Only no one vacationed in Bonn, not even Korean tourists!*"

For a few minutes, the colonel gave himself over to his dessert. Once he'd conquered that challenge, he blurted out, "You can't even imagine the consequences of this whole ordeal. Some of them are unbelievable. One occurs to me now. Max had a colonel friend who happened to be from my class, Newton Cordeiro. A complicated character, that guy. He worked with us at the SNI until we found out about his involvement in some shady scheme, which we had to cover up. He was forced to retire and wound up at the Coffee Institute. But then it seems he started getting into stranger things. Well, to my surprise, Newton Cordeiro showed up in Montevideo and headed over to the embassy. I met up with him at the entrance. Since I figured he was there to see me, I frowned. Picture my astonishment when he brushed right past me without a single word and went straight into Max's office—without even knocking. Later I found out that he was staying with Max and his wife! He was in Montevideo at least three times. And always stayed with them."

As intrigued as I was, I instinctively sensed that Newton Cordeiro was a subject that might well derail our conversation. At that stage, I wasn't particularly inclined to raise issues involving the Operation Condor article in *Foreign Diplomatic Review*. Better to let go of this piece of the puzzle. Besides, I was tired. It had been a heavy meal. And although enjoyable, the conversation hadn't spared me from its painful resonances. As for the drinks... they just kept coming. I decided to take advantage of the arrival of the tray of liqueurs to change the subject.

"Colonel," I began, affecting mere curiosity, "did you ever meet Marina, Max's wife?"

The colonel's face disappeared briefly behind the first puff of his cigar. And there was nothing discreet about the swig of cognac he took. The combination of these two acts reinvigorated his voice.

"Marina. She came up to me at a reception one time and, without realizing what she was saying, told me that Max would arrive home from our night gatherings 'and lock himself in his office.' And she further kidded, in that husky voice of hers, 'What kind of game do you guys play, Major, that has my husband losing money at poker and then, when he gets home, forgoing his place in bed with me for some report? Just what is it you talk about while you're playing?' "

And here my old bear ended up showing that life had taught him something useful after all, albeit in the form of unresolved doubts. "Marina... Sometimes I think she knew a thing or two about us. But whose side she was on, I never figured out. Their relationship was strange, tense, at any rate. I never knew what was going on between them."

And so it came to be that dozens of anecdotes gathered during my nights out with the colonel in Vienna, as well as myriad fragments that lay dormant for years in my files, joined forces to make me a virtual hostage of my saga. As if fate wanted to reward me and punish me at the same time for my blind diligence in piecing together the puzzle I was dealing with. This is the story to which I now return, picking up in the early 1970s, when Max had first arrived in Montevideo.

# PART THREE

# 20

Having landed in Montevideo in 1970 with a crusader's spirit, suited in armor, a shield on his left arm, and an unsheathed sword in his right hand, Max found his first two weeks at the embassy a letdown. There were quite a number of staff on board and so, despite his promotion to first secretary, his hierarchical position was relatively obscure: five diplomats, as well as the three military attachés, had seniority over him, several with direct access to the ambassador. The latter did not fail to warmly invite him into his office for coffee. He also scheduled a luncheon in Max's honor at his residence for three weeks later, at which time he would also "see off the naval attaché transferred to Brasilia." The rest of their colleagues and their wives would be in attendance. At this the ambassador let slip a disparaging sigh and, before bidding Max goodbye, concluded, "You and your wife will then get to know all the members of our little diplomatic zoo."

*Three weeks*, thought Max, scarcely containing his surprise. Worse yet: the talk between the two, which he had been anticipating for quite some time, hadn't lasted five minutes. *Scheduling difficulties*, the ambassador's secretary had suggested on seeing him emerge crestfallen, before sending him back down to the first floor. For someone who had shared a moment of great intimacy with his future boss in his library just months earlier, the treatment was a slight. It occurred to him that on the occasion of their original conversation, he was being wooed. And that he'd now fallen into the less important category of the *conquered*.

As such, he was but another member of a team—led, it's worth remembering, by one of the ministry's strongmen. Although hurt, Max made a point of sending flowers to the ambassador's wife, briefly mentioning what a pleasure it would be to see her again and introduce Marina. He did the same for the wife of the minister-counselor. The couple received a polite note of thanks from each.

Despite these initial disappointments, our recent arrival knew, once again, to be patient and bide his time—aware that, sooner or later, it would come. Just as it had before. In Montevideo, however, the scene was much different. He was now abroad. And not only that: he was posted in an embassy ruled with an iron fist by one of the ministry's most feared men. Itamaraty's jargon alone reinforced his feeling of imprisonment. To begin with, he hadn't been transferred; he had been *relocated*. Furthermore, being away from the broader horizons of headquarters, he felt claustrophobic, like a sardine packed in a can.

From the minister-counselor, second-in-command at the embassy, he had received word that, by orders from above, he would be in charge of technical assistance. The news surprised him, since he had imagined that his known experience in South American matters would qualify him to join the political team. Even so, he merely lowered his head and bit his lip. They had given him an office on the ground floor, with a desk, three chairs, and a faded sofa, which barely disguised the fact that two armchairs had formerly been there also, as eight deep impressions remained in the rug, four on either side of the sofa. *Someone must have pilfered them*, Max thought, *taking advantage of the weeks since my predecessor left*. His secretary confirmed his suspicion with a cryptic smile. She would reveal more, her pose suggested, were she treated right.

Esmeralda was Uruguayan and counting the days until retirement. Her white hair and calm demeanor were representative of her thirty years of service, during which time she had been through, in reverse order, all the positions entrusted to local aides. She had started in the 1940s as the private secretary of the then ambassador and became his lover. She had gone on to work for the minister-counselor, and from there moved down, both bosses and floors, until reaching the bottom, where the youngest diplomats and assistants to the military attachés were clustered.

She would become Max's friend in a matter of days—soon finding out just whom she was dealing with. Not one to mince words, especially when encouraged, she didn't hold back her thoughts on life, men, and diplomats in particular. Such candor took Max by surprise, quickly delighting him and proving to be his only true source of joy those first few rough weeks. He liked to goad her into revealing trivial secrets about the embassy and its characters, which she meted out in dribs and drabs, always receiving some bit of information from him in return. These she would store away for future use—a game at which they were both skilled players and that would draw them even closer over time.

Esmeralda occupied a small office space next to Max's. On their first day working together, she had detected her new boss's disappointed look as he took in the mediocre paintings on his walls. "What's more, they're dreary," she had said, surprising Max, who was used to guessing the thoughts of others but not to seeing his own so readily exposed.

"To match the view from our windows," he had observed in turn. And rightly so, since the days of his arrival had coincided with an intermittent rain that brought out the bleakness of that street, which had no pedestrians.

"The rain in London brings out poetry," she had said, quoting verses by her first boss and lover who, unhappy with his transfer from England to Uruguay during the war—a transfer to which he owed his life, since his residence in London had been destroyed by a bomb days after his departure—spent his time lamenting, "but in Montevideo it's woeful water that further dampens the mood..."

*How dreadful*, thought Max on hearing the verses (loosely translated, for as Esmeralda sheepishly admitted, she no longer recalled the original English version, "which sounded infinitely better"). He envisioned the two depressed lovers in bed a generation ago, looking out at the same rain still coming down now. Yet he smiled at her and praised the poem, understanding that it represented what was left of the relationship. Then he cast aside the secretary's depression in order to concentrate on his own. *To think that I could be in Washington or Paris...*

To lift his spirits, he devoted his first days to Marina and the task of finding a home, in which he was assisted by information from various colleagues and their wives, who kindly invited them to dinner. Based on these suggestions, they got in touch with a real estate agent known by the embassy and went out house hunting. Their belongings, which had come by land and already arrived in Montevideo, were held up in customs awaiting clearance. From there it would all go into storage, until the couple had an address.

Put up at a comfortable and centrally located hotel, but one that had seen better times ("It's decent," the minister-counselor had told him indifferently over the phone), Max and Marina found themselves prisoners of a tiny room whose carpeted floor undulated beneath their feet. They were constantly bumping into one another, and whispering apologies, as if some degree of formality had covertly infiltrated their relationship. They sighed without knowing why and spent a good part of the late nights reading in the lumpy double bed, which seemed to creak with the turn of each page.

Because she was younger and more outgoing, Marina handled the situation better. Over those first two weeks, she dressed simply and wandered around the city, whether with the realtor recommended by the embassy, prescreening residences she would look at again later with Max, or in the company of some spouse of a colleague, who took turns with the other wives in this task. For that's what they were: a support group, continuing a tradition that had helped them all in the past—and that, with Marina now on the team, would benefit the families still to come to Montevideo.

Far from bothering her, the variety of companions enabled her to get to know the women's world—at her husband's professional level, of course, since the wives of the senior colleagues, and with greater reason those of the military attachés, weren't part of this collective effort, reserving their energy for recent arrivals of their stature. She took in all of these small social cues, which had gone undetected in the upper-class Rio de Janeiro society she came from, with the painful feeling that they were being employed with extra rigor in her case given that she was a Magalhães de Castro. Her surname had actually sounded the alarm at the sorority's highest levels since it put the ambassador's wife—not to mention the other members of her court—in an inferior position.

This had been the main reason the ambassador's wife tried to veto Max's assignment when, months earlier, she'd learned of the offer her husband had extended to the young diplomat. Informed of Marina's aristocratic lineage by the wife of the minister-counselor, she had asked her husband one night, while removing her earrings in front of her vanity, "Just what is it that a Magalhães de Castro would hope to find in Montevideo?" To which the ambassador, who was taking off his shoes just then, freeing his feet from the prison in which they'd been confined since that morning, had responded succinctly, "Her husband." Beneath his wife's stern look, he had added, "And, with any luck, the happiness to which we all aspire, with varying degrees of success."

In private, the ambassador was a man with a sharp sense of humor and a winning personality—a secret to which no one, not even his wife (who had stopped listening to him years ago), had access. A secret, I might add, that he guarded closely and intended to reveal only in his memoirs. Meanwhile, he concentrated on going against the tide, convinced that there was no political solution for our region without sacrifices that wouldn't be understood for two or three generations. He believed that each and every drop of blood shed in this process, which he deemed both warranted and legitimate, would be forgotten over time.

# 21

Esmeralda knocked on Max's door and went right in as usual. "The ambassador's secretary asked that you come up."

"Come up?"

Esmeralda laughed. "To heaven. To the third floor."

*The ambassador's office...* Max set aside the newspaper he was reading, put out his cigarette, and pulled on his jacket. "Has my day of glory arrived?"

"After two weeks on the job?" joked Esmeralda, who had sat back down and was now filing her nails. "I'd be surprised."

Max took the stairs, even though the small elevator was stopped on the ground floor. He went up unhurriedly, like a man who doesn't pass up an opportunity to exercise his legs, combining the habit with a moment of introspection. In doing so, he showed the world, which was completely unaware of his existence at that particular moment, as well as himself, that he was in control.

In the ambassador's reception area, the secretary was already waiting for him, barely containing her impatience. Without so much as a smile or a word of greeting, she opened the door and stepped aside so he could enter.

"Good morning, Marcílio," said the ambassador without rising. He pointed to a chair in front of him and extended his arm once Max had taken a seat.

After a handshake, he opened one of the drawers to the right of the desk and pulled out a pipe and a small round tin of tobacco. "My first pipe of the day. The doctor only allows me two. The second lends a certain charm to my lunch. But the best, of course, is *the third*, which I smoke alone at night, hidden, on the terrace. At my age, Marcílio, life's pleasures are few and far between. I live a constant paradox: secrets increase around me but secret pleasures decrease. Beware."

Max smiled at these words. And at the wistfulness behind them. He hoped that partaking in this morning ritual somehow represented an honor, being specially granted to him. The ambassador, however, didn't seem that interested in his reactions. In fact, he was gazing out at the tree branches when he asked, "Are you still ticked off with me?"

"Ticked off, Ambassador?" Max was genuinely taken aback. "Why would I—"

The ambassador held up a hand and kept him from continuing. "The assignment I gave you, technical assistance. The small office...the tired furniture...Esmeralda reciting her old poems..."

"Please, Ambassador, technical assistance is no—"

"Nonsense. You and I know that. But it was necessary."

"Necessary?"

The ambassador turned to face him. "To keep up appearances. It's the perfect cover for you. Just as it was important to keep you at arm's length for a few days. Everyone around here keeps an eye on who goes in and out of my office. And I needed to defuse the reputation that preceded you. Top assistant to the minister...top assistant to the secretary-general. You're going to have to fade into the woodwork. And the sooner, the better."

With another gesture, he again kept Max from opening his mouth. Far from being rude, it was an appeal. There was no time to lose. "At eleven thirty the colonel is coming to see me with an American friend of his. He's been after me for a week to meet this guy."

He checked his schedule and slowly murmured, as if to himself, the full name recorded there: "Daniel A. Matrone. And that *A* probably isn't for angel. He's an American from the FBI, or the CIA. The attaché knows him from his days in Brazil. According to him, they used to play golf together. Must be a lie. That attaché lies a lot. Have you ever heard of a Brazilian colonel playing golf? With grenades, maybe. Do you play golf?"

"No, Ambassador."

"Poker?"

"Poker, yes."

"Excellent. Vaz..." A pause. He had transferred the tobacco to the pipe. Now all he had to do was light the match. "Major João Vaz is that big stocky guy. He's number two to the golfer colonel. Vaz came from the SNI. But he does the PR thing—nice, friendly, and all. He's going to invite you to his poker circle. And you're going to accept. To his surprise."

"Surprise? Why?"

"Because I gave explicit orders to all the diplomats to turn down the same invitation up till now. I was waiting for your arrival."

"And I..."

"You're going to accept. And lose. Lose a lot more than win. You can win once in a while, here and there. Discreetly. They like suckers, but they're no fools."

"Forgive me, Ambassador. But I don't see—"

"I need information. From the second echelon of attachés. And sooner or later they're going to open up with you. They won't actually reveal secrets. They're trained not to."

"But then...?"

"Generally, I learn about what they know *before they do.* But I'm unaware of what they *don't* know."

"What they *don't* know..."

"Right. And that's what interests me—what they don't know. And *why* they don't know. In other words, what their bosses are keeping from them, and for what reasons. Pay close attention to the doubts, the speculations. The uncertainties."

Max preferred not to press. The subject seemed rather bizarre to him.

The ambassador struck his match. Holding it lit between his fingers, he made a further suggestion. "Bluff as little as possible at the table. And avoid falling for someone else's bluff. Break up any three of a kind you're dealt. That ought to be enough. But keep your eyes open. They're crafty at this kind of game."

The ambassador turned his back to Max again and offered his first puffs to the tree branches that almost covered the windows. "Agreed?"

"Agreed, Ambassador."

"Great. Consider this an investment. Take whatever you lose out of your expense account. In exchange, you're exempt from having to host dinners at your house. Other than for your personal friends, of course. Financially, it'll be a trade-off, with one extra advantage: your wife will kiss your feet in gratitude. Because these low-level Uruguayans who have to be entertained now and again can bore you to tears."

He turned back toward Max. "How is your wife, by the way? Marina..."

"Fine, Ambassador. She—"

"Is she surviving our den of lionesses? They're quite a bunch...as is the case at almost any big embassy. The men generally get along well. But the women form cliques separated by barbed wire and pricker bushes. Here, they're all organized by my wife. And the ladies don't suspect a thing! My wife gets quite a kick out of it. We have three rival cliques at the moment, all at each other's throats."

Max laughed and disagreed good-naturedly. "Far from it, Ambassador; they've all been very kind and helped us a lot. We've even found a good apartment already thanks to them."

"An apartment? In Pocitos?"

"No, we ended up deciding on a nice duplex near downtown. It'll be better for Marina. And since we don't have kids yet, we won't miss having a yard."

The ambassador considered the matter for a few seconds. Then he gave his opinion: "Until last year, I would have disagreed with that choice. The houses in Pocitos and Carrasco are indeed much nicer. But things have been changing in this country. Matters will soon come to a head with the Tupamaros. So far, they've been playing cat and mouse with the police. They hold up a bank here, a jewelry store there.... But now both sides are taking off their gloves. And the military is going to step up for real. The closer you are to our office, the better. You're arriving at what may well turn out to be this city's last peaceful period. In just a few months, we're going to go through a guerrilla war. Until the government falls. To one side or the other. *To our side*, as far as I'm concerned."

Silence followed, during which the ambassador devoted most of his attention to his pipe and tree branches. Soon enough, however, he changed the subject. "Has Carlos Alberto introduced you to everyone?" Carlos Alberto Pereira Campos was the minister-counselor.

"Yes, Ambassador. A few colleagues I already knew from the reception at your home last year or from meetings in Rio de Janei—"

"And the attachés and their assistants? We have an entire troop camped out here. Nine or ten of them. Almost all with wives who make you want to cry."

"I was introduced to the attachés and a few of their assistants, but there hasn't been time to—"

"The best and brightest by far is the air force general. The navy admiral, who's leaving, also became a friend of mine. He's a capable man. But this guy from the army, this colonel coming to see me now with the American, is something else. Quite a shady character. He earned his stripes with the secret police in

São Paulo, where they say he pulled off some atrocious things. Here, in less than six months, he almost managed to burn all the bridges I've taken great pains to build with the Uruguayan military. His predecessor helped with that. Now, *that fellow* was first rate."

Max shifted slightly in his chair, as though seeking a more comfortable position. He knew that such bluntness, besides being unexpected and unusual, would elevate their discussion to sensitive levels. Everything that had been said up till then, even the more mundane remarks, had far surpassed the limits of a more conventional conversation. The ambassador didn't delay in confirming this.

"Marcílio, we're going to have to be frank, you and I. Your transfer to Montevideo was decided before your visit at the end of last year, *well before*. On that occasion you were included in the delegation at my request, for one reason: I wanted to personally meet you. Files say very little about people. Your transfer was already a foregone conclusion. It only went through the ministry at the final stage, for the required paperwork. The decisions, as I'm sure you'll understand, were made *on another level*. Right?"

"Yes, Ambassador. That is..."

The ambassador directed a stare at Max, followed by a puff of smoke. "*That is...?*"

"That is, yes and no, Ambassador."

"Excellent, Max, excellent. *Yes and no.* Keep those key words in mind. They summarize your mission in Montevideo to a T. Unlike in more traditional diplomacy, there will rarely be occasion for the more comfortable and pleasing *maybe*."

They laughed for a moment, the ambassador content, Max concerned. To such an extent that, sensing the heavy atmosphere, he took a gamble and skipped a stage of the conversation to get straight to the point. "Forgive me, Ambassador, but what's the urgency?"

With the question, they drew near the heart of the matter—so near, in fact, that the silence was now filled with several puffs on the pipe, all of them directed toward the ceiling.

"The urgency, Marcílio, is that I'm leaving," answered the ambassador. "And so is Carlos Alberto. I'm going to work in the president's office, before I retire two years from now. And after that, when I leave public service, I'll give myself over to the pleasures of the private sector. I'm going to make some money. The Germans are after me with a few interesting proposals."

"Do you speak German?"

"I studied in Germany!" His response took on an inflated tone. "Before the war! You didn't bother to read my résumé? I'm one of the few at the ministry who know anything about Germany. And, before coming here, I served in Germany. I was transferred from Bonn to Montevideo!"

He soon calmed down. And in order to avoid Max's feeling unnerved by the digression, he kindly confided, "Last week, I turned down the embassy they had set aside for me. I would have died of boredom in Rome. So I made the president's office a more promising offer." He added, almost as an afterthought, "And Carlos Alberto will be headed to a new post, which is still being worked out. In other words, the two of us will be leaving at the same time."

After coming full circle, the ambassador looked straight at Max and finished by saying, "That's the urgency. We have four months to form a partnership."

# 22

"A partnership?" asked Max, smiling amiably.

The ambassador set his pipe on the ashtray and reclined his chair, which tipped back beneath his weight. "I've been in Montevideo six years, son. I arrived just before the Revolution of sixty-four."

Max was disconcerted by the use of *son*. Without exactly sounding false, there was something insincere about it. And then there was the question of this *partnership* still hanging in the air between them.

"Marcílio, in four months, I'll be replaced by a big shot from the old guard, whose name I can't reveal just yet. But it's irrelevant. What matters is that you're going to get along very well. He's polite and pleasant enough. But my replacement is coming here solely to push papers. The one running things at the embassy will be his number two. A man in whom I have complete confidence, my protégé, so to speak. We've served together twice, the last time in Germany, before I was transferred here. And he's the one you'll be dealing with. The partnership I want to form is with the two of you. Our three-way collaboration is going to work with me at the president's office and you two here. His name is Carlos Câmara. He's coming from the War College. Ever heard of him?"

"Carlos Câmara," Max mumbled to himself. "No, the name doesn't ring a bell. I knew some of the college officers at one time, they'd call me once in a while to talk, but..."

"Doesn't matter. *He's* heard of *you*. Already knows everything about you. That's the reason for our conversation today. To start thinking about this transition. If all goes well, you and Carlos will have the rare opportunity to be part of a decisive moment in our country's history." After a pause, the ambassador continued at cruising speed. "It's time for you to learn about a project we're developing here. And in the region."

"In the region?"

A few more pipe puffs, shorter, almost breathless with impatience. In an ideal world, which would faithfully reproduce the ambassador's secret desires, there would be no room for questions. Or, more reasonably, for those that repeated words whose echo could still be heard. "Let's just say, for now, that it's a delicate operation, in which we're not playing a very visible role. At most, we're *interested observers*. If consulted, we give our opinion. Based on what happened in Brazil between 1960 and March 1964. They listen, take a few notes, whisper a lot among themselves...."

"*They who*, Ambassador?" The question seemed obvious but wasn't. Max was interested in knowing more about the context of their discussion, since Uruguay had a democratically elected government. What level of the Uruguayan armed forces—because that's what they were evidently talking about— was the ambassador dealing with? His superior ignored the question, however, like the referee at a soccer game who doesn't see the blatant foul committed right under his nose.

"Every country in this region lives with its own realities, its own challenges. And many of them have nothing to do with ours. But we've already been through a somewhat similar process. And they haven't. This gives us an advantage on one hand. And an enormous responsibility on the other. We can't interfere. But neither can we be left out. It's a scenario that will require considerable patience, given that the situation here and in Chile"—*Chile*, a new piece on the ambassador's chessboard—"is going to take a while to come to a head before the unavoidable conflict."

Max waited, transfixed.

"And we're alone in this endeavor. The Americans told us they don't want to get involved. They have enough problems in Vietnam. Besides, they almost got burned in Brazil with Operation Brother Sam, and plenty of Europeans criticized their interfering in our country. Covertly, fine, they're ready to help. The way they did with us. But not outwardly. I'm willing to bet that Matrone's visit has to do with this. He's not high enough up to request a meeting with me. He's coming to relay a message."

Max realized that his five years at the secretary-general's office reading telegrams and dispatches from Montevideo had little to do with the landscape the ambassador was casually sketching around them. As though the distance separating real life from the cables were equivalent to that between a photograph in focus and a rough sketch on blotting paper.

Although accustomed to reading between the lines, and making the most out of the reports at hand, Max was startled to find himself confronting information he knew absolutely nothing about. The revelation led him to better understand the nature of the present conversation—and the direction it might yet take. The ambassador had *two* channels of communication. And Itamaraty was only one of them. The official one, as if it were a façade. Max also understood that his boss, between remarks and puffs on his pipe, was slowly luring him toward a labyrinth in which he felt completely at home—and with which Max needed to familiarize himself as quickly as possible if he wished to survive. He anxiously awaited whatever was to come.

The ambassador glanced at his watch and picked up the phone, requesting that coffee be brought in. Max sank into his chair a bit farther, although this was physically difficult considering the austere piece of furniture on which he was seated.

"Things are going to take a while. A year or two...maybe more. The game will be played with a stacked deck, with a very short break between the two"—he briefly consulted the ceiling—"*proceedings.*"

The ceiling had whispered *countries*. The boss had said *proceedings*. Max heard *coups*.

"*The two proceedings*," repeated the ambassador, as if to impose order on the voices jostling for position between them. "This interval of three months between the two...*proceedings* has already been decided. Not by us, fortunately."

"By whom?" asked Max in a thin voice.

To his surprise, the question merited a response, albeit partial. "As far as that goes, the less you know, the better. Leave that to Carlos. He's the one who's going to operate on that front. Yours will be quite different. And, in a way, more important."

Max didn't know how to take these words—whether to feel flattered or frightened.

"What matters is that, in the meantime, tensions will increase in both countries. And we're going to end up having to intervene. But as discreetly as possible. As inconspicuously as the Americans. And note that they could afford the luxury of running some risks, particularly because they always did as they pleased in Latin America. So, what's one more disaster?" The ambassador was a man of the extreme right. The remark, however, revealed his disgust for Washington's excesses.

"But not us," he went on. "We'll never be accused of involvement. That's why the fewer people who know about the schemes to be put in place, should they become necessary, the better." The gravity of the moment coincided with the ambassador's sadness as he realized that he was getting to the bottom of his pipe. He saw himself compelled to take a shortcut that would bring the conversation to a close without further delay. "Our job consists of mollifying the military," he continued, without deviating from a previously traced course. "And avoiding hasty moves."

Here Max dared to formulate a question that was missing in the equation. "And what about Argentina, Ambassador?"

Two sighs and a final puff on his pipe. And, to Max's surprise, another response—this time providing clarification. "Anything can happen in Argentina. Luckily, Onganía, according to certain international press reports, is beginning to embody the gorilla prototype. This puts our generals at an advantage, comparatively speaking. But the truth is that Peronism has strong roots. And Perón could even come back from Spain. Should this happen, he'll end up setting fire to the country and reigning over ashes. And the military will be back. This time, fiercer than ever. To stay."

After a moment of reflection, he went on. "The hatred there goes way back. It's deep-seated, embedded in chronic disillusion. There's something inexplicable about that country, extraordinary in so many ways. Something that, oddly, may explain the intensity and elaborate nature of its art, from the tango to Borges. Whatever takes place in Argentina will be more brutal than whatever happens in Chile. Although..."

The ambassador hesitated. Whether from lack of ideas or words, Max didn't know. The fact is, he turned his attention to another battle front. "That's not all: if Argentina and Chile put their historical differences behind them someday, and even join up with Uruguay, we can't be left out. Especially because, in the long run, we'll have been the pioneers of this whole process. We were the first to take the risks. Two years before Argentina! And the first to set the tone for what would come. *And is still to come.*"

Max then received the most intense look of the morning, without embellishment, wordplay, or pipe smoke.

"The picture, Marcílio, is simple: the survival of each of these countries, ours included, depends on the collective security of the four. Not that Brazil is, at the present juncture, facing the least danger. But there's no question that our future security will, in large part, eventually depend on theirs. Except that

Itamaraty isn't convinced of this. *These colleagues of ours can be slow-witted!* They refuse to understand that this entire process is linked." A feeble gesture followed, directed at the ceiling more than at Max.

"So I had no other recourse. I began to deal directly with the SNI. And even with them I had to play hardball." He preferred to remain silent about the specifics. The old warrior had fought on countless fronts.

He took another tack in the conversation. "On the other hand, once this initial phase of civil conflict is over, we can't remain vulnerable to a shared stability among these countries. And the union that might result from it. We need to join their club."

"Of which we're founding members..."

"Don't kid about this, Marcílio!" Max had never imagined the ambassador to be the excitable sort. "Especially because, in the meantime, you'll have become a notable specialist in technical cooperation, *with particular emphasis in the complex area of personnel training.* And you'll be called upon to coordinate projects that justify and ensure our disinterested participation in... *the internal problems that our friends have been facing.*"

The tobacco was gone. Only the sweet smell lingered in the air. "Not only for strategic reasons," he whispered, at peace with himself once more. "For other, equally important reasons."

"Such as, for instance...," Max ventured.

"Such as, *for instance,* creating a middle class in the region. A *reliable* middle class that will one day finally learn how to vote and thereby slash the Marxist threat by the only root that matters."

"Access to social welfare?"

"Access to the market."

Soon, however, came the condescending yet almost tender follow-up. "Okay, Marcílio, okay... *access to social welfare.* Anyway, one is tied to the other. And I'm not saying the first isn't important. But it's because of *the second* that the Americans, who are responsible for this circus around us" — *circus*, the word surprised Max — "are going to suggest that we dismantle it in ten or fifteen years. Worse, they're going to pressure us in that direction. Because, by then, the Cuban threat and the danger represented by Allende in Chile will have disappeared. And liberalism will rule once more. The region will cease to invest in arms and will buy televisions, refrigerators, and stoves instead. Or whatever else may be invented going forward. Not bad, right?"

Thankfully, the coffee was served. It came with two glasses of water and a plate with an apple cut in four.

The ambassador pulled a small vial from his vest pocket. "Forgive me, son. I have to eat a piece of fruit before I choke down this awful medicine. But drink your coffee before it gets cold."

# 23

Oddly, the *son* didn't bother him as much now. Maybe because, this time, it was offered soothingly, deceptive though it might have been. Even so, Max had been feeling unsettled for several minutes, the reasons for which he couldn't quite fathom.

A half hour earlier, he had been doing nothing other than contemplating the deserted street beyond his office window, putting off the moment when he would dedicate himself to peacefully reading the newspaper, followed by the equally pleasant perusal of the day's telegrams brought in by Esmeralda—which were waiting on his desk. Now, however, he found himself involved in a plot of at least regional proportions. In which, if he understood correctly, he would be called upon to play a rather important role. All of this, from the look of it, without Itamaraty's official knowledge. The ministry was only providing the framework, allowing the ambassador, and his eventual allies (*accomplices*, some would surely say), to operate toward an unknown goal.

Previously, he had approached such topics in an informal, almost offhanded way, and this had served him well. But now the circumstances had begun to change, and the environment around him threatened to become quite constricting. Although mildly alarmed, he could hardly contain the excitement that was slowly coming over him. He had never imagined making...*History*.

The ambassador, who was watching him closely, interrupted his thoughts. "*Yes and no, Marcílio*."

"Pardon?"

"Don't worry. The big international schemes take place at this level. On a very small chessboard, where the pieces are either black or white. There are no shades of gray or the kinds of speculating the academic community is so fond of. No *maybes*. That's what you were thinking about, right?"

"More or less."

"That's why you're here today, to begin the demystification process. Which has two aims. First, understanding the scope of our challenge. This has to do with the fact that the region, in and of itself, is of no importance whatsoever in this game. Except as a reflection of another."

"A reflection of another," Max echoed dumbly.

"That's right. To the Americans, we're nothing more than tomorrow's Vietnam. As far as they're concerned, we're just a headache that can be wiped out with aspirin."

"How come?"

"Because that's what we're dealing with here. Do you think a man like Nixon understands Latin America? Aside from the border problems with Mexico? He understands the Soviet Union and the cold war. He respects or fears China. He probably holds Europe in contempt. *But Latin America?* We're barely a blip on his radar. Radar on which Africa doesn't even exist, except for Egypt because of Israel."

"And the second? *The second aim?*"

"That one is more important. And more pleasant: getting to know the mechanism you're a part of."

Finally they'd reached the heart of the matter.

"Mechanism?" Max asked.

Having finished the apple, the ambassador now took his medicine. Then he gave three quick taps on the rim of the ashtray to clean out his pipe. Sighing, he replaced it in his desk drawer along with the tin of tobacco and took two sips of coffee. Only then did he casually remark, "Marcílio, you can't be *surprised* by all of this.... Let's be honest!" Without giving Max a chance to react, he added, "Your name was part of our plans at least two years ago, as I told you."

Max seemed as though he was having trouble believing this.

"And based on what criteria...," Max began.

"...was the choice made?" completed the ambassador.

"Yes."

"Think about it, Marcílio. These things can be painful. Although, in your case, we're dealing with character traits that I personally admire. And rightly consider assets. Not shortcomings, as some do."

"Let's have them, Ambassador."

"Your name came to my attention because of how deftly you switched sides in sixty-four. I'd even say because of the extraordinary resourcefulness you demonstrated on the occasion. A gazelle couldn't have leapt more gracefully. *Kissing the cardinal's ring*... not even I would have thought of that."

Before Max could crawl and hide under the rug, the secretary knocked on the door and entered.

"The colonel is here," she announced. "He's in the reception area." She tilted her head to read the card in her hand. "With a Mr.... Dan-iel Ma-trone," she pronounced.

"With Mr. Daniel *A.* Matrone," corrected the ambassador, with a friendly smile in Max's direction. "Make them wait a bit. And have them come in a few minutes after Secretary Marcílio leaves us."

Turning back toward Max, who was now standing, he extended a hand. A hand that sealed their partnership. "Let's see what our angel wants," he said then, before seeing Max out. "We'll continue our conversation in a few days."

Max left the room through a side door. He found himself in a hallway, where he remained for a few seconds, lost in thought. He was, in fact, stunned. So much so that he needed to brace himself against the wall for a minute.

Before taking the first steps toward the stairs, he overheard the final part of the introductions: "Call me Dan, Ambassador. Everyone calls me Dan," a voice was saying.

"Fine, Dan," he heard the ambassador replying. "As for you, you may address me as Your Excellency."

# 24

The following months, Max found himself facing serious challenges on two fronts: at home and at work. The first scenario worried him far more—perhaps because he felt unable to understand it. He merely noted that, despite the happy news of her recent pregnancy, Marina was pulling away from him, for no logical reason he could grasp.

"Pregnancy really messes with a woman's emotions," Esmeralda, to whom he opened up during a rare moment of helplessness, had told him. "Especially the first."

Max took consolation from her words, until he remembered that she had never had children and therefore came by her information secondhand.

As for work, the atmosphere was complicated by a combination of factors, some predictable, others not. Consistent with the first conversation he'd had with his boss about the Tupamaros, the civil war climate had indeed begun to intensify in the country. The government struggled to remain in place, political crises broke out, the numbers of victims on both sides increased. The military grew agitated, in many cases issuing contradictory statements.

As threatening as this scenario may have seemed, however, Max's daily routine was actually far more affected by the climate of transition that took hold of the embassy as soon as word of the ambassador's replacement got out. It was as if an entire empire were on the verge of ruin and another, the details of which remained unknown, was about to take its place. The resident vassals were left unable to figure out what was really happening around them and thus change allegiances and redirect their talents (if they had any).

In the women's realm, this state of affairs had devastating effects. The cliques all vanished into thin air, and the ambassador's wife—left in a vacuum, to her bewilderment—saw her power and influence shrink with each passing day.

The city and the country threatened to implode in a thousand ways. Yet what happened within the embassy walls seemed infinitely graver in the eyes of those who worked there.

Against this complex and unstable backdrop, the ambassador and his wife threw one last dinner for the three military attachés and all the diplomats. According to custom, they should have done so later, a few days prior to their departure. Holding it in advance symbolized the ambassador's wish to show everyone that he had no fear of the future. Or, as he said to Max in private just hours before the event, that he was grabbing the bull by the horns. And one of his greatest pleasures in this process (which he had revealed to his young colleague alone) consisted in being the keeper of the ultimate secret: the extraordinary fate awaiting him in Brasilia.

As such, of the twenty-four diners seated at the endless table, only two shone brightly in the shadows (the ambassador's wife having opted for a candlelit banquet to underscore the funereal climate to which she saw herself demoted): the host and Max. Neither the fine English china nor the numerous crystal wineglasses sparkled as they did. Even the candelabra and floral arrangements spaced along the spotless white tablecloth paled in comparison to the elegance the two men displayed.

Of all those people relegated to anonymity, Marina was, by far, the most depressed. That same afternoon, by unhappy coincidence, she'd had her fateful encounter with Nilo Montenegro downtown. As a result, she'd spent the first part of the dinner in a cold sweat, not knowing where to rest her eyes.

She and Max had just gotten back to their apartment when the conflict they were going through came to a head: Marina had spoken of running into Nilo. In a matter of seconds, she'd turned her insinuations into criticisms. For the first time since they'd met, she'd raised her voice and pointed an accusatory finger at Max. He'd vehemently denied the charges, claiming they were unfounded and merely derived from the fact that he worked at the embassy. He was in no way compromised, he assured her. But he'd been rattled by his wife's tone. And by the sadness with which she'd listened to his explanations—a sadness that, from that point onward, would follow her like a shadow. *Was it possible that his wife knew something concrete about him?*

By the next morning, Max had hurried to check the file on the actor in the embassy archives. *Nilo Montenegro...* He couldn't remember what the man looked like but the name was familiar. Had he and Ana performed onstage together? Had they all gone out one night, as often occurred in the theater world? He breathed easier on seeing that there was nothing incriminating against the man, except that, until recently, he had shared an apartment with a political activist who had sought refuge in Montevideo.

The former roommate, from what Max would glean at the poker table a few nights later, was indeed a dangerous man. He realized this when, between one hand and the next, Major João Vaz had asked the number two air force official "if the package had been shipped off," to which the young man, who was picking up his cards right then, had replied with a laconic "affirmative."

Max had had no way of connecting one fact to the other. Except that, a few seconds later, after looking over his cards carefully, the young official had put a few chips on the table and said, in a lower voice, "We're just not sure what to do with the guy who shared his digs." Once the wagers had all been made, the major, who was cleaning up that night, made Nilo a part of his winning streak. "Nothing. Don't do a thing," he'd advised, counting his chips. And added, "As far as I can tell, he's just an actor." Then he'd thrown back his whiskey. That's how a man's fate was decided in those days. All things considered, the ambassador had gotten it both right and wrong by having Max infiltrate Major Vaz's poker table. He'd erred because Max would never be able to detect, in that cohesive group, the doubts or uncertainties his boss assumed were prevalent. Max therefore had no way to supply his boss with intelligence about dissidence or distrust that might warrant being noted in that environment.

On the other hand—and here the ambassador had unintentionally gotten it right—once he'd earned the trust of his fellow poker players (the kind of trust generally established among men who belong to the same club, independent of class or distinction), Max couldn't have had better access to the underworld in which they operated with ease and chilling resourcefulness. That it was an underworld of the worst kind, Max had no doubt. It was as if those hands holding cards or chips had, just moments earlier, dealt with lives and destinies—which still pulsated around them. The only evidence Max had for this dismal impression was the amount of liquor everyone consumed without showing any sign of being drunk at night's end. To this was added the steel grip each person greeted him with on the way in and out, leading our hero to run his hands under hot water for several minutes when he got home, before filing his notes.

In his presence, officials avoided being explicit about the nature of their areas of activity. But to attuned ears like Max's, any word spoken with special emphasis gained resonance. The games and teasing further helped. "Our pal Pedro is bullshitting us tonight," someone at the table claimed. "Must not have read his instruction manual very closely," another joked. "And he still hasn't figured out that sooner or later all secrets come out," a third had concluded to everyone's amusement. "All you have to do is push the right button...," a fourth reminded them, barely containing his glee, "...or administer another sip of water," rounded out the first, closing the harmonious circle.

But when Max tried to take advantage of the camaraderie and join in the friendly banter ("In that case, I'd also like to have a look at this manual of yours," he'd suggested), the others had gone quiet.

"Nice people don't get into these conversations," Major Vaz had remarked, with a paternal smile, in an effort to alleviate the awkwardness caused by the sudden silence. To which Max, laying his four aces on the table, had replied, "Keep in mind, I have a manual of my own..." He'd then added with a semblance of pride, while collecting his chips and casting an ironic glance around the table, "...issued by the same printer as yours." These comments received a hearty round of applause.

The scene had been akin to a rite of passage. All had laughed at his presence of mind. Max had even gotten a few congratulatory slaps on the back. Not because he'd won that hand—an accomplishment in and of itself—but because he'd conveyed a clear message: they were all in the same boat. It didn't much matter that some worked above deck, sporting fancy suits or uniforms, while others, in charcoal- and grease-stained clothing, took care of the furnaces below. Without the collective effort of the group, they wouldn't get anywhere.

From that night on, Max became one of them. On an honorary basis, it went without saying. As if all he needed to graduate was to learn to deliver electric shocks with the right intensity. Or familiarize himself with the use of paddles, hot irons, waterboarding, and the parrot's perch, not to mention the police dogs, specially trained to seize the testicles of reticent prisoners without crushing them. Prisoners who arrived at the torture chambers wearing black hoods imbued, as one of them would later recall, with the smell of fear. The episode, meanwhile, had ramifications of another kind, which had led Major Vaz to take Max aside for a chat during the customary sandwich break.

"Max," he'd begun, giving the impression of walking on eggshells, "we know that you have the ambassador's complete trust. And on our end, we've heard great things about your work. Insightful investigative work, which has helped us enormously in our sphere of operation—if you know what I mean."

"Thank you, Major."

"Max, for the love of God! Call me Vaz, the way everyone else here does."

"Okay, Vaz. Anyway, thanks for the compliment."

"Right...I was thinking that you might be able to provide us with a little extra help. After checking with the ambassador, of course. But we'll talk some other time. If you have a spare minute, I'll come by your office tomorrow for coffee. How about it?"

"It would be my pleasure, Vaz."

"I have a proposal that might be of interest. As I said, it would be a big help to us. For you, it could represent..." He was at a loss for the right word, and Max had no way of coming to his aid because he knew exactly what the major was getting at. He needed a better connection with the embassy. For some particular reason. "...a departure from your usual activities," concluded the major, returning to the game table.

# 25

In the residence library, the ambassador was seated in an arm-chair, supervising the packing of his books by several uniformed men from the moving company. Max, who had asked to be seen for a few minutes, waited at the entrance while his boss finished giving instructions to the manager of the firm.

When the two men were through, Max went over and greeted the ambassador. He then announced, "Major Vaz came to see me in my office this morning. So the two of us could talk."

The ambassador was silently sorting the books and magazines he wished to donate to the Uruguay-Brazil Cultural Institute from those he planned to discard. With his index finger he pointed to the bookcase in front of him, which held the complete works of Goethe, Hermann Hesse, and Nietzsche. "All in their original versions," he said with obvious pride.

Then he invited his colleague to take a seat beside him. He let out a deep sigh, as though having a hard time leaving the realm of literature to step into the far duller real world. "Good old Vaz," he murmured. Then, shifting gears, as though just waking up, he asked, "How is he? And what did he want with you?"

Max glanced at the movers coming and going with boxes. With a discreet gesture, the ambassador instructed him to proceed.

"What he wants," Max then replied, "is to transfer one of their agenda items to us. Or rather, to me."

"*One of their...*," and here the ambassador couldn't help but laugh. "Since when does that group work with an *agenda*,

Marcílio? They work with their hands! And their feet! At most, with pliers and other implements!" The ambassador had a love-hate relationship with the attachés. One minute, he'd express his admiration, even gratitude; the next, he'd reduce them to dust. He made use of their information but resented having to depend on them to get it.

"Ambassador," Max explained patiently, "those are *my* words. He didn't put it quite like that. But that's just what the major wants: to transfer a matter of theirs to me. He'd like me to start gathering information on a couple the SNI planted among the Brazilian exiles in Montevideo two and a half years ago."

His boss sprang from dark humor to incredulousness with lightning speed. *"Like you to start?* But what kind of madness is that, Marcílio? We've never operated on that level. We work on another plane. We don't take on operational duties! We're like the SNI. *A small-scale SNI.* How exactly did you create an opening for a request of this nature, which could now—"

"Forgive me, Ambassador, but the subject came up quite spontaneously, at the poker table. The major, who's not really a bad person, as you know, called me aside. And, today, he came to see me in my office."

"So this more private conversation took place between just the two of you?"

To Max's affirmative response, he said, "Good. What exactly came out of your chat?"

Max had noticed, in these few months of working together, that his boss tried to play it cool when he came up against unexpected situations. Generally, to protect himself and keep his options open, while he absorbed what he was told.

"The couple, Ambassador. The attachés' assistants haven't been able to deliver. They can no longer extract anything significant from the two. Which wouldn't be a problem if they didn't feel that the couple is hiding something important."

"They're no fools, those two."

"The major suspects that the team in place, after all these years, no longer has..."

"...any way to objectively assess what the couple knows. Or what they think the couple knows," the ambassador finished.

"Precisely. They're practically friends these days after seeing so much of one another, although it's always on the sly. And the issue might have to do with Chile."

As Max had foreseen, the ambassador bolted out of his seat. "Chile? How so?"

"No one has been able to find out."

The ambassador began to pace from one side of the partially dismantled library to the other, avoiding the piles of books and half-open boxes strewn here and there. The movers seemed to have magically disappeared. "This could be interesting," he finally said as he came to a stop in front of Max's chair.

Max stood. For a few seconds they remained on tenterhooks, facing one another. Max was quite a bit taller than the ambassador. They looked at each other with heads cocked to the side. *Interesting, but dangerous*, they were both thinking—and for the same reasons: once certain bridges were crossed, it would be hard to turn back. Even so, the ambassador's reply surprised Max. For the first time since they'd met, his boss seemed to hesitate.

"It's a lot of responsibility for me in this final stretch. String along the major. Let Carlos Câmara work this out when he gets here. That'll be in less than a month. Whatever you two decide is fine. But the matter has to stay between the three of us. Did you tell Vaz you'd be double checking with me?"

"He was the one who suggested it. He never imagined I'd act on my own."

"That's both good and bad. Good, because it shows him to be a man of character. Bad, because it means we're going to have to keep him in the loop. And I don't like to be in anyone's back pocket. We can't run that risk."

"And he's not the only one. The team that's been interrogating the couple is going to end up having to know."

"Not necessarily, Marcílio. These projects have a beginning and an end. A command from above is enough to shut down an operation. The military does it all the time. It's part of their apocalyptic scenarios."

"Destroying the evidence? Burning the heretics?"

"Just the evidence, Marcílio, just the evidence. Not the heretics. These aren't the Middle Ages; we conduct ourselves far more discreetly. No fires, no stakes, just a simple order, no questions asked. We start or abort operations, and no one is the wiser."

As Max pondered these words, the ambassador proceeded. "In any case, an operation like the one involving this couple usually has a short life span. Once its usefulness has been exhausted, it's shut down. All it takes is a command from above. With paperwork, the process is even simpler. *It's burned.* I myself keep almost no files at all. Our Holy Alliance exists only in my head. Even so, it's more alive than ever."

Here he allowed himself a brief moment of tenderness. "You know, I'm actually liking that nickname. *Holy Alliance...*" He took a few steps around the room, this time with his hands clasped behind his back. "Now, as for Vaz: have our friend believe we're thinking about it."

He stopped and turned to face Max, who was watching him intently. "*Nothing more than that.* Try to find out the financial implications. Who would pay the couple, and so on. It's not going to be me. And I doubt Itamaraty has a budget to cover something like this."

They both had a good laugh over that.

"Ambassador," Max resumed, "I was given the impression, from something Major Vaz said, that the couple would do anything in exchange for their freedom."

"*Freedom?*"

"That's right. From what I gathered, they're here against their will. They're being forced to operate in Montevideo."

"*Forced?*" Without realizing it, the ambassador was the one breaking the rule of not posing questions that echoed words just spoken.

"Yes. The story is pretty ghastly. As always in such cases..."

The boss waited, motionless, like a tiger in the savannah. He'd already heard of almost everything in this world.

Max went on. "It seems they were imprisoned and tortured in Brazil some three years ago. The man, in São Paulo. The woman, in Pernambuco. They didn't even know each other. Then, after they'd been tortured and threatened with death for crimes that may well have been minor, according to what the major led me to believe, someone had the brilliant idea of planting them among the exiles in Montevideo. And they agreed to it. In exchange, their lives would be spared.... So, they've been working the community for two and a half years. They were made to feel quite welcome. And there's one more detail."

Here Max paused briefly. He felt embarrassed, but he laid out the final piece of information. "Before their arrival in Montevideo, the army made them marry."

"The army *made them marry?*" The ambassador was even more bewildered than Max had been when he'd heard the same story that morning.

"That's right. They arrived here as a couple, with official paperwork and everything. Not to mention signs of torture all over their bodies, the kind that assuage the doubts of most distrustful Marxists. The scars are real. Among other things, the young man lost his right eye, the woman two fingers from her left hand. They were introduced the day before their departure. And they were trained right here, in Montevideo, by the attachés and some of their deputies."

"Some wedding night they must have had!" exclaimed the

ambassador, who immediately regretted the remark and bit his lip.

"The two have relatives," Max continued, ignoring the comment, "relatives who could be thrown in jail at any point should they try to run away."

"My God! These military guys, frankly... *How diabolical!*... And to think we have to deal with these people! What a nightmare."

But pragmatism soon prevailed over dignity. "Has this at least produced any results?"

"Close to fifty jailed in Brazil these last two years," replied Max without hesitation, as if keeping count. "As a direct result of information obtained by them among the exiles. A complete success, according to the major. Two secret networks broken up. A third about to come down. And assorted intel relating to Cuba. Who's there, who's come back, and where they're hiding. That kind of thing."

"And no one suspected them? Not in Brazil? Or here?"

"Not until now, no. That must be why they're trying to put a high price on what they know: to pull out!"

"Obviously."

"And they need passports to go back to Brazil."

"Of course. And that's where we come in... the passports. Feel out Vaz a little more. Make clear we're still thinking about his request. Then talk to the air force people. First chance you get, hitch a ride on their jet so you and Câmara can put your heads together. This matter might be more pressing than we think. And not a word of this over the phone. Here or in Brazil."

Since Max didn't get up to leave, despite the conclusive tone of the last statement, the ambassador waited, watching him closely.

"It seems the children don't trust them," Max murmured, as if talking to himself and this information, more than any other, bothered him.

"The children?"

"Yes, the exiles' children. The couple told one of the military officials that the kids stare at them without saying a word. The adults seem to have swallowed their story hook, line, and sinker. But not their children. So the parents keep telling the kids, 'Say hello to Auntie Helena.... Go talk to Uncle Heitor.' But the children don't budge—as if they can sense something's not quite right. Strange, isn't it?"

"Animals have that too. A sixth sense..."

"But it might also be the couple's paranoia."

"Could be."

Sighing, the ambassador sat back down. They couldn't end on this note. If there was one mood the ambassador didn't handle well, it was melancholy. To lift his spirits, he decided to take a more familiar path. "*This thing about Chile,*" he finally mumbled, as if the topic were still in the forefront of his mind, "it could be a ruse to test border security. Find the weak spots to cross by way of Argentina. When things start to escalate in Uruguay, they're going to try to cross in droves. Without calling attention to themselves. Poor things...they won't know that they'll be jumping out of the frying pan into the fire."

He glanced over at Max, who remained silent.

"And besides this?" the ambassador asked. "What else do the attachés suspect?"

"That there are weapons. They want to know where they're hidden."

"What weapons? There are no weapons." His tone was stripped of its earlier indignation. To Max's ears, it even sounded deflated.

"They're not convinced of that. They think the weapons are buried on some farm. And they taught the couple to play checkers."

Puzzled yet again, the ambassador turned to Max. "*Checkers?*"

"The exiles organized a checkers competition. Among themselves. It was completely innocent. Except that the attachés, encouraged by their deputies, are convinced that the exiles used the games to exchange information about the weapons. They went as far as to think that certain moves had a strategic meaning!"

"Unbelievable..."

"And the couple had to learn to play checkers so they could be in the competition. They came in last, of course. And didn't find out a thing. At least not about weapons. But they wound up learning about schemes to steal passports."

"*Brazilian* passports? That's certainly relevant to us."

"It sure is. The exiles told the story laughing all the while, between one game and the next. Because the idea came from one of them, who already went back to Brazil. The whole thing started here."

"Here in Montevideo?" His tone had turned indignant again, only now tinged with concern. As if the ambassador suddenly felt responsible for a security breach that might have occurred under his watch.

"That's right. Here in Montevideo," confirmed his subordinate, eyes downcast.

To his surprise, Max experienced something he hadn't before: pleasure in provoking his boss. To this sensation was added another, also mysterious, bordering on sheer delight—*that of having him in his power.* What if he could demystify the terrible reputation that followed the ambassador like a shadow? In a matter of seconds, the man had shrunk, taking on the appearance of a frightened child. As if all the evils that occurred in the territory under his jurisdiction, particularly those having to do with stolen passports, could be attributed to him. A novelty for Max. One that would have considerable influence on his life (although he wasn't yet aware of this—and wouldn't be until much later).

To prolong the sensation, he feigned a dry cough, which led him to pull out a handkerchief. Only after folding this with care and slowly replacing it in his pocket—his boss watching as

if hypnotized—did he begin to recount: "At a leather industry
expo, about three years ago."

The ambassador leaned forward in his chair, trying to recall
the event. He was morphing from a tiger in the savannah to
a cat in a kennel. And, suddenly, filled with hope, he asked,
"Organized by the embassy?"

"Yes," Max answered casually. "By the embassy's commercial sector. Hundreds of Brazilian exporters came."

"Oh, right...right...now I remember," replied the ambassador, still speaking softly. "We even notified Itamaraty at the time."

"It seems the expo was held in the winter, it was really cold
out," Max continued. "The visitors who'd come from Brazil left
their coats in the cloakroom. With passports in the pockets, in a
few cases. Eighteen disappeared all at once. And the news spread
through the exiles' secret channels."

The pleasure Max was deriving from his boss's dismay was
almost palpable. But the only person who might have recognized
this had his head between his hands, eyes fixed on the carpet.

"The following months, no small number of Brazilian passports disappeared from cloakrooms at assorted fairs organized
by Itamaraty around the world," Max went on, resorting to his
reporter tone again. "In Paris, London, Rome, even Tokyo.
When the operations didn't go through the cloakroom atten-
dants, it was the interpreters who got in on the action."

"*The interpreters?*" stammered the ambassador, without rais-
ing his eyes from the floor.

"That's right. The Brazilians' interpreters. Our exporters
rarely spoke a foreign language. The businesses that hired the
interpreters were, in turn, infiltrated by exiles, or by Brazilians
connected to them. First sign of carelessness by the visitor, first
trip to the washroom and, *zip*, the passport would disappear from
the pocket of the jacket left hanging on the back of a chair."

The ambassador threw Max a wounded look. That *zip* was
uncalled for.

Realizing that he'd gone too far, Max adopted a conciliatory tone. "As such, dozens of exiled families could move around the world. Some even managed to go back to Brazil. Thanks to these schemes."

"Those poor people," the ambassador said softly, to Max's surprise, as he found himself confronting a voice imbued with sadness. "Deep down, they even..." The older man silenced himself in time, however. Max wondered in vain what his superior had been about to say.

Sustained by this trompe l'oeil, which had saved him from painful situations in the past, the ambassador slowly stood and looked Max up and down. Was he aware that he was truly seeing him for the first time? In any case, he took his young colleague by the arm with fatherly familiarity and led him over to the bookcase in front of them. It was completely bare except for a single volume on the middle shelf. Obeying a silent command from his boss, Max carefully removed the book.

"A first edition, son," remarked the ambassador, his voice trembling. And, substituting a definite article for the indefinite, he underscored: "*the* first edition." Then, on tiptoe and leaning over Max's shoulder, he urged him, "Take a look at the first page."

"*Der Zauberberg*," Max read aloud. He didn't speak German and thus felt unsure of his pronunciation as well as the meaning of the words.

"*The Magic Mountain*," translated the ambassador in a single breath.

Touched by his boss's emotion, Max noted that the book, published in Berlin, dated from 1924. And that just below the title, in small blue letters, almost faded by time, was a signature: *Thomas Mann*.

# 26

We knew almost nothing about the British secret service other than what could be seen on screen courtesy of James Bond and his cohorts—who were always smoking pipes and sighed more than they spoke, giving everyone the impression that the international arena was as dull as a cricket match. The CIA was the organization that stood out in the Brazilian military's realities, as well as in the minds of their adversaries. Largely because, compared to the muzzled tiger of today, the institution in the '60s and '70s was a force to be reckoned with in terms of power and autonomy. It had the authority to act almost without accountability. Its tentacles extended through labyrinths around the globe, and were, of course, pervasive in the modest backyard south of its borders—whenever some alarm went off there.

Although the agency's human and financial resources continued to favor the various fronts of the cold war, particularly in a Europe divided by the Berlin Wall and a Southeast Asia that threatened to turn into a full-blown Vietnam, it had to divert some of its energy to these inconvenient neighbors—who up until then hadn't warranted more than a routine check. The CIA's caution with Latin America was to some degree like that of a chess player moving his pawns with the king's protection in mind at all times.

To keep a low profile, the agency had set up its South American operations base not in Rio de Janeiro or Buenos Aires as might be expected, much less in Santiago (where the political temperature was rising each month), but in peaceful and discreet Montevideo. And MI6, after considering Lima as an alternative for a few weeks, followed the Americans' example.

And that's how Max, who'd already had several meetings with a CIA agent to go over the technical operations he'd be coordinating in training the Uruguayan police forces, ended up also having contact with MI6. By sheer chance—or so he thought.

In those days, Max was going through a curious stage of self-enchantment, delighted with his natural aptitude as he fulfilled his functions—functions of whose exact reach he was unaware, "for his own good," according to the ambassador. Rather than distressing him, this precaution encouraged him, for it appealed to an adventurous side of his personality that had remained below the surface until then, like a hidden talent.

At the office, he routinely reviewed his ostensive work with the minister-counselor. But he no longer had anyone to supervise the other points of his confidential agenda, which grew each day and with each new set of circumstances—given that his boss was now concerned solely with details relating to his transfer to Brazil.

In his personal life, Max had entered a peaceful phase. He had left behind the fateful night of the ambassador's last dinner, when the subject of Nilo Montenegro had struck like a lightning bolt. Reassured by the prospect of a natural childbirth, Marina seemed to have undergone a change in mood, as if impending motherhood had displaced the ghosts that once hounded her. Despite the local political instability that made everyday activities difficult, she continued her routine of reading and going to the movies. She'd made a few fast friendships at the embassy, people with whom she faced the drawbacks affecting the social life of the city's inhabitants.

Liberated from his wife's angst, our hero was feeling just fine. For the first time in years, he'd achieved a strange and fascinating sense of freedom, which would reinforce his aspirations toward loftier goals. And these aspirations did in fact materialize—in one of the country's most urban settings. Because it was in the Café Sorocabana, a bar near the Uruguayan Foreign Office, that Max's life would take an unexpected turn.

Just like Rick's Café, immortalized in *Casablanca*, the Sorocabana owed its success to the diversity of its clientele and to the fact that it represented a kind of neutral territory. On any given day, one would find second-tier diplomats from various embassies, friendly young stenographers and archivists from the Uruguayan Foreign Office, correspondents from neighboring countries (and even a few from Europe, when passing through the city), local journalists from opposing factions, and a fair number of people known to support the Tupamaros—as well as police officials keeping an eye on them. Max would often stop in for coffee and to check the latest news after his official visits to the Foreign Office.

During his five months in Montevideo, Max had been to the Sorocabana plenty of times, first brought by embassy colleagues, then by Uruguayan acquaintances, and finally, as was the case that morning, of his own volition. He had even become friends with Fernández, the owner of the place, who had just obtained a temporary liquor license—a controversial achievement in the eyes of many, since the establishment had, until then, been a café in the strictest sense.

With Fernández now vested with new responsibilities, Max had begun to share secrets about assorted drinks. Days before, they'd had a long discussion about the challenges of making margaritas. Max was appalled by bartenders who resorted to using any old kind of lime—and even worse, any old kind of salt. The Sorocabana, according to those in the know, was the closest thing in the city to a traditional Madrid café, with customers who always sat at the same tables, some of them even bringing their portable typewriters or using the space as an office, as was the case with attorneys who made appointments with clients and spent hours poring over legal documents. The marble-topped wrought-iron tables were small and round. At the back of the main room, a door opened onto a barbershop and gentlemen entrusting their hair and beards to skilled hands were commonly seen across the way. These men would return to the café smelling of lavender and flaunting their brand-new haircuts. They'd then sit at a table to complete their grooming by having their shoes shined by young boys the waiters allowed in only when business was slow.

On the day of interest here, Max and Fernández were at the bar exploring in lowered voices the possibilities of importing cachaça to Uruguay—and including caipirinhas among the drinks offered. Max had just identified the distilled sugarcane liquor as one of his country's best-kept secrets when the phone rang and Fernández went to answer it.

The patron to Max's left, who'd kept his back to him until then, seemingly involved in another conversation, turned and whispered somewhat in jest, "If you want to keep it secret, the Sorocabana isn't the best place to talk about it." He'd made the remark in English, taking advantage of Fernández's being out of earshot. And because he knew he would be perfectly understood. He wasn't disappointed.

"Secret is my middle name," replied Max in a flawless accent but in the tone of one who doesn't give a second thought to what he says. Indeed, no sooner had the words left his mouth than he'd moved to a table that had just been cleared, leaving the Brit nursing his gin and tonic at the bar.

Max proceeded to jot down on a pad what he'd just heard from the Uruguayan Foreign Office concerning a Brazilian proposal, which ran serious risk of being defeated at the UN. He was intent on quickly ridding himself of the task at hand, so as to keep his mind open to what the Sorocabana might yet hold in the way of surprises. Because he'd be willing to bet a month's wages that the Brit would be back for more. Having completed his notes, which he reread before tucking the pad back into his pocket, Max waved down Fernández and ordered another cup of coffee.

Just as he'd predicted, and now confirmed out of the corner of his eye, the fellow from the bar was making his way over to his table.

"Raymond Thurston, from the British embassy," he said.

Max stood and shook the proffered hand. After introducing himself, he invited the other man to join him.

"So, Brazil," the Englishman said congenially as he settled into a chair. He seemed genuinely captivated.

"Yes, Brazil," Max echoed, without uttering a single extra syllable.

There seemed to be an almost sensual charge to their exchange, Max realized to his delight. As if he, Max, had taken on the appearance of an attractive woman whose options included allowing herself to be seduced by a stranger. In keeping with the rituals of the tribe they belonged to, the duo took the next step and swapped business cards. After which they struck up a casual conversation.

Max was usually quite cool when confronting new situations. But this one, besides being different, was extremely delicate — as much for its potential reach as for its ill-defined boundaries. From the tone of their verbal exchange, more than its content, he dismissed the notion that the other man might be coming on to him. Yet he found himself reaching a paradoxical, perhaps even disturbing realization: that there were indeed ulterior motives behind their encounter, which was proceeding as a seduction of another sort.

During his months in Montevideo, he had, as a matter of duty, paid courtesy calls to all the diplomats at his professional level. He remembered then that he'd faced serious difficulties trying to schedule time with the counselor from the British embassy. The man, moreover, once he'd finally seen him, had shared nothing useful or original about Uruguay, the neighboring countries, or any subject relating, even indirectly, to Great Britain's foreign policy.

Max calculated that in the present situation the best defense was an offense. And so he described the frustrating interview to his table companion, who found the story highly amusing. Encouraged by him, Max embellished his version. He said that the other man's compatriot hadn't shown the slightest interest in Brazil—*the only real player in the region*, he'd hastened to add. Overdoing it a bit, he recounted that the Englishman's colleague had spoken largely of a countryside manor where he bred racehorses and had lost all interest in Max on learning that he didn't play polo.

"Ronald Barns is nothing but a pompous ass," Raymond Thurston remarked when Max finished his story.

Although secondary in the broader context of their meeting, two noteworthy events had transpired perfectly in sync. The first was Max's doing. Having decided to take the offensive, he had broken basic protocol, not to mention general rules of etiquette, by criticizing one of the superiors of a man he'd only just met. The second was the work of the Englishman, who hadn't hesitated to bad-mouth his own colleague, whose name, unmentioned until then, he'd stated loud and clear, and then proceeded to mock. More than a show of solidarity, which might have been intended to make amends, his behavior conveyed a wish to form if not an alliance then at least an initial complicity with Max. Might this tenuous link not lead to others over time?

Not bad for a first meeting, they both thought while speaking of other things. The Brit had decided to have a second gin and tonic, and asked if his companion might not consider replacing his cold coffee with something less harmful to his health. Max had given in to the suggestion and asked Fernández for a martini. They'd then toasted their respective countries.

Moving on to talk of politics, they loosened up a bit. Without going overboard, but giving outlet to his Latin heritage, Max began to gesticulate as he made his more incisive points. At those moments, the Englishman reacted the only way he felt comfortable: nodding in agreement. The two men thus followed the directions of their invisible choreographers. Since they belonged to different schools, body language wasn't the high point of this first encounter. But there were other indications of good chemistry between them. These ran like electrical impulses between their words, interspersed with opportune pauses, greeted with relief by both men. During those breaks, both would concentrate on their drinks. Or look around in search of some novelty. Max filled his passive role with discretion, while the Englishman performed that of seducer almost as a matter of courtesy.

That same night, Ray would send the following encoded message to headquarters:

*I made contact. Ronnie B. did an excellent job. He left our friend indignant with the treatment received during his courtesy call, which instantly broke the ice between us. He's taller in person than photos seem to indicate. (And not as nice as the recordings suggest.) On the other hand, he's quite refined. I detected two additional traits: an adventurous spirit and a complete disregard for money. I also sensed frustration in the air, which may be worth keeping in mind.*

*He speaks and writes fluently in four languages. He's read Pound and Eliot (whose first quartet, "Burnt Norton," he translated for a Brazilian literary magazine). He avoided making any personal remarks about his boss, other than that the man owns a signed first edition of Thomas Mann that he always carries with him when he travels. He acts as if he were waiting for something. If I had to refer to a painting to describe him, I'd say it's of a hunting dog, paw raised and tongue hanging out, sniffing the surrounding air.*

*Our cousins were pleased with this first conversation. According to plan, they're going to concentrate on the technical cooperation* operations, which have already begun. They've started a file on him. Code name Sam Beckett—as homage to that strange remark recorded last week, when he told Esmeralda he considers himself "the Samuel Beckett of Brazilian diplomacy."

We have an agent on our hands, no doubt, but as one with literary pretensions, he may be unpredictable. We've arranged to have lunch Wednesday. I propose adopting our cousins' code name for him, Sam Beckett.

# 27

Less than a week after the departure of the ambassador and his wife—an event that had filled the small VIP lounge at the Montevideo airport—Uruguay was hit by heavy rains that spared the capital but caused serious flooding and numerous deaths inland.

Prompted by a similar disaster that had befallen the country some years before, one of the attachés had suggested that the embassy provide immediate relief to the victims through the air force. The Brazilian government swiftly arranged for the arrival of a Hercules plane carrying tents, blankets, and food, along with doctors, nurses, and medical supplies. The operation was soon replicated by missions from other neighboring countries, as well as Mexico, Spain, and the United States.

Even so, the headlines and photos in local papers ended up focusing on Brazil, whose plane had been the first to land in Montevideo. It had been piloted by an air force general who had the brilliant idea of opening the small cockpit window, while the aircraft was still taxiing on the runway, to wave the colors of our flag along with those of the Uruguayan nation, a gesture applauded by those present and widely publicized on television that night.

The embassy coordinated with local authorities to implement the most expeditious ways of distributing the aid, which would be transported to the interior on smaller planes or helicopters and, in some cases, on trucks and other military vehicles. Amid all the commotion, however, the Brazilian diplomats were almost caught off guard, since they'd been informed of the unexpected occurrence only on arriving at the airport: the new chargé d'affaires, Minister Carlos Câmara, as well as his wife and young daughter, had come in on the same plane. By moving up his arrival a few days and relinquishing the inherent privileges of first-class travel on a commercial carrier in favor of a flight that everyone knew to be extremely uncomfortable, the diplomat exemplified, in the words of headlines across the next morning's papers, "the empathy a neighboring country was showing in light of the tragedy suffered by the heroic Uruguayan people."

For Max, this high-profile landing signaled something else, laden with dark omens. Carlos Câmara had really come to take command. Which was annoying in at least two ways: far from embodying the discreet role their mission would require—in Max's view, at any rate—the triumphant arrival implied an obvious change in style from the tactful way the former ambassador had worked from behind the scenes. Moreover, and this seemed just as serious in Max's eyes, it demonstrated personal insensitivity toward the future ambassador, who would be coming in from Europe three weeks later aboard a luxurious Cunard transatlantic ocean liner. An unfortunate way to arrive, if contrasted to the calamity of which the country had been a victim.

As prearranged during a secret visit Carlos Câmara had made to Montevideo, Max shook his new colleague's hand on the runway as if they'd never met, even ignoring the friendly pat on his shoulder when they passed in the receiving line. The wives too had been a part of the welcome committee, trying their best to hold on to their hats—such were the gusts generated by the propellers still in motion.

This social encounter at the airport was followed by a number of more official gatherings at the embassy, in smaller and more focused formats. First, with the three attachés and their deputies. Then, with the political and economic sectors, moving on to the press corps and public relations personnel. Max, as the head and sole member of the technical cooperation unit, was included in one of the later meetings, along with the cultural affairs team, joined by the director of the Uruguay-Brazil Cultural Institute. (The administrative staff was last in line.)

Max soon noted that he was dealing with a man who thought highly of himself. Without taking much comfort in the realization, he supposed that some good might come of it and perhaps, with a little luck, the two would find themselves on more equal footing. The inherent seniority Carlos Câmara held over him could readily be compensated for by Max's special talent, which he had been refining for years and had adapted to the particular Montevideo scenario.

Just as his former boss had done, by holding a farewell dinner long before his departure, Max decided that he too would take the bull by the horns. Two weeks after Carlos Câmara's arrival, he invited him to lunch at one of the restaurants he'd frequented with the ambassador. Câmara accepted quite willingly and suggested a date. On the designated day, Carlos Câmara dismissed the Mercedes 280 and chauffeur to which he was entitled as the chargé d'affaires—a privilege he'd lose in another week with the ambassador's arrival—and the two set out in Max's car, after heading down to the embassy parking garage via a side door.

Along the way, however, something unexpected happened. At a certain intersection, as Max was about to turn right, his guest asked him to continue going straight. As Max hesitated, he heard an emphatic "Trust me," which led him to proceed without further ado. From there on, his companion continued to direct him until they reached their destination—which was, in fact, the tree-filled patio of a restaurant. Except that it was a *different* restaurant. "Trust me," his companion repeated politely when, once again, his host tried to address what he took to be a mistake. Giving up, Max resigned himself to his fate and parked the car.

The maître d' awaited them at the entrance, respectful but not obsequious, his attitude actually rather relaxed. A stance that Carlos Câmara had learned to appreciate. "Genuinely friendly Frenchmen seek refuge abroad," he commented in a low voice as they headed toward a reserved table near a window over-looking the garden. Despite having decided not to ask about the change of venue, Max was having a hard time suppressing his discomfort. He ended up remaining silent, sensing that he was perhaps being tested. As to what kind of test, though, he hadn't the slightest idea.

They ordered cocktails, Carlos a Kir, Max, at the maître d's suggestion, a glass of champagne. They then devoted themselves to the menu. Max consulted the wine list and, mindful of his guest's choice of entrée, ordered a Bordeaux. "We're going to stagger out of here," the other man said with a laugh.

"Quite the opposite," Max assured him.

They toasted, each weighing the likelihood of being right. Carlos Câmara because he hadn't yet gotten his bearings or imagined being confronted quite so soon by his younger col-league. The drinks might thus serve as an excuse should he slip a little in conversation. Max, because he needed to come out of that meeting with a clear notion of just where they stood—start-ing with the restaurant they were now in. He needed the alcohol to inject a bit of boldness, albeit restrained, into his questions.

Carlos Câmara was in no rush to address the substantive issues. He knew that, as a matter of seniority, it was up to him to kick off the conversation that would inevitably ensue. He praised the restaurant as if it had been Max's choice, acknowl-edged the quality and variety of the menu, asked whether Uru-guay had four distinct seasons—which might lead him to choose a house rather than an apartment.

Max responded to each of these topics. He said he was familiar with this particular restaurant (emphasizing both *this* and *particular*), courtesy of the ambassador. With whom, by coincidence, he'd had lunch at this very table. He further mentioned, on the same subject, the existence of at least seven or eight other fine eateries in the city, two of them Italian, two Uruguayan. He confirmed that he'd heard the country did indeed have four seasons—although he hadn't yet experienced them—which might justify the eventual choice of a house with a garden, but he also reminded his colleague that in the current political climate, apartments were less vulnerable to Tupamaro attacks.

Without taking the bait Max served up, Câmara moved on to ask about the attachés and other staff members they'd be working with. Although he had received a file from the ambassador on each, he was interested in Max's opinion given his relatively young age and midlevel rank in the embassy. His views were likely to be more useful and open-minded than those of his former boss—which had perhaps been arbitrary given his temperament and calling.

They danced around these topics until their appetizers were brought to the table. Onion soup for Carlos Câmara, *pâté de campagne* for Max. The wine, served and approved, inspired another toast, warmer this time.

"To our friendship," proposed Carlos Câmara.

"May it last forever," joked Max, injecting both humor and skepticism into his response.

If there was anything clearly unfeasible in those dark and volatile times, it was combining the words *friendship* and *forever* in the same toast, between two strangers operating in a country that wasn't their own—charged, moreover, with a mission that might very well be defined as controversial. And that in the future, depending on the direction of the winds, could end up being classified as illegal, even criminal.

It was this realization, implied rather than expressed, that led Carlos Câmara to have a change of heart and allude to the secrecy that connected them.

"Everything is bound to go right," he said in a hushed tone, with an eye on Max, as if he felt the need to lift his spirits. Holding his glass up to the light, he added, "Good wine. Nice color. An excellent choice."

# 28

After Câmara's toast, Max had allowed a long moment of silence to elapse. But he had ended up agreeing with his companion's optimistic assessment, nodding his head in assent. Soon afterward, however, he sighed—so deeply that he felt compelled to explain.

"Yes, in theory things could go right," he acknowledged. "But in practice, everything seems so..." He tried to hand off the responsibility of identifying his concerns but was dealing with a professional. And the ball was returned to him in the form of encouraging questions: "*Vague? Unclear?*"

Given Max's silent agreement, the other decided to steer the course of the conversation. "Not really," he said. And here a new Carlos Câmara took the stage. Assertive and calm at the same time. Mindful of the need to shed light on the scene but without revealing too much in the first act. "We're relying on a scheme set up in collaboration with friends from the War College, who know you, by the way, and send their best. A scheme endorsed by the SNI and, of course, by our boss. Simple and to the point. With no greater risk of involvement. Or rather, *of eventual exposure of our involvement.*"

For a moment, they talked further of the War College officials Carlos Câmara had mentioned. They focused on two in particular. Max remembered both. But what mattered to him now were the *details.* So much so that he leaned over the table to hear them.

Carlos Câmara didn't hold back. "Our work here is going to be simple. A scaled-down version of what was done in Brazil with American assistance. Cautiously, and with a lot of money, we're going to take part, albeit discreetly, in destabilizing the government. Buying space in newspapers, running paid ads in magazines, infiltrating radio and TV stations. We're going to help the Uruguayan middle class defend itself. We're going to have them blow the whistle."

"But..."

"And we're going to support Uruguay's Colorado Party in every conceivable way, including overseeing the transfer of American funds to their electoral campaigns. And when the time is right, we'll follow the CIA's lead and help create circumstances so that the presidency itself..."

"The presidency itself," repeated Max, who was following the script scene by scene.

"...can do whatever needs to be done."

"A bloodless coup, then?" Max asked.

"Exactly. Undertaken by... *the Colorados!*" exclaimed Câmara, laughing. "Thanks to which power will subtly be transferred to the military."

"And in Chile?" Max further probed, as though playing a game in which doors were opening one by one to reveal hidden treasures.

"That's being considered. How to back the military in Chile and Argentina is still under review. The situations there are different."

"*Argentina,*" whispered Max. "But why? Are there going to be changes there too?"

"No... at least not yet. But Peronism is growing stronger. And the changeover from Eva to Isabelita, which until recently was the butt of jokes even among Argentinean officials, is starting to be taken seriously. A fascinating country, Argentina..."

Here Carlos Câmara had assumed the stance Argentineans usually adopted when referring to Brazil, that of an English lord speaking of a sub-Saharan African country, which the first world needed to treat with care and understanding while keeping the natives at bay. But he soon got back to the main point of the conversation. "Two things are of utmost importance, however. First: not a word of this to the attachés *here*. We're going to work with the ones *there*. And they've already gotten orders to keep quiet."

"The ones in Santiago."

Câmara nodded. After a brief pause, he added, "And the ones in Buenos Aires." He then elaborated: "In both cases, we're going to be limited to army and air force personnel. The navy attachés are out."

"Why?" asked Max, now in a more convivial tone, intended to underscore the conspiracy between them. He was also genuinely curious.

"The one in Santiago is retiring," answered Carlos Câmara, quite pleased with the leadership role he was gradually assuming in their partnership. His lips slowly formed a smile, then he broke into laughter. "And the one in Buenos Aires...*has a lover!* A tango dancer! The poor guy is in love! He sent the old ball and chain packing to São Paulo."

"Excellent!" said Max. "Here's to the navy!"

"They say his poor wife caused quite a scene at the airport," continued Carlos Câmara, gladly joining in the toast. "To the delight of the embassy women, who all turned out, she walloped him over the head with her umbrella as she was leaving. The women applauded, and several actually cheered, 'Well done, Cordélia!' They're horribly catty, our wives are. None of them wanted to miss the show."

"Someone might as well have fun!" exclaimed Max, prolonging the moment of mirth and levity. Both enjoyed a good laugh. Carlos Câmara seemed happy to have broken the ice between them. It was the first time he'd felt at ease with his young colleague. And Max—*why not, after all?*—had let down his guard and joined in. Thanks to a woman, and not just any woman—but a tango dancer! And to the beating taken by an admiral, no less! What a riot.

"Second point, equally important!" declared Câmara, turning his attention to the matters at hand. "Not a word about this between us at the embassy or at the ambassador's residence. I'm bringing in someone from the SNI to do a sweep. The Americans have definitely bugged both places."

"*I can't believe it,*" murmured Max, bewildered.

"The Brits too, for all we know. I didn't bring this up with our boss on my last visit to avoid offending him. Especially because, at that point, it was too late. I just don't understand how he could've screwed up like this. And did he ever! I confirmed with the attachés and the security folks at my first meeting with them. No one had thought about it. They were all as surprised as you are now."

"But then—" Max began, before being immediately interrupted.

"Yes, they know everything." Having produced the intended effect, he reassured Max. "Which doesn't matter at all. We're not competing against them. We'll simply be playing along with them. To help with a task that's basically *theirs.*"

This final remark reflected the wounded pride of the diplomat promoted to warrior—against his wishes. The traditional ally was gradually leaving the front line; there were gaps to be filled.

To console him, Max made a remark that had the benefit of stroking his partner's ego. "That explains the last-minute change. Of restaurant."

His guest smiled. "Right," he admitted. "I appreciated your choice of cuisine. I merely changed the venue." Then, after a brief pause, "For now, use the phone just for routine conversation. At this point, they already know everything about you. As for me, I'm an old acquaintance. A friend, actually, to some."

Max hesitated. *Should he mention Ray?* he wondered. *After all, he hadn't even mentioned Ray to the ambassador.... No, better keep Raymond Thurston to himself,* he decided. And he looked around, fascinated. He felt flattered that someone might want to follow him. This represented a clear shift in status.

Carlos Câmara, in the meantime, guessing the nature of his fantasies, downplayed the relative importance of what he'd said. "This is all just for appearances' sake, of course. Most likely the gringos aren't even interested in us at this level. But should they be paying attention, the message will have been delivered. My decision to arrive in that flashy manner was deliberate."

After finishing his onion soup, which he declared delicious, he continued. "But you and I are going to play it safe. Given our hidden agenda. From now on, our conversations will only take place in saunas or swimming pools. Since there are so few restaurants, they end up being dangerous too."

"In the winter, we'll remain silent," Max replied. "Because there are few pools, and even fewer saunas."

Carlos Câmara chuckled. "I was kidding!" he said. "What's essential is this: we have to be extremely discreet and keep our eyes wide open." The stakes would go up drastically. As would the bets. And the smoke was growing thicker around the gaming table.

That same night, Ray Thurston sent the following message to MI6:

*Sam Beckett has a new boss and seems overwhelmed for the time being. From what little he told me today, I was left with two contradictory impressions, which might be attributable to the conflict he's going through right now. He expressed admiration for the* man, but his mood suggested that he'd rather see him dead and buried, preferably quite far from here. I think these ambivalent feelings will be resolved over time but only in part. And we may find room to operate in this gap. I do, however, need more objective data about what we've learned thus far in Bonn with respect to the nuclear negotiations between the two countries. Not that I'm in a hurry to bring up the subject, but so as not to waste the opportunity should it unexpectedly arise.

# 29

Max didn't entertain any illusions in reviewing the tenor of that lunch, although he'd appreciated the cordial atmosphere in which it had taken place. He sensed that a fatal rivalry would one day come between him and Carlos Câmara—for they were too similar to withstand such a secretive coexistence. They would, of course, do everything to carry out the mission entrusted to them. But one of the two would not survive the experience. It just remained to be seen which.

A few days after their lunch at the French restaurant, an important social event would bring the two men together again. This was when the Cunard ocean liner *Aurora* finally reached the Uruguayan coastline and then docked a few hours later at Montevideo harbor—with the stately pace reserved for the last transatlantic vessels of its kind.

The event, much anticipated by the city's Brazilian community as well as by local society, warranted the undivided attention of the embassy—whose members showed up in full force for the arrival ceremony. While the imposing ship was still some distance from the pier, the ambassador and his wife waved from the first-class deck to their colleagues clustered below, some of whom fluttered white handkerchiefs in response.

The new boss, who sported a finely styled mustache, was the consummate grand seigneur, a nobleman of the old guard, as his predecessor had informed Max previously. Tall and stout, he came well packaged in a navy blue suit, light-colored shirt, and pastel tie, details welcomed as novelties—given how accustomed all had become to the somber hues of the former boss. He immediately acted gallantly toward the ladies, especially the older ones, who were quite taken with him, not realizing that although his flattering words were directed at them, his eyes were aimed at the younger women, who stirred in him feelings of another kind and intensity.

Marina, who was seventh months pregnant, had received special attention from the ambassador's wife, who had shown her great kindness and offered the residence for a baby shower on whatever date would be convenient for her—"*and* the baby." At one point, while still managing to offer a friendly word or two to people coming to greet her, she had a side conversation with the mother-to-be. "Do you play bridge, my child?" she asked. "No? What a shame. Bridge comes in very handy in our world." She let out another sigh, deeper and more prolonged, and offered some advice: "Take up the game, my dear, you'll enjoy it." The older woman had then smiled enigmatically and retreated into thought, before returning with, "Marriages all change sooner or later, but the cards never lie." And then came the pearl of wisdom: "The king of spades was always there for me."

Charmed, Marina figured out then and there what many would take months, even years, to confirm: the ambassador's wife had a screw loose. But it was small enough to make her eccentric, at most, and often erratic. Overall, a significant improvement over her predecessor, Marina thought, especially since there would be no vengeful cliques on her watch.

In the car on the way back from the harbor, Carlos Câmara and Max had exchanged meaningful looks that conveyed their opinion of the new boss. They'd said nothing in the driver's presence, however. But each had come to the same conclusion, and with good reason: *so much the better.* As such, the former ambassador's prediction was accurate: they'd be free to do as they pleased. Under the ideal cover, moreover: an embassy with a socially prestigious head.

This last detail was attributable to the reputation that preceded the couple. The most prominent Uruguayan families had turned their backs on the previous representatives from Brazil, as chronic antipathy had developed into mutual hostility over the course of nearly six long years. But now they were ready to embrace the new arrivals with open arms. Especially because, for some, they happened to be old acquaintances.

The ambassador and his wife were both from southern Brazil. They held land on the Brazilian side of the border and even had distant cousins in Uruguay. For these reasons, and others instinctively discerned by a certain social class, the couple was received with due respect and warmth. As a result, they'd moved up to third place on the list of kidnapping targets—right after their colleagues from the United States and the United Kingdom, but ahead of the German and Spanish ambassadors, a list periodically reviewed and updated by the Tupamaros.

The months following the arrival of the *Aurora* would be characterized by the resurgence of violence in Uruguay, which would make life difficult and even dangerous for the city's inhabitants. A diplomat from the Brazilian embassy was kidnapped (he would be released several months later, after seemingly endless negotiations that mobilized both countries and then eroded their relations). The North American Dan Matrone ("Call me Dan, Ambassador. Everyone calls me Dan") had also been captured, but without having the Brazilian's luck in the end. He was executed by the Tupamaros, who had then published detailed dossiers on him, describing the assorted torture techniques the CIA taught the local police.

As an epilogue to this time of turmoil, presented here in broad brushstrokes, it might be worth mentioning that in September of that same year, 1970, two months after the arrival of the new ambassador, Marina and Max became parents to

Pedro Henrique, delivered at Montevideo's leading maternity hospital—against the wishes of the Magalhães de Castro clan, who had done everything to try to coax the expectant mother back to Rio de Janeiro for the child's birth. But Marina, who had formed a bond of trust and friendship with her Uruguayan gynecologist, hadn't budged.

So it was that on September 7, 1970, "giving us further reason to celebrate on Independence Day," in the heartfelt words of the ambassador during his official speech, Pedro Henrique came into the world. Judging from the wails he let out, he didn't seem to like what he saw.

# 30

The covert operation undertaken by Carlos Câmara and Max would reach its climax in December 1971, a year after the facts described thus far, due to something the minister-counselor had let slip one night at an embassy garden party.

Although usually rather reserved, Câmara had been eager to share with his younger colleague what he had just learned. Truth be told, his trepidation was justified: thanks to an acquaintance at the CIA, Carlos Câmara had gained access to the transcript of a meeting that had taken place between Richard Nixon and Brazilian president Emílio Médici days earlier in Washington—during which the American had asked his Brazilian counterpart "to support the destabilization of Chile."

On the occasion, the gist of what Nixon had said was, "There are a lot of things Brazil, as a South American country, can get away with that the United States can't." According to Carlos Câmara, one of these transcripts made explicit that, were we to agree, "financial means and discreet US assistance would be made available to Brazil."

"Obviously we're not in a position to oblige," said Carlos Câmara, slapping Max's thigh with enthusiasm as if to reinforce his point. "So we pretended not to hear. *But it's the green light we were waiting for. Coming from the highest possible level.*"

Max couldn't help but wonder about the challenge they would be facing. And, with characteristic nimbleness, he had soon anticipated the next moves. The Brazilian government, having sidestepped Nixon's proposal, *was free to act*, not passing information to the US *until the process was complete*. With proof in hand, they would thus reap the benefits of the collaboration without running the risk of exposure in case of failure.

Max, at this stage, already suspected what these benefits might be. Rather than being *given*, Max inferred, Nixon's go-ahead had been *received*. At the time, the White House request had simply been posed to the Brazilians. After the formal visit was over, however, it had been weighed and analyzed with glee and thinly veiled greed. Once the excitement died down, doors would open for a covert operation. Nothing that could give rise to rumors or speculations of any kind. Rather, a small surgical incision at most, involving a limited number of players. People who wouldn't leave behind traces of any sort—or, if things went wrong, could "have their presence in Chile swiftly and categorically disavowed."

Max also assumed that, as a trade-off for a mission everyone knew to be delicate, the task force would be given a long leash—and be exempt from having to account for their actions or expenses. They would operate as an autonomous, self-contained unit. As a result, the team could be made up only of personnel in whom the heads in Brasilia had utter confidence. Personnel with previous experience in such matters. And Max felt he fit the profile perfectly.

The preparations for the Nixon-Médici meeting had been followed with great interest by the CIA's Montevideo station chief. It would therefore be closely scrutinized by the MI6 agents in that city. At the time, Raymond Thurston fired off no fewer than seven encrypted messages to London. The fourth is transcribed below, as it relates to Max—as well as Câmara (code-named "Batman") and the former ambassador ("Zorro"):

*The most substantive part of the conversation between Beckett and Batman, according to what Sam confided two nights ago, has to* do with the private understandings that took place in Washington between Nixon and Médici.

Besides what we already know, I point out that, according to Beckett, the upper echelon of the Brazilian military would have been quite receptive to the ideas discussed by the two leaders. Except that Itamaraty, "without a moment's hesitation," tossed a bucket of cold water on the excitement "in light of the broader, more permanent goals of Brazilian foreign policy." The minister of foreign affairs even threatened to resign from his job. Médici then assured both sides that the Chilean officials were perfectly capable of solving their own problems, an opinion ostensibly shared by Zorro. As soon as the minister turned his back, however, the latter was summoned "from higher up" to assume command of the operation Nixon proposed, which would be classified top secret. With the understanding that it would be spearheaded by Batman in Montevideo and implemented by Beckett in the field. Monitoring it on a daily basis, Zorro wouldn't say anything of its eventual evolution to the president (other than once the process was over—and then only if it succeeded).

As Beckett foresaw in his initial conversation with me, the agreement stipulates that only fifteen officials be a part of the group operating in Chile. If Beckett's assessment is right, the Holy Alliance so lovingly idealized by Z might be more alive—and more protected—than ever, since it now has virtually limitless resources at its disposal. Sam Beckett seems quite eager at the prospect of joining this select group of fifteen operatives who will act in Chile. Batman, who would have preferred to keep him under his thumb during this operation of potentially high visibility, was forced to rethink his position.

Moving on to the subject of greatest interest to us, let me reiterate, more emphatically, my previous appeals for access to any and all information on the nuclear topic before our hero stumbles upon it and doesn't know what to say. Not knowing how to position himself—or what to look for. I also need to make him aware of our positions, which won't be easy either, since up until now we've only talked about the issue in generic terms.

# 31

The months went by. And with them, the tensions between the two colleagues continued to escalate. Despite the close ties that joined Max and Carlos Câmara professionally, the heavy cloud of secrecy under which they were operating would take its toll. By mid-1973, there were unmistakable signs of the crisis looming between them. Max's relocation to Santiago would come about as a result of the clash.

We could sense the impending military coups that were to break out first in Uruguay, and then, a few months later, in Chile, following what had happened in Brazil and Argentina. The separate and self-contained conflicts taking place in each of these countries would ultimately affect the so-called forward observation post from which our accomplices were operating.

The uneasiness between the two men went way back, and to some extent predated the relationship. Over time, they'd irreversibly progressed from the simple level of misunderstandings to the heightened plateau of confrontation. As early as Câmara's triumphant arrival in Montevideo aboard the air force jet, Max had detected a bravado that bordered on poor taste. Not even the seemingly pleasant lunch that had followed at the French restaurant had quelled his reservations.

Câmara had no grand illusions about his subordinate either. He couldn't fathom what the ambassador, a sensible and discerning man, imagined he'd found in Max. And he regretted having to deal with someone so aloof and independent, when their mission required sensitivity and tact. They basically saw the same flaws in each other, which proved the ambassador's wisdom in recognizing the same qualities in both. So much so that, in selecting the duo, he'd been dealing with two sides of the same coin. *When push comes to shove, they won't let me down*, he'd rightly thought. And he told himself, *It doesn't matter that they'll come to hate each other. The more they dislike one another, the more diligent they'll be.*

Just as the coups were about to be staged, matters came to a head. Carlos Câmara accused his younger colleague of postponing action with the Chileans for explicit personal and political gains. Their work, he'd emphasized, was intended to be collaborative.

What little information I have about the subsequent quarrel is sketchy. Apparently Max responded by citing Sun Tzu ("A sovereign should not assemble his troops in a state of anger"). Carlos Câmara, who also knew the Chinese master's work by heart, retaliated with another excerpt of the *same* maxim and then, for good measure, fired at Max two lines from Max Weber and one from Adorno, in a flurry of citations that had infuriated his adversary by catching him off guard.

At Carlos Câmara's initiative, there would be a temporary truce between the two diplomats for a few weeks—the kind that foretells storms on the horizon. Sensing his colleague's frustration at the chasm growing between them, and perhaps foreseeing the underhanded moves his partner might one day use on him, he had taken advantage of his seniority to bend the rule about public meetings both had abided by.

Under the pretext of repaying Max's invitation, which had taken place quite some time ago, he asked him to lunch. As they began their entrées, Câmara raised a topic he'd alluded to once before, speaking openly—even casually—of a project *of particular interest to the Brazilian military.* Lowering his voice, making it virtually inaudible, he confided that it was based on an idea that he himself had originated a few years earlier, "during my days in Germany with our boss." The long-awaited nuclear topic had finally been broached.

At the first opportunity, Max had shared his thoughts on the matter with Ray Thurston. The two had spoken a few times about nuclear energy, but always vaguely. It was time to take the conversation to the next level. "I need ammunition," Max told Ray at one point. "A few poker chips so that I can at least get into the game."

In order to make the most of the revelations that conversation might afford, MI6 decided to yield to their agent's suggestion and provide Max with classified information gathered in Bonn and other cities (Washington, of course, but also Paris and Moscow) regarding Brazil's progress in the nuclear arena.

On learning that he would finally have access to this information, Max felt like a warrior entrusted with the flagship of the imperial fleet. When he next met with Carlos Câmara, he would be fully prepared. He also felt something more important, which transcended the fact itself: a shudder of pride at having been accepted as part of MI6's inner circle. It hardly mattered that Her Majesty knew nothing about him—*Raymond Thurston knew.* And had someone told him that he had lost his way, irresponsibly getting involved in maneuvers that might result in a conflict of interest with his own country—unthinkable, given his diplomatic position—he would have replied that the people trying to interest Brazil in nuclear weapons, paving the way for an all-out arms race in the region, were the reckless ones. God is known to work in mysterious ways. If Max here exemplified the saying to its fullest, it wasn't so much to align with those who opposed arming Latin America with nuclear weapons but to deal his rival what he hoped would be a fatal blow.

The fateful conversation with his superior took place a few days before Max carried out another of his missions in Santiago, availing himself, as usual, of the air force jet (whose pilots could cross the Andes with their eyes closed by now). He casually brought up the nuclear discussion with Carlos Câmara again. Only this time, *he* was the one holding the cards. The unprecedented move left his partner visibly bewildered. Recognizing the desired effect he'd had, Max couldn't resist the temptation to go beyond what Raymond Thurston had advised: he'd crossed the line between what he could imply and what was better left unsaid, referring to details he couldn't possibly have known at that stage of the negotiations between Brazil and Germany.

*Could Max be in cahoots with the ambassador on this?* Câmara had wondered in astonishment. His colleague had suddenly taken on an ominous dimension. He'd gone from being a subordinate to a rival.

Max, in turn, had seen in his superior's eyes—and read in his body language—all that had emanated from the former ambassador years earlier, when, days before his departure for Brazil, he'd been confronted with the matter of the stolen Brazilian passports. Max had noted the alarm, smelled the fear. And been fortified by both.

Carlos Câmara was convinced then and there of Max's direct ties to the CIA as well as their boss in Brasilia. And in both cases, Câmara realized he was excluded from the operation's front line. He couldn't grasp quite how this had happened. It was, as would later be confirmed, a classic case of pure paranoia. A common feeling in this sinister environment, resulting from the confined and oppressive atmosphere in which everyone lived and worked—a climate that sometimes emotionally destabilized players who put their faith in distrust and intimidation.

The wake-up call had served a purpose, however: feeling threatened, Câmara decided to act. The seeds that would lead to Max's transfer date from this period.

It just so happened that Carlos Câmara knew Eric Friedkin, the CIA agent in Montevideo, from his time at the War College in Rio de Janeiro. Câmara sought out Friedkin under some pretext or other. He spoke to his friend of his concerns about the unchecked and (from his perspective) dangerous way his subordinate was operating in Santiago.

"I never liked that guy," Friedkin said wryly, before dropping his bomb: "In contrast to the Brits, we never trusted him completely, except for training exercises."

Câmara almost fell off his chair. He swallowed and inquired meekly, "The British?"

And Friedkin, who resented the other man's silence when he would sound him out on certain topics of particular interest to Washington, reveled in the cruelty. "You didn't know? Max works for them. Even has a code name. It's not exactly a big secret."

Câmara asked for a glass of water, then stood, pulling out a handkerchief and pacing the room in search of air. Once he had digested the information, though, the two decided to join forces and burn Max. And to do it soon—before he returned from his brief stint in Santiago.

Friedkin ended the conversation with the following pragmatic assessment. "Like you, we know that he didn't do too badly in Chile. But things have advanced there and we won't be needing him anymore." After a slight pause, he'd added, "The best way for us to get rid of the guy is to figure out how to transfer him to Santiago. Which is *up to you*."

Still in a state of shock over Max's British connection, Carlos Câmara took a minute to process what the CIA agent was proposing. "Santiago? Why Santiago?" he'd stammered in confusion.

"Where better to bury him?" Eric Friedkin replied, going on to explain, "With things already taken care of in Chile, he won't have anything to do there."

# 32

Taking advantage of Max's absence (and an extra flight on the air force jet bound for Brazil), Carlos Câmara shot over to Brasilia, where he confronted his boss at the presidential palace. In a steady tone—but with a resolve that wasn't lost on the other man—he laid out on the table the nuclear dossier they'd compiled together in Bonn, from the first social contacts made to the draft agreement hidden in a secret place. Then he mentioned what Max seemed to know about the subject, keeping his eyes fixed on the former ambassador's face throughout. In conclusion, forgoing any attempt at a smooth transition, he asked for his subordinate's head.

"But why, if he's doing so well?" the ambassador countered as he lit his pipe. Being the cunning old fox he was, he hadn't shown surprise. On the contrary, he'd actually been secretly pleased by the news—knowing it would come sooner or later. And he felt a pang of sorrow for his young colleague, whose insatiable appetite and ambition he'd detected during his days back in Montevideo.

"Because he spoke of you with disrespect," Câmara replied. "And because he's working for the Brits."

Dismissing the first remark—which he deemed comparable to pillow talk, never worthy of his attention—the ambassador smiled knowingly as he pondered the second, making a passing observation: "For the Brits. Who would have thought..." Two puffs later, gaze fixed on the ceiling, he said under his breath, almost to himself, "Marcílio always had very good taste. It was inevitable that eventually he'd seek someplace better than the dump where we stuck him."

Câmara remained unflustered. For the first time in the twenty years they'd been working together, he'd scowled at his boss. And while he didn't say anything overtly offensive, his attitude had conveyed the classic *It's him or me.*

He came out on top—as expected. Largely because the ambassador had other things on his mind and wasn't one to sweat the small stuff. "But let's promote him to counselor before we transfer him to Santiago," he urged. And before Câmara could protest, he said, "In fact, I'll take care of it with the president today." Patting his friend's hand, he thoughtfully added, "So he'll still think fondly of us. Take it from me, son, with a fellow like him, that's wiser."

Câmara gave in. He'd won the battle—in terms of what mattered—and headed straight from his meeting with the former ambassador to Brasilia's air base, where the trusty air force jet was awaiting him. And he managed to land in Montevideo before Max arrived from Chile.

The next afternoon, the two met, as they always did when Max returned from a trip. Câmara listened to a detailed debrief of the political and military scene in the Andean country. Max could hardly contain his excitement. He hadn't ruled out the possibility that the Chilean coup might even precede the one in Uruguay.

After sharing their impressions, both men concluded that the sequence didn't really matter. What was important were the different aspects the processes would take on: radical in Chile, moderate in Uruguay—given that the latter would maintain the outward appearance of a democracy while the generals ruled from behind the scenes. This pleased Brazilian military heads, since it left our country better protected against eventual accusations of interfering. Moreover, as we shared a border with

Uruguay, the government wasn't particularly interested in having next door the kind of ruthless Prussian-style military regime taking shape in Chile.

A week after this conversation, Carlos Câmara crossed paths with Max on the embassy's ground floor and, in the tone of one delivering good news, slyly announced, "A telegram just arrived with word of your transfer."

Still standing near the entrance, Max struggled to close the wet umbrella he was carrying and asked in a voice he managed to keep firm, "Transfer? Where to?"

Merciless, Carlos Câmara couldn't resist teasing: "Pretending you have no idea, are you? Before you know it, we'll be hearing you've been promoted to counselor."

News of his promotion arrived by cable two days later.

*The SOBs never let up*, thought Max, infuriated. He was able to control himself, though—once again paraphrasing Sun Tzu for his own purposes: "A leader never fights when he's angry."

Payback took more than a decade. When the Brazilian press, no longer under censorship, disseminated over the course of a month a series of articles on his performance in Uruguay, Carlos Câmara was forced into a humiliating and abrupt retirement, to the joy of the enemies he'd accumulated throughout his career. He objected as much as he could, but the military, concerned with amnesty in their own quarters on the eve of the coming civil government, didn't lift a finger on his behalf. Nor did they heed his demand that the source that had leaked the stories be identified.

When the National Congress, echoing the people's indignation, had demanded Carlos Câmara's head, "as Itamaraty's number one Fascist," Max happened to be on vacation in the Aegean Sea, cruising the Greek isles—at the invitation of a coffee importer.

# PART FOUR

# 33

There are things that only madmen and children are able to fully apprehend. Young Pedro Henrique Magalhães de Castro Andrade Xavier had foreseen in his own way what lay ahead in this strange new land to which they'd been banished: before coming down with a high fever, he'd burst out crying in the Santiago airport as soon as he and his parents had landed from Rio de Janeiro.

The three had spent two weeks at the mansion in Santa Teresa, recovering from the hasty move from Montevideo. By pure instinct, the little one had sensed, rather than actually seen, the helplessness on his father's face, which was offset by the paleness of his mother's. There was no one waiting for them at the airport. *No one* other than the shifty security guards inspecting the passengers, of course. They kept casting dirty looks at the child who wouldn't stop wailing... until they were side-tracked by the eight suede suitcases with leather trim arranged in a semicircle, behind which the travelers huddled, as though taking cover in a trench.

Unlike their landing in Montevideo three years earlier, when Marina and Max had been met by beaming colleagues bearing armfuls of flowers, Santiago immediately presented itself as cold, harsh, and hostile—the face it would wear for the next two decades. There wasn't a single representative of the embassy to receive them in the crowded terminal, which had become something of a stronghold given the impending coup.

Surprised and somewhat incensed, Max went to survey the ground level of the airport. There he was saved by a driver who recognized and greeted him from afar, then came over with his boss, the assistant to the naval attaché. By happy coincidence, the official had just sent his family off to Brazil on vacation. He accommodated the recent arrivals, as well as their considerable baggage, in the van, acting rather ungraciously all the while, and accompanied them to the hotel Max indicated—the traditional Carrera in the Barrio Cívico, just steps from La Moneda Palace.

During the trip into the city, the young official hardly exchanged two words with Max or Marina. Truth be told, Max didn't recall ever having said a single word to him on any of his previous missions to Santiago. To make amends, he poured on the kindness, twice referring to the man as his family's guardian angel. The sweet talk met with silence, however. *More of a guardian than an angel*, Max concluded.

Then the driver ventured to make a more personal observation: "Things have gotten very bad here, Mr. Secretary."

"*Counselor*," Max corrected, causing the man to bite his lip and keep his mouth shut.

The first two days, Marina felt hurt not to hear from any of the embassy wives, especially since she needed to find a pediatrician for her son. Not one of the women answered the phone or returned her calls. She found it strange, if not disconcerting, as she'd spoken with several of them from Montevideo just two weeks earlier. *What could have happened since then?* she wondered, frustrated at being compelled to have her son treated by the hotel doctor.

Max, in turn, would soon be facing his own share of challenges. The ambassador's allies, or those who pretended to follow his ideals out of convenience, had struck Max's name from their agendas on learning that his transfer had been ordered from above against his will. Not even his promotion to counselor had made up for the blow to his reputation. It was seen as a consolation prize.

This group had been joined by the military attachés, whom Max had always treated with aloofness or condescension during his previous visits. Initially, at least, all had closed their doors and turned their backs on Max, Marina, and Pedro Henrique. Not yet three years old, the child was already subject to the results of his parents' ostracism.

What of the handful of liberals still at the embassy, slinking around in the shadows while they awaited transfers to other posts? No matter how hard Max tried to approach them, seeking support and practical information (realtors who would help the couple find a house, doctors who might care for their sick child, bank accounts that could be opened right away, a rental car that would make it possible to move around in a city with no cabs or public transportation due to strikes), no matter how much he quoted authors everyone had read with a passion in days gone by, his shady character precluded any casual contact with this group of dissidents.

Spurned by both of these incompatible factions, Max was living in his own personal hell. It was amid this ravaged atmosphere that, one morning, while shaving in the bathroom of his hotel suite, he heard gunfire. At first he mistook it for fireworks. But it wasn't even ten in the morning. *Firecrackers, at this hour?* he wondered. *No,* he soon realized, *those were gunshots.* And they were coming from the rooftops of buildings around the public square.

He cracked open the window and spotted three tanks just below. They were filing out of the deserted square, heading straight for La Moneda Palace. They stopped midway and remained lined up there, like huge beasts ready for a fight. Marina came over to the window, cradling Pedro Henrique in her arms. Max signaled for her to back away.

The gunfire started up again, the bullets seeming to ricochet off the tanks, which remained motionless, as though indifferent to the shots. Max looked at his watch. It was five after ten. The snipers continued to fire their weapons, only now soldiers armed with machine guns were taking up strategic positions in the square and firing back. The machine-gun bursts soon drowned out the rifle shots.

Max made Marina and Pedro Henrique sit on the floor, in the corner farthest from the window. He put pillows and cushions around the two. Keeping crouched down, he made his way back over to the window. They'd taken two adjoining rooms in the hotel. The second, a corner room, extended his view over the square. That's where he turned his attention.

Max flipped on the TV, as if needing confirmation of what was unfolding before his very eyes. But all that came up on the screen were old reruns and commercials. He rushed over to the radio and set it on a table near the windows, which he closed one by one. The sound coming across was tinny, as if far away. What made it feel close was the emotion being conveyed. Max recognized the voice. It was Salvador Allende speaking. *He was saying goodbye.* The words sounded as if they were coming from a world already relegated to History: "This may be my last opportunity to address you...."

Max listened in astonishment. "My words hold no bitterness...." Sitting on the floor, his body braced against the wall, Max shrank with each line as Allende's voice grew. "History is ours and is made by the people.... I have faith in Chile and its destiny..." The radio faded out.

Soldiers' shouts and their commanders' orders rose from the square. Two blasts followed. Max reopened one of the windows. La Moneda was in flames. The first tank had taken aim at the palace. The second and third fired simultaneously. The shells had torn gaping holes in La Moneda's façade. Smoke and dust were pouring out.

Max slumped against the wall and stayed hunched over. Later, he couldn't say how long he'd remained in that position.

He only remembered that Marina and Pedro Henrique had been quiet and still, petrified. But all of them were jolted by an explosion that shook the hotel's foundation.

Max rushed to the window. Attacked by tanks, the palace was now being bombarded by aircraft. He looked upward. Two jets were flying low over the square. With each dive, they dropped their bombs. Max checked his watch. Almost two hours had passed. The soldiers continued to fire their machine guns at the façade, in a virtually deserted square. *La Moneda in flames! Right before his very eyes...*

Hands trembling, Max cracked open the other windows and, crouching low, circled nervously along them, covering his ears with each bomb that fell, each round fired by the tanks. Speechless, he saw soldiers invade the building. He was watching something that went beyond the images. A scene that would remain etched in his mind forever. But one he wasn't able to relate to—for he had witnessed it as an outsider.

# 34

For reasons he couldn't quite explain, Max watched the fall of La Moneda as if in a trance. What had happened just beyond the hotel walls triggered a conflict in his spirit, launching him in the direction of conquests still to come.

Hunched against the wall, curled up into himself like a snail while an entire country crumbled around him, he'd realized that it was time to start over again. Only no longer from square one. And that would be the distinguishing feature of this challenge, which he'd face with the same doggedness and discipline he'd displayed on previous occasions. *Had he been used and cast aside?* He had indeed. But now that he understood the whole game, and had trump cards to play, he'd patiently bide his time. He would rise from the ashes, the same way Chile would be reborn from the ruins of La Moneda.

Hours later, in an embassy thrown into a tailspin by the events, he was the only one able to keep a level head. Sitting at his desk, with the office door closed and keeping absolutely still, he underwent what the French call a *mise au point*, a succinct reassessment of personal priorities. The fact that the first civilian bodies gunned down by the military were turning up on the sidewalks didn't distract him from the task. Nor did the despair of the local public servants around him, worried by the lack of news of their loved ones. Later, he circled through the corridors as a robot, concentrating on his world alone. The greater the commotion, the more serene he seemed in the eye of the storm.

He wasn't afraid of the CIA. He'd upheld his end of the bargain, training the Uruguayan police force, and he believed that was the extent of what he owed the Americans. He had no fears where MI6 was concerned, either, because despite having delusions of grandeur with respect to Her Majesty's Secret Service, he'd passed nothing but innocuous information to Raymond Thurston and never received payment of any kind.

He had few or no worries about the SNI, having always kept up proper relations with the organization's operatives—including Major Vaz, who would visit him in Santiago more than once (Max even held an impromptu poker game in his honor). In Montevideo, he'd reconnected with former colleagues from the War College, all of whom were doing well in their careers. And he could only be grateful for the two swift promotions his own ministry had granted him.

What he had yet to contend with was the ostracism plaguing him *in Santiago*, the causes of which he preferred to downplay. Without dwelling on it too much, he presumed that Carlos Câmara's plots might have negatively influenced his new boss. That would explain the ambassador's contempt for him. He seemed to consider Max a flunky of the former ambassador in Montevideo, whom he didn't hold in high regard.

When he got back to the hotel, Max found Marina still holding Pedro Henrique in her arms. The doctor hadn't been able to come since the area was surrounded. Max had managed to get through the barricades only because he was a foreign diplomat and a guest at the hotel. A curfew had been imposed across the land. La Moneda was still smoldering next door. Hotel management had received orders to evacuate all guests within twenty-four hours. The lobby was swarming with soldiers.

"You and Pedro Henrique will leave for Brazil tomorrow," Max told his wife with the calm of someone making a decision long since mulled over. "I won't set foot in the embassy until you've taken off. You can start packing your bags while I talk to the airline. I'll have you fly in the cockpit if that's what it takes. There's no question that you're getting out of here first thing in the morning."

"I saw the Man from the Train in front of me again," Marina would confide years later. "The one who would rescue me from the boring and predictable life of a poor little rich girl, the one who would make me a happy woman. That man had long since left the scene of my life... if he'd ever really entered it. But he'd come back. By saving my son, he was saving me. And in doing so, he settled all the debts he owed me. The others, which he'd racked up with creditors of every kind both inside and outside the ministry, he'd pay for the rest of his life. *Or not...* But he was paid up with me.

"We left for Rio the next day just as he'd promised. With Chile on the brink of war, we would never have found doctors or a hospital able to care for Pedro Henrique. They were all busy with disasters of another scale. Our poor little son was transported by an ambulance my father sent when we got to Rio. It met us on the runway at Galeão, with two doctors and a nurse on board. Within a couple of weeks, the listless little boy who could barely move and spent all his time between my lap and the bed was racing around the grounds of Santa Teresa. A month later, he was an altogether different child."

What had been a moment of profound relief for Marina was for Max an even headier feeling—brought about when a man has the rare opportunity to restore his lost dignity, no longer dragged along by events but facing them head-on. He'd never experienced such clarity of vision. But snatching his son from the jaws of death—that's the dimension Pedro Henrique's medical condition had assumed in his eyes—was only the first spark in a series that would lead him to completely overturn his status at the embassy in a matter of weeks. In order to do so, however, he had to sell his soul to the devil for the second time since 1964—now at a dirt-cheap price: he traded it for uranium.

The bottom line is that, while gazing at the burning ruins of La Moneda Palace, Max had resolved to give in to the appeals of his old friend Newton Cordeiro. He would negotiate a deal with the colonel. In Chile, he would give Cordeiro what he hadn't been able to provide in Montevideo: the contacts needed to open particular doors. In this case, businessmen connected to the Chilean military, who might be interested in certain valuable raw materials Brazil had at its disposal—and to which Cordeiro had access, thanks to one of the countless shady deals made under the dictatorship.

Max asked for little in exchange: full pressure on Itamaraty, at the highest level, so that he could oversee the embassy's commercial sector. Carte blanche. Not having to run his projects or cables past the ambassador. There was already at least one such precedent at the ministry: the commercial sector in New York operated independently. This might be considered in Santiago too, by orders from above.

Well aware through his friend the colonel that wheeling and dealing in sensitive material had been going on for years in military circles, Max had no qualms about imposing his conditions. He truly believed he wasn't asking for much. And he was right. But at the time, it was what he needed to clear a path that would serve him at this new stage of his career. In promoting our exports, he would find refuge against the slings and arrows suffered in the political trench he'd been moving in until then. He would hibernate in this more appealing environment while he honed his connections—which would later bolster his slow return to power.

In negotiating with Max, Newton Cordeiro quickly grasped that his friend was in a vulnerable spot. Realizing he could include an additional item in the package being considered, which would help him solidify his reputation with the Brazilian business community and his military colleagues, he asked Max to use his position to stress among certain Chilean groups the need, as he put it, "to remove some roadblocks and set up others."

Max didn't like the idea. It was vague enough to hold a hidden agenda. But he ended up agreeing. And promised to arrange occasional gatherings of businessmen from the two countries, during which the Brazilians—ostensibly in Chile for commercial purposes—would share their experiences in the field of repression. Experiences that would facilitate the settling of accounts the two countries' armed forces weren't always able to support—from lack of interest or mandate. Operations that, in the case of Brazil, for example, would put a stop to attacks and kidnappings. Or which, in the case of Chile, would discourage covert union activities, not to mention movements that might generate instability among landowners. Projects, in sum, that would meet with greater interest from the entrepreneurial classes. In any area that suited them.

An expert on Max's weaknesses, the colonel knew exactly what made his friend tick: ambition. There was, however, a powerful additive to this raw material—even easier to manipulate: a constant rancor. Max was motivated by revenge and seemed willing to pay any price to achieve his goals. So much the better, thought the colonel: playing his cards right, he could make whatever he wanted of Max. Or so he believed. But there's no question that at this early stage, the partnership favored the colonel.

The process that would radically transform Max's position in the embassy began exactly three weeks after his arrival. Flipping through the day's telegrams, the ambassador had been notified that "by a decision from above," an independent commercial office would be established in Santiago and run by Counselor Andrade Xavier. The young diplomat was already authorized to take the necessary steps toward this goal, which included "renting adequate off-site office space" and hiring specialists who would "enable him to perform his duties."

A second telegram authorized the acquisition of two cars for exclusive use by the commercial sector, one as the counselor's official vehicle, the other for business purposes.

The ambassador choked on each word in the telegrams—and gritted his teeth when he got to the part about the two vehicles. But he sensed that these orders had come from the minister himself and that nothing could be done other than to bite the bullet and keep quiet.

# 35

To the bewilderment of many, Max didn't seem to dwell on his triumph. Or if he took any joy from it, he kept this in check. He grew a beard and began to consider the best way of handling his new challenges—among them, weighing the practical steps his duties would require. He showed little gratitude for the congratulations he began receiving from those who had ignored him until then. And he downplayed the fact that the ambassador's doors remained closed to him—a situation that would remain unaltered until a new embassy head arrived a year and a half later.

To ensure there were no lingering doubts that he was a dedicated public servant, he availed himself of the fact that Chile was facing serious internal conflicts to zealously perform a few consular tasks until the political climate settled. He realized that the country had no way of including commerce among its priorities right then. Many nights he found himself longing for the camaraderie he had once shared with his majors and sergeants. With them at least he knew where he stood. As such, he gradually understood that there really was no avenue of escape, no way out of an environment like his for those who took shortcuts. The doors that opened as options tended nearly always to be traps.

A few months would elapse before he asserted himself, as commercial attaché or in his more veiled role as business consultant. These were difficult and shaky times for Max, despite his extraordinary about-face at the embassy.

Marina remained in Rio de Janeiro with Pedro Henrique, and our friend found himself alone in an inhospitable city. His embassy duties had him trying to locate missing Brazilians at the request of desperate relatives with no alternative but to call daily from home seeking news. Max couldn't count on the slightest help in this area from his own embassy, much less from the Chilean secret police. Among other reasons, because the latter had received mixed messages about him from the ambassador's staff.

So he tried to reach our exiled compatriots, in search of information that might assist him. This was naïveté on his part, since all fled from him (and from any Brazilian diplomat or official) like the devil from the cross. As such, he found himself groping blindly, obliged to pay numerous visits to hospitals and morgues, until finally dropping in at the makeshift prison camp at the National Stadium. The three times he was there, he returned to the embassy ashen and, as a colleague reported years later, "with his beard getting grayer."

Max was facing a precarious paradox: the more he tried to distance himself from the horror—as he prepared to don the more discreet suit of business attaché—the more the repression clung to him. Luckily for him, however, one of the military attachés—by far the least radical of the three representatives from our armed forces—had taken pity on him. He wasn't the spiteful type and so hadn't felt offended by Max's displays of arrogance on his previous visits to Santiago. He'd simply taken him, on those occasions, to be childish and insecure. Thus he'd managed to detect in Max qualities the younger man didn't even know he possessed. This perceptive official came to the somewhat unexpected conclusion that, were he to find the opening to do so, Max would go out of his way to help the exiled Brazilians—despite explicit orders to the contrary.

The ambassador—to the bemusement and increasing irritation of the attaché, who believed there were limits to a certain kind of persecution—had ordered that the embassy doors be closed to our compatriots, leaving them exposed to the violence of the Chilean secret police. One afternoon, this official crossed paths with Max in the hallway and invited him to have coffee. *Tomorrow*, he specified. *Before work*, he further emphasized. He then mentioned the name of a pastry shop located some distance from the embassy. His goal accomplished, he held a finger to his lips and moved along.

Max didn't know quite what to think. He'd detected something old-fashioned in the way the invitation had been made. Something reminiscent of a classic spy novel written between the two world wars, the mood of which could hardly be associated with the complexity surrounding them in the mid 1970s. But he felt so isolated at work that he seized the opportunity with rekindled spirits.

His enthusiasm was such that the shop was not yet open when he arrived the next morning. He wandered around, stretching his legs in the cold for ten minutes, until an employee inside felt sorry for him and unlocked the door.

The attaché arrived moments later. After a brief greeting, he sat in front of Max and got straight to the point. "Go see these people." He slid a folded sheet of paper across the table but continued to hold it in place with his fingers. "It's an embassy," he said. "I wrote down the names of two people there. And, finally, one word."

Max sensed he'd been told very little and a great deal at the same time. Little, given the scant number of words. A great deal, given the enormity of what he was led to infer. The solemnity of the moment, moreover, made him uneasy. As if there were something ridiculous—or forced—about the situation.

"Don't discuss this with anyone, not even your wife in Brazil. The lines are all tapped," the attaché warned, after glancing around. "Go by bus, to attract as little attention as possible. They open at ten. At the desk, ask for the first name on the paper. When the person shows up, ask for the second. Say that you're there on behalf of Pedro. The official will ask, 'Has he recovered from his illness?' You'll answer, 'Thanks to the medicine you gave him.' Then he'll take you to a small room. A Brazilian who has taken refuge in the embassy will come see you. When the two of you are alone, say the word."

"The one on the paper."

"Yes," the attaché had replied impatiently. *What other word would I be talking about!?* his look seemed to imply. But he'd soon gone back to his measured tone. "Explain who you are. Talk about what you do. Tell the truth, that you just want to help. Somehow or other. Tell him that *I* trust you. You can bring up my name. We're related and I'm the one who took a serious risk smuggling him into the embassy in the trunk of my car. Yes, thanks to my diplomatic plates. Now, take this and go to the men's room, memorize what's written, and come back here *with the paper*. The men's room is over there, on the left."

"Now?" asked Max, surprised and somewhat unnerved. He would have liked to hear more. What, exactly, he couldn't say. With whom would he be meeting? Deep down, he was afraid of falling into a trap. He hadn't quite recovered from the manipulations he'd fallen victim to in Montevideo.

"Now," the other replied firmly.

Max stood. Only then, on brushing past the attaché, had he noticed that under his partially open coat, the other man wasn't wearing a suit, much less a uniform. He was dressed casually, in a shirt, sweater, and scarf. It was a precaution, given the circumstances, but one that had escaped Max. And made him uncomfortable, as if he were out of his element and, therefore, oblivious of such details.

In the men's room, he had locked the door and carefully unfolded the sheet of paper. He'd taken note of the embassy, memorized the two names, and stopped short at the last word. Had he noticed his reflection in the mirror, he'd have seen his lips moving as he absorbed his lesson, like an illiterate recently introduced to the mystery of letters working through a seemingly endless text. Although he was used to operating behind the scenes, it was the first time he felt truly undercover. Wasn't he about to go against his superiors' explicit orders, after all? And become entangled in who knew what kind of collusion with the enemy?

Having done what he was told, he folded the sheet in half and tucked it into his jacket pocket. Then he washed his hands and returned to the table.

"All set?" the attaché inquired.

"Affirmative!" Max exclaimed, resorting to language he'd learned in his Montevideo poker circle. And he slid the folded-up paper back across the table.

He still didn't understand the reason behind his trip to the men's room, when he could just as easily have read the paper at the table. Especially because there wasn't a soul in the place other than the waiter and a woman moving behind a glass door leading to the kitchen. He looked suspiciously at his cup, as if the attaché might have slipped something into his coffee during his absence.

"You'll be speaking to a man whose opinions I don't agree with," the attaché said. "But he's a decent fellow. And honorable. I just don't know if he's going to help you. He may not trust you. With good reason. I wouldn't, if I were in his shoes. But it's a shot. To help you help them. Because I know that at heart you're not a bad person."

"And just how do you know that?" Max asked, quite seriously.

"Because we're alike, you and I," the attaché replied, again unblinking. "From what I know of your past. And from what I've seen since you got here. We were quick to jump on board and support the coup, without knowing why. A combination of circumstances, my wife always says, when she sees me getting depressed."

Both smiled. For the first time since he'd arrived in Santiago, Max relaxed a little with someone from work. Moved by this friendly atmosphere, he felt comfortable enough to extend his legs and ask a question that had gnawed at him all night. "But why trust me? At this point? Who can assure you that—"

"You," the attaché interrupted. "*You* can assure me."

"Even so," Max murmured, pretending to feel honored when he was actually embarrassed. Nothing had prepared him for this sort of conversation. With this kind of person. That's when he realized that he too was wearing the mask of another character. And that the scene being played out by the two of them, in that deserted café, in a city itself under siege, revealed more about the strangeness of those times than anything remotely normal.

The waiter set a basket of buttered toast on the table. The two men helped themselves to milk and sugar and sipped their coffee. When the waiter had retreated, the man looked straight at Max for the first time. "You'll be acting as *a Brazilian consul. Consul* is a title that dates back to ancient Rome, to Napoleon, to the Baron of Rio Branco—"

"The old baron would be turning in his grave if he knew what I'd been involved in," Max interrupted bitterly.

The other continued, paying no heed to the remark. "With any luck at all, you'll never forget this day." At this point he glanced at his watch and, after one last sip of coffee, he stood. "I'm going home now," he said, bringing the meeting to an end. "I mentioned that I was feeling sick yesterday so I won't be in today. This one's on you.... No need to get up."

# 36

The next morning, Max went to the designated embassy. At the reception desk, he asked for the official whose name had echoed in his dreams. They had him take a seat on a bench. When the official showed up, the receptionist called Max. Max mentioned the second name and said he was there on behalf of Pedro. The conversation went as expected, and he was led to an adjoining room, where he was again asked to wait, this time on a sofa.

There was a table with six chairs in the middle of the room. The curtains were drawn against the sunlight. A floor lamp and two ceiling fixtures illuminated the space. Max waited awhile, his eyes at a loss for anything to focus on since the walls were bare. Nor was there much in the way of decoration, other than a couple of ashtrays and two candlesticks stowed at the top of a bookcase heaped with old magazines. Ten minutes later, a door opened at the far end of the room and a tall, thin man entered. A pale apparition.

Max stood and took a step in his direction. The man sat at the table and gestured for Max to take the seat opposite him. "You're Brazilian?" he asked in Portuguese once Max was settled.

"Yes, I'm Brazilian."

The man waited in silence. Max shifted his gaze away from the diaphanous being, half expecting that by virtue of the man's unusual pallor, the walls behind him would suddenly come to life — and appear adorned in paintings, vines, or flowers. But they remained unaffected by the circumstances.

Max then took a deep breath and, in as dignified a voice as possible, said, "*Codfish.*"

The other accepted the word as if it were a greeting and nodded, encouraging him to continue.

Max started talking. He explained his situation. He wanted to help but didn't know how. He admitted that, strictly speaking, he was at a loss as to how to proceed. He wanted to at least prevent unnecessary deaths, if he could act in time. And reassure the families who called constantly from Brazil. As far as he could. But... where to start? Where should he go? From whom should he seek help? He also alluded cursorily to the difficulties he'd run into at the embassy and with the Chilean police.

The man began to smile, his eyes fixed on the floor as he shook his head slightly from side to side. "If I understood correctly," he finally said, "you're in the same boat as us: stymied by both Chilean intelligence and our own ambassador here."

"Right," agreed Max. "In a certain sense, yes."

"Pretty funny," the other persisted. "Don't you think?"

"Yes...," Max replied, adding, "*and no.*" He felt a drop of sweat forming on his brow, right along his hairline. He wiped it away and went on, in search of common ground. "But I can see why you find it..." Lacking a better word, he contented himself with repeating "*funny.*"

The man pushed back his chair as if he needed more space to think. A bit of color had appeared on his face. "I'm really sorry," he said at last, "but I can't help you. I don't even know where our people are. Everything happened very suddenly. The day before the coup, I was planning a dinner at my house, a simple get-together. Since Santiago has run out of everything because of the truckers' strike ordered by the right, and the hoarding of food staples for the black market, I had a chicken breast in the oven, a few eggs in the fridge, and was relying on my garden. I was living on the city outskirts in a house with a little yard, and my wife and I had planted kale, tomatoes, and a few other vegetables. Someone would be bringing rice with sausage, and dessert was to be taken care of too.

"A friend who came through the city on her way to our house that night saw a battalion go by, with soldiers carrying rifles and machine guns. They weren't marching in formation but were looking from side to side as if keeping an eye out for some enemy. When she told us about that, we didn't know what to think.

"Bright and early the next morning I was woken by a horse. It had broken through the fence and was ransacking our vegetable garden. Where it came from, I have no idea... it looked lost. *A circus animal*, I got to thinking, *abandoned to fate by its owners*. And it was hungry. Its ribs were showing, the creature was so emaciated. I went out to the yard to shoo it away. *And then I saw...*"

Max was held in suspense by his words.

"...in the haze, just beyond the horse slowly limping away, *I saw tanks descending single file toward the city center*. I woke up my wife and a few friends who had stayed the night since they had no means of transportation, and we were out of there in no time. Each of us took off in a different direction. I stuck with my wife as long as I could, but the DINA knew what I looked like. From that point on, we stayed apart from one another in different locations, hopping from house to house. Friends' phone lines were cut and their neighbors would rat us out as soon as they saw us come in. My wife, who's eight months pregnant, is at another embassy."

He paused and looked at Max before proceeding.

"My cousin brought me here. But afterward he refused to do anything else for me. I understand. And I'm grateful for what he did. You can tell him that for me. Things came crashing down, affecting everyone. The radios around us kept blaring: *turn in foreigners you don't trust, turn in enemies of Chile....* And even if I knew where my companions are, it wouldn't help you. Things haven't been easy for our side. What we've lost, besides lives, is hope. We used to have hope here in Chile. It might have been an illusion.... Got a cigarette?"

Max recalled one of Buñuel's early films, from his Mexican phase, *Illusion Travels by Streetcar.*

"Sure."

"Thanks."

"Don't mention it. Keep the pack."

"Got a match?"

"Here."

The other man took the lighter.

"Please, keep it."

"A *Dupont?* Are you mad? No way. I'd be shot on sight by my comrades."

The two laughed.

The man lit his cigarette and contemplated the lighter for a few seconds, balancing it in his right hand. He seemed to be reflecting on days gone by, when he might have had one just like it, perhaps an even nicer one. What else might he have been thinking about?

He handed back the lighter a moment later. He'd regained a bit more color. The time had come to take his leave, though.

"Thanks again for the cigarettes," he said, getting up. "And good luck."

Max was at a loss as to how to respond. *Good luck?* "What about your wife?" he asked.

"I don't know where she is. All I heard is that she's safe at some other embassy."

Max sensed that he was lying. As the attaché had predicted, perhaps with good reason. A woman eight months pregnant, holed up in who knew what kind of situation, with dozens or hundreds of people sharing a single bathroom, about to give birth to a child. A child who might never get to know his father...

Max would have liked to wish the stranger good luck too, but he didn't feel up to it. He merely raised his hand in a vague farewell when the man, reaching the door, turned to face him one last time. The smile he'd worn briefly was gone. Even so, he pointed to the pack of cigarettes in his hand and gave a thumbs-up. "Appreciate these," he said before shutting the door.

After the man left, the room shrank around Max. He stood and paced from one side to the other. He wanted to smoke but all he had in his pocket was the lighter. He looked at his watch without seeing the hands. He imagined someone would be coming for him. And so he waited.

A few minutes later, the official he'd met earlier returned and accompanied him to the exit. The man was in shirtsleeves and the temperature outside wasn't exactly pleasant. Yet he went out with Max. As the visitor headed down the steps leading to the sidewalk, the man's voice sounded out in the crisp morning air: "*Gracias.*"

Max turned. Everything about the man, from the glint in his eye to the trace of a smile that shaved twenty years off him, confirmed his gratitude. *You tried*, his expression seemed to suggest. It wasn't up to him to judge whether it had been successful or not. But he wanted to personally convey his thanks. And if he did so, it was because gestures like Max's, no matter where they might come from, were rarer each day.

On an impulse, Max swiftly ascended the steps and shook the man's hand. For the first time since March 31, 1964, he'd wavered—to the point of nearly losing his balance. Then he turned and went back down the stairs. When he reached the sidewalk, he casually strolled away.

# 37

For a few days, the experience with his exiled compatriot had led Max to think back on his good deed. Unfortunately, however, the acquired knowledge wouldn't take root in his heart. Max was, above all, a rational man, immune to the lure of emotion.

The attaché who had tried to help him perform his consular duties was transferred back to Brazil a month later, and Max would never see him again. The official from the foreign embassy, even more understandably, would also vanish from his life forever. As for *Codfish*, yes, our friend would see him again. *Yes...and no.* Because, twenty years later, in Brasilia, with democracy restored and those who had previously been overthrown back in power, Max had hidden behind a pillar to avoid being recognized by the now high official of the federal administration when he'd almost crossed paths with him at a public ceremony both were attending. He'd been afraid that the former attaché might have told his relative who'd taken refuge at the embassy what he knew of Max's involvement with the SNI.

At any rate, the insensitivity he showed by not making more of an effort to assist other compatriots in trouble would take its toll. Because if the gods had granted Max an opportunity to shine in heaven, the devils were also keeping tabs on his destiny and would soon reappear on the scene.

Two weeks after his redemptive adventure—as he'd classified the experience—he received an urgent telex from Colonel

Cordeiro inquiring whether he would be willing to lend a hand with a particular problem.

Max agreed, and a few days later he had a drink with his new patron at the luxury hotel where he was staying. The colonel got straight to the point: he wanted to introduce Max to a São Paulo banker who had accompanied him to Santiago. And who wished to consult with Max "on a personal matter." Max shrugged. He had no way of denying the colonel.

The banker soon joined the two at the bar. *Popped up like a jack-in-the-box*, Max thought. But there was nothing amusing about his demeanor or attitude. The games he played were far darker: he was an arms dealer.

*Thank goodness*, thought Max with relief. *Weapons...* a subject that, given its nature, was beyond his purview. Aside from the countless restrictions, some of which had been put in place by UN resolutions, this was an area overseen by the embassy's political sector. Max could, at most, direct the visitor to his colleague in charge of the matter. He was therefore happy they weren't talking about the sensitive material that had so interested his friend Colonel Cordeiro in the past and could be handled only on a secret basis. Then Max realized from the other men's silence that *there was more.*

Scrutinizing the stranger, Max discovered that he recognized him, both from photographs and by reputation. His name was Marco Ferrari and he made the most of his Italian background, displaying the personal bonhomie that helped smooth over his many flaws. He was an investor but also represented interests that kept him at the head of a large conglomerate. Last but not least, he had been one of the primary financial backers of the nefarious OBAN, Operation Bandeirante, which used torture to repress dissent and which Max had assumed to be limited to Brazilian territory. So it wasn't just weapons he wanted to talk about.

During the conversation that ensued, the man circled around Max several times, like a big fish sizing up a smaller one before going in for the kill. He showed interest in the diplomat's career and asked general questions about the country they were in. At one point, he tried to establish whether they had mutual friends. Not having come up with any, he concentrated on their shared tastes in art and literature. He also brought up sports. The only subject they didn't discuss was their personal life.

*What is this guy doing in Chile?* Max wondered as he let the conversation flow. And why was he interjecting so many pauses into what he was saying, watching Max in silence, as though seeking to determine just what he was made of? *There was definitely more to the meeting,* Max finally concluded. Might it have to do with Operation Bandeirante? But *how,* if OBAN had never acted abroad, as far as he knew?

While the man ordered another drink, giving the waiter specific instructions as to how he wanted it made, Max shot a quick question to the colonel.

"No, it has nothing to do with that," Newton Cordeiro whispered back. "In fact, I don't really know what he wants, he hasn't told me. All I know is that he needs your help."

*Help? What kind of help?*

At a discreet signal from the banker, the colonel left to use the men's room, a strategic move that drew Max's attention.

"Max, I know we can trust you," Ferrari said.

Max nodded. The use of the plural troubled him. That collective *we* had weighed heavily on the shoulders of defenders of the so-called Revolution.

"We also know that you're convinced of the importance of the war we're all involved in. A matter of *life and death.*"

Max took a sip of his drink and signaled to the waiter.

"There's a community of Brazilians here in Chile..."

Max paused, his hand still raised, like a hunting dog that suddenly stops short.

"*Exiled* Brazilians," the other man continued, dropping his voice. The colonel's absence was telling. He had obviously left the scene for a reason. "One of them..." The pause conveyed anguish more than hesitation. The confidence the man had displayed until then gave way to terrible uneasiness. To the degree that his voice, although angry, came out sounding fragile: "One of them swore to kill me. *A terrorist.* An assassin."

Max had no alternative. He suddenly found himself in one of those extreme situations that are like duels—and from which only one of the adversaries comes out standing. He pinned his opponent against a wall, as efficiently and mercilessly as possible.

"And...?" he asked.

The banker lit the first cigarette of the evening. After a long drag, he declared, "He can't return to Brazil." The worst was yet to come. "Money is no object, as far as I'm concerned."

No matter how prepared he was, no matter how long he'd been awaiting the attack, Max felt blindsided. As if he'd taken the bullet intended for the militant. And he was saddened. The worst of men always cling to a few illusions about themselves—and his had just been shattered. The other rolled on like a tank, clad in his presumption, protected by his wealth.

"According to information we have, he's in the hands of the Chilean secret police. He almost certainly killed one of our own, a friend of my mine named Boilensen, two years ago. I'm next on the list. *If he makes it back to Brazil.*" And then the inevitable repetition: "He can't go back."

In deference to his illusions, or what was left of them in that impersonal hotel bar, Max managed to curb his indignation. He dealt with his revulsion, however, finding a means of returning to the kingdom of men, by selecting a weapon with which he'd armed himself in his youth: subtle yet stinging irony. Combining feeling and diplomacy to the greatest extent possible, he honed it into a samurai's sword.

"The embassy's consular sector handles visas and passports," he began in a steady voice. "As well as legalization of documents." He silently counted to twenty. The other man grew paler. "Everything relating to local immigration is up to the Chilean authorities," he went on in the same tone. "It's up to them to decide whether an individual citizen—in our case, a Brazilian—can remain in the country beyond the time frame established by law."

The banker didn't blink. His face showed no particular emotion. Newton Cordeiro returned to his seat, rubbing his hands together. The waiter served another round of drinks.

"So, it's all very interesting, as you see," said Ferrari, in a suddenly animated voice, as if he'd been engaged in a conversation the colonel could now join. And he continued, almost tripping over his words. "But I realize it's a complicated issue. Thus my consulting you. Of course what was said here remains between the two of us."

The colonel registered these last words with satisfaction, not noticing the wounded look with which they were delivered. He waited for the conversation to resume so he could orient himself, while Max helped himself to a handful of peanuts.

"Of course," Max said at last.

They'd finished their third round of drinks in near silence. Ferrari suggested they move to a table. "Right here," he added, pointing to the hotel's restaurant adjacent to the bar, as if he were at his own home. He wouldn't stray from the prepared script; he would follow protocol to the end. Even though his teeth and gut were clenched in anger. That was the impression Max took from the meeting. The man exuded power and rage yet was essentially helpless. The hatred Ferrari felt now came across as fear.

Once they were seated at the restaurant, however, his host rubbed his hands together as if he'd regained his strength. So what if Max had refused to do him a favor? He would find someone else, even if the cost were higher. As for the young diplomat, time would tell. He had nothing to lose by waiting.

Colonel Cordeiro, who had kept quiet virtually the entire evening, then found himself having to conduct an orchestra made up of two musicians who no longer had instruments to play. He handled the challenge remarkably well and was, moreover, quite pleased with himself, having fulfilled his mission. A bridge had been built between the two men, as evidenced by the harmony reigning over the table. He put himself in charge of the pleasant conversation, which featured alternating comments from Max and the banker.

His eyes tracked the bottle of wine, which was uncorked at leisure. *A delicious dinner, a fine wine…What more could he have hoped for as grand coordinator of the evening?*

Max's thoughts, meanwhile, had drifted to Carlos Câmara. Were his colleague posted in Chile, would the banker have had the gall to submit the same proposal to him?

"Excellent choice," he said, swirling his glass and tasting the wine. "Nice color." Then he continued the conversation. "In other words, what you're suggesting, if I understand correctly, is some sort of custody. The military would be manipulated but without their realizing it. Very gently, subtly."

"Exactly," replied the banker, who wished only to put an end to that disastrous evening.

"An operation," Max speculated, in the tone of one pondering an academic question, "that, from the administrative point of view, would feed the vanity of military brass without taking any authority away from the business community."

To which the banker, as if following the same reasoning, had added, "Authority having to do with the former unions, which, to this day, must have hidden arms. Not to mention the various student organizations, whose manifestos are being printed and distributed as we speak, and the artists, who most certainly have been regrouping to produce the same plays, only now thinly veiled."

*Thinly veiled plays*, thought Max, suddenly disheartened. *Where might Ana be these days? And what would she think of that expression? Was she herself working on such plays in Rio? What would she think of him if she knew he'd been asked to commit such a crime? What would his old jazz buddies have to say were they to learn he'd been offered payment to arrange to kill a man who, in other times or circumstances, might well have been a part of their crowd?*

# 38

From the poignant adventure he'd undergone with his exiled compatriot to the nightmare he'd experienced with the banker, Max had been through two extremes in a matter of days. He regarded the first as more of a fanciful digression, something bordering on romanticism; the second, however, generated an uneasiness that refused to fade. Nevertheless, he gradually managed to concentrate on more routine assignments.

Bringing together businessmen from the two countries proved to be a straightforward and even pleasant task for Max. On the Brazilian end, the challenges were easily met, with the support of the major industrial and commercial associations. These links simply needed to be reinforced so that familiar paths could now lead to new opportunities.

The same was happening on the Chilean end, even though the local economy was still weak. But Max relied on a few solid ties in the country, derived from the contacts he'd kept with certain local upper-middle-class groups over the twelve months preceding Allende's downfall. These connections ran deep given that, on his successive visits to Chile, Max had shared with these groups the plan crafted by the CIA in Montevideo and carried out in Brazil ten years earlier—by force of which the government had been systematically destabilized.

Following the Brazilian model and, later, the Uruguayan one, the Chilean business community had operated in a way that was at once light- and heavy-handed. First, it funded strikes that paralyzed the productive sectors, creating panic among the middle class and immobilizing the labor and farmers' movements. These actions were backed by investors who in many instances received support from the CIA. As a result, nearly all of the crucial sectors of the Chilean economy had crossed their arms at one point or another, most notably the truck drivers. Without transportation, essentials wouldn't be distributed, except with great difficulty.

It was the second set of actions that would take the heavier toll, leaving countless innocent victims in its wake. These included attacks on gas lines, electric towers, and railroads, which were carried out by paramilitary groups and attributed (once again, as in Brazil and Uruguay) to extreme leftist groups.

Max had also taken part in dealings intended to manipulate the media through paid ads in newspapers and other means of communication, sending hundreds of mothers into the streets beating their pans in search of nonexistent food supplies. The protests of the *panelazos*, as they would be known in Chile, could—again, as had occurred in Brazil ten years earlier—be alternated with dramatic religious processions, which, according to the CIA, "photograph well in the international press, given how imposing the crucifixes are."

The five weeks Fidel Castro spent in Chile at the end of 1971 had been particularly useful as a means of instilling fear. "A gift from the gods," in the words of one CIA agent.

These were the trump cards Max depended on for his ostensible work as this new stage was being heralded. Considering that conservative values were firmly entrenched in power, and that the Chilean elite was already sighing with relief at the initial outcome of its successful performance, it was up to the diplomat to reap the bounty of the contacts made months before—shifting them into alignment with the Brazilian exporters and investors, who were once again migrating toward Chile.

On the Chilean social circuit during this period, Max shone. And he spared no expense, organizing fairs to promote assorted products, paying for Chilean journalists and investors to visit our state capitals, creating sumptuous receptions at luxury hotels. During the months following the coup, several local business-men and their wives became full-time partygoers, exuding a telltale relief that indicated the anguish they'd been through. Even so, they listened more than they spoke and drank more than they listened. Deep down, they were still traumatized, try-ing hard to recover from their cumulative scares.

Did Max notice how doleful these people were? That they had no radiance, not to mention mundane qualities such as flex-ibility, malice, or a sense of humor? Did he ever regret having helped—even indirectly—to liquidate the country's intellectu-als, the artists, the teachers, the students, the liberals?

Or was he so bedazzled by his own splendor that he'd become immune to such doubts, content to shine on a now deserted stage?

# 39

Max had thrown himself with such determination into projects that would reinstate him in his career that he'd neglected the personal dimension represented by his family.

In the months after his arrival in Santiago, he'd traveled to Rio de Janeiro twice to be with Marina and check on Pedro Henrique's recovery. Both trips had transpired as if he were visiting distant relatives. He'd spent his evenings listening to jazz with old friends and going to shows; Marina joined them only once. Her mother had passed away recently, which didn't help matters. It had shrouded the Santa Teresa mansion in sadness and further tainted Marina's mood with uncertainty.

Rather than bringing the two together, these visits had pushed the couple farther apart. Pedro Henrique had treated his father with curiosity, not tenderness, giving every indication that he was more interested in his daddy's new beard than any other aspect of him. What would befall Marina on her return to Santiago was already looming on the horizon, for Max did nothing more than reinforce the indifference with which he regarded her—lost as he was in his own labyrinths.

He continued to act like a blind man where his wife was concerned.

She didn't complain, having given up long ago. She just didn't know exactly which direction to take. She saw herself reduced to the dimensions of a woman from olden times, even predating her mother's era. Someone observing her closely and wishing to give her a gift, for instance, would have chosen a shawl. Marina seemed to have aged prematurely and grown frail along the way.

Ignoring his wife in Montevideo had been a mistake. A mistake that hadn't had significant consequences. Keeping up this attitude, however, turned out to have far more serious implications. Because Marina would eventually come back to Chile. Weary and worn-out. And life would resume its course, only now much more painfully.

Two months after leaving Santiago, Marina returned from Rio with Pedro Henrique. The boy, who had been speaking for quite some time, refused to say *papai*—a problem that didn't faze Max in the least. For Max, his seeming indifference toward his son did not mean that he didn't love him. All of his energy was devoted to his projects, none of which included the child at that stage. Max imagined they'd be *buddies* (as he put it, seeking in language the intimacy lacking in their life) once the boy learned to read. Then they would chat about Monteiro Lobato, Mark Twain, and Jules Verne.

On the way from the airport, Max and Marina talked about the mood prevailing in the city. The political atmosphere, according to Max, was reminiscent of Brazil post-1968, only with a greater number of troops. Max pointed to the military's gray uniforms, as well as the carabineros' green fatigues, colors conspicuous everywhere in the city, conveying a message to all social classes alike, whether they supported the regime or opposed it: those men, with their uniforms, weapons, and ideas, were there for the long haul.

The cool and detached tone with which he made these observations left Marina depressed. She was pleasantly surprised, however, on arriving at the house Max had rented in a residential neighborhood, the name of which she found appropriate to their circumstances: Providencia. When the car pulled up in front of the yard, she perked up and woke Pedro Henrique, who had napped in her arms the whole way. Still groggy from the plane ride, which had been followed by endless delays in customs and a long, winding car trip, the child had rubbed his eyes and blinked at the sprawling residence, clearly having no idea where he was. Marina, in turn, was looking at the house next door, being touched up by two painters. Thanks to their work, Max explained, the traces of bullet holes would "disappear at last." Lifting the suitcases out of the trunk, he added, "Unlike the body the shots were targeting."

Since she looked at him without understanding, he explained. "It wasn't on the sidewalk five minutes, barely enough time for the man's wife and daughter to embrace the deceased." His wife remained silent. "In less than twenty-four hours, the poor women had packed their bags and vanished from the neighborhood. From what I later learned, the house was repossessed. It belonged to a high-level official from Allende's administration."

Holding Pedro Henrique's hand, Marina mustered the strength to climb the steps to the entrance of her new home. In due time, however, the three would settle into a kind of routine, including seeking a nursery school for the child—made easier by the support of the embassy wives this time around. The family bought furniture, since what they'd had in their Montevideo apartment could scarcely fill their much larger house in Chile.

The violence associated with different forms of repression would be felt in the country for many years, with the military committing all kinds of barbaric acts. Occasionally, dispersed opposing forces made attempts on the lives of government officials. All in all, however, the embattled atmosphere of the first few weeks had begun to dissipate by the time Marina and Pedro Henrique came back. And although the city hadn't quite returned to normal, it was adapting to the new times.

The National Stadium remained full of prisoners. It was widely known that additional captives were being held in the military barracks. The names of the infamous Tacna and

Arenal bases, among many others, were whispered on the city's street corners. The secret police themselves referred to the José Domingo Cañas detention center as "a torture chamber that ran like clockwork." Officers were spotted on the patio in shirt-sleeves, playing cards between one interrogation and the next.

The cinemas, theaters, and restaurants were gradually reopening and, to the astonishment of those suffering or being persecuted, these establishments had a growing clientele. Yet something had to have changed in the ambience of such places, Marina imagined. Something almost palpable, perhaps con-veyed through conversation—which no longer flowed freely, thus depriving the city's bars and cafés of their charm. Talk was instead carried out in hushed voices, suggesting a degree of intimidation. Occasionally, however, it came across as boom-ing, even raucous, as though commemorating victory. Never-theless, to those working in these establishments, simply seeking to make ends meet each month, it might have seemed that there was some semblance of routine in the air.

Marina would always see the country in her own distinct way, however. "The worst thing that happened in Chile," she told me years afterward, "came as time passed. When terror became the norm. And people stopped seeing. Some, out of ignorance. Others, by choice."

Listening to her, I remembered an article I had read recently, about certain photos in which everything appears normal because of what's been left out. Like the scenes of Paris dur-ing the German occupation, where what matters isn't so much what is shown in the image—but what isn't there. The cou-ples sipping coffee along the Rive Gauche or ambling hand in hand in the Bois de Boulogne are not in themselves notewor-thy. Except for the fact that, just steps away, at the exact same time, hundreds of Jews—men, women, and children—were being boarded onto trains and sent to concentration camps.

# PART FIVE

# 40

That conversation with Marina took place in 2004, three decades after her time in Santiago. We were on a walk around Lagoa, in Rio de Janeiro. She told me that, as a foreigner in Chile back then, she was an observer who led a privileged life and was spared the ordeals suffered by a significant percentage of the population. An observer, nevertheless, who considered herself entitled to examine the subject from the perspective of one affected by it. As if the violence committed against others had gotten to her.

"The worst came with the slow consolidation of this sad process...." She searched her memory for words that would best describe what she had witnessed. "The level of violence unleashed by the extreme right in Chile took everyone by surprise. The brutality was blatant. The Chilean military never hesitated. And where they weren't able to move in, they allowed paramilitary forces to operate. Without restrictions. Without the onus of having to answer to the government." She shook her head.

"It was all a mystery to me, considering the histories of the two countries I lived in. We weren't in a place like Argentina, where coups were common. Or even in Brazil, where we'd endured various forms of authoritarian rule. Chile, along with Uruguay, was a nation that was considered 'the Switzerland of South America.' And by pitiful and tragic coincidence, I ended up living in both of these Switzerlands, seeing the two of them sink into the same abyss just three months apart."

The sun was out in Rio, the kind of winter sun that comes and goes between the clouds, ideal for the leisurely stroll we were taking. The statue of Christ the Redeemer atop Corcovado remained blanketed in the distance. The vegetation on the hillside appeared vibrant in the early morning light, however. The city was a sight to behold, the way certain ancient ruins become a source of wonder, stripped of vanity and confident in their beauty.

"The atmosphere was stifling," Marina went on. "An authoritarian arrogance could be felt in the air on the most casual occasions. Not to mention the formal ones, which were always heavy and somber, even when they supposedly celebrated something light: the national holiday of a neighboring country, the opening of an art exhibit, a music or film festival. It was as if. . . as if a gray cloud had settled over the nation for good. The Chileans already tend to be sort of gloomy and depressed by nature. Imagine wrapping them in another layer of melancholy, which affected them all, even those who supported the government. It hung over the entire society, dividing families and friends, undermining the country in a thousand ways. Not even the prosperity that would gradually follow (as it invariably does for a certain social class in these situations) could compensate for this type of loss. It ended up silencing an entire generation."

Her speech had taken on a solemn tone. Marina was no longer a jean-clad friend ambling alongside me—and I soon understood why. My companion was gathering strength, like an athlete gearing up for the final sprint.

"The only reason I didn't go out of my mind, despite the nice, comfortable life I led, was that I met up with Paolo. The Italian photographer I told you about. That's when I really lost it. . . ."

My friend's eyes avoided mine as she struggled with an adolescent sense of shame.

"We struck up a conversation at a party hosted by a French colleague of Marcílio. At one point, completely out of the blue, he said to me, 'If there's one country where I don't want to put down any kind of roots, it's Chile.' And then he added, 'Paradoxically, it's also a place I haven't been able to tear myself away from for almost four months.' And with that, he cast his lure, in the form of a challenge: 'I feel alive thanks to this apparent contradiction.'"

*How many vulnerable women had he used the same lines on?* I asked myself.

"It was a ridiculous remark," Marina continued, now quite ready to delve into this part of her past. "But, on the flip side, I could relate because, unlike Paolo's experience, the contradictions of my life were slowly killing me.

"Three parties later, we met again. This time I was ready: I downed two glasses of wine when I saw him come in. With that, I built up the courage to broach the subject from my point of view. I mentioned his paradox. At the time, he didn't even seem to remember. I brought up mine. Then he remembered and led me up a set of stairs to the apartment terrace. Marcílio had stayed below with a group of friends. On the terrace, Paolo gave a naughty grin and pulled from his pocket a small canister, which he set on the railing. Then he wet his finger and held it up to check the wind. And he made his pitch: 'If you want, we can combine our contradictions. It's more fun than trying to figure out what we have in common.'"

She fell silent at this point. But she soon got back to what she was saying. "I took the plunge. For almost a year. That's how long I was involved with him. And with cocaine." She smoothed her hair, as if it needed tidying. She was a respectable lady, after all. With grandchildren...

"Meanwhile, Marcílio was busy with his private war. He was always at war. Overtly or covertly. Against Carlos Câmara, against his former boss in Montevideo, against the whole world.

Against himself, when it came down to it...And it was hardly worth it. Because, back then, he'd already gotten everything he wanted! He'd set up his office, hired his team, bought his cars, and received an entertainment budget from Itamaraty that was the equivalent of what the New York office got. So our house was always full of Chilean businessmen, Brazilians, even journalists.

"And Paolo was always there, with the crowd of journalists and photographers. Because he ended up making friends in that environment, more for the coke than for his talent, I suspect. Marcílio found him quite amusing. He treated him as a rarity, something between an objet d'art and a purebred dog. Our living room was always packed, no small feat, given the country's devastation. It was the beginning of Marcílio's social prestige, which he would build up from then on like few others.

"In Montevideo we'd hardly had anyone to the house except close friends and even then not very often. I think that had to do with Marcílio's job in technical cooperation. I never knew just what he did there, but"—she paused briefly and threw me a sideways glance, as if gauging my reaction—"we certainly had no social life. Whereas in Chile...no one at the embassy could believe it. Newton Cordeiro, whose influence continued to grow in certain circles, had more than repaid the favors Marcílio had done him. And despite his being a foreigner, the colonel had opened doors for us. Because money talks. The funds came from São Paulo businessmen, some of whom became friends of ours at the time. Nowadays, every so often I'll see one of their names cited in connection with the financing of torture in Brazil....

"Be that as it may, thanks to their money, and the middle ground established by Newton Cordeiro, who was a pro at such things, Marcílio had access to the upper entrepreneurial class. They were at our house around the clock, having lunch or dinner with Brazilians passing through, with whom they'd then spend hours locked in endless conversation, smoking Cuban cigars.

"The ambassador didn't understand any of it and was consumed by envy. Besides the military leaders, the only people he spent time with were the countless priests, whose masses he attended with his wife and children, and a handful of horribly boring traditional local families. Marcílio used to kid that when they were invited to dinner, they would show up covered in cobwebs! The guy had a great sense of humor.... But one thing is clear: the ambassador couldn't come to terms with Marcílio's standing." She gave a laugh. "They say the man would pace the hallways snorting, 'I want to see our business stats next year. That's what I want to see.' And, from what I heard, there was always someone to reply, 'By next year, Ambassador, our counselor will be long gone.'

"Marcílio kept a desk available for Newton in his office. Did you know he was killed a few years later in Beirut, or Damascus, selling arms? That's right—he was a dealer! There he'd be, twice a month, in Santiago! Always with his entrepreneurs in tow. He'd shower more and more lavish gifts on Pedro Henrique, who didn't even like his uncle Newton. That's what he wanted the poor boy to call him—*Uncle Newton,* can you believe it? Pedro Henrique couldn't stand the colonel."

"Wise child," I managed to whisper, in somewhat of a daze from all she'd spilled.

"The ambassador had attributed Marcílio's change of status at the embassy (which he referred to as 'one slick move') to his colleague at the president's office, our old boss in Montevideo. Carlos Câmara must have been the only one to realize the appointment had originated elsewhere. As Marcílio would say whenever he talked about him, 'He must have been just waiting for the shot that would take him down.' And true enough, a few years later, Carlos was forced to retire. When the military fell. Because of all those articles that came out about him in the press, written by who knows whom. Carlos still had another fifteen years of career ahead of him. He blew it."

# 41

Every time I recall our walk around Lagoa in 2004, and think about the plane crash in Europe that would take my friend's life later that year, I'm struck by how Marina's revelations foretold her farewell. Maybe because of the wistfulness I could feel between her words, even at the lighter moments of our conversation.

By that morning in June, Marina was no longer living with Nilo Montenegro and hadn't for some time. Yet she was doing quite well. She'd lost weight and didn't look anywhere near her age. She'd been rejuvenated once she'd gotten close to her kids again, after having lost custody during the divorce upon their return from Washington.

At the time of the separation, Pedro Henrique was eleven, Maria Isabel about five. Max had gained custody in the courts after a painful legal battle, which the social columns had followed with the tenaciousness usually reserved for celebrities. Based on some of the ugly details that came out, and others he invented, Max had poisoned his children against Marina for years, which had made contact between them difficult. The few days the children spent with their mother, moreover, contrasted with the stable lifestyle their father was able to provide them abroad, not to mention the standard of living they were used to as the children of a diplomat. This differed from Marina's situation, as her social standing had slipped following her father's death not long after his bank went under.

It was only once they were adults (and themselves married) that Pedro Henrique and Maria Isabel reconnected with their mother. And even then the relationship remained in flux. The reason was simple and said a lot about Marina's character: she had never revealed to her children why she'd left—much less what kind of man they had for a father.

"You understand, it was something I couldn't talk about," she confided along our walk. "If they have to know someday who their father really is, or was at one point, let them find out for themselves. Not from me. That's why the fight for the kids' affection was always so uneven between Marcílio and me. In their eyes, I was a mother who had abandoned ship. After creating a home with them in three different foreign cities, I had thrown in the towel and broken up our family." She stopped walking and looked out over the water of Lagoa.

"For years my kids associated Brazil, where they only settled on a more permanent basis in 1981, with a home that was no longer *ours* but rather belonged to a threesome that would alternately have their dad or me at the head. Later, the kids found out about my involvement with drugs, thanks to Marcílio, even though I'd cleaned up my act by then and had been sober for more than ten years. He didn't need to do that."

We resumed our walk. "I heeded my father's advice as long as I could and focused on my kids. Until there was a point, in Washington, when I couldn't take it anymore. The last straw was when Max had the nerve to invite a CIA operative to have lunch with us, thinking I wouldn't be able to tell. The guy didn't need to have it stamped on his forehead. The look in his eye was enough, and the crew cut. That's when I left. I packed a bag, picked up the kids from school, and went straight to a hotel. And from there to Brazil.

"The truth is, I'd checked out a long time before that. Since Montevideo. Since Nilo.... Paolo was just a passing thing, exacerbated by my discovery of drugs. The rupture, the internal kind that bleeds without anyone's noticing, happened with Nilo during our encounter in Montevideo. I never recovered from what happened on that street corner."

I remembered that evening in 1983, more than twenty years before, when Marina had mentioned that first rocky period of their marriage, in Uruguay during the early 1970s.

"Today I no longer know if I stuck around so long because of the kids, or my aging dad, or because I felt I was somehow to blame. Maybe I was hopeful... or afraid. Sometimes I felt like a character in a 1940s gangster movie, one of those noir films the two of you were always going on about—Itamaraty's own Barbara Stanwyck or Ida Lupino. Marcílio was never physically abusive; he wasn't that type. But he hurt me in a much deeper way. In Montevideo, I started to drink more heavily. All of which would later explain Paolo. Anyone could have seen it coming...."

"The acclaimed photographer!" I exclaimed, with a hint of envy I chose to disguise.

"Laugh all you want, but Paolo was an interesting guy. And he led a pretty wild life back then, before he met me. He came to Chile by bus, from Bolivia, where he'd done a photo shoot for *National Geographic*. He had a kilo of coke in his backpack. A kilo! I don't know what he was thinking. He told me the stuff had come from the Indians he'd befriended after living with their tribe for so many weeks. Could have... The fact is that he arrived in Chile a week before the coup. In other words, two or three days before us. An Italian journalist, a tourist, no one bothered to go through his bags, which held more dirty clothes than clean ones and a few souvenirs he'd hidden the drug in.

"Days later, all hell broke loose in Santiago: there were bombings, tanks, shootings, corpses in the streets. What to do with the coke? He could hide it or flush it down the toilet. He decided to hide it. So he removed one of the tiles above the little balcony near his room, waterproofed the package, and tucked the stash under the roof of the hostel where he was staying. Then he hit the streets with his camera. Allende was dead, Pinochet and his posse had seized power, and Paolo had a massive amount of coke hidden just outside his room. Minus what he'd snorted before heading out."

She glanced over to make sure I was still following the story, then went on. "Marcílio and I were stranded at our hotel. Pedro Henrique was shivering with a fever. The day after the coup, the two of us took off in a hurry for Brazil. I don't know if I was dreaming or not, but I think smoke was still rising from La Moneda."

"Might well have been," I said.

"Paolo later told me he managed to reach the burning palace with great difficulty. He must have passed right beneath our windows. And then he realized that he'd forgotten to put film in his camera! That's how far gone he was . . . a professional photographer! Trucks piled with corpses were passing by, passengers in cars were waving handkerchiefs, singing or shouting, loudspeakers were announcing the curfew. Shots rang out in the streets, hundreds of rounds were fired; protestors were chased, cornered, and gunned down right in front of him. And he had no film in his camera. He began to take photos without film, he was so high.

"He was eventually arrested by a patrol. They yanked the camera out of his hands, smashed it with the butts of their rifles, had him strip, and went through his clothes, leaving him squatting naked for an hour at the police station. But they ended up letting him go, he howled so much. . . . Crazy, and Italian to boot—it was too much for the first day of civil war!"

I pictured the Italian, racing through the city streets, dealing not with the horrors but with the impossibility of recording them. Marina, not far from him, in her hotel room, worrying less about what was going on outside her window than the sick child in her arms.

"When I dove into my affair with Paolo, I sometimes hoped that Marcílio would discover that I was leading a secret life. To replace the one he'd inflicted on me."

"I was in Los Angeles at the time," I said, in an effort not to leave her completely alone amid her memories. "My first post. When I heard you were getting involved with drugs, I was concerned, knowing things weren't going well between you and Max. I thought you were going to go under."

"I did," she replied, laughing. "And I started to enjoy experimenting with other things too. I tried acid, mescaline, mushrooms.... Marcílio had no idea. He was always too busy. Thanks to Cordeiro, he'd boxed the ambassador into a corner and was now the all-powerful head of the commercial sector. As long as he could call home at the last minute and ask me to throw together a formal dinner for a dozen people, and then find everything all set, flowers at the center of the table and waiters on hand, the rest didn't really matter."

The breeze had blown hair into her face, which she smoothed back. "When did you find out about Paolo?" she asked then, a bit more relaxed. "When I told you about him at my apartment in Jardim Botânico after my dad died?"

"No," I answered, in the same casual tone. "Long before then, in Brasilia, at the ministry. Around the time things started to go sour between the two of you. I found out from some of the diplomats' wives. I just couldn't understand how Max didn't—"

"*Suspect?*" she interrupted. "Marcílio paid no attention to me!"

Soon, however, she turned to the topic that had insidiously slipped into our conversation. "The diplomats' wives..." She sighed. "Pathetic women, with few exceptions. Someone should write a book about them one day. A coffee-table book, underwritten by Yves Saint Laurent, Gucci, Valentino, Paco Rabanne, Givenchy, Chanel... Squeezed into their leather or suede skirts, tottering on their high heels, flashing almost identical scarves, bags, and belts. How they craned their necks, keeping an eye on one another...." She paused, lost in memories. "And to think that I was one of them," she said at last. "It's not easy being the wife of a diplomat. At least, it wasn't back then. Today it's different. Nearly all of them work or are in school. Some even join the foreign service. And do a better job than their husbands. But in my day..."

She sighed again. "What's awful is that they depended not on their husbands—which was natural in our generation—but on their husbands' accomplishments. The more successful their spouses were, the fuller of themselves the wives became. And the wives of the failures, the ones who weren't promoted, or were timid and awkward, tended to shrivel, like wilted flowers. They would try to blend into the background and were the last to serve themselves at buffets. On the other hand, they were also the first to take lovers, as if wishing to punish their poor husbands for the humiliation..."

"...they'd suffered, thanks to them," I finished.

Her voice sounded feeble. "It was a perverse system, based on incredibly backward values. In the case of the all-mighties, everything happened with class, by way of loudly whispered words, upturned noses, solemn gestures, looks dripping with irony and indifference. They only realized their true worth once their husbands were dethroned. Then they'd disappear for two or three months, go on a diet or have plastic surgery, and discreetly slip back onto the scene. Just like actors who accept supporting roles once they lose their memory or get old."

From my less than responsive state, she must have realized that she was going overboard. And wearing me out. Enough so that she toned down her remarks.

"There were exceptions, of course, radiant women full of life, university professors, visual artists, writers. But they were the minority, viewed by the others with distrust."

"As threats, perhaps."

"Maybe...I don't know."

"What about Nilo?" I asked, trying once more to avoid going against the light on that beautiful morning the gods had given us. "When did you two meet again?"

We'd stopped at a coconut stand. Marina didn't answer me right away. "After the disastrous scene in Montevideo?" she finally asked.

I nodded.

"I didn't see Nilo again until 1981, when I came back to Rio, having already decided to leave Marcílio. I happened to run into him at a restaurant in Leblon. I've always been nearsighted and my glasses were in my bag. It took me a minute to recognize the man approaching the group I was with. Until he hugged me. The best, warmest hug I've ever gotten in my life! At least that's how it felt at the time. As if nothing bad had happened between the two of us. But this time I didn't let him disappear around the corner. We left the restaurant arm in arm. My friends understood, some even applauded. We left the party and went straight to bed. He had a huge bed."

We had a laugh over that. Christ the Redeemer poked out of the clouds for a few seconds to bless the long night of passion between the two and then withdrew again.

"Early the next morning, he asked me to forgive him for that afternoon in Montevideo. He explained that a few days earlier, his best friend had been kidnapped at his front door. And been taken back to Brazil in an air force jet."

"In an air force jet?"

"That's what he said. He was convinced that our embassy had taken part in the operation. The attachés for sure, or at least one of them. And the ambassador was probably in on it too. That man was evil. Anyway..."

For a minute, she seemed to have lost her train of thought. I let her pick it back up on her own.

"It seems officials came from Rio to help the Uruguayan police with the kidnapping. At the time, Uruguay was still a democratic country. At least on paper. Their coup didn't happen until later, in June of 1973. I remember it well. But the two armed forces had been collaborating for years. And the police in both countries as well. Because of the Brazilian exiles who were living there. Which explains Nilo's horror when he saw me associated with such people.

"Today, there's a lot of talk about Operation Condor, but these countries were collaborating long before then, although informally. Operation Condor might just have been its most radical manifestation. And the Argentinean military had yet to come up with that insane practice of hurling prisoners into the ocean. Very sick people indeed." She smiled with bitter irony. "A lot has come out on this subject in the newspapers recently. As time goes by, we end up finding out everything. Or almost everything. Not in detail. But the big picture."

"What about Nilo's friend?" I asked.

"Henrique or Antonio...I don't remember his last name now either."

Having finished our drinks, we left the empty coconuts and continued our walk. It was Sunday. A few bicycles zipped by us.

"In Montevideo, Marcílio kept me trapped in his web," she commented. "A soft and comfortable web. Whenever one of the threads broke, he would draw close to me again. Enough to give me a shred of hope. And when that wasn't enough, we'd end up in bed together. I always had the feeling he was thinking about other things at those times, though...."

"Other women?"

"*Other women?* No...I don't think so. Maybe...My impression was that he was thinking about other things. He always seemed busy. And he was never able to completely disconnect from his problems. Or from his ghosts." She stopped, again facing the water.

"But we carried on. At some point, in Chile, he sensed that I was becoming more distant, not to mention anxious and irritable. Coke has an edge to it.... We had a serious fight when I leaned over to get the salt shaker at a dinner party one of his business cronies was hosting and a drop of blood dripped from my nose onto the white tablecloth. The host turned pale, as did the people nearby. The cartilage between my nostrils wasn't in great shape, and I'd spent the afternoon snorting. All I remember is the terrible silence that fell over the table, from one end to the other, while the person sitting next to me tilted my head back and lent me his handkerchief."

After another pause, she returned to her past. "On the car ride home, Marcílio berated me for what he called, in his usual manner, *an unpleasant incident.* I didn't say a word. And he didn't push it. But at home he brought up the subject again. He seemed suspicious more than annoyed. As if *something strange* might be going on with me." This memory seemed to have been particularly painful.

"The next day he came to his senses. 'After all, nothing serious happened,' he said, by way of an apology. 'It was an accident that could have happened to anyone.' But now I was the one who didn't want to talk. That's when he began to see me for the first time ... and realized that he might be starting to lose me. Not that he suspected anything or anyone. But I think his sixth sense finally kicked in. And it was high time! In a matter of days, fear grew into alarm and then panic. After all, I was the one with both the social and emotional clout." Her voice didn't carry the slightest trace of victory, only tremendous fatigue.

"From then on, he made an enormous effort to win me back. By coincidence, Paolo's coke ran out around the same time. We must have snorted a half kilo each in twelve months. And the crazy fool decided to go back to Bolivia to get more. I lent him some money. But he never returned. We weren't getting along very well by then, I suspected he'd had other affairs.... Anyway, the fact is that he never came back. He might have been caught crossing the border with the stuff. Or been killed in Bolivia. Things weren't easy there either...."

A long silence ensued. It was, in fact, quite a story for someone who had been brought up at the traditional Jacobina School and been a member of Rio de Janeiro's elite country club set ever since childhood. Now there was a gaunt woman pushing sixty beside me, looking as if the scenes she'd just shared had taken their toll in years.

"Be that as it may, I decided to wait awhile. Besides giving up the coke, I cut down on booze and drank only socially. I started to do yoga. Marcílio, with this whole business of working in the commercial area, had also changed, no longer prone to the bouts of melancholy he suffered from in Montevideo. He kept dealing with the same old scumbags, of course, but they were better dressed, some liked opera, had table manners; in a few cases, they spoke other languages. So overall, our life wasn't that bad.

"Marcílio had an entertaining side, which you knew well. He was funny, sophisticated, pleasant to be around. Socially, he treated everyone as equals, with an intimacy that fascinated people. In the meantime, there had been a change of ambassadors. The new boss was a good guy and had nothing whatsoever to do with Pinochet's gang, the way the last one did. Anyway, things were finally improving—not for the country but for us, in our little world. And the next thing I knew, I was pregnant. Our sweet Maria Isabel was born a few months before we were transferred to Washington."

# 42

We continued to walk slowly and steadily, as befits older people concerned with avoiding potholes and other perils in their path. Until Marina gathered the courage to ask, "Did you ever manage to find out anything... anything *more concrete* about him?"

I'd been bracing myself for the question for years. I knew it was bound to come sooner or later. Just as I knew that, when the moment arrived, I'd try to handle the subject with the precision of a surgeon opening Max's belly in search of a tumor. I didn't intend to mislead her about the patient's condition, but I tried not to say anything to depress her further. I had to give her *something*, however. Especially since Marina knew that I hadn't stopped seeking the key to the puzzle that, for better or worse, connected us. Although she had left the diplomatic scene following her divorce, I had remained.

"I've come to some conclusions," I finally ventured. "Nothing that enables me to put together a full picture. At any rate, I prefer not to poison you with the details. Particularly because, for the time being, they're incomplete."

Given her disappointed look, I took her in my arms and said, "Marina, Max's story is like a curse: it follows me. His secrets hound me, but in fragments. That's how I feel: hounded by fragments of *his* past. It's as if someone, from heaven or hell, won't leave me in peace. Every six months, I get wind of something new about him, or a door opens onto some madness relating to him, or to the world he was caught up in."

"It's a devilish world, isn't it?" she said.

I decided to get ahead of her. "I can tell you about something that happened last year, under the current government. A sad incident, more than anything." I paused. I was offering her something personal. Personal and recent. In lieu of the unvarnished answers she was craving.

She said nothing, so I went ahead. "I was in Brazil when my youngest daughter graduated from the Rio Branco Institute."

"I forgot to congratulate you!" she interjected happily. "A daughter in the foreign service...third generation...quite impressive."

"It sure is. That was in April of 2003. The Workers' Party had won the elections a few months earlier and was finally in power." I hesitated briefly to decide the best way to revisit the moment. "Graduation month at Rio Branco varies slightly from year to year," I continued, "but it always coincides with a date known in Brasilia as Diplomats' Day, usually celebrated in April or May at the Itamaraty Palace. Once the formal part of the ceremony in the lower level's auditorium was over, all of us—the president, officials, diplomats, graduates, and guests—headed to the second level."

"Where Burle Marx's hanging gardens are!"

"Exactly. We walked in a slow procession, taking the stairs up toward the large terrace where the reception preceding the president's luncheon for the newly graduated diplomats and their families was to be held. At that gathering, small circles of people cluster in conversation and then wander, alone or in pairs, from one group to another."

My lens had covered the middle ground. Time to zoom in. "And it was in one of these groups that I found myself face-to-face with Max."

"Our big con artist," Marina joked nervously.

"Our con artist," I agreed, "who greeted me as warmly as ever and..."

"*And...?*" she pressed, seeing me stop as if faltering.

"...and took me by the arm with his usual familiarity, steering us to the long railing overlooking the esplanade, all the while congratulating me effusively on my daughter's graduation. Not quite sure how to react, I just let him lead me along."

"The vantage point that overlooks the Congress and Senate buildings," Marina echoed. "And directly faces the Ministry of Justice. A fine setting for a conversation between the two of you. *Power, justice...*"

Things would progress more smoothly if Marina didn't interrupt me. The frequency with which she did so, however, conveyed just how tense she was. As if she wanted to know—yet was afraid to hear—what I was about to reveal.

"Max professed to regret that we hadn't seen each other in so long. I didn't say anything. Then he cut to the chase. He wanted to know if I held a grudge for the two hours we'd spent together at a wedding reception in Alto da Boa Vista twenty years earlier. I thought it best to say no, so as not to rehash bygones with him, especially on that particular day. In order to placate him, I actually said that, on the contrary, I had good memories of the get-together." I closed my eyes for a moment, then proceeded. "We stood in silence, watching the cars pass along the esplanade. He knew I was lying. And in his company I experienced the paralysis one feels in certain nightmares. I wanted to get back to my daughter's side as quickly as possible. I was afraid that Max's insistence on staying with me would ruin the beauty of the day and what it meant to my family."

Marina nodded.

"It was that feeling of powerlessness," I continued after a moment, "that led me to have a change of heart. I took a sharp turn in our conversation, even running the risk of being impertinent. I told your ex-husband what I really thought of him. And I told him just how much it bothered me that, despite his political maneuvering, or because of it, he'd ended up having such a successful career."

"Marcílio must have been less than amused."

"As usual, he refused to be strong-armed and stood his ground. Then I ended up saying that under normal circumstances, if we lived in a serious country, he would have been exiled. Or forced into retirement. The way Carlos Câmara was—"

"Oh, boy," Marina interrupted. "You really—"

I cut her off. The last thing I wanted now was to get off track.

"As I continued, Max bristled with each line. My harangue was much longer than I'm recounting to you here. Definitely harsher and more detailed. His spine stiffened completely when I brought up Carlos Câmara. Max seemed to be made of stone. Leaning on the railing, I held firm, maintaining the tone of one keen to wrap up the subject. I said that, for me, he had been at least partly responsible for what had happened in the countries he'd been in back then with his poker buddies, whom I got around to calling 'pathetic allies.' He and other colleagues, whose names remained unknown until recently. Then I went back to criticizing the fact that Câmara had been the only one to shoulder the blame and be repudiated by the ministry—by the whole institution of the ministry—and by his colleagues as Judas. Because that was all too easy. A known crook was made a scapegoat and the rest of the herd moved along in peace. It was easy and, above all, practical. Not to mention convenient. And you know what his reaction to these affronts was?"

"No," she answered in a neutral tone, "but I can well imagine."

"No, Marina, that's just it. *You can't imagine.* That's why Max continues to be the great con artist he is, the greatest of them all: he's always pulling another rabbit out of his hat."

She kept quiet, waiting.

"With the self-confidence he exudes like few others, he told me, 'Carlos Câmara went to the well once too often.'

"And, like an idiot, I fell into his trap. Fortified by carefully crafted words, I laughed and said, 'Forgive me, Max, and I'm actually sorry to have to tell you this, considering our old friendship and the good times we had together—some of the best of my younger days—but I've never seen anyone go to the well as often as you.' I looked at him smugly. 'So come off it!' "

Marina closed her eyes. She'd witnessed such scenes countless times. She just hadn't imagined that in this instance I would be the victim.

"At that point, Max baited me with a common line. 'Carlos was thirsty for power,' he said matter-of-factly."

Not a peep from Marina. The stage was all mine.

" 'You don't say,' I scoffed, savoring my victory. 'And how about you, Max? What were you thirsty for?' "

Marina was now staring at the ground. She kept her arms crossed, as if the wind were picking up around her.

" 'The same, of course,' he replied, smiling even more broadly. 'Only poor Carlos...poor Carlos went to the wrong well.' "

"Ever the magician." Marina sighed. "Unrivaled, as always."

"I was so stunned that I automatically repeated his line. Even worse, Marina, I managed to turn my echo into a question, which ended up dousing the indignation I was feeling: 'Carlos went to the *wrong well?*' "

I had the impression that Marina wasn't even listening to me. Like someone who looks away from heavy or upsetting images on a movie screen or the nightly news.

"After giving me a good-natured glance, Max repeated, 'That's right, he drank from the wrong well.' And he concluded, 'He only saw what was directly in front of him. Whereas...' "

I finished describing the scene to Marina. Turning his back on the ministry esplanade, Max had slowly rotated, a motion I had to follow, given how close to him I was standing. And he'd gestured broadly with his arm from right to left through the space in front of us. His fingers glided past Burle Marx's suspended gardens, descended to the people on the marble terrace—lost in their hopes and longings—and, without lingering, moved over the circle formed by the president and his entourage, all lively and elated. With the elegance of an orchestra conductor, his hand then swept past various groups of men in tailored suits, hovered over well-coiffed made-up women, reaching the new graduates and their relatives, until finally landing on the works of art, which ranged from Aleijadinho to Portinari, from colonial furniture to Persian rugs. Once his panorama was complete, he leaned toward me and whispered, "... Whereas *this* is what I pursued."

*There you have it,* he seemed to be saying as he saluted me with a slight bow of the head, instantly transporting us both back to the age when aristocrats and diplomats had mingled in the sumptuous palaces of the past, all dressed up in lace-trimmed outfits, hiding their fists behind smiles and music—the same fists that, in our time, would have to answer for the violence that had engulfed us for twenty years.

Unlike his peers, he had been among the privileged few to live in the present without, at any moment, losing sight of his future. Whereas we ... we had remained suspended in time, tied to the past, facing realities that had nothing to do with our values. How could we envision the future if the present reflected fear, torture, and resentment?

# 43

"My poor friend," Marina said at last, hugging me, as if wanting to give closure to the pitiful sequence I'd just described. Soon enough, though, she raised her voice and protested, "In the meantime, you did a complete about-face and responded just as any diplomat up against a wall would: you simply avoided my question. I asked—"

"I know," I replied somewhat flustered. "You asked if I'd found out anything more concrete about Max. You still want an answer?"

Marina decided not to press. If she wanted to reopen old wounds, she no longer had a way of doing so that morning. We got up from the bench where we had sat for a moment.

"Did you read his speech?" She'd changed the subject while staying on topic. Given my silence, she specified. "Have you read it? The most recent speech?"

"On disarmament?" I asked in a distant tone.

"No." And she paused awhile. "On human rights," she said finally.

"In Geneva?" I inquired, my interest piqued. "No, I haven't read it. Why?"

"The kids showed me the transcript, all excited. The two of them are so proud of their dad.... You have to see how he lambastes the military regimes of the past and the atrocities committed"—here she made air quotes with her fingers—"*in those terrible times.*"

"You don't say," I answered, warming up to what Marina was implying. Much as I tried to deny it, Max continued to fascinate me. For the quality and variety of his flaws, whether these were rooted in pure cynicism, as was the case here, or stemmed from more subterranean sources. "Unbelievable, isn't it?"

Marina agreed.

"Good thing the generals and the cardinal, to whom he owes everything, have already met their maker," I added in a cheerier tone.

"They were the ones who commanded and countermanded the country," Marina recalled in a voice that almost sounded admiring. "Not to mention the corrosive effect of the greed they awakened around them."

"I read a line about Eichmann in the *Economist* the other day that applies to almost all of them: 'Like most of his fellow Nazis, he was monstrous only when fate gave him power.' " Marina still had Max on her mind. As for me, I proceeded in my futile and solitary effort to settle my score with the past. "And to think that the only one of the five president-generals who could have aspired to be a statesman would be the same to declare that 'torture was necessary.' "

Marina interrupted me and brought up what was troubling her. "The kids didn't understand my silence when I finished the last page of their father's speech on human rights. I couldn't say a single word. I couldn't even try." Without hiding the bitterness overtaking her, she laughed. "They must have thought I missed Marcílio . . . and the charmed life we'd led together! I'm told that people in the president's office are *still* enthralled by him. And that Marcílio's reputation in these upper echelons continues to grow. They say his name has been considered for second-in-command at the Foreign Ministry."

"Secretary-general?"

Marina didn't even acknowledge my surprise. She'd gone back to her own lonely track. "A guy who spent part of his life persecuting union leaders and intellectuals and who now gets posted to our top embassies abroad. He denied passports to many—that much I know. And he may have done worse. Far worse..." A long look in my direction, a final silent plea for an answer. I chose to follow the flight of the birds over the sailboats. "He's even admired by the former guerrillas he fought," she exclaimed. "He's applauded, praised for his speeches. He continues to hoodwink everyone!"

We both burst out laughing. Then a novel feeling came over me. Marina seemed to be sensing something similar. Max, who until then had kept us apart—lost as we'd been in decades of doubts and uncertainties about him—had suddenly left the scene. With that, he had drawn us together. The laughter had freed us from his story, making room for us to create our own—if we so desired. No matter how modest and tentative it might be. This unexpected emotion took us by surprise.

We kept walking. In a totally different frame of mind now. I took Marina's hand in my own. And she, just as naturally, interlaced her fingers with mine. A young couple with a baby stroller and two other children was heading in our direction. The small family soon passed by us, the mother smiling at the baby, the father cleaning his sunglasses, the kids having fun.

"Felipe!" the dad shouted. "Don't go near the road! Stay by your sister..."

We watched the five moving along, the boy zigzagging down the sidewalk with his arms out like an airplane, dashing from one side to the other, the worried father hurrying to close the space between them, the mother pushing the stroller, and the little girl carefully sidestepping holes to keep her pristine shoes from getting dirty.

"That's what I imagined having one day, when I got married." Marina sighed, as if returning to her senses.

We continued with our morning stroll. Christ the Redeemer emerged from behind the clouds once more. From the looks of it, to stay this time...Life went on, with its joys and sorrows. Always moved by memories that would never completely fade. Memories that, with a little luck, might prevent the dead from being forgotten. And lead some of the living to pale amid the guilt overtaking them a bit more each night.

"Should we head back?" Marina suggested. "It's getting late, isn't it?"

These were questions that had to do with the realities of our present but that would in no way affect our future. Or so we thought.

"Okay," I answered. After a minute, I added, as if to myself, "But it was a delightful walk."

Looking over my shoulder, I said goodbye to Lagoa then. Not knowing that I was also saying goodbye to Marina forever.

"It was so nice to see you again," she said softly, looping her arm through mine as we crossed the street. "When will you be back in Rio?"

"Soon," I promised confidently.

When we reached the opposite sidewalk, I hailed a cab and gave my friend a long, affectionate hug. A hug that, ever since her death, means more to me with each passing day.

# 44

In 2006, nearly two years after Marina's death, when I was stationed in Los Angeles for the second time, I went back to Rio de Janeiro to visit my children. Leafing through the pages of a newspaper on the way there, I came across the announcement of the funeral mass for Colonel João Vaz's wife. I called him when I arrived. Ever since meeting in Vienna, we'd exchanged Christmas cards and spoken a few times by phone.

At first he wasn't able to place me in his circle of acquaintances, for he was still suffering the impact of his loss. But once I tried to explain my absence from the mass, and mentioned our time together in Vienna, the colonel, to my embarrassment, began to weep over the phone. "My poor Matilde," he sobbed. "You can't imagine how touched she was by the teddy bear you sent our grandson!"

"Who must be a big boy by now!" I exclaimed, trying to rally him. "He must be ten or eleven, right?" I had actually forgotten about the bear I'd sent his grandson — essentially a tribute to him, the colonel, and the big-hearted way he'd lumbered along the streets of Vienna in search of our restaurants. But it seemed the stuffed animal had left a lasting emotional impression on the veteran's memory.

"It was the first gift that made Ernestinho laugh and clap his hands together!" He then began to speak of his other grandchildren, now totaling three. His sadness seemed to lessen momentarily. Memories rooted in the pleasures of the table quickly followed and he soon invited me to dinner. We agreed to get together two nights later. The colonel recommended a restaurant in Ipanema, the name and address of which he had me repeat. He said he'd take care of the reservation and expect me around eight. "I can't guarantee a fireplace," he joked before hanging up. "But the food is quite good."

I arrived at the restaurant a little late on the designated night. The colonel was already seated at a table in the rear and signaled me over with a jovial wave. As I approached, however, I noticed that it was with difficulty that he rose to greet me. He had aged quite visibly. An entire decade had elapsed since we'd last seen one another, and at his stage of life the years usually take a toll. Even so, he gave me a big hug, which immediately whisked us back to our nights in Austria.

After speaking briefly of his deceased wife, we attacked our caipirinhas. Within minutes, we were engrossed in lively conversation. At some point, he showed me photos of his grandkids. "This one here is Ernestinho," he said with open pride, sliding a picture of a chubby young fellow under my nose. He followed up with a few comments about his daughter and son-in-law, who didn't live far from him. "Which is convenient, given the onset of old age," he acknowledged a bit wistfully.

Soon enough, however, the invisible link that had brought us together in Vienna came up in conversation. "How about Max?" the colonel asked. "What do you hear of him?"

I said I hadn't seen him for some time but that I'd been following his career from afar with the same admiration.

"Admiration and bewilderment," he joked, eyeing me as he took another sip of his drink.

But the conversation had yet to wind its way through assorted de rigueur topics before returning to the subject. We talked about Brazilian politics and the economy, which individuals were rising and falling on the power scale, of soccer victories and upsets.

Once dinner was served, Max joined us again, only this time accompanied by a supporting actor, another old acquaintance of ours, Eric Friedkin.

"Max was always a source of fascination to Eric," the colonel remarked, as though speaking of another mutual friend. He looked up from his plate. "How's your food?"

"Excellent." And it was.

I took advantage of the lull to acknowledge, in the same warm tone, the new character's entrance from the wings. "Eric Friedkin! The CIA's station head in South America!"

"Chief of station, or COS," he corrected, with a mouthful. "Those were crucial years in our region. The toughest stage…"

He glanced to both sides since one never knew who might be listening. For in those days, the hunt for the Fascist witches had dropped from its lofty platform of political righteousness to the trivial level of beauty salon gossip. (*"That guy? Don't even tell me, hon. They say he was one helluva torturer,"* and then, after a furtive pause, in an even lower voice, *"during those heavy years of repression."*)

"…after our military movement in sixty-four," he finished at last. Pleased with his retrieval of the formula he'd been resorting to since our times in Vienna, he concluded, "He settled in Uruguay and from there he followed the developments in Montevideo, Chile, and Argentina."

*Followed*, I mused, taking great pains to keep the smile frozen on my lips.

Luckily, we were interrupted right then by an acquaintance of the colonel, who took him aside and expressed his condolences. After which the two got caught up talking in a corner, while I retreated into my thoughts. Still under the effect of the casual way my host had mentioned Eric Friedkin's activities, I recalled Max's outburst at the infamous wedding reception more than twenty years earlier, when he had drawn on Merce Cunningham's genius to establish a parallel between the coups taking place in the region and a choreographed operation inspired and coordinated by the CIA.

Apologizing profusely, the colonel returned to his seat. He seemed quite pleased with himself. "A former colleague from the army," he explained. "He invited me to a reunion of the old guard. To see if we can improve the retired officers' pensions."

After waving over the waiter, he asked, "Should we move on to beers?" Perhaps keeping tabs on his own wallet, the congenial colonel had discreetly turned down the wine list the waiter had tried in vain to hand him. "Now, where were we?"

"Eric Friedkin. And his admiration for Max."

"Right. But *admiration* isn't quite the word. It was more of a periodic *fascination*. Sometimes he would be impressed by him. But generally speaking, I think he was more *intrigued*. As if he couldn't place him in any given context. He wasn't alone in that. And yet he considered himself an excellent judge of character. He was never wrong. After all, that's what he'd been trained to do." And with a smile of virtuousness, which age alone confers on men who have been up to no good but may escape hell nonetheless: "That and *to deceive!*"

Perhaps regretting the snide remark, he quickly added, "You can't believe how moved I was by his phone call when he learned of Matilde's passing." He recalled the old family ties, strengthened by Eric's daughter, Nancy, who had become Ernestinho's godmother. "I'll always remember the winter nights in Montevideo when we'd roast marshmallows on sticks in our fireplaces. The girls were little and loved the fun of it."

I averted my eyes from his, which were suddenly teary, and wondered what else Eric Friedkin might have been planning to roast those particular nights, with other kinds of sticks, after singing lullabies to the two daughters.

Meanwhile, the colonel seemed ready to get back to the subject at hand. "He was extremely clever. So clever that, where

Max was concerned (and this he only confessed to me years later), Eric simply had the *British* approach our friend. That way the CIA stayed out of it. With an added benefit: he gave Max the illusion that he was his own man, that he was outsmarting everyone. Funny, isn't it? In other words, on the surface, for training the Uruguayan police forces, the CIA used Max and Itamaraty. But on the sly, the agency allowed the British to find out what Max really knew. Eric had a French name for the maneuver. It was called a trompe something or other."

"Trompe l'oeil."

"That's it. Do you guys use that at Itamaraty too?"

"All the time. Long before Machiavelli and Renaissance painting, early sixteenth-century diplomacy invented the trompe l'oeil. It was based on a kind of visual engineering, which works to trick the eye and..."

"I see," said the colonel, showing little interest in these details.

I decided to press further. "But what did Max know in the end? That was so...so important?"

"Nothing, at first."

"Nothing?"

"That's what was so curious. It was the Brits who gradually put him on the trail to what they wanted to know. To what *the Americans wanted to know.*"

"In what area?" Ten years earlier, in Vienna, the colonel had limited himself to saying that Eric had "somewhat unintelligibly" mentioned "uranium smuggling, nuclear energy, and Germany" in the same sentence. But I thought it preferable not to evoke that particular language right then.

"I know it's been many years," he said, after choosing the less soiled end of his napkin to wipe his mouth. "And that this story is old. But it remains secret. And your colleague is still active. Our famous Max. If the subject becomes public, he may wish to retaliate. Although people who live in glass houses..."

Here he had a timely recollection. "By the way, I met up with him a few months ago."

"With Max? Where?"

"At the funeral of our former ambassador in Montevideo. The Caped Crusader, they used to call him. After retiring, he went to work for the Germans." He laughed, as if introducing the Germans into the equation amused him for some reason. "The old man worked for them right up until he died. And he left behind a book of memoirs, in which he didn't even try to hide his political preferences. The funniest part is that we, at the SNI, had a file on him the size of a truck." Renewed laughter, the source of which I had no way of identifying. "He left out the best part of his book..." He continued to laugh alone. It wasn't possible that such joy could be attributed solely to the Germans, a people who may have their redeeming qualities but aren't known for their humor.

"So what's the lowdown on the ambassador?" I inquired.

"It's hilarious. But you won't hear it from me."

We'd had so many beers that he gradually gave in. Deep down, the colonel loved a good story. Especially if it strayed beyond the confines of security protocols. "He had a hobby."

"Oh, really? What was that?"

"Photography."

"You don't say."

"He had a small studio on Avenida Marechal Floriano, not far from Itamaraty, over near the Colégio Pedro II. They say all kinds of kinky activities went on there. Little schoolgirls in uniform and everything."

"Don't tell me, Colonel."

"The Caped Crusader had a second hidden agenda. Even hotter than the nuclear reactors."

"Nuclear reactors?" I asked innocently.

The colonel tried to backpedal, but it was too late. He'd already said too much. He hung on to the studio like someone clinging to a life raft. "He was up to no good in that studio with the little girls. And he photographed his exploits. The girls playing with themselves. Or with him, two, three, at a time... Until one of the mothers informed the police. Then we had to intervene. The girl was twelve years old."

"You personally?"

"*Me?*...Oh, no. I didn't even know him in those days. I only found out about this much later. Years after returning from Montevideo, that's how secret it was. No. The orders came from above, from the highest level."

"Who would have thought...and the nuclear reactors...in Vienna, you..."

"What nuclear reactors?" How to go back? He tried to sideline the issue.

"Eric is the one who knows about that."

Cutting him slack, I said, "The man who always knew it all." Given his silence, I resorted to the past. "During one of our conversations in Vienna, you said that—"

But the colonel was no fool. He dealt with my persistence by taking refuge in his recent sorrow. "Eric's phone call really got to me. I'd forgotten that he too had lost his wife. My daughter had to prompt me. My dear Betty..." Another pause. And finally, the seed of an idea, perhaps to free himself of my questions, without being rude to the teddy-bear guy. "Incidentally..."

Given all I'd learned in Vienna about conversation with the colonel, I simply continued to nurse my warm beer.

"...He's your neighbor."

"Eric Friedkin? *My neighbor?*"

"Yes. Didn't you say you're stationed in LA? For the second time? So you must know the area pretty well. He lives near San Diego. It's less than two hours on the freeway. Right on the border with Mexico. The other side of Tijuana. Dreadful place Tijuana is, by the way."

"Who would have thought," I couldn't help but murmur. I was truly surprised. Eric Friedkin...at my disposal, if I so desired. Served up on the finest tray—one provided by a mutual friend. It was the kind of news that generates both curiosity and unease.

The waiter approached with the check. The colonel firmly prevented my taking care of it. "Your money is no good here!" he exclaimed, grabbing the bill.

Returning to the subject that now seemed to be thrilling him—and troubling me: "I'm going to send an e-mail introducing you to him as someone I trust. You'll enjoy talking with Eric. And he with you. Eric is nothing like a typical CIA agent these days. On the contrary, he's become an old dinosaur, just like me. Not that he's changed in his way of thinking, he hasn't changed in that respect. But he's mellowed, lost his edge." His eyes beamed, overtaken by a childlike enchantment, as if seeking forgiveness in the past. "Yes, Eric's mind is the same, I can tell from his e-mails. And from Nancy's comments. A true relic these days. Still sharp as a tack, of course. But stopped in time." The comments weren't exactly promising. On the other hand...?

The colonel was now carefully reviewing the check, moving his lips as he tallied the figures lit by the table lamp. Once the inspection was over, he deposited a few coins on the plate and asked, "Who else can afford not to change with the times? Only Eric."

# PART SIX

# 45

In my parents' time, a man in his sixties was considered old. Yet the adjective could hardly be applied to the individual who greeted me in my office—though he was close to eighty. The man who shook my hand seemed to have no shortage of energy.

That was my first impression of Eric Friedkin. Partly because of his gaze and bearing, and largely because of his physique, probably the result of a daily exercise regimen. His expression, moreover, conveyed both calm and aloofness, a curious combination that in no way diminished the sincerity of his smile. His suntan, in turn, suggested a retirement spent on three-mast sailboats, perhaps traveling distant seas. And his crew cut, which had upset Marina years before in Washington, had ended up going with the whole look quite naturally.

Like Colonel João Vaz, he was tall. But in contrast to his friend, he had no fat on him. He entered my office and crossed directly to my desk with the composure of someone who, if required, would proceed with the same stride out over the horizon, unfazed by the window and whatever might be awaiting him some forty floors below. Also unlike his former companion—who had soon taken on the persona of a trained bear in my view—he couldn't be compared to any tamed animal.

"Delighted to meet you," he said, as I welcomed him.

He could have sat in a chair in front of me or shared the sofa a few steps away. Still smiling, he waited for me to indicate my preference. I chose the sofa. As we sat side by side, the secretary who had showed him in returned with coffee.

"Brazilian coffee!" he exclaimed in the same jovial tone. "At least I hope so..."

I apologized for having kept him waiting while I was trying to finish a report about to be sent off to Brasilia. I added that I hadn't expected him to arrive so soon after his call.

"I phoned from the lobby," Eric told me in a hushed voice, as if sharing a secret. The line could have meant *so you couldn't escape*. Or illustrated how spontaneous he was.

He must have registered something of my surprise, for he went on to explain. "Once a month, I take the San Diego Freeway and come have lunch with my friends in Los Angeles. Old colleagues from work, all retired like me. And your building is one of my favorite places to park: there's always space. From there to making the call was just one short step."

After a brief pause, he continued. "Besides, yesterday I got a new e-mail from our mutual friend. João..." His pronunciation had been midway between *João* and *John*, slightly more toward the latter.

"He wanted to know if we'd been in touch yet. The fellow seems eager to have us get together. Which is quite typical of him..."

We laughed a little, me without knowing just why, him in honor of old times in Montevideo. *Good old João*, his look seemed to say.

As expected, we went on to talk about the colonel. I described how I'd met him in Vienna and mentioned what had led us to become friends in a city that had at first seemed hostile to us—at night and in the wintertime, at least. I indicated that we'd gotten together since then and emphasized our recent dinner in Ipanema, trying to fill in the gaps with details about his recently deceased wife, his daughter and grandchildren. Especially—

"Ernestinho!" he cut in. "Ernestinho Vaz! In honor of one of João's former bosses. Ernesto..."

He'd set the ball up so I could spike it. Since I said nothing, he himself returned with a deflated "...Geisel."

In the meantime, I took a sip of my coffee, allowing the former military president to beat a hasty retreat so we could resume our pleasant conversation without his shadow looming over us. Eric didn't blink but registered what had happened. I appreciated his tact. And began to pay closer attention to him.

I noted that he seemed at ease, looking around him with satisfaction, lingering over the paintings, prints, and posters from previous years of the São Paulo Art Biennial. Then he concentrated on the windows. Seated where he was, he couldn't see much other than the blue sky. Even so, he found a way to express his admiration.

"The thirty-eighth floor! You've got a beautiful view from up here. Buildings this tall are becoming common in the area. Before, there were only the ones in Century City, and a few miles away, in Westwood. Other than downtown, of course. But the smog there tends to be unbearable." He knew the city well, even though he visited only on occasion.

"When I lived here the first time," I remarked, "more than thirty years ago, our consulate was on Wilshire, only farther down, across from the old LA County Museum."

"I know the building you're talking about," he exclaimed happily, as if there were something curious and unexpected about this new coincidence. "I usually park my car there too. It's called the Mutual..."

"...Benefit Life Building," I completed.

We laughed again. Ernesto Geisel, no. The Mutual Benefit Life Building, yes. We were groping our way in utter darkness but without being anxious or fearful of one another.

I glanced at my watch. Marina's old question about Max came to mind: *"Did you ever manage to find out anything... anything more concrete about him?"*

"Do you have plans for lunch?" I asked. "With your friends...?"

"I didn't call anyone. In fact, we rarely do. Because the time and place never change. We show up there the last Friday of each month and meet in the bar. Sometimes we end up at a table for ten or twelve. Other times, there are only seven or eight of us. Some of the fellows bring their wives, if we know them or they happen to have been in the same line of work. There are those who never bring their spouses. Or are widowers, as I am now. It varies a lot. And that's part of the charm. Of course, over time the circle has been getting smaller. But no one dwells on that..."

He got back to my question. "That said, I would be happy to join you for lunch. As long as it's on me."

"Absolutely not," I replied good-humoredly. "We're on Brazilian turf at the consulate, don't forget. I'm the one who calls the shots here. Do you like Italian food?"

Following his positive response, I said, "There's an Italian place nearby, on the other side of La Cienega. It's usually terrific. And it has an excellent salad bar," I added, paying tribute to his physical fitness.

I then asked my secretary to book us a table. Eric seemed visibly pleased at the prospect of good pasta.

Later, in the packed elevator, we kept to ourselves. Like Max (and Colonel Vaz), Eric was a good head taller than I was. In the States, everyone was at least a head taller than me.

The restaurant was called Caffe La Strada. Our entire building went there, for a beer or a quick bite. The place saw a good crowd at night too, and had live music: a trio on piano, bass, and drums.

It was across the street. Side by side, we waited for the light. The sun was out, it was Friday, the weekend forecast looked pleasant. I almost regretted that our outing was so short since it's rare to saunter along the sidewalks of Los Angeles, a city where they say there are more cars than people. We were in no hurry. One rushes toward the future, not the past.

"So you belong to the growing species of adopted Californians, then," Eric remarked, chuckling.

He was strolling with his hands in his pants pockets, his partially open beige blazer revealing a long-sleeved white shirt. His shoes were suede. He could have been a retired TV producer. Or a respected member of the Mob. All he needed in the second case were dark glasses and a chain around his neck. He was already sporting a thick gold pinkie ring.

"Yes," I replied. "I lived here from 1973 to 1976." *In another time, another life,* I thought to myself. "It was my first post," I added. "I liked the city so much that I came back. Three decades later."

"Is that so?" he asked, intrigued. "Foreigners usually prefer San Francisco. They find it charming, more inviting. Easier to get the hang of."

"It was definitely hard at first," I acknowledged. "Took me a while to get used to the freeway system. The city seemed to have dozens of centers rather than just one. But I learned. Later, when I started taking night classes at UCLA, I made a few friends. Then things got easier."

"What did you study?" he inquired amiably. He was asking the obvious questions and seemed to be having fun in the process. All along, though, he appeared to be showing genuine interest in my answers.

"Film," I replied.

"*Film?!*" he exclaimed in surprise. "That's unusual. For a diplomat."

"I'm not your usual diplomat."

In the meantime, we had arrived at La Strada. One of the waiters, Alberto, a generally sullen fellow (but who had become a friend of mine as a result of our shared passion for soccer), greeted us at the entrance. As part of his routine, he pointed to a few sidewalk tables, beneath umbrellas. But we preferred to be inside.

"Very nice," Eric murmured as we entered the dimly lit dining room. The place was small but tastefully decorated. A Neapolitan song could be heard between snippets of conversation here and there. A few good tables remained open, including one in a corner reserved for us.

The owner stepped out from behind the counter and made his way over to us.

"*Il signore Giovanni*," I said, introducing him to Eric, who shook his hand.

"Eric Friedkin," he said in turn. "My Brazilian friend spoke of your restaurant in glowing terms."

Giovanni showed gratitude for the kindness, alluding to close ties between Italy and Brazil. As Alberto came over to let us know the day's specials, all I could think was, *I'm done for, we're already friends.*

At odds and annoyed with myself, I sought refuge behind the menu. It wouldn't be easy to steer the conversation, I kept thinking, as I wavered between lasagna and spaghetti carbonara. I heaved a sigh, as if something on the menu were giving me trouble.

Eric then sighed himself. I imagine, in his case, from the variety of choices he was facing. After a certain age, I've been coming to realize, the ideal menu is limited to five dishes. Clouds hung over our gastronomic adventure. But I had no reason to complain. Worst case, we'd eat well and say goodbye after small talk. Nothing wrong with that.

Eric wanted to know if the portions were large. He explained that he didn't usually eat much at lunchtime. And pointed to the salad bar I'd mentioned. We decided to go with salad and split the lasagna. That way we'd have room for dessert. At Alberto's recommendation, we placed that order too: cannoli Sicilian style for Eric, tiramisu for me. Followed by two espressos, decaf for him. So much for that.

Or almost. "Any wine?" I asked in my capacity as host.

"No, thank you, I have a long drive back home. But I'll gladly have a bourbon before the meal. And a Diet Coke with the lasagna." I ordered a glass of red wine.

Alberto gestured to me. He had something to tell me but didn't know if he should approach. With my eyes, I encouraged him to speak up. The more interruptions, the better. Alberto then availed himself of the arrival of bread, oil, and olives to exchange two or three lines with me in Italian, a language I speak poorly but understand well.

Once he moved away, I whispered toward Eric, "Soccer…"

"I could tell," he replied, adding, "I spent many years in South America. It was impossible to survive, back then…"

To this day, I don't know whether his pause was intentional.

"…without knowing something about soccer."

*Balls, bullets…*, I thought to myself.

"They were wonderful years," he went on, now seeming to be in an introspective mood, after putting a few olives on his plate and passing me the bread. "Complicated, full of challenges. And, as is always the case, full of rewards too."

For now, he was sounding me out. Using a philosophical tone, which might turn melancholy or light—depending on how I weighed in. The bridge between us had been built by someone he trusted and was therefore solid. But the reference to my film studies and time spent as a student during such a turbulent period in California had possibly shaken his convictions. He slipped along this particular flank like a soldier crawling beneath a barbed-wire fence.

"Tell me a bit about your experience at UCLA in the seventies. Must have been a fascinating time."

Depending on what choice I made, I might focus on the end of the Vietnam War, which I'd watched day after day on TV, disaster after disaster, body bag after body bag; perhaps mention the Watergate saga, which I'd also followed with my friends and neighbors, celebrating Nixon's resignation by popping open bottles of champagne.

These were topics Eric too had followed, only from the other side of the electric fence that separated us—given that he was already a prominent figure at the CIA at the time. During those same years, in Montevideo, he had met Colonel João Vaz—and Max—in the secret capacity of station chief of his agency.

Were I to go in that direction, I would expose myself straightaway, as well as my personal beliefs—and then pay the price of watching our conversation die out. On the other hand, I could very well present myself under the guise of a bureaucrat without in any way being unfaithful to the truth. I was a diplomat, after all, trained to observe political scenarios in other countries—without judging them. What are the duties of a consulate if not lending assistance to its nationals, granting visas, legalizing documents, and, beyond that, fulfilling tasks in commercial and cultural promotion—two areas that had been under my purview in the seventies?

What I couldn't do, however, was hesitate. My guest had already eaten three of his four olives. That's when I had an inspiration and decided to answer his question indirectly, letting him reach his own conclusions. I described an incident that had happened to me, one that left a deep impression for the intensity with which it had unfolded. Something Eric would interpret his own way, bringing me into his fold or not. Without either selling my soul to the devil or suppressing the mortification the episode had caused me. All I had to do was leave out a few details.

The incident, to describe it in full, had taken place at a Joan Baez concert. I'd been obsessed with the singer-songwriter since my teens. Besides being beautiful, pure, innocent, and sensitive (to my young eyes and romantic spirit), she'd launched another of my idols—Bob Dylan—to fame. Her wonderfully lyrical yet simple music had roots in old English, Irish, and American folk songs. Back then, however, protest themes were prominent in her repertoire. The outdoor concert was held at an improvised amphitheater on the UCLA green. And there I was, ecstatic amid the crowd, living one of my dreams.

At some point, to thunderous applause, Joan Baez got to ranting against military coup leaders. And there were plenty of them back then. Setting aside her guitar, she suddenly called out, "Is there anyone here tonight from Greece?" Several arms shot up, with clenched fists. Roars against the Greek colonels and cheers for democracy followed, added to chants and booing of the brutes.

"How about Chile? Anyone here tonight from Chile?" Again, arms and fists were raised. There were shouts against Pinochet, cheers for Allende. "And Argentina?" she yelled. More fists, jeers, and cries of death to the gorillas. She then made one last call: "How about Brazil? Anyone here tonight from Brazil?" I remember having raised my arm with enthusiasm. And catching sight of another dozen amid the crowd. We were celebrated too, getting our own share of cheers, *vivas*, and applause. We felt noble in our outrage.

When the music started up again, several people came to hug me and offer their boundless solidarity. They wanted to know if I needed assistance of any kind. A priest offered to help rescue, with a private plane, any relative of mine who might be hiding out in the Amazon jungle. A young woman gave me half her hot dog and the dregs of a bottle of warm beer. A guy handed me a lit joint ("keep it," he insisted) that I felt obliged to take two hits off, choking and coughing. I thanked them all, moved by so many gestures of friendship and selflessness, feeling loved by this sea of humans.

I passed the joint along but rather than getting swallowed up by the crowd, it kept making its way back, which led me to take a few more drags. The pot, which seemed to be first-rate, made life seem impossibly beautiful. In my mind Joan Baez and Joan of Arc blended into one and the same muse. And that muse, part artist, part warrior, was singing to one troubadour soldier alone — me.

Everything had gone along splendidly until the couple sitting beside me, after much conferring, as if hatching a plan between them, asked if I needed a job. Given my state of euphoria, I replied no, that I had a job, thanks very much. Not satisfied to leave well enough alone, I felt compelled to inform them that I worked at the Brazilian consulate.

"*At the Brazilian consulate?*" the couple replied in a single voice, completely bewildered.

"Yes!" I confirmed happily, my eyes glued on Joan of Arc, who was winking at me just then. "At the Brazilian consulate!" I repeated with pride.

"*For the gorillas' government?*" the two persisted as though stunned.

"Yes!" I repeated, not paying attention to what they were saying, worshipping my muse.

Their bewilderment turned into disgust, as if I'd just escaped from a leper colony with the explicit goal of infecting everyone around me. In a matter of seconds the news spread like wildfire, with shouts of "Informer! We have an informer here!" I was shoved multiple times and kicked at least twice, then grabbed by the collar and shaken mercilessly. Until a security guard turned up and got me out of there.

More than the pain and dismay, it was the looks of hate and contempt that astounded me. Pushed along by the security guard, a big guy who kept his hands squarely on my shoulders, I forced my way through the people I came up against. With every few steps the anger around me subsided, because the groups I was now passing didn't know exactly what had happened, among other reasons because they were all stoned.

I had yet to recover my peace of mind, however, and struggled to explain to the guard, who kept ordering, "Go on, man, go on, don't stop and don't look back," that while working in business and culture, I'd kept a wide berth between me and the Brazilian military. "Just shut up and walk, man, just walk!" he barked.

The snubs directed at me seemed not just unfair but incomprehensible, feelings exacerbated by the pot I'd smoked. After all, how many of my Brazilian idols' concerts had I been to in Brazil without anyone's requiring an ideological affidavit from me? Was the only form of protest to take up arms and rob banks or kidnap ambassadors? And what about the young UCLA students around me? Had they done anything beyond their political masturbating to be able to sleep peacefully at night?

In describing the scene to Eric, I chose my facts and images carefully. I left out the crowd's exuberant chanting and cries of protest against the generals and eliminated the pot from the scene. I concentrated on my elation at having the opportunity to see a live performance by an artist I'd admired for years — and knew only from recordings. And on the bad vibes that had set in around me when, responding to a casual question by the people sitting next to me, I was almost lynched by an army of justice seekers.

When I was done, Eric tipped back what was left of his bourbon and made a single comment, which I took as favorable since it seemed to strengthen my credibility. "California wasn't exactly a reliable state back then. Between then and now, those kids learned their lesson. Today, some of those guys who almost lynched you probably own the building where you work."

*Maybe...*, I thought to myself, as our lasagna arrived.

Sealing our first trace of complicity with an affectionate pat on my back, Eric proposed, "What do you say we visit the salad bar? That will give our pasta time to cool."

He leaned over my shoulder and confessed, "I liked Joan Baez a lot too." Then he added, "My daughter stole all my records of hers. They were small, forty-fives. Remember those?"

# 46

Eric Friedkin didn't live in San Diego proper but a half hour away, in the town of La Jolla, which the locals casually, even nonchalantly, referred to as "a seaside resort community." It was justifiably proud of its beach nestled into cliffs intersected by canyons—a setting that made the community's property value one of the highest in the country.

The Eric Friedkin I saw there looked quite different from the man I'd had lunch with three weeks earlier in LA. He was sporting Bermuda shorts, a Hawaiian shirt, and Docksiders without socks. He walked over to my car as I was parking. Before even greeting me, however, he'd cast a stern look at the blazer I was wearing. His first words, upon shaking my hand, while I was still in the process of locking the car, were aimed at this particular part of my outfit. "Let's ditch that jacket right away or the neighbors will think you're with the Mafia, which is serious stuff around here."

I couldn't help but laugh at the joke, recalling that I'd associated him with the Italian underworld at our earlier meeting.

"No Jews, or members of the Mob, in our neighborhood..." The additional comment made me cringe.

He went on to talk about his home. "You have no idea what trouble my wife and I had buying this house, the way the community here is so closed. And that was back in the eighties, if you can believe it. Despite our having been introduced by mutual friends, the realtor looked rather suspiciously at the 'public servant' I scribbled under 'employment' on the form."

He remembered his role as host in due time. "What would you like to drink? Would you prefer to stay inside or should we go out to the pool? I have a nice table with a big umbrella."

"I'll have a vodka tonic with a twist of lime. The pool sounds like a good idea. Let's sit out there."

With that, we crossed the room and headed toward the back of the house, first making a stop at the bar, where I sat on a stool while Eric fixed our drinks.

"A vodka tonic... wise choice, wise choice," he murmured to himself.

The kitchen was right behind the bar, separated from the living room by a counter. Talking all the while and now alluding to our lunch ("I really liked that Italian restaurant and already went back, with a few friends, last Friday night"), he headed to the refrigerator and returned with a bottle of vodka, which he placed in an ice bucket.

"Tall glass?" he asked. On seeing me nod, he indicated, "I'm going to join you in the vodka, only I'm going to have mine straight. And note that I usually only drink—"

"Bourbon."

"Did Vaz tell you? He'd never drunk bourbon before, but he ended up liking it. A good guy, our Vaz..."

When it came down to it, we had nothing in common, Eric and I, other than a Brazilian colonel for whom we both had a soft spot. Except for that, what connected us had yet to be defined, stemming as it did from a feeling of unease rooted in distrust. I had just driven almost two hours to his house, in what would likely be a fruitless pursuit of answers to questions I might not even be able to formulate. I had no clue to his motives for inviting me. But the one aspect of human nature that always thrills me is its unpredictability. And Eric Friedkin was about to toast me with a fine example of this trait, so rare these days.

"You don't really like me at all, do you?" he asked serenely, taking a first sip of his vodka.

I was so ready that I answered point-blank, "No, Eric. Not one bit." And found myself able to add, "It's too bad, but that's how it is."

He averted his eyes and took a second sip of his drink. A heavy silence followed.

"You know," he said at last, "for a long time, I thought someone would come. To kill me. Me and my family." He chuckled, as if belittling his old fears. "For years, I went around armed. I kept a gun and a grenade in every room of the houses we lived in. Then I got over it. No one came. And the world changed.

"Five years ago, when I saw the first tower of the World Trade Center collapse before my eyes, I raised my arms to the TV screen, as though trying to hold it up with my own hands. Then, watching the second tower fall, I had a horribly selfish reaction. I thought, *I'm off the hook.* Who would be interested, now, in settling scores with an old man like me, who took part in prehistoric wars compared to those being waged today? A man who served a CIA that had nothing to do with the current one? Where people knew each other's first names, and electronics had only just come onto the scene?"

# 47

Now that we knew where we stood, the conversation gained in intensity.

"Vaz told me you would be particularly interested in Max," he said.

"That's right. He was my best friend at one time. I was very young, I'd just joined the ministry, where he was already shining like few others."

"I know."

"You know? How? I never told Vaz. In fact—"

"Vaz is no fool, you know. All those dinners in Vienna..."

The comment saddened me. I'd appreciated the colonel's ingenuous, almost innocent manner with me, and hadn't imagined there had been anything calculating about the old bear then. *But...* it was also possible that it had been Eric, not the colonel, who had come to that conclusion.

"Another of your trompe l'oeils, Eric?" I prodded, laughing.

He liked it. He was vain. Instead of reacting, however, he opted to throw a few pieces of chicken on the barbecue, which he surrounded with an assortment of sausages. He'd put on an apron for the job. For a while, he moved back and forth between the grill and the table where I was still sitting. With each stop at the table, he'd take a sip of his vodka, toss the salad of lettuce, cucumbers, radishes, and tomatoes, and check my drink—which, depending on its level, he'd refill with more ice or vodka, leaving it up to me to add tonic water.

At the grill, he leaned over the meats, turning them as needed, then faced me to make a comment or two, almost always having to do with his progress on the grill ("We're getting there," "Do you like your meat well done?"). Or he'd come up with some generic remark about the neighborhood.

He explained to me that *La Jolla* was a corruption of the Spanish *La Joya*. He told me the local university was strong in oceanography, a field his son-in-law had majored in, but computer science had become just as important. He spoke of the countless golf courses in the area, complaining that there was now a nudist beach beside his.

"You wouldn't believe the ghastly sights we're exposed to," he said miserably. "Cellulite, lard, huge potbellies...Few young people can afford to live around here. And when they do show up, they come from far away. To surf."

I also learned that Gregory Peck, Cliff Robertson, and Raquel Welch had once lived nearby.

"How old is she these days?" I asked, simply to say something.

"Raquel Welch? She must be past her prime," he answered, bending over a chicken thigh. "During the Vietnam War, the photos of her in *Playboy* were already circulating in the trenches. They were traded as the gold standard."

*Vietnam*...Eric was trying to lure me in. That conflict had stifled *our war*, silencing the social demands that cried out for solutions, and sinking our region into a downward spiral for two decades—at the expense of countless lives. For now, however, I decided to wait. If Eric strolled through La Jolla in Bermuda shorts and Docksiders, I wouldn't be the one to venture back to the alleys and torture chambers of South America with weapons in hand.

"We have a few politicians too. One of John McCain's twelve houses is here. They say he stands a chance of being elected president. I ask you, how is it that a guy *with twelve houses* has the balls to run for anything in today's world? Even in this country? He'll only win if the Democrats choose that black guy as their candidate. The one with the Muslim name."

While I pondered the implications of this last tirade, Eric continued to mine this ethnic vein. From the Muslims, he moved on to Arabs in general. For a few minutes, he went back to talking about discrimination against Jews, a topic that seemed to amuse him. Given my silence, however, he gradually lowered his voice to the level of a whisper, which now reached me only intermittently.

Between the pool and the fence that divided his property from the neighbor's was a single tree, whose branches were swaying with the breeze. At that point, I'd already downed two strong vodka tonics without having been offered so much as a peanut. Struggling to stay awake, I closed my eyes for a few seconds. To my delight, the foliage grew thicker and denser, spreading into a canopy over the yard. I suddenly found myself in a Bolivian jungle. Che Guevara was handing me a grenade. And showing me how to pull out the pin.

"I read your letter," I heard a voice say from far off. *What an honor*, I thought. *Che has read my letter.*

"You did," I answered happily, lost as I was between La Jolla and La Paz.

My eyelids were heavy as lead, but I cracked my eyes open for a second. There was Eric standing at the grill. I straightened up as best I could in the chair.

"Inspired pages," he went on in the same distant tone. "A bit naïve, like every outpouring made under the influence of alcohol, but beautiful nonetheless. It's a shame they went unnoticed for so long."

He turned toward me, as if wishing to emphasize what he had yet to say. Now he had my full attention. "So very long…"

Just like Max, he knew how to make the most of his pauses.

"…thirty-three years. The age of Christ."

He turned back to the fire, leaving me lost in doubts. *Inspired pages...Outpouring under the influence of alcohol...Christ...* What was he talking about? And why was he so keyed up?

It was going to be a long afternoon. Which wasn't in itself a bad thing—since I'd regained at least some energy—because there was nothing modest about my agenda: it ran from the nuclear power Brazil had tried to obtain in the 1970s to the number of deaths Eric was responsible for during his time in South America. Between the two extremes, we'd meet up with Max. But there was no hurry. Particularly as other topics cropped up around us.

In my case, I would have liked to know how Eric compared the quagmire of Vietnam, in which he'd served dreaming about Raquel Welch, to the quicksand his country found itself buried in currently in Iraq and Afghanistan. Once again, however, my lunch companion veered off in an unexpected direction.

"You know," he said, picking up my plate from the table, "men like us are a dime a dozen. But men like Max are hard to come by."

Back at the grill, and without turning around, he announced, "Our lunch is ready. Chicken or sausage?"

"Sausage," I answered promptly.

He brought me a plate with two plump sausages, moved the salad bowl within my reach, and pointed to the tray with oil, vinegar, and salt. That done, he excused himself. "I'll be right back. Forgot the ketchup."

Fortified by the sausage I wolfed down with a few cucumbers and tomatoes in Eric's absence, I decided to mull over his words. *Men like us...* But I didn't get past the first line because Eric, who passed by me again on his way to the grill, took it upon himself to repeat the second.

"Men like Max are hard to come by." His back to the table, he shook his head from side to side as he put food on his plate.

His body language reminded me of Max at our dinner in Alto da Boa Vista, when my old friend had moved in that same vaguely paternal way, as if to say, *This kid will never change…*

I found myself thinking that, in the space of a generation, thousands of people south of the equator had been imprisoned, tortured, and killed in the name of priorities long since forgotten. Who would answer for the fatal gale that had precipitously taken them all? Who, in Brazil, to cite one such scenario, would face a camera to publicly lament what had happened, as Robert McNamara had with respect to the horrors caused by the Vietnam War?

What had occurred four decades earlier in our region had remained suspended in time. What place could there be for dramas now relegated to the academic world—on a planet deprived of memory?

Eric finally came over to the table with his plate, on which, after much deliberation, he'd placed a single piece of chicken and two sausages. I looked at him as though seeing the man for the first time. On the surface, he had nothing whatsoever to do with Max, as I well knew. But on some other level, more difficult to define, the two seemed like brothers. Born of different times and backgrounds—but blood brothers nonetheless.

The vodkas on an empty stomach—now replaced by beers—propelled the journey I was making within the parameters drawn by Eric. It was a journey that was in some ways strangely mollifying. What was odd, I noticed, weighing the pauses and silences, was that Eric seemed to be undergoing a similar experience. Maybe he saw me as the knight errant who had knocked on his castle door in search of something buried in his conscience. I'd given him the choice of arms, and my host had left his spear and sword aside—in favor of booze.

He kept a full glass of bourbon on the lower shelf of the bar, as I'd noticed earlier on my way to the washroom. That explained why he'd forgotten the ketchup. And returned to the kitchen in search of mustard. And, later, had gone to get napkins from a cupboard. Eric drank vodka with me and bourbon with his ghosts.

Instead of the attempts on his life or his family that Eric had awaited in vain, fate had sent him a simple clue hunter. It hardly mattered that these clues related to Max, for the two men had dwelled amid the same horrors. Our duel had been limited until this point to a few lines fired at random, interspersed with platitudes and traded barbs.

Now, however, Eric was eating. Slowly and in absolute silence. Once in a while, he threw me a glance, but with the placid air of someone contemplating a soothing stretch of landscape. I might as well have been the second tree he'd always wanted to plant in his yard.

# 48

"Was it really *that difficult*, Eric?" I asked at last.

"What?" he replied.

"To survive."

"I beg your pardon?" he said stiffly. Then he sighed, as if stalling for time. So I went ahead.

"Today, as I was parking my car, you tied me to the Mafia on account of my blazer. Then you bad-mouthed the Jews a couple of times, which is awkward when it comes up gratuitously in conversation. After that, you criticized Arabs and Muslims alike, and derided your country's possible future president as 'a black guy,' striving the whole time to create an unsettling atmosphere for my visit. Not satisfied, you puffed out your chest mentioning 'men like us,' suggesting a shared past that exists only in your mind."

He held up his hand. "Actually, I thought I was *praising you*. Making you part of a group I'm proud to belong to."

I set aside my almost untouched plate. No one, whether versed in etiquette or not, could fail to see the gesture as a rupture.

"Eric, out of respect for your age, the willingness with which I came to visit you, and my overindulging in your excellent vodka..."

"...which you diluted with tonic water, ice, and lime, when it's supposed to be drunk straight..."

"...which I diluted with tonic water, ice, and lime, when it's supposed to be drunk straight," I repeated in the same tone, quite ready to set aside my four decades of diplomatic life and for once give it straight to someone I despised. "You wouldn't by any chance *be fucking with me, would you?*"

To my surprise, he laughed at this, and then replied evenly, "By seeing us as equals? Far from it. We're equals, yes, if Max is our point of reference. As he seems to be. Just as he seems to have been the reason for your visit here today. Not to mention the dinners in Vienna."

He'd gradually raised his voice. I pulled my plate back toward me and continued to eat, listening—but keeping sight of my immediate priorities.

"If we take Max as our reference," he persisted, and here his voice took on an almost aggressive tone, "we're equals. Because we believe in something. Whether that something is different, or even diametrically opposed, is irrelevant. What matters is that we believe in *something. Max didn't believe in anything.* Except himself. You of all people should know that."

After a pause, he added, as though talking to himself, "I never kid around. That's why I'm still alive today."

I thought of Marina. It was as if she'd been with me all along, seated at the table with us.

"That may be, Eric. But even so, you did a complete about-face and avoided answering my question."

"On the contrary," he said coldly. "I spoke up even before you started fishing for information. Shortly after you got here. And you pretended not to understand."

"When?"

"When I came right out and said that *I had read your letter.* That's the difference between me and the guy you met three weeks ago. I read your letter. And saw who you were."

I waited a beat, to see how far he'd go. He didn't hold back.

"And more than that: who you've been all these years. And still are."

"Well, that's great, Eric!" I exclaimed. "I've always wanted to know who I was. Who doesn't? At one stage of my life, I even underwent therapy to look into this big mystery. Maybe you can enlighten me on the subject."

He leaned over and looked me in the eye. Not hostilely but steadily. He knew I was flying blindly, that I knew nothing about this letter he kept pulling out of his sleeve, the way a poker player would an ace of spades. But then he stood and went over to the grill again. No longer as chef but as a man intent on doing some serious eating.

While he helped himself, he told me that, on receiving Colonel João Vaz's e-mail about me, he'd realized my name sounded familiar. Between forkfuls, he said that he'd always had an excellent memory. And added: "Like your friend Max." Except that his own gift, according to him, was beginning to fail. That's why he hadn't been able to make the connection, no matter how much he racked his brain. But my name rang a bell; of that he was fairly certain.

Given that I was Brazilian, he continued, gnawing on the drumstick gripped in his hand, he supposed he might have met me during his stint in Rio. He told me he'd become friends with Carlos Câmara during that time. Having recently arrived from Bonn, Max's future superior was teaching at the War College, where Eric sometimes also gave classes. When they'd met up again some years later in Uruguay, Eric had warned Carlos about Max, whom he knew quite well by then. "Keep your eyes open," he'd said, not mincing his words, "the guy will suck the blood right out of your veins."

As I listened to him talk, I became increasingly aware of the bones being ground in front of me, the skin being ripped, the chunks of meat being chewed. Eric had polished off all the chicken he'd grilled. For a man who had described his appetite as "frugal" three weeks earlier at lunch with me, he certainly packed it away. I had the uneasy feeling that his hunger had grown in proportion to my silence. There was, however, a positive side to what was happening: the pieces of my story were finally starting to fit together.

The Café Sorocabana (*"I used to go there all the time,"* he revealed at one point, *"long before they served liquor, and was among those who maneuvered behind the scenes to revoke Fernández's license, reckoning that we needed lucid people on the job, not drunks"*); the wiretapping of the embassies; the code names Zorro, Sam Beckett, and Batman; CIA and MI6's hesitation to avail themselves of Max, since both agencies considered him unstable, *"given his extraordinary ambition, which meant he would have not one but several agendas of his own"*—all this information and more began to surface as though awaiting me for years.

Revelation gave way to revelation. Eric had me under his spell, not only because of the content of what he was saying but also because of his distant, haunting tone. He might have been leaning over an old family album, identifying people, lingering here and there to mull over their journeys and misfortunes. At one point, he reminded me that a good deal of what he was telling me came from documents that had already been declassified by the National Security Agency, and that the rest would soon come to light as well. Pointing over to his garage, he added, "I have my own archives, which I've been carrying around with me for years as insurance."

In the meantime, we'd cleared the table and scraped the leftovers into the trash bin. While I'd brought in the plates, utensils, and glasses, Eric had zealously cleaned the grill, using gloves, an old dishrag, and a can of spray. Then he'd lowered the lid. It wasn't yet three o'clock. From the other side of the kitchen counter, Eric said to me, "Now we need to figure out what to have for dessert. Pecan ice cream. Or fruit…I can offer you melon or grapes. *Seedless* grapes, in my mind the greatest invention of recent times."

"I'll go with the grapes," I said.

"Wise choice, wise choice," he again murmured to himself. He opted for the ice cream.

Then, with bowls in hand and no further explanation from Eric, we headed farther into the house, crossing a small room with bookcases, two sofas, and a TV ("our family room," he said, as if his wife were still alive), and turning into a hallway, at the end of which was a door.

I could see it led to the garage. Or, as Eric made a point of saying, "to my past."

# 49

Metal shelves ran from one end of the garage to the other, divided into rows and crammed with boxes with numbered labels.

Waving his ice cream spoon in the air like a conductor's baton, Eric explained, "I devoted years to putting my papers, photos, negatives, and microfilms in order. And I managed to get it done. My wife was a great help. I never would have been able to organize this archive without her. Today, I'm a shadow of what I once was. After she passed away two years ago, I didn't set foot in here for months. But I ended up coming back. The prodigal son returns home."

He paused ever so slightly and indulged in another spoonful. Was it possible that he harbored no doubts whatsoever about his decades of active service? Or was he trying to keep his ice cream from melting?

He soon proceeded. "A small part of the archive could in theory be accessible to the general public. Newspaper clippings, photos, copies of innocuous reports. There's a confidential part, which is gradually being declassified by the government. The rest, more than half, and don't ask me which because I couldn't even tell you at this point, is secret. All mixed together, intentionally. Maybe out of spite. The wheat and the chaff are scrambled together amid the dozens of boxes in this garage, which will one day go back to Langley, as specified in my will."

After a bitter laugh, he concluded, "It's going to be one helluva job to sort through all this material. This cursed legacy will be my revenge, for having been sent home before my time, after so many years serving my country. Let them sift through the paperwork for months, if not years! And may they be frightened by what they find!"

Now I was the one who was frightened. I'd accompanied him, slowly munching on my seedless grapes, thereby giving the impression that nothing out of the ordinary was going on, as if we were strolling along the Champs-Elysées on a spring afternoon, not surrounded by the tragic spoils of bloody battles. The labels went parading by my eyes without my daring to linger over them: *Allende, 1968–1969*; *Allende, 1970–1971*. After 1972, the boxes were classified by month (*Allende, January–April 1972*; *Allende, May 1973*). The labels on the last—the smallest of all—hit me the hardest amid that grim collection of memories: *Allende, August/September 1973*. At the end of the same shelf devoted to Chile, names of familiar martyrs (Miguel Enríquez, Tucapel Jiménez, José Carrasco among them) and others, unknown, appeared. There were labels designating paramilitary groups, torture centers (*Arenal Base, Casa José Domingo Cañas*), regions and islands (*Dawson Island, Puchuncaví, Chacabuco*).... Still others referred to informants or individuals who, according to Eric, needed to be watched ("You have no idea how many people we had to keep an eye on"). Many bore enigmatic titles.

An entire shelf was devoted to the Chilean secret police and the infamous names of those who had served in the dreaded organization: Contreras, Krassnoff Martchenko, Fernández Larios, Osvaldo Romo Mena, Mario Jahn Barrera.... Some had only numbers, all in blue ink circled in black, or code names (*Zulu, Orpheus, Zapata*, and—the most curious of all—*Onassis*). I counted three boxes with the label *MIR*, undated, and another three for Letelier, Bernardo Leighton, and Prats. Cuba and Fidel were relegated to secondary spots on the next shelf. I remember one box in particular: *Cuba—OSPAAAL, 1966*. "The Cuban stuff wouldn't fit in three garages this size," joked Eric. "But, fortunately, the island wasn't my problem."

I went past at least four boxes devoted to General Pinochet and one to his family. Five shelves, from one end of the garage to the other, had to do with the Uruguayans, most with the Tupamaros (namely, Raúl Sendic) and the dictators and torturers of the time (Bordaberry, Gregorio Alvarez, Manuel Cordero). The Argentinean Montoneros also figured prominently.

Eric kept talking all the while. His words reached my ears in counterpoint to our steps, receding only when he took another spoonful of ice cream. He'd finish it eventually, though, and his speech would soon be deprived of its pauses.

We'd reached the Guevaras. They took up an entire set of shelves in one of the rows. His "African phase" was there, from his passages through Mali, Guinea-Conakry, Ghana, Dahomey, and Tanzania to the guerrilla warfare he'd been a part of in the Congo.

"Copies of field reports," Eric explained when he saw me slow my pace. "From colleagues stationed at African posts. Not everything that's here has to do with me, of course. But in Montevideo, we received copies of reports from countries that were in some way connected to us."

Having finished my grapes, I wondered what to do with the bowl. "Set it over there." Eric pointed to an empty shelf near the door.

We traveled up and down the aisles of his doleful bazaar, reaching the far end of the garage, then moved up the next row back toward the door. I estimated that we would finish the whole trip in nine or ten more rounds.

"You have no idea what it's like to be born trapped in a system," Eric said at one point. His tone had changed. It was no longer assertive but had veered off on a more evocative path, which required attention on my part. Eric had finished his ice cream and set his empty bowl next to mine. He licked his fingers before wiping them on his Bermuda shorts. "I don't say that as an apology. I don't owe anyone an apology."

Had the man who'd held his hands up to the TV screen when he saw the World Trade Center towers collapse finally stepped onstage?

"To be born trapped in a system," he repeated. "For a man like you, a man who was young at the time, the world was a chessboard where pieces could be freely moved based on faith or idealism. But we..." Another pause.

Frustration prevented him from keeping up the appearances he'd relied on during lunch. He seemed to need air. "We were at war," he said at last.

He vented with the conviction of someone who had experienced day-to-day life in the trenches. He knew what he was talking about. The war, for him, was no abstract phenomenon. I'd seen plenty of awards for acts of bravery hanging on the walls of a hallway on my trip to the bathroom. He'd killed Vietcong, lost friends, even been wounded. In sum, he'd seen death up close. It hardly mattered if it came wrapped in an ideology or not, or whether the ideology was right or wrong. When the time came, the horror would always be apolitical. Two adversaries suddenly confronting one another, wielding weapons in the middle of the jungle, couldn't both be right. Or both be wrong. In a split second like that, what difference did it make where the truth lay? What mattered was to be the first to fire. And hit the mark.

"The cold war was hanging over our heads," Eric said quietly. "Today, if you look back, with a minimum of goodwill and forgiveness, you'll see what we escaped from. Because, no matter how crazy you may be"—another glance at me, which I returned with a cordial smile—"you can't simply go on admiring our comrade Stalin as before, right? Or condoning Mao's cruelty, which caused millions to die from starvation. Historically proven facts, which explain what's transpiring in certain parts of the world nowadays. Or can you?"

Put that way, I couldn't. So I agreed without feeling I'd surrendered any space on my chessboard. "No," I replied, "I can't."

He exhaled deeply, as if he'd won the first round.

I then felt obliged to add, "The problem with this kind of reasoning, as often happens to be the case, is the broader context in which such matters are analyzed."

I had to bite my tongue, given the crap my highfalutin words were hiding. But there was no other way. And I had to take it to the end, increasingly aware of the ditch I was digging between us. "Its *dynamics*, and the necessarily shifting perspective of those... *those watching.*"

Eric stopped in the middle of one of the aisles, in front of two boxes, on the labels of which I could read *Jorge Videla, miscellaneous* and *Alejandro Lanusse, correspondence with Galtieri.* He set his clenched fists on his waist, which was rather comical since he was in Bermudas and Docksiders and looked more like a tourist indignant over a canceled reservation than a war hero offended by the rhetoric of an academic.

"And what exactly do you mean by that?" he asked angrily.

I faced the same options as usual, in analogous situations. Grab the bull by the horns? Or negotiate a strategic retreat? Better negotiate.

"Eric, I don't think this is the time, or the place, for us to get into this kind of argument. I was merely trying to say—"

"*Bullshit!*" he burst out furiously. Immediately, however, he apologized. And I, in turn, raised my hand as if to say, *Forget it.*

"Did abuses take place in South America?" my host asked, throwing his arms open wide. The indignation was directed at his boxes, not at me. Facing the general silence, he himself took charge of answering. "Of course! You bet they did! Why? Because we couldn't always choose our partners down there.

And, often, these turned out to be the worst sort of people. Do you think we were mad about Pinochet? Or Contreras? The corrupt military we had to deal with in some of these godforsaken countries, including yours?"

A bit more and I'd feel sorry for Eric and his companions. But the moment didn't lend itself to irony.

"*War*," Eric said heavily. "We were at war. And there was no time to lose."

He'd returned to the start of his verbal digression. I waited to see if he'd end there—or head off in another direction.

"There was no time to lose," he repeated, as if gathering strength before climbing a hill. "Either we snuffed out the fledgling Communist movement in South America or we would have to contend with *two* guerrilla wars on opposite sides of the planet. And we didn't even know if we could win the one *we'd been involved in for years*. But if the Orientals knew how to play dominoes, so did we. And we decided to set up *our own game* in your neck of the woods."

Here I recalled Merce Cunningham's choreography, brought up by Max twenty years earlier. But Eric went on: "*The right-wing dominoes*, we joked. We went in through Brazil in sixty-four and from there all the countries toppled one after the other, just like a house of cards: Argentina in sixty-six; Uruguay and Chile in seventy-three (a good year for us); Peru at some point, I no longer recall just when; then Argentina again in 1976 (after the brief and pitiful Perón hiatus); and so on. A beautiful domino effect...just perfect. We worked the guerrilla warfare in our backyard with gusto. Without firing a shot or losing a single man."

Given my silence, he continued down the slope.

"We were used to conventional wars. We'd won two at once, against the Germans and the Japanese. But a guerrilla war was a whole other ball game. Two, in fact...and on a continental scale. No way would we have managed!"

I couldn't help but put in my two cents. "And both quag-
mires," I suggested, "just like today in Iraq and Afghanistan."

He seemed taken aback by my interruption, so caught up
was he in his past. He closed his eyes for a moment, having
been confronted with words that cut across time and projected
him without warning into the challenges of the present—like a
miner who can't handle the blinding light after days of despair
in a dark shaft.

"Maybe so," he finally conceded, lowering his head. "Maybe
so. Today's world...today's CIA..."

He fell silent. And cast a tired look over the contents of his
garage. A look devoid of pride—and, who knows, perhaps even
bewildered. A bit as though, as a result of our tour, he'd reap-
praised a legacy that had brought him only joy until then.

Suddenly I stopped short. I had just passed a box on which
I'd hastily read *Nuclear Agreement, Brazil-Germany*. I was so nervous that I worked up the courage to excuse myself to use the
washroom, promising I'd be right back.

"Don't worry," I heard Eric say behind me. "I'm not going
anywhere."

# 50

"Is that the 1975 agreement?" I asked as casually as possible when I got back.

"In a way, yes. Better known among us as '*Everything you always wanted to know about Westinghouse's feelings toward the CIA but were afraid to ask.*'"

Impossible not to laugh. But I soon added more seriously, "Right. You guys lost a boatload of money when the Germans signed the agreement with Brazil."

"Billions and billions of dollars," Eric confirmed. "And for years they accused us of having screwed up. Even though"—he pointed to the box in front of which we'd stopped—"even though this box contains not the final agreement from 1975, as you assumed a moment ago, but drafts of the original document we managed to copy in Montevideo *years before the agreement was signed*. And even though we sent *everything* to Langley."

"And then what?" I asked in surprise.

"Then nothing. The CIA did nothing. *Not a thing.* They simply sat on the information. Maybe Westinghouse, which had already won the bid for the nuclear plant..."

"Angra 1."

"Yes, the Angra 1 nuclear plant. Maybe Westinghouse was convinced that with this first victory, the rest of the deal was in the bag. It was in the bag, all right. But in the *Germans'* bag. And it was your friend Max, our very own *Sam Beckett*, who put us on the trail."

"A double triumph. Or a single blunder?"

"I don't even know anymore. It was a complex operation, involving smoke and mirrors, the unwitting participation of your former ambassador in Montevideo and his partner Carlos Câmara, not to mention the role played by the British agent who was working with us. Each had a part in the equation, which would earn me a medal of honor and a handshake from Richard Nixon a year later."

"Despite Westinghouse's failure?"

"Yes...," he replied, "*and no.*"

Then he spilled the beans. "I ended up getting embroiled in the whole Brazil–Germany nuclear issue by mere chance. Courtesy of an indiscretion by your ambassador. The only one he committed in almost six years in Montevideo, poor guy. As I was listening to the recordings we routinely made, a comment of his on the phone caught my attention. I started to concentrate more on everything he said. And put together lines here and there. Until gradually discovering, to our utter bewilderment, that *he* was the bridge between Brazil and Germany on the nuclear subject. Who would have believed..."

"Really, it doesn't make sense."

"*Except for one detail*, which eluded our people at Langley, given how low Brazilian priorities are, and were, for us. The ambassador had served in Bonn before being transferred to Montevideo."

"Yes. But...that in itself doesn't..."

"Exactly. Yet this kind of detail would *never* have gone undetected if we'd been dealing with a Russian diplomat, for instance. Or an Eastern European. But since he was Brazilian, no one saw..."

*Being a part of the third world had its advantages*, I couldn't help but think....

Meanwhile, Eric pressed onward. "How could we have imagined that the German–Brazilian nuclear connection would go through *Uruguay...*?" he asked.

To be honest, the possibility would never have occurred to me either. And I doubted that even today anyone would have connected such seemingly unrelated and disjointed facts.

"Once red flags had been raised, I went into the field. And quickly saw that the ambassador operated of his own accord. At least initially. I'm not saying he disobeyed ministry orders *but that he acted without its knowledge.* He counted solely on the support of a group of military officers, close to the president, with whom he exchanged messages we eventually decoded. And on Carlos Câmara. Even though we were friends, Carlos had never broached this subject with me in Rio. Nor did he in Montevideo. Unlike Max, he was a professional. And a true patriot."

He took a deep breath, like someone paying tribute to a fallen comrade. He allowed himself to linger a bit longer on this digression. "The ambassador too. Only, he was a loose cannon. Vaz later told me some unbelievable stories about him."

His eyes, laden with suggestions and malice, sought mine. Would I by any chance be interested in taking a break for a few spicy details? *No?* Too bad...

"The old man had studied in Germany, before World War II," he went on. "He'd made friends, some of whom had survived the conflict, even come out quite well. Several found themselves at the head of their old industries. Washington asked my opinion: what should be done? It was my idea to bring the British secret service into the game. So we wouldn't be exposed, should suspicions arise. The Brits owed us a few favors."

*Favors for what?* I wondered. Something relating to the future Falklands/Malvinas problem? Too late; Eric had already moved on.

"It was Max, then, who connected the dots for us," he said, his eyes shining jubilantly. "*Not even realizing it!* That was the beauty of the whole thing."

To my surprise, he grabbed my arm, as if celebrating a victory. A strange show of intimacy for a man like him.

"Max served us up the crucial information we needed to find the drafts of the agreement. We knew the ambassador had them, because we'd tried everything on the Bonn end, to no avail. The ambassador's copies were our only hope. But no one could figure out just *where* that maniac had stashed the papers, or the microfilm. We put Ray on Max's tail."

"Ray?"

"Raymond Thurston. An agent from the British secret service. We partnered on a few projects. Nice guy. And an excellent agent. He ended up becoming friends with Max. Which would later cost him his job."

Here Eric drummed his fingers on the box, as if to rekindle my interest in it. "It was a move worthy of James Bond," he said affectionately.

So it was then, three hours and six sausages after having crossed the threshold of his home, by which time we'd already downed countless vodkas and beers, that I managed to return to the tragic Brazil of the 1970s. Not by way of familiar topics, as I'd envisioned. But by having been hurled behind the scenes of the nuclear negotiations between Germany and Brazil. In a certain sense, just as had happened to Eric forty years earlier.

# 51

Eric moved right into the topic, as though in a rush. *The State Department and the Pentagon were alarmed*, he told me, as if I could dispense with preliminaries in such a complex matter.

Although involving the peaceful use of nuclear energy, with no evident threat of danger, the issue had serious implications all around. On the German side, it demonstrated a kind of independence Washington found unacceptable since Westinghouse was known to have already won the bid for Brazil's first nuclear plant and assumed the market was theirs. On the Brazilian side, it represented the first explicit rupture with Washington since the military takeover in 1964. An incomprehensible—and equally unacceptable—show of independence.

"But what was the difference?" I asked, trying to familiarize myself with the subject, which I'd known little about at the time and couldn't quite recall. "What distinguished the two countries' offers? In terms of the equipment?"

Eric looked at me as though sizing up a small child he didn't particularly care for. "To make a long story short," he said after a resigned sigh, "we wanted to sell Brazil what we called *turnkey nuclear plants*. In other words, facilities fully equipped for immediate use. But without any technology transfer whatsoever. You bought them, installed them, pushed a button, and presto! The plant was up and running. The rest of Latin America would be gnashing its teeth in envy and we'd then sell fifteen more plants just like it to whoever could pay."

He winked at me. It was, in fact, an interesting proposition. For the Americans.

"On the other hand," Eric continued, "the Germans proposed a whole *nuclear program* to Brazil, with several plants. Eight in all, which would operate based on a method they were in the process of testing. A method that would allow for the transfer of technical know-how."

"What method was that?"

"Easy, my friend... That part came later. First there was a preamble."

It was nice to note that Eric was treating me with the same bonhomie Colonel Vaz had shown in Vienna. *Take it easy*, my dinner companion had said one night in that same tone.

"Until the seventies, uranium was enriched by gaseous diffusion," he continued. "A new, more efficient and less expensive method was being developed, though. Using ultracentrifuge."

*Ultracentrifuge...what a word*, I thought, looking around me and trying to imagine how many more mysteries those boxes might still yield one day.

"Only three countries in Europe had had access to that technology. And Germany was one of them. They'd formed a partnership with the other two. That was the technology Brazil was after."

Step by step, we were approaching the core of the matter.

"But at the last minute, the State Department pressured one of the partners, and when I say pressured I mean with an arsenal of persuasive arguments..." A glance in my direction, to make sure I was able to appreciate the firepower a country like his could bring to bear. "It pressured one of the two other partners to prevent Germany from transferring the technology to Brazil. And the Germans reneged. They were forced to back out of the deal."

The most important, however, was still to come.

"Here's where things began to heat up. Instead, and in utter secrecy, the Germans offered the Brazilians what they presented as 'a promising alternative method' they'd been developing on their own to separate out the uranium of interest. Because that was the issue: separating the wheat from the chaff. This method experimentally developed by the Germans was called *jet nozzle.*"

I must have looked lost, for Eric made a vague gesture that meant, *Don't even try to follow.* But that didn't keep him from giving me a short lesson. "There's still no equivalent for the term in Portuguese," he concluded at last. "What matters is what it represented: transfer of technology. In the field of uranium enrichment."

"Washington must have loved it," I joked.

"Indeed," he concurred. "The agreement with Germany foresaw the construction of eight nuclear power plants in association with KVD, a subsidiary of Borgward-Stitz. German interest in the project was twofold. Financed largely by you (which was in itself pretty humorous), they were testing a uranium enrichment process that would raise their standing in the international community—if it worked. And they would still be guaranteed participation in the entire cycle of the project in Brazil, which meant they would ultimately be partners of the commercial plants. Beyond the exploitation of uranium and its enrichment process, these would involve construction of heavy equipment at an extremely high cost. Not bad, right?"

The first world certainly knew how to defend itself.

Eric picked up his pace. "The Germans weren't unaware of what the Brazilian military wanted. They quickly realized that they'd pay whatever the price might be. So whether in good faith or bad, they ended up negotiating with your country something they were still testing—and that would never work for their clients' top secret nuclear purposes."

"Why? The Germans aren't known to be irresponsible peo—"

"Because, as I said, they were still working on the technology. But since they were confident that they'd eventually get it right, they felt they were acting ethically. Except that we were up to speed. We knew they had no way of getting there. And that, as a result, Brazil couldn't benefit from the technology, despite all the German nods toward a breakthrough that would never occur."

Eric let out another of his sarcastic laughs and said, "A friend of mine who's an MIT professor asked me, completely incredulous, 'Do the Brazilians actually believe that? Are they going to buy it?!' " Then he added, "The ones who ended up on top in the operation, besides the group employed at that firm you all created at the time to manage these projects..."

"Nuclebrás."

"...that's the one...were the banks. The banks made a killing on the operation. Mostly American banks, I might add. German ones too, of course. And even British. Not to mention the Brazilian ones that dealt with them. Huge loans were made to Brazil during those years. Don't forget that back then everyone needed to get rid of their petrodollars...."

Eric paused briefly before continuing. "It's a shame this less visible side, the whole business of bank transactions, can't always be monitored. And denounced. The side that always has shrewd operators behind the scenes. You wouldn't believe the role our countries' major banks played, two of them in particular, in these negotiations. And how much they raked in..."

He'd spoken as if the investors and their usual sordid games hadn't been part of a larger scheme—in which he, Eric, had himself been involved.

"The banks never lose," he went on. "Neither do we. We, the American government.... In my day, anyway. We never lost."

His conclusion was as pitiful as it was unexpected: "Maybe that's why we stand alone today...isolated as hell...unable to deal with a world that for the most part despises us."

# 52

I allowed a good long moment to pass, so Eric could deal with his mea culpa and let it go in peace. Then I turned my focus back to Max, coming full circle, as it were. Fatigue was beginning to set in. Gripping as the topic was, I would have preferred to get out of that garage. It was getting late, moreover, and I still had a long stretch of highway ahead of me.

"That James Bond tactic you mentioned," I said. "Can you tell me about it?"

He didn't hesitate; he even seemed to relish the opportunity. I almost suggested that we return to the living room to hear the story in more comfortable surroundings, but I caught myself in time, sensing that in the mind of a man like Eric, absurd as it might sound, certain subjects *belonged* in that setting. Brazil and Germany, together once again, only this time as hostages in a La Jolla garage.

The challenge, as Eric explained to me then, had consisted of finding out the state of negotiations between the two countries, and where the corresponding documents might be located. On four occasions, the CIA had sent teams, disguised as plumbers, construction workers, or meter readers from the electric company, to comb the ambassador's residence. They knew the documents had to be there, whether in hard copy or microfilm, since they'd turned the embassy's office upside down more than once in the dead of night and found nothing.

As usually happens in urgent and desperate situations, the

hoped-for miracle came about by chance. When Max, in one of his conversations with Ray Thurston, mentioned for the second time the existence of a rare edition of Thomas Mann, which the ambassador never failed to carry along when traveling, a light-bulb went off in Eric's head. *That could well be it*, he thought.

At first, not even he had faith in his hunch, it seemed so pre-posterous. He soon remembered, however, that the ambassador was a man from another era. And that his literary preference for authors like Maurice Leblanc and Conan Doyle, who often favored the obvious in formulating their puzzles, might well have inspired his choice of hiding place. His CIA colleagues had also rejected the tip, deeming it ridiculous. They hadn't yet entered the age of state-of-the-art technology but could never have believed they were kept in check by such a childish ploy. As such, more than a few had fallen prey to the ambassador's smokescreen—which would have held up had it not been for Max's calamitous intervention. And Eric, for lack of a better option, had decided to investigate the possibility. The microfilm had been found tucked in the back cover of Thomas Mann's masterpiece, on the eve of the ambassador's departure. "We barely had time to copy it and slip the original back into its hid-ing place," Eric concluded with great pride.

"But not even," I asked, leaving aside the singular aspects of the operation, "not even after reading the documents were you able to prevent the countries' negotiations from going through?"

"I did my part," Eric answered laconically. "What happened afterward was out of my hands."

Here he hesitated a minute, the way Colonel Vaz would every so often in conversation with me in Vienna. The halt wasn't quite like the lumbering old bear's, though it was just as solemn and imbued with a touch of sadness. It was, I realized then, the pause of the elephant heading to the graveyard to die—with nothing more to lose. Or hide.

Indeed, where would Eric go after La Jolla, if not to the

cemetery? Following in the footsteps of his far more illustrious neighbors? Yet unlike them, without the generous eulogy of a newspaper obituary? On the contrary, forgotten even by the agency that had turned its back on him?

"The Brazilian military wanted the atomic bomb," he said at last. The grande dame was finally taking the stage. "The secret was somewhat of a joke," he added. "We always knew the bomb was the driving force behind the agreement between Brazil and Germany. We, meaning the CIA. And we also knew that with the Germans, you wouldn't get very far. With Westinghouse, on the other hand, who knows? A lot of easy money would come into play.... Loopholes might open, certain secrets could end up in the wrong hands...."

There was nothing ironic about his tone. Quite the contrary. He hesitated, hoping to recount the facts as faithfully as possible. Who else could he talk to about such matters these days?

"There was a group within your military that thought of nothing but the bomb. An influential bunch, close to the president. And there were, naturally, those who defended the use of nuclear energy for peaceful purposes. But those guys represented a majority solely at your Foreign Ministry."

His eyes were gleaming again. It was obvious the subject fascinated him.

"The military's argument was simple and to some extent made sense. They'd come to the conclusion that they'd done us a favor by overthrowing the Goulart regime. A *legally constituted* government, as they kept reminding us whenever they could. And that this favor might yet hatch additional plots in other countries in the region. As in fact had been the case in Argentina, Uruguay, Chile, and Peru in subsequent years."

He looked at me. He would have preferred that I draw my own conclusions and spare him from further embarrassment. Despite understanding his reasons, I decided to let the words come from his mouth.

"If we wanted further results elsewhere, though," he continued, eyes fixed on me, "we would have to pay the price. The chain of events had its cost."

And he went ahead, while I wondered how far his delirium would take him. Because imagining that a small contingent of Brazilian Fascists had been responsible for the series of coups in a number of South American countries was as unrealistic as denying that these same countries were capable of destroying themselves without outside help. Buying this story served, at best, to feed another fantasy—that the CIA had had a limited role in spawning these disasters.

Oblivious of my thoughts, Eric kept going. " 'Besides the US and the Soviet Union,' alleged the Brazilian military, 'didn't England and France have bombs? Wasn't India almost there?' " Eric paused briefly. "Ultimately, there was zero support for the Brazilian bomb. The matter was never even broached with our president, which infuriated your military, put your ambassador in Washington in a jam, and left Westinghouse high and dry."

After a good laugh, he grew serious again and added, "The Brazilians refused to understand *our* position: the last thing we needed, at that stage, was a nuclear country in our backyard. Not to mention the arms race that would inevitably ensue in the region. The Argentineans, the Mexicans, the Venezuelans, everyone would want their own bomb."

Eric leaned toward me, as if someone in La Jolla might hear us in that closed garage, surrounded though we were by shelves and boxes, and said, "Thus the complication Bonn represented. Because things snowballed when that German of yours became president. Ernesto Geisel...And your ambassador in Montevideo presented to the president's staff the nuclear project he'd been trying to cook up unsuccessfully for years with Bonn....
That's when things got rough. Because, after our resounding *no*, Germany came back with a disturbing *maybe*."

# 53

Another pause. "Regardless of how strongly we believed the German nuclear technology would prove ineffective, we were worried. First, because we weren't one hundred percent sure it *wouldn't* work. Second...second, because we had no way of pressuring your government. That was when we began to realize the danger in dealing with excessively closed regimes."

Ah...now we were getting somewhere.

"The widely proclaimed Brazilian political thaw began there. But it was born in Washington, long before it surfaced in the minds of Brasilia's supposed wise men. Because, with the military in power, we had no access to the key decision makers. And for matters of this magnitude, lobbying wasn't an option. There were no governors, senators, congressmen, investors, journalists, or others we could pressure. We tried to swap out one general for another, during one of those 'preelection' phases of yours, and failed. True, the fact that our candidate was a perfect idiot didn't help much. But we had little choice, considering the available options...."

We both laughed at this, him lightly, me with a clenched heart. We'd finally found common ground, Eric and I. Albeit narrow. But it had been worth the wait. Eric began to perk up again.

"For the first time since we'd become a world power, for the first time since we'd called the shots wherever we wanted, except behind the Iron Curtain, our hands were tied. Leaving out Cuba, which by that stage was just a pebble in our shoe (and had more to do with elections in Florida than with Fidel and his proselytizing), our hands were tied in our own backyard. Tied by our own doing, with our foolproof nylon rope! For having helped put that bunch of incompetent jackasses in power...pardon my language, it's the bourbon talking...." He corrected himself: "I mean, the vodka."

That was too easy. The producers of the big show had put up their circus ring around us, after which—two decades later—they'd decided to stage their show elsewhere. Without giving so much as a second thought to the revolt that would soon tear down the tattered tent they'd left behind.

"Eric, don't you find this all just a bit much?" I asked. "An entire continent transformed into a blank screen, on which you all drew whatever scenes you wanted? Isn't that a gross oversimplification of a reality—"

"But that's exactly what happened," he retorted, laughing. "On a larger scale than we were used to, of course. When we intervened in other countries' internal affairs. As occurred routinely in Central America, starting with the Panama Canal, Guatemala, et cetera. Putty in our hands, that's what South America became at one point, whether you like hearing that or not. Putty in our hands...And it couldn't have been any other way. The Cuban crisis had ceased to exist, Allende had been overthrown, and the threat of subversion was no longer an issue for us. There were other challenges now. And the main one entailed doing away with centralized nationalist governments."

The irritation coming over me was reminiscent of the conversation I'd had with Max twenty years earlier in Alto da Boa Vista, about this very subject. Eric must have picked up on something in my facial expression, for he became somewhat conciliatory.

"It's not that the student movements against the military, the marches, the protests, the courage of the press, and so forth, didn't matter. Of course they did. But the decisions were all made in Washington in terms of the big picture. Because the details..."

"The details were up to us."

"Right."

"And Max? Where did he fit in all this?" I finally asked.

Eric smiled sympathetically. "As you've probably guessed by now, I never actually liked the son of a bitch."

Had he noticed the unease that had taken hold of me? Probably. Because rather than coming across as aggressive, the line had sounded affectionate. As if Eric were turning to Max to draw us together. After all, he knew very well that my ties to Max were more personal (and went back farther) than those that connected me to João Vaz. The colonel had opened Eric's door to me. But the person who'd opened Eric's heart, insofar as he could be said to have one, was Max.

"He intrigued me," Eric acknowledged. "He didn't seem to fit in anywhere."

He watched me for a minute, then went on. "Not with us, when he helped train the Uruguayan police with your corporals and sergeants; or in your embassy, where he was always butting heads with Carlos Câmara. Certainly not in Vaz's poker circle, from what our mutual friend told me. When it came down to it, the only person who actually liked him was Ray." He patted the box again, as if Raymond Thurston could hear him from within. "It's not that Max changed his personality to suit each environment, which was a virtual requirement in the game we all played. But there was something peculiar about him. He didn't seem comfortable in any of his skins."

Eric shook his head briefly before continuing. "I never quite understood what he was after. He didn't seem to believe in anything, except maybe in himself. Even so, I have my doubts... To believe in ourselves, we have to be grounded in some kind of reality, goddammit! I wouldn't have been able to keep going otherwise."

Eric seemed genuinely puzzled by Max. Yet he regained his posture and asked, "So where does your friend find himself these days?"

"Moscow," I replied. "He's the ambassador there."

"*In Moscow?*" Eric responded in awe. "Not bad."

"Not bad at all," I agreed. "With any luck, he'll end up in Washington again."

# 54

"That was where we were destined to meet again, Max and I," Eric said. "Six or seven years after he left Montevideo. One night, a few months after my so-called *retirement*, when I was still living in Washington, gauging my future prospects, I went with my wife and two other couples to the Cellar Door, a jazz club in Georgetown. The club isn't around anymore. Buddy Rich always used to play there. So did Dexter Gordon, whenever he came to Washington... At some point, I went to the men's room. And on the way back, I passed by Max. I recognized him despite the beard he'd grown in the meantime. Max is the type of person who doesn't go unnoticed, even though nothing about his appearance stands out. Have you ever noticed that? Curious, isn't it?"

I hadn't thought about it, but it made sense.

"He was alone, sitting on a stool with his back to the bar, his eyes on the musicians. I took a few steps in his direction and stopped almost in front of him. The room was dark, but the bar less so. He didn't recognize me right away, even though it hadn't been that many years since we'd last seen one another. He was surprised when he realized it was me. And greeted me effusively, which was nice. I thought he'd held a grudge from his time in Montevideo. But he looked quite happy.

"We traded the classic *Fancy meeting you here*... and got to chatting. He told me he'd been living in the States close to four years and was the deputy at your embassy. 'Fine career you've got,' I remarked. 'Number two in Washington at your age, not bad.' He laughed again, modestly this time. I told him then that I'd left active service but was doing consulting work. I asked if he was expecting anyone, to which he replied no. He thanked me for the invitation to join our table but made clear that he preferred to remain at the bar. He'd be leaving shortly, he added, and wouldn't be staying for the second set. We exchanged business cards before saying goodbye.

"I thought I'd never see him again, but a week later he called and asked if my consulting allowed time for extended lunches. He wanted to have me to his house, only he was living in Chevy Chase. It wasn't all that far, but the suburb was somewhat removed from downtown. 'Lot of snow out that way,' I commented, trying to get out of the invitation. 'A lot of snow,' he agreed, but he insisted. The following Friday, I left my car at the embassy parking lot and we drove to his house together."

Eric paused to catch his breath. Quite possibly he was also gauging how much to tell of the encounter.

"It was snowing pretty hard. At first, we were kind of quiet, other than a comment now and then about the city, its traffic, its museums and galleries, and, above all, its jazz clubs. I found out that he loved jazz, which I hadn't realized. He knew a great deal about the subject, as far as I could tell. I still didn't have any idea what he might want from me, since, for obvious reasons, we wouldn't be able to talk about old times, as usually happens in these situations.

"Along the way, we chatted about US politics. Maybe that's what he was interested in, as the embassy's number two. Trading playing cards with someone he assumed to be an expert on the subject. I also got to thinking that he might want to sound me out as to what kind of file the CIA had on him. Because, at one point, he'd said something like, 'Sooner or later, things are going to end up changing in Brazil.' He might have been concerned about that. We talked about Jimmy Carter and what he represented on the American political scene. We spoke of Iran, of the student demonstrations against the shah, of the dead and wounded, and what all of this might lead to. Then we moved on to terrorism in Europe, the assassination of Aldo Moro, the return to democracy in Spain, those kinds of topics. All things considered, we managed to avoid Uruguay without much effort."

Eric described that day as though he were reliving it. "The snow was falling more heavily by the time we arrived. The house was big, one of those typical suburban homes. There were toys piled up in the front entry and hallway leading to the living room, but no children in sight. They were at school, Max explained, before noticing that it was cold in the house too. Actually, it was colder inside than out, or that was my impression, given the dampness. He quickly apologized, looking rather surprised himself."

*The unexpected, which always makes its presence felt at the wrong time.*

"His wife came out to complain, having just realized herself that there was a problem with the heat. Evidently, she'd gone back to bed after taking the kids to school. Annoyed, she barely acknowledged my presence and glared at me. I found it strange, thinking maybe Max had forgotten to say he'd be bringing a guest to lunch. Why else would she treat me hostilely, without even a hint of a smile? For someone like me, who had spent so many years living in South America, a stern look from a woman was a bad sign."

I took a deep breath, frightened by what would be coming next. My poor, dear friend Marina. Just what had she gotten herself into?

"At any rate, I picked up on the unpleasant vibe between us, or between the two of them, I don't know. Max and I had a drink. During lunch, his wife rejoined us. And once again, she hardly spoke to me. Or to him, as a matter of fact...Max, however, was quite lively. He'd opened a bottle of red wine and talked for all three of us. There were indications he'd be invited to work in the president's office when he returned to Brasilia. At the recommendation of one of his former bosses. He mentioned that the move would be very good for his career. But there was something strange in the air, something that went beyond his wife's silence. At one point, Max leaned toward her and softly asked a question in Portuguese. It sounded like, 'What's up with you?' Or 'Anything wrong?' I didn't detect the slightest animosity in his voice. Just concern. He sensed she wasn't quite herself yet had no way of identifying the cause. And the damnedest thing is that he was right, as I well knew, something was indeed wrong. Because even if she didn't know me, I knew her a little too well. And although she had no way of knowing that, she'd sensed it. A matter of instinct."

*The hour of the wolf...* I thought. Why not? If it was snowing so heavily out there? And the climate inside that house had also proved to be quite chilly?

"Years before, at a social dinner a few days after his arrival in Chile, Max had told an agent of ours that he would no longer be cooperating with us as he'd done in Montevideo. Training the police forces. He'd been polite but firm. He claimed he'd changed sectors within the embassy. When I was informed of the fact, I suggested that my people keep an eye on him in any event. Standard procedure, even when the split is on friendly terms. One of my colleagues handed the task off to the Chilean secret service. And they tailed him.

"After a month, the Chileans determined that he was clean. He had indeed taken charge of the embassy's commercial affairs, with a brief stint in the consular sector. So I ordered the operation to be suspended. But the Chileans continued to track Max on their own, now on a weekly basis. Three months later, I received a curious message from my agent in Santiago. There was something on Max's wife that might be of interest to us. I asked what it had to do with. And then the photos arrived. Personal delivery, marked top secret. In an envelope addressed to me."

It was the most delicate moment of our conversation. Either I put on the brakes right then or we'd all be tumbling downhill, Marina, Paolo, Max, and me. To this day I have no idea why I kept quiet. It wasn't out of morbid curiosity, or lewd voyeurism. I simply remember that I felt completely helpless, unable to react.

"The envelope contained a series of photos of Max's wife snorting cocaine with a young Italian man. According to the DINA report, the two got it on several times a week at his place, in the morning or afternoon. Sometimes at night, when Max was traveling. And there was coke aplenty. The police did a sweep of the apartment while the Italian was attending a party at Max's house. He'd been to several social dinners at the couple's home. From the photos (some even taken at Max's house), the two men appeared to get along with one another. The sentiment was probably forced in the Italian's case, but genuine in Max's.

"The cocaine was of the highest quality, as analyses revealed. The DINA team went over the Italian's apartment with a fine-tooth comb. The guy wasn't a dealer. As the police gradually discovered, he'd give two or three grams to friends in exchange for some favor. At first we didn't know where the stuff had come from. Until our bugs recorded that the Italian was planning to go after more. So I had my agent alert our people in La Paz. And we never again heard of the poor guy. Even though the Italian embassy in Bolivia was always asking for our help. Just our bad luck that the fellow was the nephew of an Italian senator. These mishaps happen sometimes. And there was nothing we could have done. The Italian ended up at the bottom of Lake Titicaca in a burlap sack with a weight tied to his feet. We never imagined it would come to that. But at the time we were also interested in discouraging trafficking, even among sometime users. His Indian friends went down with him, poor wretches. Each in a burlap sack."

*How many others had suffered the same fate?*

"At any rate, it ended up being very unsettling having lunch with that sullen-faced woman, whose personal life I knew so much about. Who was now blatantly snubbing me, as if she sensed what had happened at my doing. Odd, don't you think?"

Another pause to collect his thoughts. "At some point during lunch, my embarrassment did in fact make me uncomfortable, as if I were invading her privacy simply by being there, seated at her table. Especially since, along with the photos of the two snorting coke, I'd received many others of... well..."

It was too much, even for him. He had the decency to change the subject then. And veered down a path that allowed me at least to catch my breath. "But the strangest part of that lunch happened later. After dessert, which we ate alone, Max and I. Because his wife, what was her name again?"

"Marina."

"That's it... *Marina*. She didn't stay for dessert. She excused herself, got up from the table, and left without waiting for coffee. And so we went back out to the closed-in porch, where we'd had our drinks earlier. The only more or less warm part of the house, I might add. When we'd arrived, Max had brought out an electric space heater."

I knew that at that point, Marina was up in her room packing her bags. In a few minutes, she'd leave that house for good.

"The yard was lovely, all covered in snow. I've always liked snow. Outside the city, of course. Nice and white, the kind that doesn't turn into mud, making our lives difficult. We were standing out there, the two of us, holding our coffee cups, in front of the picture windows overlooking the deserted yard, when he apologized for his wife's behavior. He said something like, 'I don't know what's gotten into her.' I waved it off, indicating he need not worry about it. We must have both let out a sigh, meaning *women*..." Here Eric smiled.

"Then, maybe to shift gears, Max pointed to a snowman in the middle of the yard. 'My kids say that's me out there,' he said, laughing. And I laughed too. Until I looked more closely. The snowman had no eyes, nose, or ears. No carrot or other vegetables. The poor thing didn't even have arms, the kind made with twigs or sticks, nothing. It was just two balls of snow, a big one for the body and a smaller one for the head. That was it."

"A work in progress," I ventured.

"Maybe... I don't know... I found it strange. I'd had three glasses of wine at lunch and remember kidding with Max, 'That snowman needs a drink,' to which he replied, 'Who doesn't?' With that, we finished our coffee, I hit the loo, and we returned to Washington.

"On the ride back, our conversation revisited the international scene. This time, as I recall, we talked solely of the Camp David Accords, and wondered if we'd finally see a longer-lasting peace process in the Middle East. It almost seems like a joke remembering that today.... At no point did we mention Uruguay. And at no point did the omission bother us, or seem to represent anything out of the ordinary. It was as if the country, where we'd once lived, had been wiped off the map. As in fact it was. For many years."

He'd made the remark in the tone of someone who'd had nothing to do with the fraudulent 1973 elections, which had led to the dissolution of Congress and the suspension of the Uruguayan constitution, as well as the banning of the unions, censorship of the press, and all kinds of upheaval, resulting in imprisonments, torture, and deaths—in a process that had put the military in power. He spoke as if he hadn't financed the opposition and the country's conservative forces, to the tune of millions and millions of dollars, and destabilized the government in countless ways, just as he'd done in Chile for years. Instead, he'd studied his fingernails, as if suddenly realizing that they were due for a trim.

# 55

He'd actually said, *the country had been wiped off the map.* I'd heard him quite clearly. And noted something in his tone, which suggested a rupture with the past. It was hoping for a lot from that man, I know. By that point, however, I was exhausted. Drained by the conversations, the booze, the comings and goings in the labyrinths of that garage and its secrets, the painful references to Marina, what had been said and left unsaid. . . .

It was time to leave. Weariness had set in for good this time. The heat around us, moreover, had become unbearable. An hour earlier, when Eric had flipped the light switch in his garage, he'd also turned on a temperamental air conditioner, which hadn't been up to the task. How could it, considering the ultra-centrifuge energy contained in each of those boxes? We ambled down the last aisle of shelves toward the door that would take us back to the house. Just as I was starting to rehearse my good-byes, however, Eric stopped in front of a box. I raised my eyes to the label he was pointing at. And there were the three magic words, along with their corresponding numbers: *Sam Beckett, Montevideo, 1970–1973.* The symbols reverberated with the intensity of an epitaph.

"A present for you," my host announced formally, lifting the box into his arms. With the offering, Eric was neither claiming victory nor surrendering. He knew I had judged and condemned him. But he sensed I hadn't crucified him. And that in itself, at the end of his life, was enough. As such, he was now offering me a gift for having shown mercy, by not dealing him the coup de grâce he might have imagined he deserved.

"*For me?*" I asked, not knowing how to react.

"Yes for you. Who else? This is where I found you."

"The letter..."

"A copy, but perfectly legible. Faithful to the original you wrote Max on April 5, 1973. Thirty-three years ago."

The reference to the exact date cast a solemnness on the scene we were going through. As if it dignified Eric's belated appearance on the stage where he'd performed for so many years. The final act... except, of course, for the one that would eventually bring together his daughter, son-in-law, and a few friends from his Friday lunch group one rainy afternoon at his grave site.

"At the time, none of my Montevideo agents had the patience to read that letter. It was in Portuguese, a language I alone of our group would have understood. Even so, it never made it into my hands. Because, in the eyes of whoever tried to decipher it, it seemed confused and repetitive. And, at first glance, it was."

A letter... *My* letter.

"After our lunch at La Strada," Eric continued, "I had the idea to take a look in the Sam Beckett box. Vaz had mentioned your interest in Max quite often. That's when I found the letter and saw your first and last names. And then..."

And then the former agent had done some fieldwork. "It seems it was never read through or analyzed. Even so, it had generated a file, which had passed right under my nose. And been signed by me, when the material was archived. Something stuck in my head, amid thousands of names, numbers, dates, and cobwebs."

He smiled at the memory. He seemed just as tired as I was and, after locking the garage door behind us, headed with relief to the bar.

"I read the first lines. That was enough. Enough to become curious. Despite how shaky my Portuguese is. If I barely speak Spanish these days, imagine my Portuguese..."

I now recalled the letter's existence, although I had no idea as to its content. I merely knew that I'd written it. And sent it to Max in Montevideo. Had it been intercepted? But how, if I'd used the diplomatic pouch? Max had never responded, and I'd ended up forgetting about it. I was transferred, moreover— to LA, in fact. My attention had turned to other priorities. California... The films, the music, the bookstores, the museums and galleries... Being able to breathe, read a newspaper without having to look for hidden meaning between the lines, without having to search for news of the dead or disappeared...

"I asked Nancy to fax the letter to Vaz's daughter. And Betty sent us the translation by e-mail a few days later. In the message addressed to my daughter, she said that her father had been moved by what you'd written. João always was very emotional. And he must have gotten worse with age. That's how—"

"That's how...?"

"That's how the Eric you met at the consulate, and took to La Strada, isn't the same one hosting you today. Just as, in my view, you're not the friendly diplomat I had lunch with three weeks ago. Not that you're no longer friendly... or a diplomat. It's just that... you're not *quite you*, are you? Do you follow?"

"Yes... *and no*," I replied. They were rhetorical questions, at any rate. What were the chances I had anything in common with the young man who had written that letter? That was the only question that mattered. Let my host resolve his own existential problems—if he had any.

From the bar, Eric offered me one last drink ("for the road"), which I thanked him for yet turned down. He had set the box on the counter. I went over and picked it up. To my surprise, it was light. Curious though I was, I hesitated to take it. It didn't seem advisable to accept anything, of any kind, from that man—under any circumstances. I hadn't come on anyone's behalf. Not the dead, not the disappeared, not my friends, ministry colleagues, or peers. Were I to accept his gift, wouldn't I be absolving Eric of a portion of his sins?

Reeling from these doubts and still recovering from the exhaustion that had come over me, I decided to buy time and asked a question. "But, Eric, how did you come by this material? And why did you feel the need to...?" It was the best I could do. Leave the question hanging.

# 56

He seemed more relaxed, lighter even, as if he'd just unburdened himself. After all, thanks to me, there were now only four hundred seventy-seven boxes left in his garage — other than those hidden in his conscience. Seated on one of his sofas, he held his glass loosely in his right hand as if still grappling with my question. I settled into a chair facing him, firmly determined to leave in five more minutes.

"We photographed everything," he murmured, after a swig of bourbon.

"Photographed?" I repeated in a low voice. "Max's things?"

I wasn't feigning surprise. Eric, for his part, seemed unaware of my bewilderment. Or pretended he hadn't noticed. But he needed a second swig to proceed.

"Max and his wife lived in an apartment near the center of Montevideo," he said at last. "A duplex. Every time they went away for the weekend, to Uruguayan friends' haciendas or to Rio, hitching a ride on the air force jet, they'd give the servants the time off. Unlike MI6, I didn't trust him. Or the information he passed off to Ray, vague or useless more often than not. This, of course, was *before* he led us to Ali Baba's cave. Without even realizing it..." The recollection didn't bring him quite the same pleasure as before.

"The building was secure, with bars on the windows, solid locks, and armed guards at the entry. But with our contacts at the Uruguayan police running interference, it wasn't hard to spend a night in the apartment going through papers and photographing whatever seemed useful to us."

Suddenly he laughed, struck by a memory that lit his face with a childlike expression. He hesitated to share it with me, though. Afraid, perhaps, of entering dangerous territory. But the story seemed too good to die with him and be buried with his bones in San Diego. "One of the agents opened a drawer in her nightstand and immediately closed it. He was a young guy and turned completely red. I went over to see."

This time, however, I got ahead of him. And before he could go on, I cut him off. "She died two years ago. In a plane crash."

His eyes widened. "She *died*?"

"Two years ago," I repeated. "In a plane crash. Into the ocean. Near the Greek coast."

He hesitated for a moment. Was he thinking, as I was, of the two deceased, one at the bottom of a Bolivian lake, the other lost in the depths of the Aegean Sea? Was he thinking of everything hurtful—and demeaning—that he'd revealed to me about both, just earlier, in his garage? Was he thinking of the photos he'd spoken of as if he'd just developed them in his secret lab—and hung them with clothespins to dry? They were images that should have been respected, regardless of their nature. And that he had helped defile.

They were stories that didn't even belong to him, pathetic as they might have been. The two deceased watched us, wide-eyed, from the depths of their respective bodies of water, as if all that remained of them was the ability to show indignation—an ability now projected with the intensity of headlights cutting through the darkness. The sensation was so strong that Eric closed his eyes, while I kept mine fixed on him. Two human beings who had intended no evil awaited an explanation that would never come.

"I'm really sorry to hear that," he finally said, as though returning to his senses. After another long pause, he struggled to regain his lecturing tone, albeit in a wearier voice. "Once the film had been processed, we sorted through the material and got rid of what seemed superfluous. Your letter, although long and unclear to my agents, ended up staying on the stack. Simple carelessness, if you ask me."

It was obvious he wanted to be done with the subject. Although he'd had no hand in Marina's death, the same couldn't be said with respect to poor Paolo.

"I was half drunk when I wrote that letter," I admitted.

With relief, he grabbed the life jacket I'd tossed him. "One of my agents said something to that effect. Before giving up on his reading, he even added, 'This guy must have been loaded, he went on for pages writing about a brother and a sister on a bus.' "

*A brother and a sister on a bus...* An initial image slowly emerged from the past, but it came from so far away that it seemed to belong to another world, not just another time. A fleeting image, which a flame might illuminate before giving way to darkness.

"At that time, in Brazil, we had no one to vent to," I continued. "At least, I didn't. And Max... *Max was my best friend.* I was worried about him...the rumors that were starting to go around. The letter might have had to do with that too. The news of his transfer to Santiago hadn't gone over well at the ministry. In the minds of many, he'd sealed his fate once and for all."

Eric nodded in agreement. This time without giving me the sense that he was being critical or feeling uncomfortable. I'd even say he smiled in a fatherly sort of way. *You'll see*, his eyes suggested. Except that, like me, he was exhausted. It had been a very long day.

We both stood and walked toward the door, Eric with my box in hand. When we got there, he opened a closet and handed me my blazer. Then he gave me the box and shook my hand. We exchanged one last look. End of chapter. *La guerre est finie.* He remained standing on his front stoop while I negotiated the steps down to the sidewalk.

"What store did you buy your crystal ball at?" he shouted from above, once he saw me opening the car door.

"Crystal ball?" I yelled back, not knowing what he was talking about, while I set my gift on the backseat.

"The one that allowed you to see so far ahead, in 1973. The one that led you to write your letter..."

"Oh, *that* crystal ball," I joked back. "At an antiques shop in Brasilia. It was called the Nightstand. But it closed years ago. Went bankrupt. It dealt with the past. And the past, back then, had no future."

"It was good to see you again," he said with one last wave.

"Give me a call one of these days," I replied, before shutting the door. "When you come to LA for lunch with your friends."

But he never did.

# 57

Back at my apartment in Santa Monica, after three hours on the San Diego Freeway, I flung open the living room windows to take in the sea breeze I thought I needed to pull myself together, and set my trophy on the dining room table. I kept pacing around it, like someone circling the cage of an unfamiliar animal. For a while, I limited myself to weighing the pros and cons of opening the box that same evening. I strategically chose to put off the decision and took a shower. Then I made some tea and turned on the television.

Having reached my sixties, I was no longer so sure I wanted to meet the young man who had addressed Max all those years ago, just before heading—full of hopes and dreams—to the city where he now found himself once more, only tired and old and approaching the end of his career. The idea that a cycle of this magnitude could open and close around me was distressing. Far more than the difficult hours I'd spent with Eric—or with Max three years earlier, at my daughter's graduation. The two men, moreover, had slipped away from me like water running between my fingers. It was in the nature of these characters to forever elude us. Wasn't that the story of my country—and the entire region—only on a larger scale?

What would I say to the young man waiting inside that box? That the individuals responsible for the disasters that had befallen our generation were still alive and kicking, as if nothing had happened—and that, to add insult to injury, many remained

in power? More than once, in the hours following my visit to La
Jolla, I caught myself glancing over at the table, as if the package
sitting there had a life of its own and, mindful of my indecisive-
ness, was patiently biding its time. The reflections coming off
the TV screen were coloring the box with successive hues.

I remembered a scene Max had described to me years earlier, during one of our late-night conversations, a prehistoric
vision of sorts, which occurred right after the coup of '64. He
was lying on his bed in the old apartment he shared with his
mother in Humaitá, thinking of the possibilities that had suddenly and unexpectedly opened before him. Minutes earlier,
he had received a phone call from the secretary to the Cardinal Archbishop of Rio de Janeiro concerning his future. What
had given the scene its added dimension had been the Coca-
Cola sign blinking on and off at the bakery shop across the way.
The red light had lit up his face every two to three seconds,
leaving him alternately immersed in shadows, which, as a good
reader of Stendhal, he had deemed "appropriate to the historical
moment."

Now it was his cardboard box that was undergoing a similar
effect. Except that the target was no longer Max's face, but his
past. Or what was left of it in this Californian version that I'd
come into by chance.

When I finally decided to open my treasure, I found that the
box contained copies of the telegrams Raymond Thurston had
passed on to MI6—the kind of communications now declassified by the US government. And my own letter, from another
era... The rest basically consisted of Max and Marina's phone
bills and bank statements, correspondence between Max and his
mother, and memos on work matters unrelated to my former
friend's covert activities.

Some of Ray's telegrams are excerpted in this manuscript,
sprinkled amid its chapters. As for the photocopy of my letter, it
was indeed perfectly legible, as Eric indicated. It even faithfully

reproduced the perforations certain characters had made on the original sheets of paper, as if specific keys on my typewriter had been struck in anger. In the transcription that follows, I've italicized a few words that I'd underlined by hand at the time, markings the microfilm captured less clearly. On rereading its content—which I did only after moving from tea to whiskey—I recalled that, at the time, I'd considered eliminating the P.S. inserted by hand just below my signature, thinking it too long and kind of corny. But omitting it would have meant retyping close to twenty lines on the last page—and at that point I was dead tired. So I kept it.

I chose to leave the postscript in the present manuscript as well, above all because it underscores a sentiment: that the joys of great milestones, such as those of my youth—man's landing on the moon, for instance, or the widely hailed end of the Vietnam War—rarely compensate for our individual losses. Because the former ultimately leave us indifferent, becoming impersonal fragments of history. Whereas the latter continue to affect us, fatally—and forever. I had been fortunate, however. Unlike so many people in our country and region who had lost friends and relatives—if not their own lives—I'd merely lost an idol from my younger days, as it happened, the one I'd looked up to the most.

There are deaths that snuff out a single life. And others that, like military coups, finish off an entire generation.

# PART SEVEN

My dear Max,

Here I am, in the apartment you're familiar with, on yet another night in Brazil's heartland, sitting in the living room that serves as my library, dining area, and guest bedroom. The absolute silence around me is surreal, even though it's not yet ten p.m. by my watch.

Any other city in Brazil, or elsewhere in the world, would be alive and hopping at this hour. Brasilia is in a deep slumber, however. How many decades will it take before our capital finally wakes up?

I feel like a privileged witness to this deserted stage, as I've just spent a good long while at the window, smoking and watching a still life in which only the night doormen shuffle by, not even a stray cat honoring us with its presence. A landscape made up of the fronts and backs of low buildings, all identical, which seems to imprison me in an enclosure of cold light and concrete—the perfect urban metaphor for the political system we live under.

It's unbelievable how these homogeneous residential areas lend themselves to this role and replicate the Fascist realities we're all trapped in. Not to mention the monumental Esplanade of Ministries with its glorious structures—which today serves as the setting for parades and other demonstrations of patriotism rooted in oppression. One day, though, this architecture will breathe again, without a single brick having to be moved from its place.

I'm hoping that you've made headway in your translation of Eliot's quartets. I liked the excerpts I read and have never understood why it's taken you so long to try your hand at the second quartet. Especially after the fine reception your rendering of the first deserved, in 1970. Or was it 1971? But beware:

*traduttore traditore,* etc., etc. So much for small talk, even though it does have its place in our line of work, doesn't it?

I decided to write you this letter for two reasons. The first is that I've just been betrayed, which is always disheartening, and am reeling from the pain of having been passed over. To make a long story short, I lost the opportunity to be transferred to Geneva. A shame, because there I could have continued in my areas of interest, which bring me such satisfaction—among other reasons by keeping me away from the thorny world of politics.

As a consolation prize, I was offered Los Angeles, where I could work in the consulate's commercial sector. At first, I didn't know what to do. But after thinking it over, I accepted. It might be interesting to dive headfirst into California during this amazing, tumultuous time the US is going through. Nixon and the Watergate mess, the American debacle in Vietnam, the pro-test marches, feminism, the Black Power movement…Maybe that will all compensate for the more challenging work in Geneva, and LA will prove to be stimulating. At least I'll be able to hear a lot of good music there, from Bob Dylan to Joan Baez, not to mention the classics, as well as the movies I'll have a chance to see after so many years of censorship in Brazil.

But the second reason I'm writing to you is, by far, the more important. It has to do with things that I never seem to be able to tell you personally when we see one another. Not that you intimidate me. *It's the issues themselves that are unnerving.* Something serious happened during our last meeting—and I can no longer keep quiet.

The rumors about your upcoming transfer from Montevideo to Santiago stunned me. You must have noticed my uneasiness. Max, the likelihood of a military coup in Chile increases every day. Just as it does in Uruguay. *Everyone knows this.* The two countries' newspapers cover nothing else—and if ours say little about it, it's because they're being censored, not because of lack of interest or concern. I don't mean to come across as a champion of truth and sacred values, but I'm afraid that you'll end up confirming the suspicions of everyone, within the ministry and beyond, who believes you're working for the right. *Working for them by choice.* And that, willingly or not, you may become part of the intrigue being talked about at the ministry, scheming said to be inspired by your boss in Montevideo.

Since I have no way of meddling in a decision you might already have made, my only recourse is to relate a certain story to you. A very simple story, which may somehow convey my feelings about what's happening in Brazil these days. There's nothing exceptional about my characters: a lower-middle-class brother and sister from São Paulo. The boy was around twenty, the girl eighteen, when they went through their ordeal. The facts were told to me by the boy first. Two weeks later, by his sister. And finally, sometime after—in the presence of their mother, with whom they've been living here in Brasilia, ever since they were able to relocate—*by both.* Each adding to the other's sentences. *A montage!* as the boy proclaimed at the end of what seemed more like a theater production. (He's a film student of mine at the university; we became friends after I showed his class *Battleship Potemkin* and we got to talking about Eisenstein and Pudovkin during the break.)

The brother and sister are truly fond of one another. And, from what I gathered in talking with their mother, that's been the case ever since they were little. It's unusual to see that explicitly among relatives, even close ones—for me, at least, it was a novelty. In my family circle, we were always more reserved where our feelings were concerned. And that's what moved me about this story: its emotional undertone.

The episode they took part in, or found themselves ensnared in, much to their surprise, happened in São Paulo, more than four years ago, right after the military tightened its grip. And that's what made me think of you, because we met around then—when you elevated me to "lunchable" status.

The facts, then, took place back in those days, toward the end of December '68. One afternoon, when the two were at home (and their mother fortunately wasn't), the boy writing a paper for school, his sister ironing a skirt, they suddenly found themselves thrust into a nightmare: they were forced apart *without having time to utter a single word to one another*. Informed on by a militant who had been jailed and tortured, the boy barely escaped through a window at the back of the house where they lived on the city outskirts. He jumped a wall and disappeared into the woods.

He was no terrorist. He'd graffitied a few walls, participated in protest marches, those kinds of things. But it so happens that, under torture, people end up turning in their own mothers—to whom they attribute the worst crimes. They'll confess anything to make the electric shocks stop. Can you imagine what it's like to be shocked in the balls for hours on end? Or to have an electric wire shoved into your urethra and see four guys falling over laughing around you while you writhe in pain on a floor soaked with your own excrement? That's what happened in the case of my student's comrade. He held out as long as he could and then gave up several names out of pure desperation.

For nearly a year, neither the mother nor the sister had any news of the boy. They knew their home phone was being tapped and sensed they were being watched. During this entire time, without arousing suspicion, they kept a close eye on friends and acquaintances, seeking any sign that would restore their hope. Trips to the hospitals and prisons turned up nothing. The same was true at the army quarters and police stations. Like many relatives of political prisoners and other victims of the system, they had no powerful friends. They didn't know people who could assist them in any way. They concentrated their thoughts on him alone. Was he dead or alive? And, in either case, *where*?

Then one afternoon, on a bus stuck in traffic in downtown São Paulo, the boy caught a glimpse of his sister sitting at the back. He lowered his head and considered the possibility that she might have been followed. The thought couldn't be dismissed because, in the meantime, he'd taken part in undercover operations and was now seriously wanted by the military. He reckoned that they might be able to exchange at least one look. To do so, however, it was vital that his sister not be startled when she saw him.

Taking advantage of the flow of passengers getting on and off, the boy, who was standing near the driver, gradually moved toward the center of the bus. And stopped there. Every so often he'd glance toward the back, but without lingering on his sister. Flanked by two older women, she remained absorbed in her book. He waited, relying on his right eye to let him know when to act. Each time the bus slowed, he noticed, his sister would lift her head from her book to make sure it wasn't her stop. He realized that this was simply a reflex, common in public transit riders absorbed in their reading, and that it would be repeated every time the vehicle stopped. There would thus be an opportunity for eye contact, depending on the gaps between people.

Now, Max, try to visualize the subtlety of the scene the boy went through. He stood still in the middle of the bus. Bringing his left hand up to his chin, he began to rub his index finger over his lips, "the gesture," as he put it, "of someone lost in thought." An unconscious motion suggesting peaceful musing. Thanks to which, at the decisive moment when his trusty eye gave the signal—confirming that his sister had suddenly seen him—he was able, in profile, to raise his finger for a second, "in a vertical line that went from his chin to his nose." With this, he sent a clear warning, which made the girl keep her eyes glued on her book—"a novel," in her words, "that now anchored her."

They continued the ride that way. Profoundly joined, profoundly apart. For an indefinite period of time. On a trip that was in no way connected to the space or the men and women around them, "as if the bus were floating," she said. (Of the two, she is more introspective, poetic; whereas he's practical and objective, a man of few words.) Once past the danger of an undesired gasp or a destabilizing surprise, they felt they could steal *another* look. Brief as it might be, they knew it would take place in slow motion, as if it had a life of its own—and time on its side.

It fell to the brother, then, as he signaled the driver for the next stop, to let the girl know that the precious moment was approaching. She remained immersed in her book and nervously wondered if there might not be an opportunity, at that split second, for a quick smile. But seeing him still in profile, wearing the same stern look, she decided to let him take the initiative. She promised herself that, whatever he did, she would try her very best to mirror his expression, so that *he could see in her eyes a reflection of the love they shared.*

It's a sappy image, you'll say. Maybe so...but it touched me like few others. Because life, when it comes down to it, is about these very moments. And that's how things went. Just as that was how mother and daughter, clinging to one another that afternoon, regained the strength to await the day they'd all be together again. It didn't matter anymore how long it would take. Something had happened to restore a sense of order. The two women learned then to have faith. They felt that the boy would take extra precautions from then on, to spare them further pain—after having brought them utter joy.

And that's precisely what he did, distancing himself little by little from his clandestine life. He changed his name and, with the experience he'd acquired while undercover, met his family again in a safe place. Eventually, they found refuge here in Brasilia.

Max, when this story was recounted to me by the brother and sister together, in its third and final version, they reenacted the experience for me, each reliving details from his or her point of view. As if they were two cameras capable of simultaneously revealing the images and secret pulse that connected them, they celebrated their feat, presenting it as if it had all been a game. It so happens, however, that on the previous occasions, *when the event had been told to me by just one of them*, there had been nothing uplifting about those scenes. They were imbued with the anxiety both had faced. The narrative had been the same, but it was perceived through the prism of fear.

That's what led me to tell you this story. More than the images of the dead and tortured, more than the lists of disappeared, more than the accusations reported by the newspapers, what happened to these young people illustrates the absurdity that's taken hold among us. Because if the image of a defiled body makes us think of death—and horror—the scene between them is all about life. There had been just two possible outcomes in the tiny, almost invisible scene they went through. Love and hope, on one hand; torture and death, on the other. In the middle, emptiness.

*How could we possibly have reached this point in our country? In the name of what? How could it be that one half of our population is dying from hunger and the other from fear?* The fear is real here, Max. Anyone living in Brazil feels it up close—unlike someone who's abroad, like you. Information travels by word of mouth, despite the censors' efforts. And conveys vivid images. A father suddenly gone. A voice missing at a university. A bride led to the altar by an uncle or a brother. A teenager who comes home for lunch but fails to show up for dinner. Year in, year out—nothing changes. On the contrary, it gets worse. All of these absences taken together weigh heavily and clamor—not so much for revenge but for explanations. Yet none is provided. Not a word.

Unlike our pleasurable diplomatic missions (and you'll forgive the grotesque comparison), they produce permanent absences, Max, *which never allow for the joy of reunion*. They don't bring peace or tranquility. Quite the opposite, they deepen the despair of everyone involved. I'm afraid that the seed planted in our midst in '64 will give rise to a sickly tree, the branches of which will end up multiplying out of sight. If pruned, they'll grow in other directions, poisoned by the same evils.

The day will come, of course, when things improve. In five or ten years. Sometimes I dread that moment almost as much as the present. *Sad to say, isn't it?* Fears evolve; they change with times and circumstances. They retrace the path that led them to panic. Then they're reduced to misgivings—and a permanent feeling of uneasiness. Caused by an impunity that will last and explain the crimes that will be committed in the future. *Ah-ah!* you'll say. *Who dares to make such cavalier predictions? Who? Our good old friend on the Johnnie Walker Red label,* Max, the one who never fails, as you'll recall. The Striding Man from our Old Highland Whiskey, his hat tipped to you. Who proves to be more prophetic with each shot... Who else could it be? Or do you think I'd have managed to write this letter completely sober?

I'm off to bed now. So I can wake up early and pick up the papers from Rio at the newsstand. Censorship remains rampant, but even so it's possible to glean things here and there. They're pros, our journalists. At least those who still resist... Some manage to convey plenty between the lines, using that tiny space to project deafening screams only a few of us can hear.

Speaking of which, have you been an eyewitness to much in Montevideo? Anything you can tell me about? How many weeks until the coup in Uruguay? And in Chile? Will these two countries shift the uncomfortable attention of the international press away from Brazil? I never find the courage to ask you these questions in person. It's easier by letter. But don't feel obliged to respond.

Kisses to dear Marina and sweet little prince Pedro Henrique. And a brotherly hug to you.

N.

PS:

The FM station that kept me company throughout this letter has started to play "Imagine" again. Ever since the song was composed, the radios seem to play nothing else. All around the world and even secretly in countries where bans are in effect. So much has happened since we first met. From Woodstock to man's landing on the moon, from feminists burning their bras to the first cries in defense of the environment, from the eternal struggle for human rights to the fatigue of those who cashed in their chips and latched on to this or that system. Today on TV the news reported that the twin towers of New York's World Trade Center (110 floors each!) have just opened for business. There was also coverage of "the beginning of the end" of the Vietnam War.... How many years of darkness and uncertainty still await us? What explanation (I no longer dare to say "lessons") will we leave for those who come after us? Will we blame the cold war for the deaths and torture that occurred *on this side* of the Berlin Wall? And when the wall comes down one day, in two or three generations, as it must, won't its fall reveal an infinite number of others, dividing the planet into not two but two *thousand* sides? Walls, fences. *This side, that side.* With so many walls, I sometimes find myself questioning the difference between one side and the other. *That's when I know it's time to stop drinking and go to bed!* But to end with "Imagine," what will the world be like when John Lennon is surrounded by diapered grandchildren and then great-grandchildren? Will we be closer to or farther from his verses then? Will they have lost their relevance? Or will they remain as meaningful and poignant as ever?

# ACKNOWLEDGMENTS

I am indebted to Judith Gurewich of Other Press for her remarkable editorial suggestions, which gave this English edition of my novel a smooth narrative flow while further balancing and focusing its content. I am also grateful to my Australian publisher, Henry Rosenbloom, from Scribe, who had his curiosity piqued by a story dealing with a forgotten war in South America—which resulted in the first English publication of a book originally written in Portuguese. Equally heartfelt thanks go to my agent, mentor, and longtime friend Thomas Colchie, to whom I owe much more than these few lines can possibly convey. Elaine Colchie's editorial expertise also greatly enriched the text. My sincere gratitude to Kim M. Hastings, who faced the many challenges inherent to the translation with imagination and tenacity, added to a rare degree of professionalism and dedication. To my new colleagues at Other Press who shepherded my manuscript through the different stages of production, Yvonne E. Cárdenas, Keenan McCracken, and Cynthia Merman, my deep appreciation. As for my wife, Angelica, love of my life, I wish to say that, as editor of the ten books I have published in Brazil, she has more than paved the way for the literary journey we have covered together in these past two decades.

*Edgard Telles Ribeiro* was born in Brazil in 1944 and graduated from the Diplomatic Academy in 1967, when he joined the Brazilian Foreign Service. Prior to that, he was a journalist and film critic writing in Rio de Janeiro. The author of seven novels and three collections of short stories, several of which have won major literary awards in Brazil, he currently lives in New York.

*Kim M. Hastings* is a translator and editor based in Connecticut. She lived in São Paulo for several years, studied Brazilian language and literature at Brown University, and holds a PhD in Spanish and Portuguese from Yale. Her translations have appeared in *Words Without Borders*, *Review: Literature and Arts of the Americas*, *Two Lines*, and *Machado de Assis*, among other publications.